ARY OF
LIA

P9-DBO-621

Journey
of a
Cotton
Blossom

Journey
of a
Cotton
Blossom

MURRAY
LIBRARY

OCT 2016

J. C. Villegas

BROWN BOOKS
PUBLISHING GROUP

© 2016 J. C. Villegas

All rights reserved. No part of this book may be used or reproduced in any manner without written permission except in the case of brief quotations embodied in critical articles or reviews.

This is a work of fiction. Any similarity to real persons, living or dead, is coincidental and not intended by the author.

Journey of a Cotton Blossom

Brown Books
16250 Knoll Trail Drive, Suite 205
Dallas, Texas 75248
www.BrownBooks.com
(972) 381-0009
A New Era in Publishing®

ISBN 978-1-61254-883-8
LCCN 2016939809

Printed in the United States
10 9 8 7 6 5 4 3 2 1

For more information or to contact the author, please go to
www.JCVillegasBooks.com.

This book is dedicated to all those who have struggled to be themselves; all those who have faced racism and prejudices; all those who have been bullied or abused; and all those who have lost their lives due to bullying or prejudice. My close friend AJ was bullied all through middle and high school for his race and for being gay. Regretfully, I was one of those bullies. I was struggling with admitting who I was, so I turned on someone like me with the anger I held for myself. He did not deserve the treatment he received. No one deserves to be treated like they don't matter. No one deserves to be bullied. No one deserves to be harassed, beaten, or murdered because of prejudice. To all the LGBT community, to all the African-American community, to all the communities out there belittled and thought of by some as "less than," and to every young person in every community who is struggling with bullying and prejudice, know that you do matter. I wrote this book for all of you . . . for all of us.

Acknowledgments

I would like to thank my wife and parents, who fully believed in me from the moment I had the relentless dreams that brought this book to me. You three urged me to follow those dreams, and for that, I am thankful.

Catalina, you stood by my side and had faith in me. You never once thought that I couldn't do this. You never discouraged me. You held me up when I was struggling. Your encouraging words and love resonated loudly. You are the epitome of what a spouse should be.

Mom and Dad, thank you for helping me through this process. Both of you have always encouraged me and urged me to listen to my dreams and follow them. You've always taught me that God will show us the way when the time is right. You taught me to trust in myself, those feelings, and the journey. Mostly, you both have taught me the definition of unconditional love. Y'all have always shown me that I am loved for who I truly am. I have always felt that love and the pride you both have for me. Thank you for that. That is a gift that so many are wrongfully deprived of.

I am extremely grateful for all three of you. You are my support and my family.

Guillotine

The gavel of society has come down, severing my head from my neck. I am forced to choose between what my brain has been conditioned to think and what my heart knows to be true.

1

The Chains of Sunday

One early Sunday morning, the day of God, in a small southern town known as Clarksville, Mississippi, a beautiful baby boy was born. Most the people of the town were at church. They were praising God, as all good, God-fearing Christians do.

This baby boy cracked open his beautiful, bright eyes for the first time while his mama held his warm, tiny body, full of energy and life. He was God's gift to the world that day. She cradled his head with one warm hand while staring deeply into his soulful eyes and realized she never could have imagined a love this overpowering.

His sweet baby smell and his spirit were intense and special. His mother possessed an inexplicable knowledge that he had been put on this earth to be a great presence among humankind. She knew he deserved a strong name. *Joseph it will be,* she thought to herself. It was as if God had leaned down and whispered the name directly into her ear: "Joseph."

Like any mother, she wanted the very best for her first child. She was just a young girl searching for guidance; nevertheless, she felt the deep love for her child that consumes a mother.

With church letting out in town, the young mother knew that everyone would soon be meeting her freshly born baby boy. She was not ready to share her gift from God, but she knew she would have no choice. There was tension in the air, thick and almost tangible, as the people returned from church.

The mother's immense love turned to intense fear for her new-born baby boy. She was afraid that he would be stripped from her arms like she had been from her own mother years before. Her first instinct was to take little Joseph and run before the "owners" returned from having given "praise" to God. Even though she was weak from giving birth alone, she had that motherly drive to grab her boy and run. For a brief moment she had a fantasy of teaching Joseph to walk and talk and then watching him grow into a wonderful man. Then she snapped out of it. She knew she needed to get away before it was too late. That raw, motherly drive inside of her was screaming, *Run, run!* while trying to claw its way out to save the infant.

As the motherly instinct broke free, she covered herself and grabbed Joseph tightly, preparing for escape and the salvation of their lives. She leaped from the bed in which she had given birth, slinging placenta to the floor. As she took her first step with a huge jolt of momentum, she felt a taut jerk and fell to the ground face-first, protecting Joseph's tiny head from the blow with her own childlike hand. She was abruptly reminded that she was chained to the bed like a disregarded work animal. There was no saving little Joseph, her only love, from what was sure to come.

2

The Sweltering Delta

Clarksville, Mississippi, was a big cotton producer. It was a small town in the Delta, known as "the Golden Buckle of the Cotton Belt." Big producer of cotton meant big plantations, and those big plantations came with rich, white aristocrats whose sense of entitlement was thicker than their wallets.

If you had visited the South that summer of 1943, you would have felt the humidity and caught a whiff of the mint juleps. A mint julep is a drink most southerners can tell you about: a mixture of bourbon whiskey, mint, sugar, and water. In the town of Clarksville, as in most southern towns at that time, you would see a Baptist church on every corner with a large plantation nearby. Funny thing is, while most southerners know about those mint juleps and most southerners are Baptist, every Southern Baptist knows that alcohol and Baptist are not supposed to go hand in hand. Yet they seem to mix well and very often despite alcohol's supposedly sinful nature.

You could stroll by the picturesque white antebellum homes on your way back from church, a church-held event, or one of the few other activities available in town. You see, in small-town Mississippi, most of the activities revolved around the Baptist church. These antebellum homes are still famous in the South for their regal white columns and grand stature. There is beauty and darkness to them. You can see the exterior beauty of these magnificent structures, but then it is as if you can almost feel the evil that has happened within those walls.

In those days, you would see people working in the large emerald yards with the perfectly manicured rosebushes and cotton-blossom-covered fields. You might have seen somebody sweeping the white, wooden front porch with somebody else slowly rocking in a chair while sipping on a mint julep. It's a great drink for cooling oneself down on a hot, humid Mississippi summer night. Chances are that you would not have seen the aristocratic owner sweeping the porch, working in the yard, trimming the roses, or tending to the cotton blossoms out in the field—only the "workers," laboring in that sweltering Mississippi sun.

They were called "workers" because slavery had been abolished almost eighty years earlier, although there was no telling that to the people of the Deep South, particularly those in Mississippi. They were a bit behind on those pesky things called civil rights. Mississippi would not vote to ratify the Thirteenth Amendment, abolishing slavery in the United States, until 1995, but missed the big step of actually filing it. A Freudian slip, one might say. The Thirteenth Amendment was adopted in 1865. One hundred forty-eight years later, on February 7, 2013, Mississippi finally, officially abolished slavery. It is fair to say Mississippi procrastinated a bit.

The "workers," as they were legally called, were still treated very much like slaves in 1943. They were treated dreadfully inhumanely, less so than one would treat a mule. The owner of one fine plantation in particular would be the one in that rocking chair looking down off his porch at you while sipping his mint julep. You could almost feel his delusional beliefs of superiority and judgment burning your skin while you strolled past. He was casting those proverbial stones with his judgmental god right by his side, or so he believed with his false grandeur. Religion is a funny thing in the South—always has been. There were people such as this plantation owner, Richard Kingsley, who bent religion to fit their personal agenda. Never mind what Jesus really thought or taught.

Yes; this hot, humid summer of 1943 was the summer of Joseph's birth in the Delta on a sweltering Mississippi day. This was not a good place to be born a little mulatto boy, as they called them, but only when being polite. This region was known as "the most southern place on earth." The self-proclaimed "grand" white aristocrats called people of mixed race mulattos or, more commonly, Negros. That is, only if they had to be what we now refer to as "politically correct," which, most of the time, they did not. Being known as "the most southern place on earth" still has its bad and good associations, but in the time of Joseph's birth, it was mostly bad for a little boy like him.

3

Joseph Kingsley

Joseph Kingsley was the full name of this beautiful baby boy. He was breathtaking. He had soft, mocha skin with a full head of curly hair, dark as the night was long. The touch of his skin was like caressing the finest of silks. His eyes were glossy and held a hint of blue. His mother was sure they would turn a beautiful chocolate brown just like her own. If you stared into his eyes, it was like you could see straight into his soul and directly into heaven. He surely would grow into a man who would drive the women wild. At birth, his last name was that of his birth mother, Dove. However, he was the Kingsleys' baby now.

You have heard the name of Richard Kingsley before: the aristocrat sitting on his porch with judgment in his eyes. The Kingsleys were a very well-known and influential family in the Delta and much of the South. They owned a highly successful cotton and soybean plantation in Clarksville.

Margret Kingsley was the woman of the house. She was a tall, skinny white woman. Her face was pallid, and her cheeks were sunken, with bright pink blush and pale, chapped lips. She resembled a made-up corpse right before the burial. She, along with the other ladies of the local church, was fixated with being skinny and being the "best" of the local societal women. She was successful in her labors to do so. She looked like a skeleton—one with bright, rosy cheeks and blonde, frizzy hair. She reeked with an overwhelming scent of patchouli, a pungent, earthy, and slightly sweet smell that, when overused, overpowers all your senses. Mrs. Kingsley used more than one person should ever use. If the wind caught her right, you could smell her a half mile down the road.

Mrs. Kingsley had insisted they change Joseph's last name if she was going to be forced to raise that "mixed beast," as she referred to him. She would not have a child in her home bearing the last name of Dove—the horror and the shame. The associations were just dreadful to Mrs. Kingsley. Her husband, Richard Kingsley, had humiliated her once again in the community, bringing shame upon the family. Surely all the townspeople were gossiping about this one. Mrs. Kingsley would have to skip a few more meals to make up for this humiliation.

Mr. Kingsley was a great, hard-nosed businessman. He was feared around the South for his harsh business tactics and his refusal to be told no. This was why they had such a successful cotton and soybean plantation. Some businessmen could get a sale solely on their charm or looks. Richard Kingsley had neither. He was fifty-two years old and didn't look a day over sixty-five. He had salt-and-pepper hair that he parted to the left side with a thick but not very effective hair product of some sort. His hair always looked like it needed a trim. He, too, had rosy cheeks. His, however, were not from too much blush. The pinkness was from too much bourbon whiskey. He had a fine love for his bourbon.

Mr. Kingsley also had a potbelly that protruded from his pants because he wore his pants too low and his belt too tight. He usually smelled like an unpleasant collaboration of strong cologne, bourbon, and cigars, but at least it was the finest of cigars. With that kind of money and power, he would not be caught dead smoking anything but the best money could buy. One can only assume he wore so much cologne to camouflage the whiskey smell, but unfortunately for everyone, it just made a rude, obnoxious, and festering stench of its own. Because of his lack of looks, style, or grace, not to mention his horrid smell, he needed his hard-nosed tactics to be successful in business. He could, at times, be a slight bit compassionate, which was shocking to most, but you sure wouldn't hear of that compassion from a little thirteen-year-old girl named Claudia Dove.

Claudia was an innocent and shy young girl. She had been born at a neighboring plantation and sent to work at the Kingsleys' when she was ten. She spent several years there before giving birth to her son. She helped out in the gardens and the fields. Claudia had a very tender manner to her, and she was a hard worker, one of the plantation's best. She was one of those children you might look at and long to hug tightly because of the sweet sadness you could see in her eyes. You could tell she'd had a rough life, but she only spoke of positive things . . . when she spoke at all.

Claudia's face was soft like a rose petal, with dark, chocolate skin to be envied. Her hair was usually brushed down flat, though stray hairs would pop out all over. If you ever had the chance to see her clean and all dressed up when she was a young adult, you would swear she was one of those fancy models out of France that the magazines sprawled all over their pages. Unfortunately, no, Claudia did not know of the minute compassionate side that was said to exist within Richard Kingsley. She learned the wrath and evil that was within him by simply uttering the word "no" in his presence one afternoon when she was only thirteen years old.

Nine months after that day, and a lot of healing later, Claudia gave birth to her baby boy. Even though Mr. Kingsley was not pleased to have a new baby, he told Mrs. Kingsley, "I cannot bear for it to be raised by that lying nigger."

Claudia had told a few others about her brutal rape. Of course, Mr. Kingsley denied it.

"Why would I need to rape a little nigger girl when I *am* Richard Kingsley," he said in an indignant tone.

Richard Kingsley had decided to force his wife to raise little Joseph as their houseboy.

"He can help you in the house, and you can train him just as you please. Once he is around eight, you will have your perfectly trained house nigger," Mr. Kingsley explained. "What woman would not want that?"

The dreams that Claudia had for her and her boy were stolen when he was stripped from her arms by Mr. Kingsley. Now her hopes for his future had seemingly vanished, because he would now be raised as a house slave for the Kingsley family. The dreams of her and her son together were gone, and her dreams for him alone were gone, but unfortunately, she would always have the nightmares of Richard Kingsley forcing his whiskey-soaked body on her while stealing her innocence with every thrust of his pungent, sweaty body pushing against hers.

4

Colds, Cries, and Sweet Lullabies

When Joseph was just a baby, he was no more than a nuisance to Mrs. Kingsley, even though the only way she knew he existed was when she heard him cry a few rooms over. Mrs. Kingsley and the women of her social circle did not dare raise children even if they were their own. Why in the world would they waste their effort on children when they had nannies and maids? That's what the help is for, right?

Joseph spent most of his days with his nanny, Berta. Without Berta, he would never have known the touch of a loving hand or an embrace. The Kingsleys surely were not giving those out. Berta loved and raised Joseph as her own. She always kissed his soft, sweet head before putting him to sleep while singing to him the song her mother had once sung to her, a familiar African-American lullaby that had been passed down for decades:

O, go to sleepy, sleepy, li'l baby,
'Cause when you wake,

You'll git some cake,

And ride a li'l white hossy.

O' de li'l butterfly, he stole some pie,

Go to sleepy, li'l baby, and flew so high

Till he put out his eye.

O, go to sleepy, li'l baby.

This was an old lullaby that had been passed down when Berta's mother was a little girl. If it were not for Berta, Joseph would have been a different man when he grew up—very different—but he had Berta's guidance as a young boy. The love and guidance of someone can make all the difference in the world for a child, and it did for Joseph.

Berta was an elderly lady of seventy-three years old, and a rough seventy-three years it had been. She had lived most of her life in Clarksville. Her skin was worn from all the years out in the sun. Her hands were rough from the hard life of working the fields day in and day out, but they were gentle enough to rock Joseph to sleep every night. She was moved out of the field and into the house to work once Joseph came into the home. What great luck it was, she thought when she was put inside to raise Joseph. Someone of her age should not be out in the sweltering sun doing hard, manual labor.

After meeting Joseph and seeing how the Kingsleys treated him, she learned her move inside was not just about her at all; it was about God wanting them to save each other. Berta always looked tired and worn, but whenever she laid eyes on Joseph, her eyes had a sparkle in them. There were countless times that Berta risked her own life to protect Joseph from the strikes of Mrs. Kingsley. She would use her own body as a shield for little Joseph, each time risking retaliation that could result in her death.

Mr. Kingsley was not home often. When he was, he was too in-terested in his whiskey to care about the boy. You could say that Mr. Kingsley forgot that Joseph was alive, which was a sad truth and a blessing all in one. That was one less person from whom Berta had to protect Joseph.

Mrs. Kingsley and Berta early on came to a mutual understanding about Joseph. One night when Joseph was only two months old, he developed an awful cold. All night, he screamed. No matter what Berta did, she could not comfort the boy. She rocked him, gave him milk, and even gave him an old cold remedy her mama had used on her when she was a young girl. Nothing seemed to ease his pain, so scream he did.

The screaming woke Mrs. Kingsley, a hideous beast when awakened. She was like a bear being disturbed from its winter's slumber. She rose out of her bed sniffling and rabid. She flung on her pale blue night coat while shoving her long, bony toes into her silken, laced night slippers. She then proceeded to storm down the staircase, screaming.

"Shut that fucking little nigger up before I shut him up myself!"

Clearly, the Christianity was seeping from her pores as she shrieked with fury about this tiny baby scalding with fever. She burst into the nursery where Joseph and Berta were. Still screaming, she picked little Joseph up and violently shook him.

"Shut up, I say, shut up! You will listen to me, nigger!"

She threw him down and raised her hand back as far as she could with the full intent of striking this two-month-old baby boy until he submitted and did as he was told. Just as her hand was coming down knuckles first, she felt an abrupt force grab her. Berta had tired of using her back as a shield, so she grabbed Mrs. Kingsley's wrist as hard as she could and, in a deep, almost possessed-sounding voice, said, "If you evuh touch dis boy like dat again, I will kill you. I know dat dey will kill me fo it, but I have lived my life. Dis boy has not, and I will make sure you are dead cold before deys ever make it to me."

Mrs. Kingsley turned white as a ghost, even whiter than she already was, if you can imagine that. She turned around without saying a word and quietly went back up the stairs to her room, most likely not to go right back to sleep. Surely she was just lying in her bed awake, stricken with fear, reliving every moment of what had just happened and knowing Berta meant every damn word. For weeks after that, Mrs. Kingsley had fingerprint-sized bruises on her wrist as a gentle reminder of the lesson she had learned that night. Mrs. Kingsley never again laid a hand on Joseph as long as Berta was around.

5

Tea Parties and Oak Trees

Joseph had an interesting childhood, to say the least. Growing up, he saw all kinds of politicians and other important people come through the doors of the Kingsleys' home. Joseph and Berta would just sit on an old wooden bench in the foyer and watch all the important businessmen and the politicians come and go as deals were made and lost and drinks consumed, only to reappear hours later, in some cases, on the floor. Not all of the guests could hold their liquor. Many became sloppy very quickly and provided great entertainment for Berta and Joseph.

Joseph was now a young boy of ten. His days had come to include several things; schooling was one. A teacher hired by the Kingsleys came to the house to educate Joseph. They felt that if he were not well spoken enough to meet their standards, he would embarrass them.

Work was the other thing that filled Joseph's days. He worked odd jobs in the house, but he knew that when Mrs. Kingsley was aggravated with him, he would get sent out into the sweltering sun to pick cotton in the field or perform whatever job could be forced on a boy of that age. This happened more often than not. He still had the light in his eyes and his strong spirit, but he no longer had that tender baby skin. His hands especially had lost everything childlike about them besides their small size. The hard labor stripped him of that. His hands were rough and rugged like a grown man's hands, with blisters and calluses all over them. He was also quite muscular for a boy his age.

One particular summer day, he had been in the yard all day doing different sorts of chores, such as trimming bushes, chopping wood, and caring for the animals. He was exhausted. Then he heard his ill excuse for a mother, Mrs. Kingsley, yell his name. This was the only mother he had known since he was taken from his biological mother the day of his birth. He had not seen her since, nor did he know who she was, because she had been sent away after mentioning her rape. The kiss and tight embrace of Claudia's motherly love had been stripped away from him.

Berta did her best to show him love. She did as best as she knew how within her restrictions. Being affectionate toward Joseph in the presence of Mrs. Kingsley was forbidden. This was just another way that Joseph was mistreated. Tragically, he didn't know the difference between Mrs. Kingsley's treatment and true motherly love.

Mrs. Kingsley screeched from the porch, "Come here, boy!"

Joseph knew he better make it fast before he angered her.

"I need my tea. The church ladies will be here shortly for our prayer meeting," Mrs. Kingsley spouted. "Make it hot but not too hot, and don't embarrass me as you did last time the ladies came by."

Joseph always tried his best for her, but at times he would get nervous and clumsy, especially when people came by. He was still at that tender age where he wanted to please. He wanted everyone to be happy and proud of his work.

Mrs. Kingsley's church lady friends arrived. They were a breed all their own, infamous for praising God's name and, in the next breath, gossiping and judging the misfortunes of others. By the way, they believed that if someone was black, poor, or different from them, it was a vast misfortune.

All the ladies, Mrs. Kingsley included, always walked with a sense of entitlement and placed their indignant looks of shame upon others they deemed less worthy. These ladies would not even look directly at little Joseph. They would simply ignore his existence unless he was pouring their tea or doing whatever task they'd burdened the boy with. How could they acknowledge him? He was not as "Christ-like" as they, or so they delusively believed.

Mrs. Kingsley called Joseph to bring the tea.

"Boy, bring the fine ladies and me our tea."

The reason Joseph was always more nervous when Mrs. Kingsley had guests was because he was expected not to embarrass the family with childlike mistakes. What ten-year-old makes childish mistakes? He slowly walked the serving tray, balanced with the teakettle and the cups on their little saucers, to the small table situated in the middle of the ladies' "prayer" (gossip) circle. The whole time he was walking over, you could hear the tea sloshing in the kettle. The shaking of his nervous little hands was creating a rattling sound from the cups and the kettle top clanging against each other.

Joseph finally reached the table and set down the tray. He carefully poured the tea to ensure its evenness in each cup. As he handed out the teacups to the ladies with his unsure and shaky hand, one lady did not properly secure the cup in her hand. Down went the good china, as Mrs. Kingsley called it. It was as if everything happened in slow motion, the teacup plummeting while Joseph just froze, petrified of what "he" had just done. Before anyone knew what had happened, the tiny teacup was in a hundred pieces all over the floor. Steam rose from the ground, created by the tea's heat against the cold hardwood floor.

Mrs. Kingsley jumped up, reared her bony knuckles back, and swiftly struck the back of her hand solidly against Joseph's little face, right across his cheek, knocking him backward. Just before he was sure to fall to the ground, Joseph caught himself on the arm of a chair occupied by one of the ladies.

Mrs. Kingsley had scanned the room, ensuring that Berta was nowhere to be found, before she slapped Joseph. She could still remember that cold, firm grip on her arm. She was not going to make that mistake again. No, Berta was nowhere to be found because she was bedridden in the little house out back. She had been feeling ill lately and was forbidden to come into the main house out of fear she would infect the others. It was no matter to the Kingsleys that Berta was not ill with something contagious. It was just their excuse so that they would not have to deal with it.

After Joseph caught his balance on the arm of that chair, he ran from the room, trying his best to hold back the tears. All the while, Mrs. Kingsley was profusely apologizing for Joseph's poor behavior. "I am so embarrassed. You can't find good help anymore, and it is so difficult to train them just right. Don't y'all agree?"

All the ladies nodded in agreement as they resumed their conversation about training the help like they were circus animals.

The incident had passed, and the ladies continued with their "prayer" meeting while another member of the help cleaned up the shattered china and hot tea. One lady, Mrs. Sheryl Barnett, said, "Did you see the Smiths in church on Sunday? I cannot believe they are not too ashamed to show their face after they lost their farm. If I lost all my money, I would not show my face to a soul."

"Oh, Sheryl, really? How unfortunate," Mrs. Walton replied, trying to mimic sympathy.

"It's true," Mrs. Barnett said. "Gerald and I watched the bank men come and take it all. How embarrassed they must feel; just a shame."

Mrs. Henryson chimed in:

"Well, did you hear about the Johnsons, who lost their baby this month? They were due in just a few months. Bless their hearts. I wonder what they did wrong for God to want to take their baby. It's just sad to me that people can't follow in Jesus's footsteps. If they did, maybe these horrible things would not have happened to them, and they could be fortunate enough to still have their baby."

"Amen!" the others exclaimed, as if there were the slightest bit of care or actual praise behind the word.

Mrs. Walton asked, "Have you spoken to them since they lost the baby?"

"Oh, Lord, no, but I will put them on the prayer list for this week. Maybe the church can send them a card, and we could all sign it," Mrs. Kingsley said.

The ladies all agreed that a "heartfelt" card was a grand idea. They could keep their distance while giving the illusion they gave a damn. Fakeness at its finest. They were doing God's work after all, right? The grotesque gossip and self-delusions of grandeur continued like this for more than an hour. This was their specialty: to belittle people while leading them to believe that they held actual concern and that everything they did was done in His (God's) image. In actuality, they were like a tornado to his image, shattering it like a windowpane.

While the gossiping in Jesus's name continued inside, Joseph was outside in his favorite spot. It was under a grand, majestic live oak tree with wide-spanning and winding branches that reached out on all sides as if trying to touch the corners of the earth. Joseph wished he could stretch out and touch all the corners of the world. Besides being an inspiration to Joseph, this oak also gave him great shade and comfort when he went there to think or to cry. This was where he solved all his boyhood problems, even though most of them were issues no one should ever have to deal with, especially a child. The tree protected and embraced him when he most needed it.

Joseph would always go to this spot to think. He constantly wondered what else life had to offer. He just knew there was more. His purpose on this earth was not serving the Kingsleys—it was something much greater.

Joseph always felt a great sense of injustice. As he sat under that regal oak tree, he thought about an unjust world. This should not be a recurring thought pattern in the mind of a ten-year-old child, but that was all little Joseph could think about. He felt destined for a different life.

Joseph touched his cheek to wipe the warm tears as they rolled down his face. His cheek was still hot and red from Mrs. Kingsley's bony knuckles. Joseph had been slapped many times in his short life, but this time, it was different. It changed him forever. It sparked uncharted thoughts—dangerous thoughts for people in the Kingsleys' position, because these types of thoughts were ones that could spark a revolution of change.

"Why would I be raised by parents like them? Why me?"

Joseph was talking to that voice inside of him, or maybe to God; at that age, it was all one and the same. He had questions—hard ones. God had better answer up. He wanted to know why Berta could not be his mama. Why couldn't he and Berta live in a big, pretty house like the Kingsleys'? He'd always had a sense that how he was treated was wrong even though he did not know anything different. He felt deep inside that this type of treatment was not right, and a feeling deep inside is where the truth always starts.

Even though Joseph was not sure what he thought about God at the moment, God was to be thanked for Joseph's depth. He was very perceptive and spiritually deep for a ten-year-old. He always thought of a better life and changing how things were. This slap had been almost like a slap of awakening into reality. A slap of courage; a slap to create change in this world as he knew it.

6

Berta and the Little House

Joseph had been lonely lately without Berta around. She had been ill for almost a week now, still banished to the little house out back. The little house was an overly endearing term for a place lacking just that—endearment. Joseph had called it that since he was much younger, but in actuality, it was the slave quarters. Nowadays, it was called the quarters for the help, but everyone knew what it was even if they didn't want to admit it.

Little boys need constant entertainment. Without Berta, Joseph would quickly get bored. He had no one he could talk to or with whom to observe the goings-on of the house. He was a very mature ten-year-old, mostly because he was forced to be, but Berta had also started to deteriorate mentally, as many elderly people do. This allowed him and Berta to develop a friendship-type bond. It was strange to see an eighty-three-year-old and a ten-year-old getting along as best friends, but that's what they had become. The human condition requires companionship, and it can adapt to those needs. These two even developed their own language so they could laugh at all the antics that would happen in the house, especially when the Kingsleys were entertaining. They would use their eyes and hands to communicate. The two had slight hand signals for almost everything. You needed to pay close attention to notice anything was being communicated. This was important for their safety.

Berta always made Joseph laugh. She would tell him stories of the past and encouraged him to dream his own future. Whenever he questioned Berta about why things were the way they were, why they were treated differently, and why they couldn't live in a nice big house and have people do things for them, Berta would tell him: "Boy, you always do for yourself, be strong, and don't depend on dem others to give you a leg up in your life or to do your work for you. You can have what evuh you want, but no great man was built on laziness—and you will be a great man. The future is your dream. It can be what evuh you want it to be. You can change what evuh you set your mind to. Don't listen to dem Kingsleys' rubbish."

These words of wisdom stuck with Joseph. They made his questions and the anger of his situation grow stronger. His sense of injustice was fueled by these words of empowerment. This kind of talking and thinking was forbidden at the Kingsley home, as well as in most of the Deep South, for African Americans or anyone not of pure Caucasian descent. They did not take a liking to free thinking or dreaming of a different society, because the Kingsleys and those of a like mind were quite happy with the way things were. If people like Joseph started thinking for themselves, they would see how weak-minded and ignorant people like the Kingsleys were, and they would change their entire universe. Why would the Kingsleys want change when what they had was, to them, an almost perfect society? If the "workers" dared to dream, it could shatter the perfectly deluded reality they lived in every day. Joseph was a dreamer, and no one would stop his dreams. He would start to pull at the strings of an already unraveling societal structure very soon, but for now, he was missing his only friend.

Joseph decided to get up from the ground beneath that oak tree, wipe his tears, and sneak off to visit Berta. For days, he had been asking Mrs. Kingsley when Berta was going to get to come back to the big house. Mrs. Kingsley would just shrug off his questions and answer with an irritated and rash tone.

"Soon, boy, soon."

He was tired of waiting for soon. Joseph hatched a plan to sneak off when no one was looking. He headed to the little house to see Berta even though he was forbidden by the Kingsleys to do so. He was always one to follow the rules the Kingsleys had dictated for him. However, in this instance, he missed his friend too much to care about the rules.

Joseph was also pissed and hurt by the abuse Mrs. Kingsley had dealt him in front of all those church ladies. It was humiliating and dehumanizing. Joseph was now feeling defiant and rebellious. This was the perfect time to sneak off: he was outside alone while Mrs. Kingsley was inside, busy gossiping about the whole town. Mr. Kingsley was away on business. The mixture of sadness, anger, and opportunity is what made him decide to make his move.

He quietly snuck off behind "the big house," as he called it, through the tall cotton all the way to the little house in back. He glanced around slyly, as if he were on a covert mission, before he hopped up onto the porch. He quickly opened the creaky door and slipped in. His eyes needed to adjust to the lack of light in the windowless room. The only light came from the cracks in the wood on the walls and in the floor, where you could see straight down to the sandy ground. Some tall weeds had grown up through a few planks.

As Joseph looked around, he noticed how tiny and worn the room was. Even though he had never been loved or treated well by the Kingsleys, he had become accustomed to elegant surroundings, so this was new and different to him. He had been here once before—the day he was born—although he had no memory of that or of the inside of this wretched place.

It was a crowded space with a multitude of beds. It looked like someone had played a vigorous, piece-cramming puzzle game of Tetris to fit it all in there. The stove and one bed touched, that's how jam-packed it was. He wondered how someone could warm a pot of tea or coffee without setting the bed on fire. The whole room smelled of sweat, blood, and thousands of tears. Joseph wondered how anyone could sleep there.

Suddenly, he felt a hand reach out and touch him. It was cold and fragile. There was not much flesh covering the bones. He jumped and started to scream, but then he heard a weak, shaky voice.

"Joseph?"

Without missing a breath, Joseph said, "Berta, is that you? I have missed you. When can you come back to the big house with me? I am lonely, and I have no one to talk to there. No one likes to talk to me. I have no friends but you. I want you to come back with me. It's much nicer in there. Why do you have to stay here? It's so little and scary. It smells funny, too. Why don't you come with me?"

Berta waited until Joseph was done with all his questions, which he blurted out as if they were never-ending. Even though they were friends, she still knew he was just ten, and in her experience, ten-year-old boys had a lot of questions. Berta reached out and very tenderly touched Joseph's face. Tears fell from her eyes and down her old, sunken, sun-worn cheeks.

"Joseph, I need you to be a big boy. I need you to follow your dreams. You dream big, now. You hear me, boy? You know all da time you wander off in your mind, and your mind tells you dis ain't right? You listen to dat voice in you now, ya hea. Don't let anyone hit you or treat you like you less than dem, because believe me, boy, you are not. You are as good as dem people or better. You have a bigger heart than dem people, and you know how to think on your own. You're a smart boy, and I want you to act like one.

"Don't stay around here and waste your whole life like I did. The only good thing I did by stickin' around here was meetin' you. Even if I had tried to leave when I was younger, and dey had killed me for it, my Jesus has a better place for me than here. If I had went to spend my life scrubbin' Jesus's feet, at least he would talk to me nice, he would look me in my eyes, and I would have a nice place to lay my head at night. I don't want you to get my age and feel this regret, boy. No person should be dis age and still answerin' to someone else.

"You need freedom. You deserve to be free of all dis just like your mind tells you so. So you listen to that voice inside. You leave, and you make a difference for you and for people like you. No needs in continuin' like dis. You are strong. I believe in you. You, little boy, are my hero. Now you need to start actin' like it and be your own hero."

Hearing this, Joseph felt inspired and confused at the same time.

"Why do you tell me this, Berta?" he said. "I don't want to leave, because I don't want to leave you. I will stay as long as you do. If you really want me to leave, we can go together. You are my best friend. You are my only friend. Without you, I don't have a friend, and I am very lonely. Please, Berta, don't make me go alone. Don't make me leave you."

Joseph said this while becoming increasingly panicked and confused. Berta took a shallow breath and uttered, "Don't be foolish, boy."

She then reached out and took Joseph's warm little hand into hers while tears streamed down her face. "Joseph, you won't be alone; I'll always be with you, but in a different way. I know dat you would never leave me, but I have to leave dis place now. I will find you again, don't worry, boy. You'll be much loved one day, but I have to go now. I can't hold on any longer."

Joseph, in a confused and nervous voice, questioned her. "But Berta, where are you goin'?"

Berta squeezed his hand. "My sweet boy, I am headed to wash Jesus's feet."

Berta died that day and was buried out behind the little house. There was no funeral, but when no one was around, Joseph went out with tears in his eyes and picked some of those blooming cotton blossoms and laid them on her grave. He had no idea of the irony and depth of laying those blossoms there—that's the funny thing about being a kid. He was just ten years old and thought they were pretty. He knew how much Berta liked pretty things.

7

The Rose Vine

Joseph's life for the next few years was pretty normal, considering his circumstances. He worked, and then he worked some more. Joseph was also starting to physically develop into a handsome young man. His deepening voice sure sounded like that of a young man. Thanks to Berta, he had learned how to carry himself like a fine good one, too. He was very polite to everyone. Unlike most of the others around whom he had been raised, Joseph believed that all humans were equal; therefore, he treated them as such. He treated people politely. He clearly had no respect for those who treated him poorly, so saying he treated them with respect would be an overstatement, but polite would be the correct word.

As Joseph grew older, the anger inside him grew stronger, like a volcano waiting to erupt. He still lived with the Kingsleys, spending his days growing more resentful of how his life was turning out. His want for something better was incessant. He knew there was more out there for him, but it was as if all his desire and anger were festering, waiting for the perfect storm.

It was a beautiful spring day. The sun was warm, the birds were chirping, and all the flowers were in bloom. It's as if all life comes back to the world during the spring. The sounds, the smells, the warm touch of the sun on your skin with sweet scents of honeysuckle tickling your nose; that is the essence of spring. Joseph appreciated all of this. Spring was his favorite time of year.

This perfect spring day, Joseph was out tending the garden. He didn't mind this job. It got him outside to enjoy the weather on days that were this beautiful. He also liked to watch life come about. He lived through the plants. He watched them grow into everything they had been put on this earth for. He made sure they were healthy and got all the care needed to thrive. Likewise, he yearned to be able to grow into what he had been put on earth for without repression. He was almost jealous of the plants. There was nothing there to hold them back from their full potential. There was, however, one rose vine that was Joseph's favorite. It was held back by rope and wooden lattice to force it to grow the way the Kingsleys desired. No matter how much they tried to train it to grow a certain way, it still pushed through that lattice and grew however it pleased. This rose vine reminded Joseph of himself.

Mr. Kingsley had been sick the last few days, so sometimes during the day he would sit and watch Joseph work. Joseph did not like this one bit. He enjoyed being out there alone, able to appreciate life and nature without being watched. Nature was one of the only things he was allowed to fully enjoy. No one could notice that he took pleasure in it, so they could not stop him.

Joseph did not like the way Mr. Kingsley stared down at him with judgment and disdain in his eyes. He felt a heaviness from Mr. Kingsley's sinister energy. It was a dark gloom pushing down on him, his mood, and his spirit. He could feel the negativity clinging to his body and the poison slowly seeping into his pores. You could see his body slowly starting to slump from the cloud of darkness weighing down on him. His shoulders slouched inward, his back hunched over, and his head sunk straight down into his shoulders like a tortoise's.

The vile presence lurking over him was one way to ruin a nice spring day that he was otherwise enjoying.

This is some kind of shit, Joseph thought to himself. *The one thing I enjoy, and this drunk is out here staring at me like he wants nothing more than for me to mess up so he can scream at me.*

Mr. Kingsley was an angry, miserable man. He loved nothing more than to force his misery on others. It is said that misery loves company, and on this day in particular, Mr. Kingsley was apparently very lonely. He just loved to assert his power and control over people. One could even claim that he used his privilege of power for evil.

Mr. Kingsley just sat there sipping on his stagnant glass of whiskey, warmed by the sun, while tiny beads of sweat formed on his upper lip. He took his fat tongue and licked the beads of sweat off his lip, believing it to be little drops of whiskey that had escaped his mouth.

He leaned forward and muttered, "Boy, what's wrong with that bush?"

Joseph could not hear or understand his drunken mumbling. "Sir?" he politely responded.

Mr. Kingsley drunkenly hollered, "Ya def, boy, or ya just stupid? I said, what's wrong with that bush? I told you and all the other ignorant niggers that this here bush should climb up the wall, as it is supposed to. You can't get one damn thing right even if Jesus himself had taught ya how.

"If you want something done right you have to stand over somebody and make sure they do it nowadays with these lazy, damn niggers. Is that what ya tellin' me, boy?"

It was no mind to Mr. Kingsley that it was a vine, not a bush, and Joseph was pretty positive the saying was "If you want something done right, you have to do it yourself." He would not ever dare tell this to Mr.

Kingsley, though. He just allowed the ignorant old drunk to think he was right. It was just a known understanding that the Kingsleys, and people of like minds, didn't dare do anything themselves. God forbid they participate in manual labor. Joseph knew not to talk back, but at the time, he was also at a loss for words. What do you even say to a drunk who isn't making any sense? Joseph sure didn't know.

Mr. Kingsley stood up, a bit wobbly at first. He pulled up his slightly dirty khaki-colored pants so that his entire backside was again covered. He slowly stomped down the stairs of the porch and went around the corner of the house. He was headed toward the shed on the back side of the house.

Joseph was scared and confused. "Where is that drunk headed?" he uttered to himself. "Did he forget what he was doing?"

He wanted nothing more than to continue working, but he was paralyzed from the fear and anticipation of what Mr. Kingsley was up to. He could feel the intensity in the air. Even though the sky was cloudless, it was as if darkness had covered everything in sight. Mr. Kingsley rounded the corner of the house with nothing more than pruning shears.

What in the hell is he doing? Joseph thought. *Is he coming to work? Surely he would not lift a finger in this yard.*

He had never seen this man work in the yard in his full fourteen years on this earth.

Mr. Kingsley walked up and demanded, "Give me your gloves." He snatched the gloves from Joseph and put them on his own hands. "Here, boy, this is how you do it."

He started to hack at pieces of the rose vine, shredding all the beauty it once possessed and stripping it of its individuality and freedom. He was even slicing off the blooming rosebuds. There was no method or reason to his madness. He was just wildly shredding.

Joseph watched as Mr. Kingsley butchered everything beautiful about this oppressed but willfully strong-growing vine. Mr. Kingsley continued with his oh-so-helpful dictation.

"Now you grab it, boy, and pull these limbs off."

"But I have no gloves," Joseph said.

"Does it look like I care that you have no gloves? I don't give a shit. You do what you're told, boy," Mr. Kingsley said.

Joseph started to tear at it vine by vine, ripping them off the main stem. His hands were bloody and torn from the thorns slicing into him as he yanked at these tough vines. Some of the vines would just rip through his hands and snap right back into place. Their strength and resilience shined through. It's not known if Joseph was more upset by the pain or by the fact that this free-spirited living thing was being torn down in much the same way the Kingsleys had tried to tear him down his entire life.

Mr. Kingsley stumbled a bit as he reached to cut the thickest of the vines from the stem. Out of nowhere, he started to strike Joseph with that vine. He attacked Joseph like a rabid dog foaming at the mouth, consumed with delirium. The first strike hit Joseph in the face, just over his right eye. He winced and cowered down while raising up his hand and forearm to protect his face. Rageful, Mr. Kingsley just kept hitting him over and over with the vine, striking him all over his now bloody and shredded body.

"You and these goddamn plants will listen to me! No one disobeys Richard Kingsley! No one!"

Mr. Kingsley finally ceased his madness. What was only minutes had seemed like an eternity. For the first time in his life, Richard Kingsley had a look of confusion in his eyes. He was not sure what he had just done. After all, this was his son by blood. He sat down, slumped over, and placed his hands to rest on his knees. He sat there for a moment, out of breath and wheezing. That was the most exercise he had seen all year. Joseph stood there with his bloodied face and body, preparing for more while silently praying it was over. Mr. Kingsley uttered something that was barely audible. Joseph thought maybe his mind was playing tricks on him, but he could have sworn that while Mr. Kingsley was slumped over there, through his wheezing, he'd uttered, "Sorry, boy."

One can't help but wonder what might have triggered Mr. Kingsley to lash out like this in the first place. Was it that he could just sense the dormant rebellion and strength in both Joseph and that rose vine? Mr. Kingsley's character and personality were so weak that he could not handle anything that challenged his authority, whether it be a plant or a person. Neither Joseph nor the once-stunning rose vine was weak: both had a strong desire to grow however they pleased.

This was not just any spring day in Clarksville, Mississippi; no, this was the spring of Joseph Dove. This was the day he started to blossom into a strong, independent young man. This marked the day he started to allow himself to bloom into what he was always meant to be. All that anger and drive he had held within himself would someday help him to join one of history's most noble struggles for civil rights and equality.

Joseph, for the first time, thought, *I will be free!*

8

Joseph Dove

After that day in the garden, Joseph refused to be known as Joseph Kingsley anymore. Of course, he could not voice this to anyone in the Kingsley home. He did not have liberties such as personal choices or opinions in the Kingsley household—or anywhere in much of the South. No; if you were colored, you were expected to just put your head down and do as you were told.

Racism was bad in the South, but it actually grew in Mississippi during the 1940s. For far too many people, voicing opinions or trying to make personal choices was literally a life-or-death situation. Joseph had changed his name to Joseph Dove, but only in his own mind. He liked to wait till he was alone just so he could hear himself say it out loud: "Joseph Dove." Oh, what a nice ring it had when he said it out loud. It excited him how it rolled off his tongue so eloquently.

A few months prior, Joseph had found an old letter that talked of his birth mother. It even listed her name: Claudia Dove. *What a beautiful name,* he thought. He had never before heard of her or known anything about her. No one in the Kingsley household ever spoke her name. Even though Claudia could have offered so much more love to Joseph than the Kingsleys could ever muster, they were disgusted by her and believed her to be less than human. With the letter in hand, Joseph now possessed her name and a location where he believed she might be. He had a new mission—to find his birth mother.

After Claudia had been vilely raped and given birth to Joseph, Mr. Kingsley had sent her away due to her speaking about what had happened. He couldn't chance the possibility of even one person believing all the "lies," as he put it, she was spreading. Even though slavery had been abolished long ago, that was not the reality for many in the Deep South. No one was truly free. The lack of educational opportunities, combined with poverty, racism, and unadulterated hatred, kept African Americans enslaved to these rich white folks. It had been easy for the Kingsleys to sell Claudia to a man in Doddsdale, Mississippi.

Jim Oscar Westridge was a cotton plantation owner and a United States senator. This sounded like it might not be too bad of a place to be sold to. Assuming for a moment that the sale of a person could ever have a silver lining, this might be one. Senator had a nice ring to it, but Joseph would soon find that this couldn't be further from the truth. The only thing that was ringing over at the senator's house was hatred, bigotry, corruption, and an evil that saturated everything.

The letter Joseph had discovered a few months earlier was not a letter at all but a bill of sale listing his birth mother's name along with where and to whom she had been sold. This was all the information Joseph needed, because he was finished with all of this plantation life and the malicious treatment he had received since he was old enough to form memories. He knew deep down in his soul that treating a human like that wasn't right. He had made up his mind that he was getting out of there.

Joseph had big plans for himself and his mother. He was going to travel to Doddsdale, get his mother, and take her off that plantation. They would get a home of their own and live together happily ever after. Isn't that the dream: to live in a peaceful place full of love and acceptance, free from hatred, with no one beating you or raping you, no one monitoring and controlling all your actions, no one screaming at you or breaking you down to the very core of your soul and existence, where everyone in the home is treated as an equal? Isn't that everyone's dream? It was Joseph's. How nice it must be to enjoy a more simplistic dream of getting an education, getting married, and living happily ever after. Even though Joseph did occasionally fantasize about those things, he and many others did not have the luxury of making those dreams their main focus. Some were consumed with prayers and dreams of surviving another day; others dreamed of and prayed for death.

Over the years, Joseph had come in contact with a little bit of money here and there, and if you save, money slowly adds up. People would drop money out of their pockets or handbags while enjoying a spot of intoxication at one of the Kingsleys' famous soirees, attended by the most prominent and wealthiest of the South. They would dance and mingle in handcrafted gowns and luxury suits tailored to perfection. They loved to be seen and to boast about their money through lavish things. They would often stand around and marvel at how the poor were able to live without all these possessions.

"Poor things. How could they ever be happy? Bless their hearts."

Although these statements sound endearing, in the South they are nothing more than insults. There is no true concern or care in these sentiments.

Joseph could not grasp how they needed these material things to make them seem happy. This troubled him. Many of the people Joseph encountered at these parties had such deep, embedded misery. They muffled it, for a moment, with the shiny new objects they purchased for themselves. Joseph noticed that shiny things easily distracted them, just like a parakeet with a sparkly spoon. Parakeets love shiny objects.

Shiny objects and arrogance were the only shallow pieces of happiness these people could grasp. Their arrogance was manifested in a manner of grandiosity. They had manipulated themselves to believe that they were superior to others, including Joseph. They clearly lacked greatly in a little department called morality.

Joseph thought that, having all this money at their disposal, surely they would never miss or even notice when they dropped a quarter, especially while they were rapidly ingesting the finest wines, champagnes, and liquors that money could buy. A quarter was too small to hold significance to these "fine" people. Joseph would capitalize on these opportunities when they arose. The morning after a soiree, he would find the misplaced money and tuck it away somewhere safe.

Joseph had a great hiding place for the money. There was a loose board in his room upstairs he'd found one day while hiding under his bed from the Kingsleys' shouting. Mr. and Mrs. Kingsley had many of these infamous fights. The level of screaming and abuse was something the worst of quarrelers would shriek at. However, they would not dare fight in front of others. The simple thought of the shame and embarrassment this would bring to the family was unspeakable, even though everyone knew of their verbal brawls. No kind of gossip could slip past these townspeople. The Kingsleys didn't regard the help and Joseph as people; so, even though Joseph was in the house, they still considered this being alone.

Joseph despised the arguing and fighting. All he had been through had not hardened him. He still had his gift of sensitivity. It could even be argued that this was his greatest gift of all. It allowed him to have profound depth and to show the same compassion to all living beings. He wanted to battle for those that needed help. Because of this, all the reckless fighting greatly upset his tender soul. That was why he always hid under the bed in his room upstairs when their arguments got aggressive.

This day, he ran to his bed and dropped down to his hands and knees quickly, shuffling into his safe haven. As he slid under his dome of protection, a nail snagged his sagging shirt. It was a new shirt, so he knew he was going to be in trouble when the Kingsleys found out. In most families, it was a known fact that little boys and girls alike got holes in their clothes from time to time. Kids could be very rough on clothing. Clothing was not meant to last forever—but it was in this family. Joseph was in a panic. What should he do? Thoughts of pure fear raced through his mind. *What will they do to me?*

Just at the peak of his anxiety, Joseph looked down and noticed that the board with the nail sticking out was loose. He realized that the board could be lifted, so, out of childish curiosity, he pulled it up and revealed a nice little cubby between the floor and the downstairs ceiling. This was a great treasure because now no one would ever have to find out about his shirt. He was saved. He removed his shirt and stuffed it in his newfound hiding spot. This became where he hid the cigar box he used to stash his money. A fine cigar box it was, because, as we all know, Mr. Kingsley smoked only the best.

At times, Joseph felt guilty for not returning the soiree guests' dropped change. Not returning the money was not of the highest moral order, but he was just a young boy during those times. He had not yet developed a mature moral gauge, but he still had more morality than the guests from whom he profited. In his older years, he would return money even when he felt they didn't deserve it, but as a young boy, he knew no different. There was something that just didn't seem right about it, but what's a boy supposed to do? That money could help him someday when God gave him a path to save himself. He had very wisely learned in his short existence that God would provide a path, but the only person who could save him in this life was himself. "Be your own hero." That was what Berta had so wisely told him right before she died.

In some rare cases, other members of the help would give Joseph money for his birthday or other special occasions. It was only a penny here and a penny there, but that added up over the years. He felt very special on those exceptional days. The money itself was not special to him, even though he really appreciated it; what was special was how the money made him feel. That warm, fuzzy, loved feeling didn't come along very often during his childhood, especially after Berta died. If other help didn't do kind things for Joseph, who would? Not the Kingsleys. They were too hateful and stingy with their money. Mr. Kingsley's thought process was, *That could be good whiskey money; why waste it on the boy?*

Most young boys would spend every cent they got on a coke or some candy. Not Joseph; he was a little planner. He started saving the day after Mrs. Kingsley struck him so hard. That was the day he knew he was going to liberate himself from that horrible place. He had been plotting ever since. He had also been slowly collecting first aid supplies in case he was injured in his escape or during the journey to his mother.

9

The Great Escape

It had been about an hour since Mr. Kingsley had brutally beaten Joseph, who was still experiencing the unpleasant sensation of stinging and burning throughout his body. His clothes were ripped and stained with blood from the thrashing. He was leaving this shell of a home; it was time for him to fly. He was going to wait until Mr. Kingsley passed out from all the whiskey he had been knocking back all afternoon. After the immense amount of energy he had expended beating Joseph, he was surely due for a nap.

Joseph snuck into the living room, where Mr. Kingsley lay. He had finally passed out on the couch. Joseph was positive Mr. Kingsley was fast asleep because of the obnoxiously loud snoring coming from his gaping mouth. His fat, whiskey-filled belly was sucking in and swelling out, resembling that of a hippopotamus. Everyone knew this was not an animal to piss off.

Mr. Kingsley had gifted the couch pillow with a small puddle under his gaping mouth from his incessant drooling. He tended to drool a lot when he took alcohol-induced naps. Mrs. Kingsley would have had a fit because these were the nice pillows, not fit for him to lay his drooling, sweaty face on. Everyone knew that would ruin silk.

Joseph looked around to ensure Mrs. Kingsley was nowhere to be found. Earlier in the day, she had gone out with the church ladies for lunch. She would surely be gone a while because there was a whole lot of gossip to catch up on around town. Good gossip was hard to resist.

This was the perfect opportunity for Joseph to make his escape. All the excitement and fear of the unknown nauseated him. His rough hands were shaking, and everything looked a little hazy—surreal, even. He tried to stay in the present and keep it together. He rushed to his closet and grabbed a brown duffel bag that he had packed months before. He had been waiting for the right moment. Each night before bed, he would add and remove things from the bag, keeping it current and always changing his mind about what to take. He had a few summer clothes, a few winter clothes, the first aid kit he had cobbled together, an old canteen filled with water, and his cash, safely secured in the cigar box. The time was coming soon, so that week, he had collected some rolls from the dinner table along with several apples and two handfuls of dehydrated deer meat. That should do just fine for his journey.

Joseph had also packed a small teddy bear Berta had given him when he was a baby. It was a little worn and missing an eye, but it made him feel comforted and safe. He still slept with this bear even though he was fourteen, but he would not dare tell a soul that.

Joseph threw his brown duffel bag over his shoulder and crept his way down the stairs, his heart beating immensely faster with each step. If he were caught, the beating he'd receive would be like nothing he had ever experienced. He might not ever have another opportunity to escape this place. It was easy to get trapped but hard as hell to escape.

He could still hear Mr. Kingsley sucking in the walls with his snoring. The stairs creaking sounded like an orchestra striking up.

Each creak sent chills up his spine. Once he finally made it to the end of the stairs, which seemed like an eternity to him, he peered around the corner, looking for Mrs. Kingsley. He did not see her, and he had not heard her car pull up. With their rocky driveway, he could hear a car slinging rocks the second it turned into the drive.

Joseph crept past the living room, where he could see the couch Mr. Kingsley was consuming. Joseph ever so gently slipped past him and into the foyer. The front door was within a few feet. He was trying with all his might not break into a full run, which was what his mind was screaming at him: "Run!" He knew that if he ran, it would surely wake the sleeping drunk. So tiptoe he did.

He finally reached the door. With his hand shaking uncontrollably, he reached up and turned the knob. When he started to pull the door open, it let out a loud, piercing scream. He froze, waiting for a reaction. His face flushed, and his heart felt like it was about to explode. There was nothing. No movement.

"Oh, thank God," he whispered to himself.

He slipped out the door, made his way down the porch steps, and then stopped and looked around, ensuring the coast was clear. It was, so Joseph took off running down the gravel driveway. *Freedom!* he screamed inside. He was not yet far enough away from the house to be completely safe, but, boy, it sure felt good. He was finally off to find his real mother.

Joseph had been walking several miles on this old dirt road to freedom when he heard the most awful sound he could think of.

"Joseph Kingsley, what in the hell do you think you are doing?"

He was frozen in fear; he knew that voice even better than his own. He slowly turned his head to reveal the nightmare he knew to be true. It was Mrs. Kingsley, finally returning from her lunch. A thousand things flew through his head too fast for him to process.

All of a sudden, Joseph felt a warm sensation over his body: a courage; an anger. It was an adrenaline he had never felt before. Then he screamed at the top of his lungs: "Joseph Dove! My name is Joseph Dove!"

He turned and continued to walk away down the dirt road. Mrs. Kingsley was dumbfounded and had no response. She had seen the fire in his eyes and was a bit scared of the anger she saw in him. Last time she saw this kind of rebellion and anger had been with Berta— dear, sweet Berta.

When Joseph turned to walk off, he felt shock and pride. Mrs. Kingsley watched him walk away in her rearview mirror, and the strangest thing happened. A tear formed in the corner of her eye. It fell down her face, leaving a streak of white where it washed away the makeup. It had all happened so suddenly, before she could stop it. Somewhere along the way, through all the hate and mistreatment she had forced upon him for fourteen years, she had grown fond of having him in the house. Now she feared she would be in the house all alone. She knew Mr. Kingsley was never there, even when he was physically in the house.

Mrs. Kingsley quickly swiped her hand across her cheek, wiping away the only sign of humanity within her. She then drove off, never looking back. Somewhere deep down, she actually felt some sense of care and love for the boy. Or maybe it was just sheer self-loathing.

10

Blind Love

Joseph had a new pep in his step. He was on the road to finally meet his mother and—don't forget—the good senator. He had played this scenario out in his head a thousand times. He would show up and talk to the senator. Joseph would start by explaining to the man how it was his dream to live with his mother in their own home. He would then present the senator with all the money he had saved as payment for the release of his mother. It clearly would not be much money to the senator, but out of the kindness of his heart, he would indeed oblige. With such a convincing young boy in front of him, how could he not? He was, after all, none other than a great senator of the United States of America, bound to uphold certain standards. He then would hand Joseph his money back and say, "Why don't you keep this and use it toward your new home together?"

Joseph went over and over this scenario in his head. Every day on his long walks toward Doddsdale, this was all he could think about—this and what his mother would be like. He pictured himself walking up a long, gravel driveway with a majestic white home sitting at the very end. As he walked up, he could see a very regal-looking man with a white beard smiling and waving at him. It must be the senator. He seemed so welcoming and warm.

On the right-hand side, just before the house, there was a giant oak tree like the one under which he'd found refuge at the Kingsleys. He pictured his mother on a swing hanging from that large oak tree by two ropes that held a piece of wood between them, functioning as a little seat. There she sat, swinging so effortlessly. She looked flawless. She was wearing a beautiful, flowing white sundress with little yellow and pink flowers all over it. She had a beautiful, soothing yellow cotton blossom in her hair, a slight touch of soft pink caressing the tips of its petals as the sun did her face. She would see him and immediately know that he was her baby, her one and only, stripped out of her arms at birth. She would run to him, and tears would fall down her face out of pure joy and overwhelming emotion. He would reveal to her his plan to talk to the senator, and they would then go get a home together, where they would live happily ever after.

He continued to walk down the road to Doddsdale with these merry thoughts dancing in his head. This was a rarity, so he was really enjoying himself every step of the way. He felt like the sun was warming his heart and soul, with God smiling down on him. He was on the top of the world in this moment.

Joseph had calculated it would take him about three days to walk there. That included time to stop for sleep and to eat some of the snacks he had packed. However, he did not believe he would be sleeping a whole lot because of his sheer excitement. He had also set up a water-drinking schedule to ensure he would not run out. He had hopes that he would run across a fountain or hose on his journey so he could refill. Of course, he would need either a fountain approved for the colored or an unattended hose. This was a "kind" way of saying to the non-Caucasian community, "You are not human. You are afflicted with something we don't want to catch." This was all Joseph had known. These laws had been in place long before his birth. He found them ridiculous, but it was not something he was going to rebel against alone as a young black boy in the South. That would be a death sentence.

During the early spring in the South, temperatures can range from hot to cold within a few hours. One day you could be in shorts, and the next, layered in coat and pants. This was why he had packed himself a range of clothing options.

Joseph was making great time. Sometimes he walked late into the night, when it was just him and the stars. He found it so peaceful. He was able to take in everything around him on his journey. The beauty overshadowed the dirt he stirred up with each step. He was amazed at all the oak trees, the large, blossoming magnolias, and the sweet smell of the honeysuckle that lined his path. Occasionally, he passed a little farmhouse, but overall, it was just him and nature. He felt a sense of safety in its embrace.

Joseph did not often pass by people or cars since he was in such a rural area, but when he did, no one paid him much mind, which was good. He knew not to look anyone directly in the eye. This is the same cautionary information for if you were to come in contact with a leopard. If you look a leopard in the eye, it sees it as a challenge and will attack. Oddly, the same went for these townspeople in the South. The difference is that a leopard does not discriminate.

These people did discriminate against those they lovingly re-ferred to as "the Negros." Never mind if it was an adult or a child. Growing up, Joseph had heard many horrific stories about people he knew being attacked. He had even seen this ignorant brutality several times, so he learned to keep his head down and stay quiet. That was how you stayed alive in these parts. Fortunately, the people he passed probably just figured he was the new help for a neighboring house. The townspeople in these areas sure liked to gossip, but they didn't care too much about who had or didn't have new help.

Joseph sensed that he was getting closer to his destination. He knew he had walked a long distance. According to his calculations, he should be arriving sometime the next afternoon. It was a hard walk, but luckily, he was a strong boy. He would just keep walking south until he reached that Doddsdale sign. After that, it would be smooth sailing. It was as if he could not walk fast enough, but he knew he had to pace himself. He didn't want to overdo it and become sick or excessively hot. That would require too much of the water he'd brought. He still had not come across a fountain or hose he could use to refill his bottle. He had been very sparing with the water, but, boy, he sure was thirsty. If it had been summertime, he never would have made it.

The sun was starting to go down. He knew he would need his energy for all the excitement tomorrow, so he decided to hunt for a safe place to sleep. He wandered off the road and found a hay barn in the woods. Though he checked around for signs of activity in the area, he saw none besides some livestock tracks. This would work great: shelter and safety. There was a bit of loose hay on the ground. It was a tad moldy, but dry. He gathered some into a pile. It would make for a comfortable bed for the evening. It was way better than just the tough ground, which was how he had slept the previous two nights.

It hadn't taken him long at all to find this place, which allowed him to sit and enjoy the sunset. He could not remember a time in his life when he'd ever been happier and able to enjoy life without fear of retaliation. He thanked God for this moment, and he really took it all in. He even talked to Berta a bit. He sure wished she could be there with him to enjoy this sunset. She would have loved it.

As the sun went down, his appetite rose. He reached into his bag to pull out dinner: deer jerky and a roll. He was about to take his first bite when he heard screaming in the distance.

"You get back here, you little ingrate! I will find you . . . I don't care. Just go out there and be with the loose niggers!"

Joseph then heard footsteps steadily getting closer. His heart jumped. All his elated emotions that he had been feeling were gone in an instant, replaced by fear. The footsteps sounded like they were in a full sprint, and the crunching sounds of the leaves and pine needles rapidly got closer and closer. Where was he to go? Where was he to hide?

He was panicked and had no clue what move to make. Just then, he remembered the large rolls of hay in the corner of the barn. If he hurried, he could bury himself behind them. He jumped up, grabbed his bag, and darted behind all that hay. He burrowed in as quietly and quickly as he could. He became very still, but so did the footsteps. Listening intently, he then heard what sounded like sobbing coming from the front of the barn.

Who is crying in here? he wondered.

Was he hearing things? He wanted so badly to see who it was and what was going on, but he stayed put. His fear overruled his curiosity.

About fifteen minutes had passed, and the sobbing continued. Joseph's curiosity was growing stronger by the minute. He had also grown weary of being so still. A fourteen-year-old does not have that kind of patience—at least, this fourteen-year-old boy didn't.

Joseph hated when people cried. He always wanted to make it all better. He was a caring young fellow. Between his curiosity and his sympathetic heart, he could no longer remain hidden. Beside him, there was an opening between two of the hay rolls. He pushed himself up to the opening by grabbing the wall and one of the rolls of hay as leverage. He could only see through the crack in the rolls one eye at a time, but he was able to see a young girl. She looked to be about his age. She was sitting there sobbing, her rosy-cheeked face buried in her hands.

He wanted to help, but he did not want to frighten her. He just softly said, "Hello. I am Joseph. Don't be scared."

The girl turned around with a look of sheer fright on her face. She started to scream.

In a panicked voice, Joseph said, "No, please. I do not want to get into trouble. I just escaped where I grew up, and I am on my way to meet my mother for the first time."

He should not have been so divulging, but it just blurted out of his mouth so fast, like he had no control. Her face shifted. He could see a slight ease come over her.

"My name is Sarah," she responded in a soft, unsure tone.

"May I come out?" Joseph asked.

"Yes," she uttered with a little hesitance and a wee bit of curiosity in her voice.

He crawled out slowly so as not to spook her. He walked out from behind the hay and sat down on the opposite side from her in the front of the barn. He wanted to keep his distance so she would not feel afraid; also, honestly, girls still scared him a bit. Since he had not been around many, he was not sure how to act around them yet.

They talked for a few minutes—only small talk. They shared a giggle here and there. This went on for a few more minutes. After they had both loosened up a bit, Sarah decided to ask Joseph a real question, one that carried a lot of weight.

"How did you end up in one of our barns?"

He could have given her a simple answer, but instead, he just spilled it all out. He told her the whole story, feeling he could trust her. He'd gotten a sense of who she was, and he felt oddly comfortable with her, as if they had been friends forever.

Joseph started from the bitter beginning and did not skip any details. During his whole story, it was obvious how caring and attentive she was. At times, it looked as if his tale could be physically hurting her, she was so empathetic toward him. She thought of him as brave, and at the same time, she hurt for him. As Joseph was finishing his tragic story, he thought to himself that Sarah might be hungry or thirsty, so he offered her some of his water and food. He knew that he did not have the water to spare, but he could not resist offering her whatever she might desire.

He had never met someone this beautiful. Sure, she was a pretty girl on the outside. She had long, curly golden hair and skin like a newborn, with sun-kissed cheeks and light chocolate eyes that could make anyone stop in their tracks. He was almost positive he could see heaven through her eyes, and it seemed she felt the same way about his. She was very physically attractive, but he did not really notice this until after they had talked a bit. He had never felt this way with anyone. She was so easy and fun to talk to. She was intelligent, she made him laugh, and she seemed to have such a gentle spirit, which Joseph picked up on easily. Those qualities were why he found her so beautiful. They enhanced her outer beauty. Everything about her was perfect to him. Joseph sat there with the hope the night would never end.

It was very strange in that day and time that Sarah never once seemed to even acknowledge that Joseph was black and she was white. It was as though they were just old friends with no cultural barriers between them. So Joseph decided to ask Sarah a question that was tickling his curiosity. "Why don't you care that I am a Negro?"

This was a colossal rarity in this area. It was something Joseph had never seen or experienced. Without hesitation or discomfort, Sarah answered his question:

> "My daddy is a very hateful man, and it got worse after my mama died. I always heard him being hateful to all the people at my house—calling them names, screaming at them—and I heard him beat them. The horrid cries they let out still haunt me. There were times that people just disappeared. I knew not to ask questions, partly out of fear for my own safety and partly because I didn't want to hear out loud the answer that I already knew to be true.

"Sometimes the screams kept me up at night. I would just lie in my bed and cry for them. I would lie there and imagine that I had all the bravery and strength in the world and that I could run out there and save every last one. Many were my friends; they were more like my family than my blood father. They loved me and accepted me for who I was. I would imagine that I was able to save the world one person at a time, all while just lying in my little bed, helpless to their cries. My daddy often does the same thing to me because I, too, do not fit his standards of perfection."

Joseph stopped to ponder to himself. How in the hell could this girl not fit her father's standards? *She isn't black, she is surely Christian, and she seems to be smart.*

These were the only criteria for perfection Joseph had known: white, rich, and Christian. Society had taught him these were the standards by which all people were measured. If you had this holy trinity, you could rule the world. This was what Joseph had grown up with: the falsified view that if you were not white and not Christian, you failed. Joseph was coming to the realization that, in the eyes of society, only white people could reach perfection—the true, "Christian-ly" standard of Jesus. They paid no mind that Jesus himself had not been white. It was blasphemy to speak of such. Joseph, too, thought that Jesus had been white because that was what Mrs. Kingsley had taught him.

Sarah continued to explain. "I don't want to grow up to be a mean, hateful person like my daddy. I feel like we are all the same. I heard a kind voice and a gentle spirit when you spoke to me. That is all that matters to me. I was given a gift to not see the differences in people. I can judge them based only on their actions and their spirits. You can believe me when I tell you that I truly do not see color, because I am blind."

Joseph had no idea. He stumbled for the right words to say, and nothing came to mind. He just uttered, "I am so sorry."

Sarah smiled and said, "It's nothing to be sorry about. I view it as a gift. Maybe if I had my sight and was not different from others, I would not be able to be so open and accepting of people. Maybe if I could see, I would not feel a connection to those viewed as different. I might end up like the rest of them. I don't ever want that. I like being different. It allows me to see things in ways that many others don't. It allows me to open my mind to all that is out there and to what God has in store for me without manmade rules directing me. Instead, I am able to think outside the rules and allow only God's guidance to lead me."

Joseph was in pure awe of Sarah. She was so wise, way beyond her years. He had never heard anyone speak like this before. She spoke with no barriers, no judgment, and no hate. She spoke only with love. He knew at this moment that this was the girl he wanted to marry. Never mind that he was a fourteen-year-old African-American boy and she was white. Joseph just didn't care. He knew what he wanted, and he knew what he felt. He also knew that God hadn't spent his time making both of them only to place barriers on their love, no matter what society had taught them. He knew there was nothing wrong with how he felt; to him, it did not matter what anyone else thought. Sarah also felt that warmness and a special connection to Joseph.

The night was growing shorter, so they agreed to find each other once they were old enough. They scooted closer to one another and lay down with their heads tilted toward the stars. Joseph explained to Sarah all the shapes that the different stars made and what they looked like when they twinkled.

Both secretly wished things could be different. Sarah reached over and grabbed Joseph's rough, teenage hand. She caressed it once with her thumb, and they fell asleep hand in hand. The next morning, just as the sun was coming up, Joseph looked over at Sarah while she was still sleeping. He felt so warm and happy inside. It was a bitter-sweet moment. He had found his soul mate in this world, but soon, he would have to leave her. Sarah slowly opened her eyes and smiled with the sweetest, most honest smile he had ever seen. She suddenly jumped up.

"I have to get back. My daddy is going to kill me." She leaned over to Joseph and said, "Don't forget our pact. When we hit eighteen, we come and find one another."

Joseph smiled as big as a boy could.

"Yes, yes, I cannot wait," he said, nodding his head in 100 percent agreement.

He quickly forgot that she could not see that nod and dashing smile, but this made no difference to him. Sarah leaned over and lightly kissed him on his cheek. His entire body turned red, and he felt hot all over. He was as giddy as could be. He thanked her and told her he would never forget this moment. Sarah smiled, then took off, hurrying back down the path from which she had appeared. This was the greatest moment of his life up to this point, and he swore to himself that he would never forget this feeling.

Joseph was very sad as he started to pack up his bag, preparing for the last stretch of his journey. He stopped and reminded himself that today he was going to meet his mother. This shifted his mood and lifted his spirits. As he was placing his things in the duffel bag, he noticed that, miraculously, his water had refilled itself. Sometime in the night, Sarah had sneaked up to her house carrying his water canister. There at the water spigot right outside her father's bedroom window, she'd filled Joseph's water. If her father had awakened, all horror would have occurred. Joseph might have never seen her again. Sarah had risked all this for him. She knew he was special. He felt now that he would no longer thirst for water or unconditional love.

11

The Dragon's Lair

Joseph picked up his brown duffel bag, threw it over his shoulder, and headed back out to the old dirt road that led straight to his mother. He looked back and took a deep breath. He wanted to savor this feeling. He did not want it to become dim and fade off slowly into the depths of his mind like a distant, forgotten memory. He scuffed his worn, dusty shoes along the rocks to slow down his walking and linger a little longer. He was continuously looking back, wishing to relive the whole experience or just to see Sarah one more time. There was nothing there but his shadow staring back at him in the morning sun.

He said to himself, as if he were talking to another person, "Get it together. Today is the day you go meet your mama."

This helped him return to the present and focus on what was ahead of him. He turned forward, leaving Sarah and his shadow behind him. He was left with only the faith that, one day, Sarah would be in his forefront again, but for today, he must continue his journey as he walked down the road toward Doddsdale.

For the first several hours, he walked like a zombie, steadily heading south with his head slumped slightly, staring at the ground, deeply entrenched in thought. There were just miles and miles of mindless walking in front of him. The path was straightforward with no obstacles blocking his way. This had allowed his thoughts to absorb him. He then heard the faint sound of a dog barking in the distance. This quickly snapped him out of his nearly trance-like state. He noticed how far he had gone. It seemed like he had been walking for mere minutes because his mind was overflowing. He had become so engaged in his thoughts and dreams while also planning details of a variety of situations.

Oh, yes, Joseph had planned out the meeting with his mother and their time together. He also had a new preoccupation: planning out his desired future with Sarah. Ahhh, Sarah: his new love. Over the past several hours, he had mapped out their lives together, which would have humiliated him if anyone were ever to find out. He had planned their wedding, what their home would look like, and the children they would have. He even threw in a family pet. He dreamed of them having a dog, even though he was slightly allergic. He was indeed a giddy young fellow who felt the sensation of being in love. He envisioned his future laid out in front of him. Now that he was on his own, the possibilities were endless.

Around the time his dreaming and planning finally subsided, he looked up, and there it was—the greatly anticipated grand sign for Doddsdale. He could not believe he had made it. The exhilaration of this moment flowed through his veins. He noticed that the sign was way smaller and less impressive than it had appeared in his mind, but no matter; the excitement and joy overtook him. Oh, Doddsdale. This was the place where all the dreams he had been visualizing for years could start to become reality.

There was not a whole lot to the town of Doddsdale. It appeared as if an iron had flattened the whole area. It was easy to see clear across town. However, to see across town would not have been difficult even if it had been located in twisting and winding hills, for Doddsdale was a tiny place. He'd thought Clarksville was a small town. Clarksville felt like a booming metropolis compared to Doddsdale. This would surely make his feat of finding the senator's place a whole lot easier. No time to linger. It was time to find and meet his mother.

Joseph had dreamed of having a real mother his entire life. He yearned for that warm embrace, the unconditional love, and the guidance that he had missed out on for so many years. The only guidance he had had since Berta's passing was the guidance he heard from within. Thankfully, his intuition and internal guidance were sound and normally steered him in the right direction. Soon, oh so soon, he believed he could have all that he had dreamed of for years. It was right at the tip of his rough fingertips.

Joseph was so close. He sensed his mother's presence gently caressing his mocha skin. It did not matter to him that they had not laid eyes on each other since his birth. The bond between a parent and a child can be very strong, even if they have lived apart for the child's entire life. Sometimes in life, you find that you just have that special connection with someone, and you can sense when they are near. This was how Joseph felt about his mother, and he believed that the feeling was mutual.

Even though Joseph sensed his mother's nearness, it provided no compass. He was not certain which direction to go to find the senator's plantation. It was a small, rural town with a population of just 190. It was not much of an actual town. It was mostly country land without the convenience of directional signs, so Joseph was confused on which way he should go. Straight ahead, backward, left, right? He could spend hours wandering around trying to find the right home. That was assuming there was more than one large home to choose from, but Joseph didn't know. He could leave the Doddsdale town limit without even knowing it and end up searching all over the Delta.

It was Joseph's first time to ever leave the confines of Clarksville, so he was confused to begin with. He was also beginning to tire from his full day of walking. Frustration with his predicament set in. Joseph knew not to ask any of the white folk for directions for fear of repercussions. The rule of the land was not to speak to someone white unless spoken to. However, Joseph had not yet passed anyone, which in his situation could have been a very good thing. There were those certain people, the horrendous variety, who might have treated him maliciously.

Just as Joseph's frustration peaked, a boy around the same age as him happened to walk by. He was slightly excited to see someone. Plus, Joseph took into account that the boy was alone, black, and close to his same size. There seemingly was no threat present. This could be his answer to which direction he should explore to find the coveted home of the senator.

He thought, *Surely this boy would know where the senator lives. I should ask him.*

We all experience times when we want to say something but freeze and then repeat to ourselves the same words over and over, wishing we could just spit them out until it becomes almost impossible to say a word. It makes us nervous, and it feels absolutely ridiculous for no good reason. Joseph was doing this to himself and simultaneously telling himself to shut up and spit it out already. Joseph finally blurted it out as if he were shoving something out of his chest through his mouth.

"Excuse me? Do you know where Senator Westridge lives?"

See, that wasn't so hard, he thought in a mocking and scolding manner.

"Yeah, he lives up the road, where the big flag is hanging," the boy said.

"Thank you," Joseph responded.

The boy crouched his head and shoulders real low while leaning in toward Joseph. "Pssst—you don't wanna go there," he whispered. "People that go there never leave."

Joseph tilted his head slightly to the side and crinkled his forehead with a look of puzzlement.

What does he mean they never leave? I am free, and I can do as I please, he thought to himself with an indignant tone echoing in his head.

He decided to ask the boy. "What do you mean, they never leave?"

The boy took a quivering breath and responded, "You see, it's like they get stuck there. There are these invisible chains that are chained so tightly, you can't never leave."

Invisible chains? How can you have invisible chains? Joseph wondered. Nothing this boy was saying made any sense. *There must be something wrong with him. Maybe he had a little something to drink, or maybe he is just crazy.*

Joseph kept all this to himself and tried not to let his face show his feelings of judgment and mockery. He told the boy, "My mama is there, and I have to go get her."

The boy nodded his head back and forth slowly as if he felt sorry for Joseph and was disappointed in him. He looked Joseph in the eye with a bit of sadness. "Good luck. I guess I'll be seein' you again," he said in a whisper as soft as a faint rustling in the distance.

Be seeing me again? No matter. He was not going to fixate on that for too long. He was on a mission: Operation Save Mama. He did not have patience or time to fixate on someone's craziness.

As he was leaving to walk off, the boy said, "By the way, I'm William."

Joseph stopped and turned. He looked into William's tattered and worn little face. "I'm Joseph, but I am leaving after I get my mama."

Joseph was somewhat defensive over William's insinuation that they would meet again. That went against his whole plan, and to veer from the plan was not acceptable in Joseph's book. He hadn't diligently worked on this plan for it to fail him now. *What in the hell is this boy talking about?* Joseph just stared at him with perplexity. William could see the confusion in Joseph's face, but he offered no further explanation.

They both turned and headed in their separate directions. Joseph continued in the direction that William had pointed out to him. As he turned and began to walk, he continued to think, *What does he mean, they get stuck? Invisible chains?* He could not shake those statements even though he tried. No matter; he was on his way to go unstick his mama, no matter what that crazy boy had said.

The closer he got to the senator's house, the more excited and anxious he became. His pace got increasingly faster. He was so close to breaking into a run. Then, like an image from a dream, there it was before him—the thing he had been walking toward for the past three days. On the left was the huge flag, flying strong in the breeze. Its red, white, and blue waved in the sky, the X-shaped stars rippling on top of the waves. It was almost as if the flag were clapping upon his arrival as it popped in the wind. It was the flag William had told him to seek out. It was attached to a large, slightly tarnished metal pole buried deep in the ground.

The flag was on the corner of a gravel driveway by the road, as if its job were to welcome you when you arrived. After days of walking, he had reached his destination. He stopped to take a deep breath and relish in the moment. This was a huge accomplishment for a boy who had lived his entire life controlled. He had broken out to seek what he had always dreamed of: his mother and freedom. He felt proud in this moment of accomplishment. He had made it all on his own.

As he rounded the corner into the driveway, he saw this magnificent house. The yard was covered with elaborate gardens and extraordinary flowers. There were enormous white columns in the front of the house. The stature of these columns was such that it seemed as if they could have supported the entire structure all on their own. There seemed to be a great level of order at this house, apparent from the first glimpse. Everything had a place. The entire outside of the senator's residence and the yard were pristine.

Joseph was ready to sprint up that stretched driveway when the strangest and most unexpected thing happened. When he took his first step, he felt a chill come over his entire body. It felt like a hand was on his chest and was physically pushing him backward off the driveway and back onto the road. It was an intense pressure like he had never experienced. No matter the order that was seemingly seeping from this estate, all it did to Joseph was place his body and emotions into complete chaos. It appeared tranquil but felt like turmoil. What could it be? He attempted to shake off these feelings as he had previously tried to do with William's statements. He wanted to keep moving forward, and he was able to do so, but a distinct heaviness weighed on him.

He desperately wanted all that he had imagined to come true. He wanted it so badly that he was willing to ignore all the warning signs and even alter reality in his mind to fit his agenda. He was searching for signs that would fit the expectation he had for this day—any sign. A hint of hope was all he needed.

He then scanned the yard with one sweep of his head, searching for the large oak tree that hosted his mother. She was supposed to be right there, swinging in the wooden seat tied by ropes from a stout, sturdy branch protruding from the tree's body, as he had imagined. Suddenly, there it was. The large oak tree was right where he had envisioned it. His mother was nowhere to be found, however; just for a second, he'd thought he saw the swing hanging there. As his eyes adjusted, he noticed there was no swing at all—it was just a lone rope dangling in the air.

What he had envisioned was quite conflicting, to say the least. One rope would have held memories of childhood fun and innocence. The other rope held only memories of screams, hatred, evil, death, and sadness. It held such a disturbing level of fear and intimidation just hanging there, slowly swaying in the wind. Was this the point—to strike fear and intimidation in him? Joseph had always heard stories, but in his lifetime, he luckily had never come into contact with one of these ropes being used for what it had been purposed: vile murder.

What is it doing there? Maybe it is just for show, Joseph thought. He had seen people hang these in their yards or somewhere on their vehicles as a form of "decoration." Joseph felt they were trying to strike fear into people to prove dominance, but he knew it just proved ignorance.

As repulsive and distressing as it was, Joseph did not want to see it for that. He was still trying to be positive, and he was searching diligently for the bright side. That was assuming that you could see something not of pure darkness in this situation, but Joseph, in a sense, just burrowed his head into the sand and refused to see the negative. He only wanted to see what would support his mission. That noose did not fit into his plan. His desire to meet his mother overruled all logic. He quickly brushed off all the signs that were right in front of him and kept walking toward the house.

Sometimes in life, you are shown all the right signs, but you ignore them anyway. You have to open your eyes and your mind to see them. These were not the types of signs Joseph wanted, so he chose to proceed blindly, pursuing his plans. He was too invested in his emotional state to see what needed to be seen in that moment. His eyes were sealed shut.

No matter what emotions and sensations Joseph attempted to suppress, he couldn't deny that things felt so strange here. There was an unnatural presence about the place. You could almost hear the silent screams in the wind. He spotted a few shifty eyes lurking from behind corners and from within the cotton fields. He had imagined that he would immediately recognize his mother. No one looked familiar, and no one seemed as friendly as he had imagined. Everyone seemed downright creepy because of their silence and skulking. It felt like he was walking into a dragon's den. Everyone was hiding and remaining quiet to keep the dragon sleeping so it would not awake and destroy the village. It was the most eerie feeling he had ever felt.

All of a sudden, Joseph felt a strong sensation of panic. His fear and intuition were starting to break through his bullheadedness. His pace slowed tremendously as he tried to process it all. *Maybe I should turn around. Maybe I should listen to that boy, William.*

Just as he turned his head, looking back at the road while contemplating the idea of leaving and running far away, he heard a boisterous voice call out. "Hello there, boy! Can I help you?"

Joseph whipped his head back around, looking toward the house. All the spying eyes had vanished. A man was standing there, smiling on the porch between two of the attention-commanding columns. He was a slightly tubby-looking man with circular, metal-frame glasses that fit snuggly on his rounded, mushy white face. His face drooped a bit, sagging around his mouth. He had dark hair with a few strings of salt mixed in. It was swooped to the right side like a gentle wave.

His was a very charming smile with the whitest teeth. He was wearing a chocolate-brown suit with a matching tie and shiny brown loafers. The loafers had a bit of dust on them, but you could still see the fresh shine on them gleaming through the dusty layer. *He looks a bit cartoonish*, Joseph thought. He was reminded of a character he had once seen in a comic at the Kingsleys—Droopy the saggy-faced dog. Because of this likeness, the man no longer seemed that scary to Joseph. He gave off an impression of warmth, although Joseph still felt unease.

"Come here, boy! Come closer so we can talk. Do you need something? I would be happy to help you with whatever you need."

Joseph hesitantly started walking toward the man. This was exactly how Joseph imagined things going, but he couldn't help but feel that something was not right. Maybe it was his gut, or maybe it was just William's words continually echoing in his head. Nonetheless, he was uneasy. He dragged his feet every step up that driveway.

When Joseph reached the top of the driveway, there stood "Droopy," smiling. "Hello there, boy. I am Senator Westridge. What's your name?"

Joseph was fidgeting, and he stuttered a bit, muttering, "J-Joseph, sir."

The senator nodded his head and said, "Well, it's a pleasure to meet you, Joseph. Don't be afraid, boy. We can be friends. Now, what brings you to these parts of Mississippi?"

Joseph started to tell him the whole story, as he had done with Sarah, but then he stopped himself before blurting it all out. He needed a good read on this character before divulging his life story. "I came in search of my mama," Joseph said shakily.

"Why would you think your mama is here, boy?"

"Well, sir, I come from Clarksville, and when I was there, I read a piece of paper that said my mama was sent here to work for you years ago."

Senator Westridge touched his chin with his finger and thumb in a slow stroking motion. "Huh? Well, isn't that the darnedest thing. Have you ever met your mama or seen a picture of her?"

"No, sir, I haven't," Joseph said, his head hanging.

You could see the wheels turning in the senator's head. "Well, let's see what we can do about that, Joseph. I am sure we can fix that. What is her name, boy?"

"Claudia Dove," Joseph said with a hint of confidence in his voice. As Joseph spoke her name, his spirits lifted and the unease started to fade. The more they talked, the more Joseph's level of comfort with the senator rose.

"Claudia Dove, you say? Yes, I believe there is a woman by the name of Claudia Dove that lives here," the senator said, boosting Joseph's level of comfort a bit more.

Joseph felt he was going to leap right out of his skin. His level of excitement was almost uncontrollable. "Can I see her? Can I?" Joseph said in a childlike tone, almost shrill from the excitement.

The senator shook his head with disappointment. "If it were up to me, we would run out there and let you meet your mama right now, but she is not here," the man said. "She has been on a trip for a couple of days, but don't you worry. I expect her back any day now."

Joseph was disappointed to hear this, but he reasoned that, considering how far he had come and how long he had waited, what was a few more days? He decided now was as good of a time as any to tell the senator about his plan, so he took a deep breath and whipped out his inner businessman.

"Senator, sir, I have saved some money, and I was thinkin' that maybe I could give it to you, and when my mama comes back, she could come with me, so we could get our own place."

The senator didn't miss a beat. "Well, I couldn't take your money from you, boy. It's illegal to take money for folks these days. You can't just buy and sell folks like you could in the good ole days, and I have to uphold the law here, son. I am a senator now. But when your mama returns, if she would like to leave with you, you will both have my blessing."

Joseph couldn't believe it. It was all as he had envisioned, but the feeling was even greater than he could have imagined. Maybe people in these parts were a bit nicer than what he was used to, even though it was just thirty or so miles from where he grew up. Those thirty or so miles were starting to feel like a lifetime.

Joseph was gripping his moneybox in his hand so tightly that the tips of his fingers were turning white.

The senator looked down and saw the box. "What's in the box you're holding? It looks like some damn fine cigars you got there."

Joseph smiled and said with a hint of pride, "No, sir, it's my money."

The senator nodded with a smile. "Well, would you like me to hold on to your money for safekeeping until you are ready to leave with your mama? I would be obliged to do that for you, boy."

Joseph hesitated just for a moment, but then he thought to himself, *What would this man, a United States senator, want with this little bit of money I have?* Joseph had already been told that he could keep his money and leave with his mother. As the senator's hand was already reaching for the box, Joseph hesitantly said, "Oh . . . OK," while he handed his box over to the oddly ready hand of the senator.

The senator eagerly said, "Good. It's settled, then. You will stay here until your mama returns, and I will hold on to this for you for safekeeping until you leave. Now, let me show you to your room."

Joseph nodded and followed the senator around the corner.

"Now, I have many people that live here, but for now, you can stay in your mama's house."

My mama's house, Joseph thought.

Oh, how wonderful and mystical it all felt. It was so surreal to him.

12

Crazy or Controlled?

A gravel pathway next to the mansion led to a quaint little house beside it. This smaller house was offset by modest-sized, meticulously kept flowerbeds in the front on each side of the steps leading to the tiny front porch. It was picturesque. Everything looked so well kept—almost too well kept. There was no chipping paint, no rotting wood, not a single weed to be found in the flowerbeds. There was not even a speck of dust on the porch. This was an odd occurrence, seeing as there was a nearby gravel path and a gravel driveway. The level of perfection was almost eerie. The Kingsleys' house was well maintained, but this borderline perfection was achieving another level.

The senator walked up the steps to the front door, motioning for Joseph to accompany him. He opened the door and walked in while Joseph stood back in the threshold, looking around the room. The first thing he noticed were flower paintings hanging on all four walls. The inside reminded him of something that Mrs. Kingsley would have decorated, which gave him an odd sense of comfort.

This little house was a studio-style home. There were no walls besides the exterior ones. This space was where all the house's belongings were located. To the right of Joseph was a brass bed with a flower-patterned bedspread, keeping with the paintings' theme. The only thing not pristine in the house was the brass bed, which had several tarnished imperfections, but even that seemed a perfect fit.

The house was particularly lovely for its being help's quarters. From what Joseph had seen before, this was not even comparable. This house had an unfamiliar level of arrangement, detail, and style. It reminded him more of a place the Kingsleys would have used to host their guests, not their help.

"This is where you can lay your head and your bag. I hope you like it," the senator said while smiling.

"Like it? I love it!" Joseph said.

He couldn't help but think that his mother must love this little house, too. He always imagined her loving all things flowery and really taking interest in all the beautiful things life had to offer. He was so warm inside thinking that this was how his mother had been able to spend her past fourteen years. He had long worried about if his mother was OK, and he would just fixate on the sure hell he had imagined that she had been living in. What was there to worry about? It was perfect.

Just as Joseph was dreaming of the good life, his thoughts were interrupted by the senator.

"Now, to stay here, I am going to need you to help out around here like the others."

"Sure," Joseph said.

He would have done anything asked of him now that he was able to stay in his mama's house; the senator had a sneaking suspicion this was true.

"I can do anything you need since you are being so kind to me," Joseph said.

"I am glad to hear you say that," said the senator, now grinning as he walked out the door. "I will have William bring you some dinner, and then you need to rest. It will be a big day tomorrow."

With that, the senator left, shutting the door behind him.

Joseph stood in that perfect little house, a huge smile on his face. He looked lost in euphoria. Pure joy. In the space of less than twenty-four hours, he had met the apparent love of his life and finally felt at ease with his mother's situation, and he would soon finally meet the woman who had brought him into this world kicking and screaming.

The three-day journey's exhaustion finally caught up to Joseph, and he walked over to the ever-so-appealing brass bed. He gently laid his body across it while caressing his hand over the pillow. It was so soft and cushiony compared to what he had felt the last few nights, spent on the ground or on a barn floor.

Joseph finally settled in a bit and had a moment to reflect. He was trying to process everything that had just happened with the senator. It had all happened so fast. Then it dawned on him: *Did the senator say "William"? I hope it is not the same William.* These thoughts flooding in shattered his euphoric feeling. If this was indeed the same William, this could bring what Joseph feared. *Did he tell the truth, or was he just crazy?*

Joseph was scared to find out whether William was correct. *What could this mean for my mama and me? What would that make the senator?* Joseph's head was spinning. He did not want to see or think any more about this William character.

Everything that day, mostly, had gone according to plan, other than William's lingering words, which circled in Joseph's head like a hungry vulture ready to pick at the dead carcass of his dreams.

Joseph lay there for a while, but it was not too long before there was a knock at the door. He knew it must be the William fellow that the senator had told him about, bringing his supper. He was quite hungry, but he preferred to starve than to open the door to his possible fears. He stood up and slowly pulled open the door, and there stood William with his dinner—the very same William. Joseph's face dropped. His pupils dilated as fear took him to a new realm.

"Hello. Nice to see you again," William said in a rehearsed voice. "Here is your supper." He had had personality and life in his voice earlier. Now it was just a monotone puppet. Joseph wondered who was pulling the strings.

Joseph was trying desperately to convince himself that William was a crazed liar. He was bargaining with his own mind, but for now, he was out of chips. Joseph tried to convince himself that maybe William was just there as a prank to scare him. Joseph quickly turned to anger as a defense. *What is he tryin' to pull?* Then, in a moment of uncertainty, he thought, *If it was so damn bad, why would William say all these awful things about the senator and his house, then come back here to work when he was clearly free earlier to roam far away? Why would he be here unless this was a good place to live?*

The senator had treated Joseph with respect and given him a great place to lay his head. Joseph was agitated. He just wanted his mama so they could get the hell out of there. William could keep the senator all to himself, in Joseph's opinion, but Joseph wanted answers.

"Why are you here when you told me to stay away?" Joseph spouted in a clearly irritated tone.

"I done told you. My chain brings me back," William said. "You have a good night now."

Joseph just stood there, dumbfounded and a little nervous, unable to respond. Was William insane, or was he somehow being controlled in a way that Joseph couldn't see? None of it made any sense.

This haunting thought kept Joseph awake for hours even though he kept telling himself he had a big day tomorrow. Every time he reminded himself of the senator's words, "to get good rest," it would place him that much further from sleep. Finally, he found a remaining chip deep in his mind. He made one more bargain with himself so that he could rest. He told himself to just enjoy the fact that he was finally there and block out all this William business.

All he had to do was to help out for a couple of days and wait for his mother to return. They would then be free to leave together and live a happy life. He knew this to be true because the senator had told him so. It was that simple. Joseph was finally able to drift off to sleep with the words of William locked safely away in a closet deep in his mind.

13

Into the Gray

Aweek had gone by since Joseph had arrived at Senator Westridge's plantation, and a long week it had been. Joseph had been working in the fields every day, just as the senator had asked of him. Joseph's patience was wearing thin, though, with this waiting-on-his-mother-to-return business. Every day while he worked, he secretly watched for a woman that might be his mother coming down the drive. His eyes would eagerly glance around every time he heard a noise in the road or the driveway. Still no sign of her. That strange pressure he'd felt on his chest since he arrived was still with him. He was convinced it was either nerves or excitement, but he was not going to allow it to ruin this good thing he had going on.

Day after day, though, the senator was able to build more trust and a deeper level of respect in Joseph. It was the little things that reeled Joseph in. The senator would smile at Joseph, treat him courteously, make eye contact, and say things as simple as "Thank you" or "You're welcome." It was unlike what Joseph had experienced. The Kingsleys never smiled at him, made eye contact, or told him thank you. Their actions toward him were always sharp and distant. Joseph's thoughts about the senator were, *Who would be that nice if they were someone that could not be trusted?* Joseph always knew he could not trust the Kingsleys. There was no mystery there; it was black and white. With the good senator, Joseph was entering into the gray.

For the past week, the senator had greeted Joseph with the same smile and courteous behavior as the first day they had met. Joseph's respect for Senator Westridge, with his polite and seemingly gentle demeanor, was blossoming. Before Joseph knew it, he was on a schedule with the rest of the workers. He was up before sunrise, out in the fields tilling the soil and planting the cotton seeds one strenuous row at a time. It was springtime in Doddsdale, but the temperatures were steadily rising. In the South, the temperatures get high and the humidity gets even higher. Being in the direct sun all day performing manual labor can take a toll on one's body, even for a young boy.

By Friday afternoon, Joseph was exhausted. He had always had to work for the Kingsleys, but he was quickly learning now that he had had it easier than the other workers who worked those fields for the Kingsleys all day long every day. By comparison, this was brutal work, and Joseph was exhausted and hungry. The mixture of tiredness and hunger are never a good combination for one's mood. Even the nicest of people can snap.

At one point, Joseph stopped working long enough to wipe the sweat off his brow. His eyes glared with frustration and defeat. He was ready to quit and leave this place, ignoring the reason he'd come there.

Just when Joseph's spirit and patience had reached wit's end, the senator stepped out onto the porch. "Joseph, why don't you come on up here, boy!"

Joseph perked up a bit at hearing his name called from the very lips of the man he was coming to care about and respect. He couldn't help feeling special with his name being called in front of everyone. It was his name and no one else's. Too eagerly, he took his hoe and ran over to the large wooden barn behind the house. He placed the hoe against the side of the barn and then headed to the porch where the senator was standing. He quickly hopped up onto the porch, energized by his excitement.

The senator smiled and said, "Joseph, I just wanted to tell you I appreciate the good work you are doing here. I see you work hard. You're doing a fine job, boy."

Joseph's spirits were immediately lifted.

"I wanted to let you know that I heard your mama is heading back this way. You should be able to meet her very soon."

Hearing that perked up Joseph. Unfortunately, with the senator, there was always a "but."

"But until then, would you please keep up your great work for me? It helps me out so much to see such a driven young man out there. I am sure you are an inspiration for the others as well."

Joseph stopped and thought, *Maybe I am an inspiration for the others.*

"Now back to work, son. We don't want to lose this sunlight, do we?"

Joseph hopped off the porch with a whole new pep in his step. His ego had been stroked, and his mama was on her way. Senator Westridge stood back and watched Joseph run out into that field, looking like he was heading to frolic on the beach. The senator walked over to the rocking chair on the porch; he sat down as he sipped on his perspiring glass of bourbon on the rocks. The grin of accomplishment on his face was a sign he knew he was on the right track with Joseph.

Anyone who has experienced the wrath of the deceptive knows the signs to watch out for. The more naïve they think you, the easier it is for them to capture and devour you. Until now, Joseph had experienced only the type of cruelty that was in his face—outright hate and evil. He had never experienced the variety masked with false care and phony kindness used to obtain a more obscure goal—one that could capture your soul. Joseph was naïve, and the senator was blindly leading him right where he wanted Joseph to be. Joseph would soon learn firsthand the wicked webs of deception that could be woven.

Webs are designed to trap prey in such a way that the prey can never break free. Sit and watch an unsuspecting insect fly right into a spider's web. The insect never sees it coming, while the spider had this masterful plan all along. Upon the insect's first impact with the web, it is clear it doesn't know what's hit it. Panic sets in, and the insect flails around, frantically trying to escape, until it exhausts itself. Its body and mind surrenders. It quits fighting.

The carefully planned attack has worked. The spider is the victor. Every once in a while, though, you will see one last glimmer of hope from the captive. It gives that one last push, that one final, desperate fight to save its own life. Something remarkable then happens. There is a pop of the web, and the captive wiggles loose. Sweet, sweet freedom is all the insect's as it flies away as fast as possible. One can only have faith that Joseph would be able to break free from the web that he was now flying straight into.

As Joseph kept getting closer to the web the senator was wickedly weaving, he still did not see it coming. He did not notice anything at all. He felt like he was on top of the world. Each day that passed, the senator asked Joseph for his help with more and more duties. It had been close to four weeks since Joseph first arrived at the plantation, and he had now become like a manager of sorts for the other workers. He was the senator's right-hand man and loving every minute of it. Anything the senator needed, he called on Joseph for, and Joseph was eager to oblige. The senator thrived on how young and impressionable Joseph was. He was the perfect medium to mold.

Joseph respected and cared about the senator, and no one in that position wants to find out that the person they respect is indeed wrong or deceptive. That is disheartening; it also makes one believe that they are weak and lacking judgment. Many times, people find it easier to just turn a blind eye. Joseph did not see any flaws in the senator; nor did he yearn to see any.

Joseph worked the fields less these days, and he was beyond pleased. No more manual labor for this fellow. The senator knew that to keep Joseph on track, he needed to change up his daily routine; otherwise, Joseph would get frustrated and choose to leave while there was still a chance. Joseph needed that extra stroke to the ole ego and the extra attention, and he functioned well with it. Joseph had always been an open book, so it was easy for the senator to read him. Now it seemed that the senator was starting to write the pages.

The senator saw that Joseph could readily become an enforcer rather than a mere worker, so Joseph's new duty was to patrol everyone. He was to ensure they were doing their job properly according to the senator's standards. He thought of his mother a little less each day. The thought of her returning drifted further and further from his mind. He now had an important job given to him to keep his mind occupied. When the senator asked Joseph to take on this job, Joseph felt beyond honored. The fact that the senator trusted him with something like this was a huge accomplishment for Joseph. For the first time in his life, he felt like someone important; he felt special. He was lost in this new feeling, and he soaked up every minute of it.

To accent Joseph's new rise to power, the senator took Joseph aside and gave him a gift. One day, he called Joseph over to the old barn out back. Joseph was a little nervous, wondering if he had done something to upset the senator. The senator had become a father figure in Joseph's eyes. Mr. Kingsley had treated Joseph as nothing more than a burden, so Joseph had never had a father figure. Now, in the senator, he did, and you always want to make your papa proud. Joseph walked out to the barn, and the senator called him inside. He was standing there with a long, thick leather whip. Joseph looked hesitant and nervous to enter.

"Come on in, boy. You ain't in no trouble. I got a gift for you."

A gift! How exciting! Joseph thought.

The Kingsleys never gave him gifts when he was growing up. His birthdays and Christmases were just more days on which he felt alone and alienated from love. Joseph smiled and hopped on into the barn. The senator looked at Joseph with a sense of importance lingering in his eyes.

"Now, this is a special gift, and it comes with a lot of responsibility. Can you handle the responsibility, boy?"

"Yes, sir," Joseph quickly answered as he pushed back his shoulders, straightened his posture, and snapped his feet together in the dirt so that they were now perfectly aligned with one another. He was now standing with a stance of pride.

"This here whip is to help you with your important job," the senator told him sternly. "You got to keep all them in line. Sometimes them niggers can get jealous of such a fine young man in control. They might think that it is them that should be in your place. This is to show them you are in charge. You are who I have chosen, not them. Can you do that, boy?"

"Yes, sir!" Joseph spouted militantly.

He handed Joseph the whip. It was an odd and sinister ceremony of sorts. Joseph grasped the whip tightly with both hands; then he gave it a crack or two just to try it out, like a kid with a new toy.

"Attaboy," grumbled the senator.

The senator gave Joseph a smile of pride. Joseph had made "Papa" proud.

"Now you get out there, boy, and keep them niggers in line."

Joseph quickly ignored the hateful words the senator spouted, making himself believe that the senator meant nothing bad by them. Joseph smiled and ran back out the barn door to his post in the middle of the field. As he stood there with his long, thick leather whip, which he thought was very cool, he watched over everyone.

He felt powerful with the whip in hand. He thought it a cool accent piece to his title. He got so easily caught up in all that, losing sight of everything that once really mattered to him. The honorable, moral-bound little dreamer was fading far away.

The other "workers" were quickly learning to dislike Joseph. He had not made a single friend other than the senator he believed to be his friend. Joseph had always had a deep desire to be a social fellow, but throughout his life, he had found himself alone. Now he was one of the bad guys, and he hadn't even seen it coming. He jumped to the conclusion that the others were jealous of his supervisory position. The senator had frequently warned him of this—the jealousy. The senator's words echoed in his head: "They are just jealous, boy, because I chose you." It was not even a distant thought in his mind that maybe, just maybe, he was disliked because he had become the oppressor, the problem, a thread in the web of wickedness. Besides the fact that Joseph had been blinded to the truth, the explanation that the problem was their jealousy was what made him feel better inside.

Joseph quickly went from being a sweet young boy to plantation enforcer. This was not what he'd risked it all for when escaping the Kingsleys. He was lost, and he did not even know the wrong turn he had taken. He had become everything he had always hated.

Joseph's new role was introduced to him by the senator in such small increments, he did not even notice the transformation. It started out with Joseph simply watching over everyone on occasion. He did not want anyone to get into trouble, so he quietly observed. They all had a twinge of fear in their eye that kept them obedient to the senator's callous rule. With little pep talks from the senator, Joseph was eventually running to tell him when someone was not acting or working "properly." Day by day, Joseph was encouraged to take more authority. He had gone from not wanting anyone to be in trouble to correcting the workers himself when they were not behaving as he saw fit. "Get back to work," he would demand with a snap of the whip.

Joseph found that he enjoyed having power instead of being the one controlled. Ironically, the senator's control and manipulation was what led him to this disturbing place; the need for power had started to wrap its corrupt grip securely around him. It was addictive, and he loved the high. As with any addiction, it had tampered with his moral compass. The more the need for power grew, the weaker he became, a slave to its rule.

14

Mama?

Two years had passed, and Joseph had lost all his charming boyishness. He was like an angry old man, never smiling and always looking vacant and numb. He was miserable but did not know the difference anymore. He didn't even look like the same person. He should have been a very attractive-looking young man, but there was no glow left to him. He had a darkness suppressing him, and he had been alienated from anyone who could bring light.

The only one that he could have a conversation with was the senator. None of the other workers wanted to speak to him. They feared him. The senator had also prohibited him from speaking with any outsiders. If he was allowed to speak to someone visiting the plantation, it was only in a monitored situation with the senator watching over him like a wolf guarding its kill, pacing back and forth with an intense and sinister glare in his eyes fixated directly on Joseph. It made others so uncomfortable that either they would quickly quit speaking to him or they learned to not engage with Joseph at all.

His conversations and interactions with the senator had drastically changed since Joseph first arrived—if you could call them conversations. The senator's soft smiles and kind thank-yous, never authentic to begin with, were a thing of the past. Stern glares, vicious words, and the barking of commands were all Joseph received. The senator was cruel and merciless. Joseph had no one else; he was completely isolated. His self-esteem that had once been so abundant was gone. Joseph had once believed he was meant to change the world; now he felt worthless, unable to offer the world anything. The senator had drilled these thoughts so deep into Joseph's mind that they had become part of his own mental dialogue. The abuser had managed to train the victim to become his own source of abuse and oppression.

Nowadays, the senator was constantly screaming at Joseph that he was not doing an adequate job. It was never good enough, so Joseph continually strived to do and be better in the senator's eyes. No matter how hard he tried, he would never live up to the senator's expectations. There was no real bar to reach. It was just a tactic to make sure he failed and remained completely controlled.

The senator would tell Joseph awful things such as, "Boy, you should feel blessed that you have someone as nice as me who allows you to work here, because no one else would put up with your pathetic lack of talent and the level of sloppiness that you continually show me." The senator would also tell Joseph that he sickened him. He made damn sure Joseph believed that he was so worthless that no one else in the world would take the time to care for him and love him the way that the good senator did.

Joseph now truly believed that he could not go anywhere; he could not escape this prison. No one else would ever love him or put up with his worthlessness. All of that had formed a gray dome of ugliness and self-detestation that was suffocating his spirit.

In turn, Joseph had become harsh and unsympathetic toward others as well as himself. He had brief moments of clarity in which he wanted to unearth his old self, digging deep below to excavate that boy who had once shined so bright. However, as the web was intended to do, it kept him trapped. He feared what the senator might do; he feared where he would go; and he feared who, or what, he had become. All this control, fear, and abuse had festered inside him until it morphed into pure anger.

Joseph began to take out his deep-seated anger and internal turmoil on the workers. No leniency for laziness, as he called it. He now stood in that field like a dictator, holding the whip of dominance strong in his hand. He cracked it often to remind them who was in control, although, ironically, he had an absolute lack of control within himself. He was vacant, chaotic, and cold. He had barely dreamed or thought of his mother in months. The senator had made Joseph into his spiritless puppet, yanking at the strings as he pleased.

Yes, Joseph was angry, but he had never used physical violence. He did not find it necessary; he also did not have the stomach for it. The senator was pushing him further each day to become more vile. He craved to see the escalation of Joseph's cruelty and anger. It was like a game to him. How cruel could he make one good-natured boy? It was like getting a sweet pup and training it to be a vicious fighter.

One cold and gloomy February morning, just four months before Joseph's seventeenth birthday, he was patrolling with a watchful eye over the workers slaving out in *his* field. Joseph had become so tired of the cold gloom cast over Doddsdale and himself. He had grown to loathe himself and what he had become. A tiny light deep inside of him wanted to bleed through, but it was relentlessly being suffocated.

While he was patrolling that morning, his mind swarmed with anger and frustration. Just at the pinnacle of his rage and angst, one of the women in the field caught his attention. She had stopped working and was slightly slumped over. It appeared as if she were exhausted and needed to catch her breath. His first thought was to question if she was all right, but that was quickly overshadowed by irritation that she was not doing as he had instructed. This was the one thing he had control over, and he took it seriously.

"Get back to work!" he demanded. Why was this lady acting up? She was not listening to his clear demands.

The senator, as usual, was not too far away and was witnessing this event. He screamed to Joseph as if Satan was spewing from his mouth. "Are you going to let that nigger get away with that?"

Something snapped in Joseph. His eyes turned cold and lifeless. A beast had taken over his soul and was raging to get out. He stomped over to the woman while she was slumped over and grabbed her tightly by her arm, cutting off circulation. He jerked her toward him, flinging her body. He dragged her through the field as she stumbled and lost her footing along the way, dragging her toes behind her in the dirt.

All the while, the senator watched in delight. Joseph and the woman went into the barn behind the house. He threw her onto her knees in the dirt. He forced her on all fours like an animal and told her to keep her head down. He pulled her shirt over her head and then stood there, motionless.

By now, the senator was standing in the doorway of the barn with demented gratification dancing in his eyes as he said, "Do it, boy! Don't let that mongrel control you."

Joseph was not sure if he was equipped to do what was expected of him, but then he heard the voice of the senator continually echoing in his head. "There is no room for weakness here. Are you a coward or are you a real man, boy?" With that, Joseph reared back and began to strike her with his whip, his symbol of dominance.

It began mildly. Then it was as if something very dark seized him. He felt this intense heat over his entire body; he was blank. Joseph was gone, and the fury from all his past, everything he had been through, came out screaming through that whip. It shot out like an electric current of pure rage. It flowed from his body through the whip onto her stripped back, over and over again. Everything that had ever happened to him was projected out onto the tender flesh of this helpless woman.

As the woman screamed out in sheer pain, Joseph felt the release of all his emotions departing through her mouth as cries of agony. He had never felt so exhilarated and sickened all at the same time. He stopped himself just short of pure insanity while her blood dripped off of his hands and arms.

The senator walked off with a grin full of pure evil.

The woman was weak, with blood dripping off her sides and forming bloody streams in the sand. Then, with anger, feelings of betrayal, and bravery, she turned her head, looking over her left shoulder and up at Joseph. Her eyes were soaked from tears and laced with pure disgust. "Didn't your mama teach you any better?" she said in a frail voice.

It was in that moment that the light shattered through, and it all rushed back to him in an instant. It exposed the memories of why he had left the Kingsleys' house, why he had come here in the first place, and how that beating from Richard Kingsley had given him the courage to try and change it all. He was supposed to be helping himself and others, not turning into this monster he had become.

As the woman stared at him with disgust and hurt in her eyes, he saw a familiar glimmer, and he felt something strange. As quickly as the rage had come, it dispersed, and his knees gave out as he almost fainted. He fell to the ground with his body shaking uncontrollably. All the while, the little boy inside of him screamed with fury and wrath because of what he had done. He grabbed his face and started to cry in agony, smearing her blood all over him. He thrust himself forward so that he, too, was on all fours. He dry heaved and vomited; each splash of sickness sprayed dust and a spatter of her blood back in his face. He looked up at her with tears rushing down his cheeks. They left streaks where they had washed away the dust and blood.

Snot was streaming out of his nose and pouring off his upper lip onto the sandy floor. Vomit-filled saliva dangled out of his mouth from his pouting bottom lip. He looked at her with defeat in his eyes and uttered, "Mama?"

Joseph was in sheer shock, disgust, and horror of what he had done. With tears, vomit, and his mother's blood covering his face, he began to punch himself brutally. It was one blow after another on his cheekbone, which was beginning to collapse. His mother reached up to grab his arm.

"No, son! Stop it! Stop it!"

Joseph again fell to his knees and screamed. It was a scream that shook the ground and bellowed all his raw emotions. "I'm so sorry! I'm so sorry! I'm so sorry, Mama! How could I do this to my own mama? I deserve to die!"

Joseph began to punch himself again. He knew it was what he deserved. Claudia was crying as she reached for Joseph's arm.

"Son, please don't hurt yourself. You don't deserve this."

"Yes, I do. I don't deserve to live."

"Son, please, you got to forgive yourself. I forgive you."

Claudia reached over to him with her arms open, and Joseph crumbled into them.

When Claudia realized this was her son, she forgave him instantly. She knew this was not his real character, and she believed he had been misled and brainwashed by the depraved senator. The son she had been longing for, year after year, was finally in front of her. She had wished better for him, but she was nonetheless ecstatic to finally be with him. Joseph was happy, too, even if he couldn't enjoy it at that moment.

15

Eyes Wide Shut

onths had passed. Winter had turned into spring, spring was
turning into summer, and things had changed for Joseph since
that horrid day in February. They had changed a lot. Joseph was no
longer patrolling the fields. He was no longer lost in the façade of the
person that the senator had tried to mold him into.

Joseph was attempting to rediscover himself, but in doing so, he
had to discover the new version of himself as an adult. He was no longer a little boy. He was becoming a striking young man. He had made
some friends at the plantation, and he was at work alongside them in
the fields. They had been forgiving toward him; they had seen it all
happen before. William was becoming quite his buddy. What Joseph
had been through had happened to William as well.

Again working in the very fields he used to control, Joseph had
to do almost twice as much work as the others to avoid being severely beaten by his old friend, the whip. The senator did not like it at
all that Joseph refused to be his puppet any longer, but Joseph could
only refuse to do so much before it became a danger to his own life.

He just remained focused on changing himself for the better. He was learning to let go of all the harm done to him as well as all the harm he had done unto others. He was slowly shaking free from the remaining strings of the web. He knew it would take time, but he was determined. He was not going to let himself or anyone else get in the way of his goals again.

Everything had become crystal clear to him since that February day. The dark veil of denial was lifted from his eyes. For the first time, he noticed that the flag in the front of the house was not a welcoming symbol at all. It was the ole southern symbol for racism, hatred, and ignorance. It was the Confederate flag, flying high as if to say, "I want you to know that I hate anything that is different from myself." As the senator had always said, "We gotta keep those niggers separated and controlled." This flag, for him, was representing just that—his falsified beliefs of superiority.

Joseph also now realized that the dangling noose disgracing that beautiful oak tree out front was not merely a sadistic form of "decoration"; it was also one of the senator's methods of striking fear into the workers' hearts. It was his tormenting tribute to all the innocent people he had ferociously slain there. He left it hanging to remind the others what would happen to them if they misbehaved.

The horror stories of hangings that had taken place in that front yard still circulated the plantation and for miles around. Many of the older workers had watched in horror as one of their family members or friends dangled by the neck, swinging back and forth while trying to break free, soaking in every last bit of torture before departing from the merciless agony. Most of the survivors who had witnessed at least one of these horrid and unspeakable tragedies still had vivid nightmares, accompanied by piercing screams right before waking up soaked in sweat and covered in tears. Some of the survivors killed themselves, some became alcoholics, and the lucky ones just became numb.

Yes, this was the type of souvenir the senator liked to keep. He was all about the mental control, no matter how he went about it. He could pretend to be your friend to get what he wanted, or he could drive fear into the depths of your core. He enjoyed it all, but Joseph's eyes were now wide open.

Joseph had decided to ask for the money he had originally given to the senator to hold for him on the day he first arrived. He had just a shred of hope that the senator had some type of human decency deep inside him. Joseph was wrong, though. When he did muster up the courage to ask for his money, the senator nearly fell out of his rocker, he was laughing so hard.

"Boy, you really thought that I was going to save that money for you, didn't you? Hahahahaha, you really are an ignorant, monkey-lookin' son of a bitch. You ain't got no money. The night you showed up here, I paid a whore with that money to be my little nigger bitch."

The senator was such a ruthlessly cruel man. He had eagerly waited for the day Joseph would ask for his money. He wanted to relish in the defeat he would see coming over Joseph's face when he told him that it was all gone. With no money and nowhere to run, Joseph's options were slim.

Some days, Joseph held the positive outlook that he would one day free himself from there, and some days, he felt defeated, like he would be trapped there forever. Still other days, death seemed like a more humane option. Joseph spent his days trying to find a way to safely escape this prison. At times, he believed prison itself might even be a pleasant escape from this hell. Without money or a place to go, it was nearly impossible for Joseph to plan an escape, but he was patient and tried to stay positive. It was a task made easier because he now had some allies.

Joseph had always dreamed of going to college, but that was just what it was—a dream. He did not believe that college was an attainable goal for a broke mixed boy from the Delta of Mississippi. He was falling into complacency.

He did love to learn, however, and he found that he also loved to teach. He had discovered this because the senator had had Joseph tutored every Tuesday right up to the day he quit being the senator's puppet. Just as the Kingsleys had, the senator thought it important for Joseph to sound educated as long as he was going to be around house guests. For those several years, a teacher had come to the house and taught Joseph all that schoolbooks had to offer. Ironically, the senator had not planned for Joseph's education to benefit Joseph more than it did himself. It was known that the senator would never do anything to knowingly benefit anyone besides himself.

Joseph's teacher, Mrs. Macon, never missed a Tuesday. She was a sweet older lady with light-colored, curly hair and glasses a bit too big for her face. She had a gentle smile, and she'd really taken a liking to Joseph from the first day she met him. She could see that Joseph was something special, and she was pained as she saw him gradually change from the sweet, hopeful boy he had once been. She wanted to help keep that hope and light alive inside of him. She would give him little compliments here and there to boost his pride. Joseph was brilliant in his studies, and she saw this. She hoped he could someday fulfill his dreams to change the world. She believed he would, too, but to convey this to him was difficult with the senator's watchful eye always right around the corner.

Mrs. Macon was deeply concerned when the senator stopped her from continuing to educate Joseph. She pushed as much as she could to convince the senator otherwise, but he was having none of it. She found a way around the senator, however. She was also tutoring the senator's son, Henry, so when she came on Tuesdays, she would make an extra lesson plan and sneak it under a big rock for Joseph. Sometimes there would be a test in place of the lessons. Joseph would eagerly take the test, then leave it back under the rock for her to retrieve the following Tuesday.

Joseph looked forward to those Tuesdays every week. As soon as he got his new lessons, he would run back to tell everyone what they were going to learn that evening. There were three others with whom Joseph had become close. They also loved to learn, and Joseph loved to teach them. They would have to wait until it was dark, and then they would sit around in candlelight while Joseph taught them the new lessons he had received. They would learn it all—mathematics, history, grammar, and the sciences. It really helped Joseph bond with them: William, an elderly man named Jeremiah, and Joseph's mama. Joseph finally got to bond with her.

No matter how happy Claudia was to be with Joseph, she always encouraged him to find a way out of there so that he could have a better life. She wanted what most parents do—a better life for their children than they had for themselves. She would always tell him it was too late for her, but he was still young and had so much to offer. She told him this despite the fact that she was still quite young herself. His mama loved the fact that he was getting an education, even if it was crawling out from under a rock. When he taught them what he had learned, Claudia would just gaze at him with pride exuding from her heart. Her little boy was so intelligent.

Joseph was excited to get to spend time with his mama, who, unbeknownst to him, had been there all along. The senator had been lying to him the entire time—nothing more than a demented manipulation tactic. She had never gone on a trip. She was not even allowed to leave the property. She had been living in the slave quarters out back with the other workers and working the fields every day from the time she had arrived, which was only days after giving birth to Joseph. She had been shoved into this tiny shack with a dozen other people, forced to heal in the few hours she was not slaving away.

Living conditions were horrendous. The dog had better living conditions. The dog's house was more sanitary and better constructed. That cute little house that Joseph had been permitted to stay in after he arrived on the plantation was actually a guest home. Joseph had been allowed to stay there and told it was his mother's house solely to lure and manipulate an excited, hopeful young boy. His mother had never been allowed to set foot in that house. All Joseph's fears of how his mother had been living were not only true but worse than he could have imagined. The illusions that had once been painted for him of her living the good life had been shredded into unrecognizable pieces.

Every evening, Joseph, William, Jeremiah, and Joseph's mama sat around together, talked, told stories, and laughed. One evening when the four of them were sitting around as they so loved to do, Joseph decided it was a perfect time to tell them all about Sarah. It had been three years since they had met in that barn, but he had never forgotten her. He remembered her like it was yesterday. He went on and on about Sarah and that magical evening. They were all so happy for him. He told them that he even remembered how she smelled and the golden shimmer of her hair when the moonlight hit it.

"Wait. What? Golden hair?" Jeremiah piped in with confusion in his voice.

"Is she white?" William asked.

"Yes. Why?" Joseph questioned.

"Why? Why?" his mama said with a high-pitched tone. "Because, son, that very thing can get you killed. It can get you hanged in that front yard faster than we are expected to pick cotton."

His mama was irritated and fearful for her son. She didn't want anything bad happening to her only child.

William shook his head with judgment glaring in his eyes as he said, "Didn't you hear about what happened to that boy down in Money? He got killed for just flirtin' with a white lady. He didn't get killed like they just shot him. Those boys drug him out of his uncle's house. They beat him and beat him. When it looked as if he could take no more, they beat him again. They hurt his body so bad you couldn't recognize it was a child.

"After the beatings were done, they then shot him in the head and tied him up with a noose made from barbwire. They hung him up by a fan to laugh at what they had done, and then they dumped him by the river. That is what these sick bastards did to that poor boy because he flirted with a white lady, and you sayin' you wanna marry one?

"Joseph, these folks here aren't like you and me. They don't see us like people. They see us like the trash. We aren't meant to be with white women. It's just not allowed, and it won't never be."

Joseph was horrified hearing this, and he was pissed all at the same time as he whipped back: "You don't understand, none of you! I love her, and she loves me. I knew since that day that she was made for me. Our souls are supposed to be together. We can change. We can change their minds. We are all human. Why can't we love who we love? There is nothing wrong with love. What is wrong with the world is hate. Love makes it all a better place. Love is what makes living in this place tolerable when all else has gone wrong."

Joseph went to sleep that night thinking of that poor boy from Money. He could not shake the vivid, horrific thoughts. This did not scare him away from Sarah, even though maybe it should have. It restored that fire in him that he'd once had—the fire to strive for what's right. It gave him something to fight for: equality and justice for that boy and all the others who had been murdered, tortured, brutalized, humiliated, and treated less than human. From that moment on, Joseph knew in his heart what he wanted. He wanted change, and he wanted equality. He would not stop fighting till he got it for himself and everyone else. These powerful emotions of injustice and the search for humanity helped free him from his complacency.

Every day that passed after Joseph heard that horrific account, he became more and more infuriated by all the hate and inequality he saw all around him. His eyes were finally wide open, and he saw it everywhere. There was no reason why he or any other person should be treated differently. He knew and felt on the deepest level of his core that everyone was the same; they were all human beings. It infuriated him that others couldn't just open their eyes and see it, too. The level of ignorance was almost intolerable to him. He looked every day for a way to get out of that plantation and go and change the world—go and fight for what he knew was right and moral.

Joseph had begun to hear of rights fighters who were popping up here and there. Word does travel fast in the South, especially in a small town. The news of these activists was all the buzz. It's all anyone talked about. Some were excited, some enraged. Joseph had heard that they might be coming to the South. He wanted so badly to be part of something that was impassioned for humanity. That was his new goal. That was what he wanted to do. But Joseph was still deep in the Delta of Mississippi. Breaking free from those racial chains and boundaries would be just short of a miracle.

16

Education Defeats Ignorance

It was summertime in Mississippi, and a damn hot one, as usual. It seemed all the kids around town close to Joseph's age were getting ready to head off to college. Joseph was now nineteen, and his desperate want for a higher education was almost too much to bear. He could practically smell the scent of a freshly cracked book tickling his nose. The fall semester was just around the corner, and the senator's son, Henry, was starting to pack up his things with the anticipation of leaving for college. Every year, Joseph had watched all the wealthy white kids run off to college the second they hit eighteen or nineteen, and every year, Joseph saw some poor sap sit and watch the others leave, wishing he or she could trade places for a shot at an education. This year, the poor sap was Joseph.

Most of the kids with money around the Delta attended Ole Dixie, just northeast of Doddsdale. That was where Joseph had always dreamed he would go if he had his way. Ole Dixie was known for its law program, and that was something that really intrigued Joseph. If he got a law degree, he would be able to fight the good fight in a courtroom for all those who needed equality. For those kids headed to college, however, it was not so much about celebrating the chance for a higher education and broader knowledge as it was a celebration of independence and freedom from their parents. It was as if they had not been free all along.

Joseph had heard countless tales of many "newly freed" kids getting out from under their parents' roof, squandering their parents' money, and reveling in their newfound independence through late nights with alcohol at fraternity houses. What a waste of a precious gift that others, such as Joseph, would gladly fight for. This deeply bothered him because he wanted to relish in the education that a university could provide him. He believed he might not ever get to experience any of those three precious goals: a formal education, independence, and freedom.

Considering the many obstacles he would need to battle against, Joseph often found counsel in Jeremiah, the elderly man he had befriended at the plantation.

"How am I ever going to have the chance to go to college?" Joseph would say. "I am a poor, dark, mixed boy with no formal education stuck on a plantation in the Delta of Mississippi."

This was a battle that had been lost time and time again for as long as stories were told. He was not sure if winning the battle over racism, poverty, and education was even a possibility.

Joseph was distraught about the seemingly unnavigable obstacles in his way, not to mention his not even being allowed to attend most southern universities. "The only reason I am not allowed to attend is simply for being born who God made me to be," he said.

Jeremiah nodded because he knew Joseph spoke the truth. Ole Dixie, the local university he wished to attend, did not have a desire to accept students not of the white aristocrat type. All area universities were heavily segregated. Segregation was almost like their second religion, Southern Baptist being the first, of course. In their eyes, he was just a poor ole Negro who would never amount to anything but a field nigger—although, for the second time, things were slowly starting to change in Mississippi by the forced hand of the United States government.

One sweltering hot evening in that summer of 1962, Joseph was out on the side of the house finishing his last chores for the day when he noticed a sleek black sedan pull up in front of the house. A man in a pressed black suit got out of the driver's seat and went around to open the back passenger-side door. An older gentleman stepped out of the back seat, brushing his blazer with both hands as if to wipe out any imperfections. His elegant suit screamed money and power. By now, the senator was out on the front porch to greet the man, and Joseph was curious. He could tell this man was someone of importance by how he carried himself, so Joseph snuck around to get a closer look.

"Governor, nice to see you again. Thanks for coming," gushed the senator.

Joseph had heard that the governor of Mississippi had come to visit a few times before, but he had never laid eyes on him. He had only heard stories. Governor Burns was infamous for his desire to strip emancipation and demand continued segregation.

Joseph had heard that the governor only came to visit when he needed favors from the senator. Both he and the senator had similar views on many matters, especially when it came to segregation, as most Mississippi politicians did.

The governor had a grave look on his face when he began to speak to the senator. "Let's go in and sit down, Senator. I don't have long, but we need to discuss a situation goin' on up in Lee.

"I know that you, as well as I, will hold this matter close to your heart since it is in regard to our ole alma mater. We had the situation handled just fine, then yesterday I got word that the nigger-lovin' president is rumored to get involved.

"I need you to get in his ear, or whoever's ear up there in Washington, to let them know we down here in Mississippi don't need their help regulating our schools. We are just fine with how things are run around here. We like our children being kept separate and safe from those Negro kids. This nigger boy is trying to attend Ole Dixie, and the good folks there just aren't havin' it. Too much old money is in that school, and we don't need folks afraid to send their kids to Ole Dixie. It holds such a strong legacy, and it creates such strong men, like you and me. We don't want him or his kind in our school. If we allow one Negro in this white university, then what's next? Monkeys are going to be allowed to enroll?

"It's all just absurd. As you know, he took this matter to court here in good ole Mississippi, and his case was shot down so fast it almost slapped the black off that boy, but he has taken it to the federal level now. We need to get a handle on this matter now before it disrupts our entire strong state of good, God-fearin' Christians. If I have to stand and block the entrance to that university myself, I will. That nigger ain't gettin' through."

This was right up the senator's alley because he loved his segregation. He would segregate the whole world if he could. He and the governor were right on the same page about that—a miserable page in a very demented book.

The senator was more than happy to get involved. He often spoke of it being God's will to keep the races separate. This was the excuse that so many—too many—had used to fuel their ignorance, fear, and hatred. The governor and the senator stood up and shook hands in full agreement that they needed to exhaust all measures in order to stop this threat to the Mississippi that they knew and loved—a hateful one. The senator walked the governor back out to his car, shook his hand again with an overly firm grip, as if to prove his manhood and dominance, then waved to him as he left. As they parted ways, they both had the glimmer of determination and a twinge of hate in their eyes, but they would have claimed it was Jesus's love and his calling that was glimmering so ominously.

Joseph heard the entire conversation, but he was not entirely sure who or what they were discussing, so he started asking around. Joseph quickly found out that his soon-to-be new hero's name was James, and James was indeed on the battlegrounds of justice there in Lee, Mississippi, just an hour and forty minutes northeast of Doddsdale. The news buzzing all around town—and the nation, for that matter—generated an electric excitement in the air mixed with grave apprehension. Even just a whisper of an African-American boy going to this all white, prestigious, very segregated university in Mississippi brought along excitement and apprehension. Some reveled in the thought of change; many reviled it.

Joseph desperately wanted to be with James in the middle of the battle against the deep-seated, tenacious segregation rules of Ole Dixie and Mississippi, which were being upheld by the governor, senator, local courts, and countless citizens, their collective stance based in their Southern Baptist roots. James, viewed as a terrorist against Mississippi and the Lord himself, only wanted an education and to be treated like a human being. It was exceedingly difficult for Joseph to comprehend how an entire culture could be so dangerously wrong and cowardly, joining in the maliciousness or turning their heads to the wicked and the unjust. It was as if they just blindly followed in the footsteps of those who spoke the loudest.

James won his federal court case that June of 1962. Ole Dixie and the state continued to disgracefully fight against the ruling until the bitter end. The president stepped in and forced Mississippi and Ole Dixie to allow James to attend.

The governor kept his promise to Senator Westridge. The day that James was supposed to set foot into Ole Dixie for the first time, the governor defiantly stood there blocking the front door with disgrace and hatred smeared all over his face for the entire nation to see. Joseph, along with everyone around the country, heard of all the riots and deaths that resulted because one student wanted to get an education at the university of his choice. Having a choice in the university you attend . . . what a novel idea. James was a top student and eligible to serve his country in the military, but he was considered unworthy of attending Ole Dixie.

The president had to supply James with military guards and US marshals for protection just so he could set foot on that campus. The US marshals then had to stay with James for the full year of his attendance at Ole Dixie till the day of his graduation. They all endured torment and torture for the entire duration of the year, although they didn't seem to mind. They looked at James as the hero he truly was. They were protecting a legend.

This whole revolution was surreal for so many as they watched all of this unfold. For Joseph, it was the extra fire he needed to move forward with his dreams. James inspired him and gave him hope. It made him believe that what he had always dreamed of was achievable, not foolishness as so many had told him. Still, the fact remained that it would take nearly a miracle for Joseph to ever attend college. Dreams can be achieved, however, and miracles can indeed happen.

17

Plymouth Rock

Joseph was still forbidden to be near Mrs. Macon, his teacher, but word traveled fast around the plantation. Mrs. Macon soon heard of Joseph's deep, fiery desire to attend college at none other than the now-infamous Ole Dixie. She was thrilled to hear such news, but she also feared for him when she learned of his preference. She knew it would be a life-changing decision and possibly a life-ending one, but she'd always had such faith in Joseph. She knew he could accomplish whatever he put his mind to. She knew he was meant to do great things.

One afternoon early that August, Mrs. Macon had again left something for Joseph under their covert rock. It was some information about applying to colleges. What he found under that rock of hope that day gave him great encouragement. Her belief in him also made him feel exceptional. So many times in his life, he had been subjected to negativity from people putting him down, so just one person believing in him seemed like an army in his favor.

Joseph was whistling on his way back from the rock when he caught the senator's disapproving glares. He quickly trotted to his quarters, knowing he did not want to further disrupt the beast. He sat down against the side of the tiny wooden house (the slave quarters), where he had been residing with the three others: his mama, William, and Jeremiah. Just as the excitement and nerves were settling in, a sweeping wave of devastation hit him: there was no record of his ever having attended school. He would not be able to go to college. Even though Mrs. Macon had educated him, there was no record of it—no transcripts, no grades. It had been hard enough for James to attend Ole Dixie, with all that discrimination and racism, even *with* a well-documented education and service in the military. Without such documentation, it appeared impossible. Joseph had only lived on plantations, serving people's entitled needs.

Joseph was overcome with despair, as if there had been a death in the family. Actually, it was a death: the death of his dreams. The dreams of being a lawyer, of changing the world, of teaching, and of leaving that dreadful plantation were gone in an instant.

That evening, he sat alone by candlelight, writing a teary but well-thought-out letter to Mrs. Macon explaining why a college education was not an option for him due to the lack of proof that he had ever obtained an education. He felt as if he were signing away his future in that letter. He slowly walked out to the rock to lay the letter underneath, his head hanging in gloom, his eyes filled with tears like he was laying a body to rest. To his astonishment, when he solemnly lifted the rock, he found another envelope there.

During the entire time that Joseph and Mrs. Macon had been exchanging information under this rock, not a single time had she ever left anything more than once a day. What could it be? What might this letter hold? He grabbed it and ran back to the light. He opened the envelope so quickly that he sliced himself with a deep paper cut, but he paid no mind to that. As he opened the folds of the letter one at a time, he was not sure if he should feel dread or enthusiasm.

Dearest Joseph,

I hope this letter finds you well.

When I previously left you material about enrolling in universities, I failed to mention a few things of importance. You do not need to worry about the fact that you have not had formal schooling. I am an accredited homeschooling teacher. As far as the board of education knows, you have always been my student even after we were forbidden to continue our studies. No one needs to be any the wiser. I have kept detailed records of your work and grades. All are on file and can be submitted with your application to the college of your choice. The extra tests I have been leaving for you lately were state tests that are required for acceptance to most universities.

I failed to mention that purposely. I did not want your nerves or other interferences to affect your performance. I knew you could do it, and did not want you to be your own enemy.

It is my honored pleasure to inform you that your results on these tests were outstanding. You did brilliantly, and because of this you can practically choose any college you wish. This, however, does not include other determining factors. If Ole Dixie is truly the college you choose, there will be many battles ahead, but if anyone can conquer these battles, it is you, Joseph. You're a remarkable man. I am proud to say, I was the one who was lucky enough to help educate such an intelligent and outstanding person that will help change the world.

Love Always,

Mrs. Macon

P.S. I have enclosed several applications, including one to Ole Dixie.

Joseph's eyes were once again shedding tears, but this time, it was droplets of joy rolling down his sweet face. All along, Mrs. Macon had had Joseph's best interests embedded in her pure heart. She had been recording his progress as a student of her own, even when the legality of it could come into question. Sometimes, morals and good deeds trump all. She had become his angel, watching after him. Everyone could use an angel like her.

Joseph was thrilled to find out this new revelation. He was also terrified at the thought of all this change. Even desired change can be frightening. Ole Dixie and Mississippi Delta University were among some of the universities to which he could apply. These were the closest to him and the most logical in terms of distance.

Most kids attend a college close to home, even if home was a sliver of hell. It's what they know. Ole Dixie was prestigious in the area, but it had that horrible reputation for being exceedingly racist and intolerant. The students who attended Ole Dixie were known around Mississippi as children from money, and some of these children were known to be quite cruel, especially if you were not like them: rich, entitled, and white. They would verbally—and at times physically—taunt those they believed did not fit in. Henry, the senator's son, verbally abused Joseph all the time. Henry loved to shove a shoulder into him every time they passed each other.

The occasional underprivileged kid slipped in at Ole Dixie. They had a difficult time fitting in and were picked on, but an African American or anyone of color was unheard of before James. It was a scary place to attend if you were of any descent other than Caucasian. Of course, Joseph's first pick was Ole Dixie. He would love to get a law degree, and Ole Dixie was widely known for its law program.

That evening was one hell of an emotional rollercoaster: up and down and up again, but it ended on an up—way up. Joseph was elated as he jumped up and down, telling his mama his great news. He was like a little boy on Christmas morning. He gushed to her about his opportunity. It was brief, though, because he was in a hurry to do something he had waited a long time to do.

He ran to grab the pen that he hidden under his bed and went to work on that application. Every stroke of the pen was a stroke of his confidence. He filled out every blank on that application, and he did so with such meticulousness. He would not let a simple error be an excuse to not allow him to attend. Joseph sealed his application to Ole Dixie in an envelope to leave for Mrs. Macon. He ran back out to the rock and placed all his aspirations under that lump of stone.

This rock had become a symbol of hope to Joseph. It was a symbol of progress and a symbol of freedom. Joseph was fighting against religious persecution from many of the "Christians" in the South, who insisted it was against God's will for the races to be intermingled. He was fighting for freedom and freedom of choice, and he wanted to fight for a better life for not only himself but also for those treated as unequal.

The rock was rough in places and smooth in others. It was black, white, and gray, all fluidly intertwining. With all its differences, it represented harmony within itself and the earth. This was how Joseph believed the world should be: living harmoniously. He would soon have the opportunity to try and stimulate change for the better, but all he could do now was wait.

18

Ah, Sweet Satisfaction

Weeks passed, and still no word from Ole Dixie. Every day seemed like an eternity to Joseph. He was stuck in this prison, awaiting his release papers, but today, he had other preoccupations.

A familiar car pulled up out front. It was a car that Joseph recognized from the Kingsleys' estate, leaving him apprehensive as to why that car would come all this way to Doddsdale. A man got out and walked up the stairs to the house. It was the Kingsleys' butler. One of the senator's butlers opened the door, and after a minute, he pointed out toward the field, right at Joseph.

Joseph could not swallow. His throat was defying him. The man from the car walked out into the field and up to Joseph, a grim look on his face.

"Joseph?"

Joseph hesitantly replied, "Yes, sir?"

"I was sent with some bad news for you. Mrs. Kingsley is real sick. They don't think she will make it much longer. She has the cancer.

She asked me to drive all the way out here and let you know. She also wanted me to tell you that she is sorry."

"Sorry? Sorry for what?" Joseph nearly screamed.

"I am not sure, son," the man responded. "She just told me to let you know she was very sick, and she said she was sorry."

Joseph's face was as blank as a sheet of fresh paper. He could not yet process this news. The Kingsleys' butler and Joseph talked for a few minutes, then he walked back out to the car and headed on his way.

Joseph was not sure what to say or how to feel. He first felt a strange sadness. Mrs. Kingsley had been the only mother he knew growing up, and no matter how badly she might have treated him, he still thought of her as a mother. It was a confusing time for him.

Joseph sat there steaming from rage, questioning everything he had known about Mrs. Kingsley. His mama was there with a listening ear.

"Sorry for what?" Joseph said to Claudia. "Being a horrible person to me, treating me like less than an animal, never showing me love, physically and mentally abusing me, stealing me from you, Mama, the one who loved me?"

The list could go on, but Joseph was exhausted from all the sorrow, anger, and over-contemplation.

His mama rubbed his head in a loving and comforting way. "Baby, you gotta let it go," she said. "That anger will eat you up inside. It's not good for your soul."

Joseph knew she was right, so he let it go for now, but it would be a long journey to forgiveness.

Sometimes in life, you really get down on yourself no matter what positive things might be present. This was how Joseph was feeling. It really bothered him about Mrs. Kingsley. He could not seem to shake free from the lingering sadness. He considered a trek up to Clarksville to see her before she passed. He was not even sure if he would be welcomed, but he felt like it was the right thing to do. So Joseph packed his things and prepared for the journey. It was still a long walk, but it wasn't quite as scary or exciting now that he was no longer a boy. He had learned the ways, a bit more, of the wicked and wonderful world that he knew as the South.

Two days after he received the news, Joseph headed out to Clarksville. He went to tell his buddies good-bye and kiss his mama, who told him to be careful. That's what mothers do.

As Joseph was walking down the driveway toward the dusty road, Mrs. Macon's car pulled up. He gave her a quick glance and smiled, knowing that if his look lingered too long, they would both be in trouble.

She did the same while exiting her car. Her smiles were always filled with such warmth. She whispered to him as she passed: "I heard about Mrs. Kingsley, and I am sorry for you. Even though you two were not close, I know it still must be hard."

It felt good hearing those comforting words of sympathy from Mrs. Macon. Joseph nodded his head and gave her a half-smile full of sorrow. As she walked away from her car, a packet fell from her arms. Being the gentleman that he was, he quickly went to pick it up for her. That was when he noticed it was addressed to him from Ole Dixie. *She must have dropped this on purpose for me*, he thought. He quickly tucked it under the front of his shirt and briskly headed out to the road.

Joseph wanted to open the envelope right then, but he knew he'd better wait till he got a safe distance from the senator's vision. Several miles down the road, Joseph pulled the packet from under his shirt. It was exciting to have such an official envelope addressed to him.

When he opened the envelope, there were several pages. He was afraid to read even the first page. He walked over to sit down off the edge of the road to begin reading. As he started reading, one word popped out at him: "accepted." He was in pure disbelief. "You have been accepted to The University of Ole Dixie."

Immediately, he started to whimper like a baby. His life was changing right in front of him, and he could not believe it. He had been accepted to the one university he had chosen, Ole Dixie. As he read further, he noticed that he had qualified for a full scholarship for his academic achievements, although they were conveniently all out of scholarships for the year. This was an enormous disappointment, but he brushed it off. He knew now that there was a chance of him getting a scholarship the following year. In the worst-case scenario, if he could not go to the school of his dreams, at least there was a great chance he would be accepted and receive a scholarship somewhere else.

As Joseph finished reading, he stood up and brushed off the dust from himself. He was absorbing this disappointing yet amazing news when he heard a voice yelling his name. He looked up and saw William running down the street after him.

"What is it, William?" Joseph said in a panicked tone, a sick feeling in the pit of his stomach.

"Wait up, Joseph," William said while running toward him. William was out of breath as he delivered the news. "Joseph, I got word from Clarksville. Mrs. Kingsley passed on last night."

Joseph's head dropped sullenly, and his face had a look of defeat. He turned and began to walk back to the senator's with tears flooding his eyes.

William just gently placed his hand on Joseph's shoulder as they walked back slowly together in quiet mourning.

It was as if the senator could smell defeat in someone. He thrived on the blood of the weak. As soon as William and the mournful Joseph arrived back at the mansion, the senator was standing out on his porch to greet them. The senator had a devilish grin on his face, and it seemed like he giggled to himself a bit as he opened his mouth to shout. "Hey, boy, did you hear Mrs. Kingsley is dead?"

He said this knowing Joseph already knew. He was the one who had sent William running after Joseph to deliver the news.

"I heard she suffered, but not as bad as she would have if she had seen your ugly nigger face before she died. Thank God you didn't make it."

Joseph was enraged. He felt as if he could have gone onto that porch and easily beaten the senator to death with his bare hands. Instead, Joseph showed remarkable restraint while he took a deep breath and kept walking right past the porch, ignoring the senator. He knew that if he said or did anything, it would jeopardize his very tangible escape from this hellhole. He wanted to go and use his education to fight against the likes of this unintelligent, ill-spirited person. Losing his temper now and forfeiting the chance to leave and get an education was not in his plan. He would not give the senator the satisfaction of winning.

Joseph remained quiet for the next few weeks. He tried to focus all his energy into working and filling out application after application to various colleges. Each response letter he received was the same song and dance: accepted, but no scholarship or financial help. They legally had to accept him because the president had put his foot down on this issue, but there were always loopholes for the wicked to weasel through. Most of these colleges assumed a little Negro boy would not have the money to pay full tuition. This was the spineless escape they used over and over.

Joseph's positivity on finding a full scholarship was fading. There was another college close by that was specifically for African Americans, but they would only train him in blue-collar jobs. Joseph wanted to get a law degree. He decided that if he couldn't get a scholarship, he would try to earn the money, but it seemed that would take him a lifetime. Everything looked hopeless, although Joseph was not going to give up. He started going all around town, offering his services for whatever needed to be done. He was taking a huge risk of this getting back to the senator, but he didn't care. This was his only chance.

When soliciting work, Joseph was met mostly with a no, a slam of the door, people ignoring him, name-calling, and laughter. A few people gave him small jobs. A couple of older ladies allowed him to carry in their groceries and put them up for a few cents, but the jobs were few and far between. Fall semester was out of the question, regardless of the school. At this rate, he didn't know when he would ever be able to attend.

One day, Joseph was out working in the field when he got an overwhelming feeling things were about to change. He couldn't explain it, nor did he 100 percent believe in the feeling. It did, however, help him stay positive. Joseph truly believed that God had a bigger plan for him and that God would provide him with a way if he worked hard and continued to help himself. Joseph looked up to the sky and said, "God, I hope this hard work pays off."

The tingle in the air and the freshness of Joseph's attitude were strong. One afternoon shortly after Joseph had that overwhelming feeling, a postman arrived in search of a Mr. Joseph Kingsley. He was carrying a letter that required Joseph's signature. It must be of importance.

William ran out to the field to alert Joseph of his letter. He started screaming, "Joseph! Joseph!"

Joseph's mama heard William's screams, and she immediately started crying. It was as if they could all feel the life-changing cosmic shift emanating out of that postman's hand.

Sweaty and worn down, like he was every day, Joseph walked out of the field toward the postman. Joseph was apprehensive. To be let down is a horrible feeling, but to let down the ones whom you love and who are rooting for you could be the worst feeling of all. The postman looked Joseph up and down.

"Are you Mr. Joseph Kingsley?"

"Yes, sir, I am," Joseph stated with pride and a bit of hesitance.

"Sign here," the postman instructed.

Joseph's shaky hand reached for the pen and signed his name. He felt very official; he had never been asked to sign anything before. The postman handed over the letter, and when it converged with Joseph's hand, waves shot through his body. It was an electric feeling of life rejuvenation. The return address was from a law firm in Clarksville.

He opened the letter quickly but with great care. He did not want to tear whatever enormity might be held inside. He tightly held the one page that had been encompassed within that envelope and read it aloud to his mama and William. His voice trembled as he read through the letter.

Turns out, in Mrs. Kingsley's dying days, she had drafted a will leaving Joseph $100,000 on top of a full college fund.

Joseph dropped to his knees, threw his hands high in the air, reaching for the heavens, and screamed with cries of joy and relief. No more prison, no more hell, no more abuse, and no more chains. He was born to chains and had lived his whole life according to the shackles of repression.

"No more!" he screamed. "No more!"

He was free! He was finally free. He grabbed his mama and William. They all squeezed each other with the tightest of embraces and cried. He cried and cried, and they sobbed for him. The joy that he felt was like none other, and it felt amazing.

It is not known what made Mrs. Kingsley leave Joseph this money. Was it love or was it guilt? Joseph liked to think that it was a little bit of both. Joseph promised to help William and his mother as much as he could. He was ecstatic to be able to finally help the ones that he loved.

The senator heard all the commotion and came storming out. He despised hearing such happiness ringing out from those whom he believed he owned. "Get back to work, niggers! This isn't social hour!" he yelled. "We don't get to cry and hug around here. If you like cryin' so much, I'll give you somethin' to cry about,"

This time, Joseph was the one with the grin, and he was grinning from ear to ear.

"Why you grinnin', boy? Get back to work, I said."

Joseph looked him right in his cold, dead eyes and screamed, "I don't work for you no more, you hateful piece of shit!"

The senator was stunned, his eyes filled with shock.

Joseph had the most satisfying smile as he grabbed his mother's and William's hands. They walked off the plantation, leaving the senator screaming and enraged as the flag of repression, tattered and worn, waved them adieu in the background. Joseph had never felt such a sense of sweet satisfaction.

19

Ole Flames and Fury

Some months had passed since that glorious August day of sweet freedom. Joseph was about to start the spring semester at Ole Dixie. He had bought a little house out in Lee for himself, his mama, William, and Jeremiah. That day back in August, the three of them had snuck back in the dead of night to fetch Jeremiah and bring him along. This had become their little family. No one was going to be left behind.

The day that Joseph purchased the house was a monumental moment for them. He couldn't believe he now owned something of his own. The day he signed on that dotted line, he had his mama, Jeremiah, and William with him. They all shed tears of joy that day. It was so surreal to all of them. It was surreal to Joseph that he would ever have had $19,000 to spend on his own home. As a property owner, he couldn't be prouder.

While preparing for the start of school, Joseph had spent his days working little side jobs. He also read to some of the local kids once a week. He enjoyed seeing the joy it brought to their faces in a place where joy could be hard to find among all the racism and poverty.

The other three found work at a local farm. It was a lot of the same work they had performed for the senator. The difference was that they were no longer viewed as property, and they had a home to go to at night where they were free to do whatever their hearts desired. They were also being paid a decent wage, considering what they were used to. They were all happy to have found work and to have each other. Most of all, they were happy to be free from the daily abuse of the beast of Doddsdale.

Joseph and William had become like brothers. They were as close as two could be. William was just a year younger than Joseph. Claudia had taken in William as her own. She had looked after him when he was brought to the plantation at the tender age of five after his parents had been killed in a tornado that tore through the town one spring. Claudia had instantly taken William under her wing, giving him the motherly love a child needs. One has to wonder if this helped fill that hole burrowed deep in her heart from having her own flesh-and-blood child stripped from her arms.

Then there was Jeremiah. He was like the patriarch of the family. The boys looked at him like a grandfather, and he loved them like one, too. Jeremiah love to cut up a bit, and, boy, did he love to hear himself talk and tell a joke. He loved to tell wild stories to the boys at night, but he also had a wise soul. The boys never acted too old for his stories or his wisdom. You could see the wisdom and softness within him by looking into his eyes.

Jeremiah had lived his entire life on that plantation. He had been born there, and he had seen a lot there—mostly things one should never have to see. The senator's father had been just as cruel as his son, if not worse. Jeremiah had lived a rough life, but it never hardened him. He was thankful for what he had and what he had been given. Even though he had no formal education, the life he had lived had given him a wealth of knowledge to pass on to the next generation, and there stood Joseph and William to absorb it all.

Yes—this was their little family, and they were all thankful to have one another. They each had their roles and fit into them effortlessly. Each individual was there to support the other, and right now, Joseph sure needed some support as he was preparing for Ole Dixie. He was excited, nervous, and scared to death every day. The intensity increased as the first day of school crept closer, coming at him like a freight train.

The greatly anticipated first day of college had finally arrived, and Joseph had already thrown up four times that morning. He couldn't hold anything down. He was stricken with the granddaddy of all nerves. He packed up his bag and headed out the door, scared to death. Everyone else was already at work, so he had to be his own cheerleader and pep-talk host as he drove to the campus for the first time to register for classes behind the wheel of the old Ford Crown Victoria he had bought for them to use.

After arriving at campus, he was greeted by a local police officer hired to escort him to registration and to and from his classes during the semester. This officer, instructed to stay with Joseph throughout the first few months, was not real cheery about it. He too, as many did, believed it was wrong for a Negro to be at this school. Being new to the force, though, he didn't have much choice. He had to work his way up. No one else on the force wanted this job. Frankly, the entire police force was powerless to say no to sending one of their own to do the job. Uncle Sam had been keeping a watchful eye since everything that had happened the previous fall with James, so they sent their newest recruit to do the "dirty work."

The first day was harsh. Joseph was teased and taunted. He was shoved, spat on, and called all kinds of names. People would knock his books out of his hands and stand around laughing as he picked them up. This happened again and again, and it always drew a crowd.

The things other students said to him were unthinkable. You would have thought that he was incarcerated in the hardest of all prisons, not attending a distinguished university. Even several professors mumbled racial slurs, and some were not as faint as a mumble should be. He just kept reminding himself that he was getting the education that he so desired, and that made him one happy fellow.

A few months into the semester, some of the abuse had been toned down. Disregard the ignorance, and all was going fairly well—at least the part that mattered the most to Joseph: his grades. He was taking the typical first-year classes—English, biology, history—with some law classes thrown in. He was the top student in his class, all As all around. He was proving Mrs. Macon correct that he was extremely intelligent.

Joseph had learned to block out most of the taunting. It had become like an annoying fly steadily buzzing around his head. Finally giving in to its presence, he made a conscious choice to focus on the positive in his life, although there still were days the taunting would drill its way down and get to him. How could it not?

One day in particular stood out to Joseph, and it couldn't be blocked out or erased. It all started with a group of fraternity boys. One boy in particular was quite familiar to Joseph—Henry, the senator's son, a little prick. He traveled campus with his gang of entitled assholes who served to inflate his ego even more, if that were possible. They picked on Joseph worse than anyone on campus. It was relentless torment day in and day out.

Every time Joseph saw them coming, his entire body tensed up with knots in his stomach. After those encounters, Joseph often ended up in the bathroom, heaving. The officer in charge of protecting Joseph was more like Barney Fife without morals: following Joseph around with a lack of concern, tripping over his own feet, and fumbling his words.

The day that could not be wiped from Joseph's mental slate started with the typical torment aimed at him. Spineless, uncreative jabs were thrown at his character. Joseph always stood there like a man and kept quiet till they were done with their juvenile behavior, but this day was different. Joseph had not gotten much sleep the night before because he had been cramming for a huge final in his criminal law class. Plus, he was in a hurry. The final was about to start, and he knew that there would be no exception for tardiness, especially on his behalf.

As the taunting began, Joseph softly spoke up in a polite manner. "Look, fellas, I am in a huge rush today. Could we please let me slide, just for today?"

The roars of their laughter broke out.

"Let you slide, huh, nigger? Let you slide?" Henry said with vile laughter rumbling in his voice. "You don't tell us when to let you slide. You keep your nigger mouth shut and be thankful for what we give you. We let you slide every day by not beating your nigger ass. I'll tell you what we will do, boy."

Using both his arms, Henry violently shoved Joseph with such force that he fell backward, stumbling over his own feet. Then the fury crept into Henry's eyes, taking over like dark clouds consuming the sky. His voice deepened an octave with an almost growling tone. "I am going to teach you what it is like when we don't let you slide, boy."

Henry and his gang were like a clan of angry hyenas viciously and clumsily attacking their prey, feeding off each other's energy. Joseph lowered his head and covered it with his hands to protect himself as the blows from their fists started coming at him one after the other. One of them kicked him in the stomach, knocking the breath from him and flinging his body to the ground. Joseph took the only defense he could, curled up in the fetal position with his head covered by his now-bruised hands.

Seconds seemed like an eternity as fearful thoughts sprinted through Joseph's mind. All the while, the useless Barney Fife stood to the side, not attempting to make any effort to stop the brutality. The officer actually got a twinge of pleasure watching these boys thrash Joseph's helpless body.

Just as Joseph thought he could take no more, he heard a woman's voice cry out. It was muffled by his arms, which were protecting his head, and by the heathens who were hovering over him with their vile saliva slinging.

The voice sounded like an angel as she screamed, "Stop! Stop that right now!" She grabbed at Henry's arm, commanding them to stop. He slung free of her grip without turning around.

She yelled, "I will tell my uncle if you don't stop this right now!"

This time, Henry turned around to see who was invading their fun. When he saw who it was, he looked surprised and made an utterance with an insincere and spiteful smile. "Sorry, miss."

Henry and the others reeked with smiles of gluttonous satisfaction as they stepped back, wiping spit from their foul mouths.

"You remember this, boy," Henry said while he turned to walk off with his cronies, laughing.

Joseph took a deep sigh of relief and wiped the spattered blood from his eyes so he could see his savior. Focusing his eyes, he looked up into her face, which was caressed by rays of light gently encompassing her head like something from the heavens. When her face came into focus, it was as if he had been lifted straight into nirvana, and he cried out, "Sarah?"

It was none other than his boyhood crush and only love. "Oh my God, I can't believe it's you!" Joseph said in an exhilarated and joyous tone, still gasping for breath.

"Joseph?"

Sarah recognized his voice after all these years, and she was elated. "What are you doing here, Joseph?"

"I go to school here."

"Me, too!" Sarah said excitedly. "My uncle is the dean here. I have not once forgotten you, Joseph. I have wanted to find you for a while. I can't believe it is you."

Joseph felt no pain. He actually forgot that he was still lying on the ground until Sarah reached out her hand to help him up, with the softest smile on her face. Joseph made his exam on time thanks to Sarah, and he, of course, made an A. After that day, the two were practically inseparable.

Joseph finished out the semester ranked at the top of his class. His family was so proud of him, and so was the love of his life, Sarah. She could not have been more proud of him. The whole family loved Sarah, and she loved them.

Joseph had introduced Sarah to his family one night over dinner the same week as their impromptu reunion. Joseph's mama, Jeremiah, and William were all nervous about having a white girl in the house. Likewise, Joseph and Sarah were both nervous for the introduction to go well. Joseph knew he wanted to spend his life with Sarah, so his family's liking her was important. The night they all met was very awkward at first, but by the end of the dinner, they were all laughing and cutting up.

The family loved Sarah; however, they were worried about the hardships Joseph and Sarah would face dating one another. This included Sarah's family not accepting that she was with anyone other than a well-off Christian white man. All that racial tension in the South intensified when you spoke of intermingling the races. People did not look kindly upon interracial dating. In fact, it was illegal in all of the southern states to marry someone of the opposite race. Joseph and Sarah felt this painful inequality to their core. They were in love and wanted to eventually marry, but that rite of passage that so many could share with their loved one had been stripped from Joseph and Sarah's future by barbaric laws and ignorance.

When Joseph and Sarah walked down the street, people looked at them as if Medusa and Poseidon were walking around town with their forbidden love. The two feared doing something as simple as holding hands or giving each other a loving pat on the shoulder. Kissing in public was out of the question. The wrath and uncomfortable stares they would receive for a simple kiss, a symbol of love, was shocking. It was unimaginable how their love could incite such hatred and chaos.

When they were out in public together, they were often subjected to shrill squawks from the street. Sarah was targeted with screams of "nigger lover," and she was often told by self-proclaimed Christians that she was going to hell. A majority of the local churches, as welcoming and loving as they declared to be, were the last place Joseph and Sarah wanted to go together even though they continued to try. Most churches prohibited their attendance together, proving they were the polar opposite of what they claimed to be: loving and welcoming.

One Sunday morning, as Sarah and Joseph were being turned away from yet another church that chose to practice discrimination instead of love, Sarah looked to Joseph with tears in her eyes.

"How can two people deeply in love affect all these other people so negatively?"

Joseph shook his head, saying, "I don't know the answer." It was so difficult for them to understand. They knew their love was real.

All the racism and whispers were an adjustment for Sarah especially. She had never lived through this. She could hear the lowest of whispers since her hearing was so keen. She had heard similar whispers of cruel prejudice before due to her blindness, but nothing of this magnitude.

Joseph had become almost numb to the repulsive slurs long ago, but it did trigger an uproar of emotions in him when he heard the racial lashings directed at Sarah. He would clench his jaw so tightly that you could almost hear the bone cracking. Throbbing headaches often resulted. At times, he would shout back in a rage of anger, while Sarah responded to Joseph with, "Leave them be. They don't know what they are doing."

Joseph was always impressed and surprised at how much peace and love Sarah had within her. She, in turn, was always impressed by how loving and positive he remained even while enduring so much. They complemented each other perfectly. They just wished others were not so blinded and could see it, too.

20

The Noble Struggle

Joseph completed his first semester at Ole Dixie with impeccable grades and was set to return the following fall for his second semester. The first semester had been difficult due to all he had endured and the constant studying, but he'd made it through.

After about a month of class attendance, Joseph was mostly ignored, other than professors occasionally cutting their eyes toward him begrudgingly and the students' whispered slurs. His English professor, Professor Black, was the only one who would voluntarily engage with him by greeting him and asking him questions in class. Joseph really appreciated Professor Black.

Joseph was proud of his accomplishments, as were his family and Sarah. He had done the unthinkable. Just a few years prior, it would have been unimaginable for any person of color to attend Ole Dixie, and yet there he was, completing his first semester. Not to mention that he was on the president's list with his perfect 4.0. As much as he enjoyed learning, though, he was ready for a break from all the ridicule thrust upon him daily. He was looking forward to summer, a time when he could work, relax, and enjoy the simple life without the daily dose of harassment to which he had become accustomed.

One Thursday near the end of Joseph's first semester, he was enjoying his lunch at a favorite bench of his on campus, where he could sit nestled among some beautiful and fragrant rosebushes. He loved to surround himself with the sweet things life had to offer while escaping the hard ridicule whenever he had the chance. From the time he had been a little boy, Joseph would seek solace in nature. It was healing to him. Every Thursday, Joseph had a short break between classes, and there he would sit, eating a sandwich that he had brought from home.

On this Thursday, he was seated on the bench, taking the first bite of a bologna sandwich—his favorite kind—when a young man approached him. This guy appeared to be in his early twenties, a little on the husky side. Joseph thought maybe he was a football player at Ole Dixie, but there was something different about him. Joseph looked up at the young man with an irritated glare because he was disrupting the lunch that Joseph had been looking forward to since he saw his mama making his sandwich that morning.

The young man introduced himself as Michael, and upon first impression, he seemed like a cool and collected guy. After he had introduced himself, Michael started in on his agenda without hesitation like a good salesperson. He was not like a normal sales guy, showing up on your doorstep in a short-sleeved white dress shirt and a tie with a vacuum cleaner. No, this fellow was dressed in a simple gray T-shirt and jeans that contrasted with his white skin. His auburn hair had a slightly unkempt look, like his facial hair and ensemble. His demeanor was very mellow. He seemed like a gentle soul.

Michael immediately expressed interest in Joseph. It was an odd feeling to have some stranger be so stricken with him. Joseph could not help but feel uneasy despite Michael's laid-back demeanor. Michael started to question Joseph.

"Tell me about the struggle you have gone through being a Negro here in the South and at this university. What did you go through trying to attend this college? How harsh has your treatment been here?"

It was not a question of *if* he'd received harsh treatment. That, unfortunately, was a given with his attendance.

"Why did you want to go to this school with all the state's resistance?" Michael continued.

Joseph had not yet had a chance to answer even the first question, nor did he know what to say. It was all so strange.

"I'm interested in all your activism, Joseph."

Joseph thought, *Activism? I am not an activist.* Joseph looked puzzled and a little bothered. "The brave man that came before me, James, was the true activist and hero who fought so hard so that people like me could have this opportunity. I merely took it," Joseph said.

Michael nodded and smiled in agreement and contentment at Joseph's humility, but he told Joseph: "You are indeed an activist, because you fought for your right—and subsequently others' right—to go to the school that you choose. You did not leave the decision up to the ignorance of the people. Instead, you stood up and fought for the greater good.

"Because you have endured all this torment in the noble struggle for equality, you, too, are helping to pave the way. If no one followed in James's footsteps, his triumphs and tribulations would have been in vain, don't you think? He wanted to pave the way for others. By taking that path, you are continuing to pave and smooth a rocky road for those behind you to follow in the footsteps of the strong leaders before them.

"This seems like the only honorable thing to do—to uphold the progress that James has laid before us. I see that same fire in your eyes: the fire that craves change as if it were oxygen. Am I right?"

He indeed was right, and Joseph knew it. This young man was strangely encouraging and passionate. At first glance, one would not believe that this type of passion could come from someone who seemed to care so little about his appearance. Maybe that was the key. It was not that he did not care about his appearance; he did not care about upholding his appearance to societal demands. This was a young man who could think for himself, peer outside the box society had crafted, and see the greater good of humankind.

Michael seemed to care a lot about Joseph's success. There was something very trustworthy about this guy, but the whole thing was still a little alarming; they had just met. It was also trying for Joseph to trust a strange white man advocating for Negro rights. Selflessness was not something Joseph was used to. He stayed open to this new experience—open, but cautious.

Joseph had noticed a strange accent on this guy. Michael was not from around there. He sounded like he was all the way from New York. So why, Joseph wondered, was he all the way down here in the South, and why was Michael approaching *him*, of all people? Joseph was intrigued and yet confused. What was Michael's purpose in talking to him? Michael then started urging Joseph to continue with his activism as part of a vital fight for equality.

Michael told him, "We are taking an imperative step toward equal rights this summer, and we at the CORE would like your involvement."

There it was, finally: the salesperson shtick. Until this point, Joseph had not been sure what Michael was selling. Now he knew that his instincts had been dead on. However, this fellow was selling nothing more than a chance to change the world.

This was what Joseph had always dreamed of: a chance for him to advocate for the equality of humankind. This was the product Michael was pushing. No lousy vacuum cleaners were involved. Joseph wanted to hear more, so he invited Michael back to the house that night for dinner so they could talk more about this intriguing invitation. Michael had done his job. He had hooked his fish and was reeling him in. Dinner it was.

When Michael arrived at the house that evening, everyone took notice of what a polite guy he was. He graciously introduced himself to the whole family with a charming smile, softening the room; then it was down to business. During dinner, Michael spoke with such enthusiasm of what he called the "Mississippi Summer Project."

"This project is a colossal step in pushing equality forward in the South," Michael began. "Our goal is to encourage Negros to register to vote and to use their voice to inspire change. We also want to set up summer schools that are higher quality than the poor, underfunded Negro schools that exist now. Education is power and the future. We really want to focus on the smaller communities here in Mississippi and reach out to lend a helping hand. Is this something you could get behind, Joseph?"

Joseph thought that this all sounded like something he had always dreamed of being a part of. *I could help all the people I grew up around and help those with similar struggles in other communities.*

Michael continued, "Joseph, we really want you to volunteer because we need strong-minded individuals who are unafraid to stand up for what is right. It has to be someone who truly grasps the intensity of the difficulties and struggles that people of color in the South have to endure."

Joseph started to allow himself to feel the gravity this movement could carry. Without hesitation, he committed his summer to volunteering for Michael. In just a few short hours, Joseph had bid farewell to the summer of freedom from ridicule and taunting, and he said hello to the Freedom Summer, which, ironically, would be full of the most horrific taunting and intimidation Joseph had ever experienced.

As dinner and conversation wrapped up, Joseph walked Michael toward the front door. When they reached the door, Michael suddenly ducked down below the little window situated at the top of the door. "I think they're here."

Michael's mood drastically shifted from laid-back to nervous and even paranoid. He insisted they go to the living room window to check the street in front of the house. At this point, Joseph was quickly re-thinking his decision to join this skittish fellow in anything. *I have invited a strange white man from the North into our house, and he is in Mississippi claiming that he wants to encourage the Negro vote?* he thought. Joseph definitely had an "oh, shit" moment. None of this was adding up.

Despite Joseph's hesitation, off to the living room curtain they went. Joseph was going to oblige with whatever this clearly unstable fellow wanted, but when they pulled back the curtain ever so slightly, sure enough, there was a black Lincoln parked across the street with two men in it watching the house. The vehicle looked very official—government, maybe. Perhaps Michael's paranoia was valid, Joseph thought. Now he was becoming a bit paranoid himself.

"Can I stay a while longer?" Michael asked.

"What are those men doing here?" Joseph questioned.

"Me and the others organizing this movement are being watched by who we believe to be Sov-Com. They have been watching us for months. I always see cars following me and men lurking around. The other two I work with say they have had the same experience. We were even being watched all the way up north. We've heard reports of others involved being watched, too."

Joseph figured this was all too outlandish. It seemed so surreal, like a spy novel. *Is this reality?* Yet there it was, right there to see—the Lincoln with the men clearly keeping an eye on Michael, the house, or the whole situation.

Joseph needed to know more. "Who is Sov-Com?" he asked.

Joseph was always one to be curious, seeking answers, and this seemed like the topic of all topics to pique his curiosity.

Michael took a deep breath, as though he were trying to calm himself before speaking. "Well, the whole explanation will sound fabricated, but I promise you it is unfortunately all completely true."

With another deep breath and a brief closing of his eyes, he went on. "Sov-Com is a notorious and exceedingly dangerous organization run by the Mississippi government. The leaders are the governor, lieutenant governor, speaker of the house, and the attorney general. That's the top of the Mississippi food chain, and that's what makes it so dangerous.

"They are the law, so they believe there are no rules. They have everyone in their pocket, it seems, and those people snuff out civil rights progress before we even have a chance.

"They are like piranhas that feed on the flesh of those who threaten their segregation. They have spies all over the country watching those believed to be involved in movements that will affect the South. They get especially violent with the activists here on their own soil. I have heard stories and witnessed them inciting police brutality toward civil rights activists, especially the Negro activists. Rumor has it that they have the White Citizens' Councils on their payroll, along with some Klan members.

"Sov-Com is a far more dangerous organization than we have ever had contact with. They have all the power, and they play dirty—I mean filthy. I fear for my life, and if you decide to join our fight, then you, too, will have to fear for yours. I can't even fathom what they might do to one of us if they catch us alone . . . or maybe I can, and that's what scares me. The brutality is vicious enough with the crowds around. This is why we always travel together. It's harder for wolves to hunt a strong herd. They wait for the straggler, the lone one."

Sarah was not thrilled hearing all this about Joseph joining this movement now that she knew his life was a chip that could be played in the fight for equality. This was not something she wanted to gamble with, but hearing all of this from Michael made Joseph want to fight harder against this wickedness. From living with Senator Westridge, he'd always known that the people inside Mississippi's government were corrupt, but this was really blowing his mind. With all the elements of suspicion and espionage, what Michael was saying sounded like a vivid delusion coming out of the mouth of someone mentally ill. Joseph had read novels that were not this creative and far-fetched.

Joseph knew he had heard the name "White Citizens' Councils" before.

It suddenly dawned on him that it was Westridge. That was why the hate-filled, racist congregation's name sounded so familiar. "I lived half of my life working on Senator Westridge's plantation. At times, the senator would host these meetings at his house."

Michael nodded and sighed. "Oh, yes, Senator Westridge was a big part in this council. He was quite infamous for his speeches and the big role he played.

"The council started out claiming it was going to be nonviolent, but then Westridge gave his appalling speech in Alabama, saying: 'When in the course of human events it becomes necessary to abolish the Negro race, proper methods should be used. Among these are guns, bows and arrows, slingshots, and knives. We hold these truths to be self-evident that all whites are created equal, with certain rights. Among these are life, liberty, and the pursuit of dead niggers.' He incited all kinds of violence with his speeches and loved every minute of it all. He is indeed an evil man. I can't imagine what it must have been like growing up with this monster."

Joseph just nodded. What was there to say? There were just too many stories of terror that he could have told, but he chose to just nod and continue talking of the present rather than relive those memories.

"Oh, yes, I know this very well," Joseph said. "I have seen that man inflict all kinds of evil and pain on folks, but I never imagined how far and wide his reign of terror went."

This lit the rage and fury of injustice inside Joseph. It burned strong. He no longer felt hesitant to help Michael, and he had never felt hesitant to help humanity.

The Lincoln sitting outside must have tired of waiting. It was finally clear for Michael to leave. He said his good-byes.

He then looked at Joseph and said, "We have a long summer ahead of us. I will see you soon."

This day marked the start of Joseph's involvement in the noble fight for civil rights that all began with the Freedom Summer.

That summer, the Freedom Summer, Joseph traveled with a few others on their great quest from county to county, talking to local citizens who would lend them an ear and an at least semi-open mind. They were trying to promote change and educate those who would listen to them. Joseph especially wanted to educate anyone of color about the immense importance of voting. He passionately preached of change and revolution to those towns. Michael and the others started to notice that people really responded when Joseph spoke. Some would stop what they were doing and attentively listen. Joseph had quickly become an excellent public speaker. It seemed so natural for him. When the others noticed his talent, they gave him the duty of speaking to the crowds, however large or small they might be. It worked out great for everyone because most of the other volunteers loathed public speaking. Joseph was not a big fan of public speaking himself, but he was good—really good.

Word traveled fast around the civil rights movement circuit of what a brilliant speaker he was. He was so personable and convincing with his convictions. You could see in his eyes that he wanted so desperately to make the people he preached to understand the gravity and novelty of this opportunity. If they would all just simply vote, they would then have the power to generate tremendous change for themselves and others.

It was unexpectedly hard to convince many to vote. Change was simply too challenging for some, and at what price would change come? Many did not want to face the torment or possible death that could accompany standing firm for their rights. In many of the counties they visited, it seemed that Sov-Com had beaten them there. They knew this because people's eyes would be consumed with fear. Now was the time to rise up in the stance for equality and just treatment, but fear paralyzed many.

The gleaming light that had shined so intensely in the beginning of summer was fading. Joseph started to feel a pestering sense of hopelessness pecking at his soul. He felt as though Sov-Com, all of its associates, and racism were starting to win the battle; darkness was prevailing, but there was still a shred of light. They would push through, power on, and stay strong, no matter the feeling of defeat they might harbor or the atrocious intimidation forced upon them daily.

It seemed like the longest summer of Joseph's life, yet it flew by. The summer's end was bittersweet. Despite all the great work they had done, there was still so much ground to cover. At times, it seemed like a hopeless plight. Joseph and the other volunteers were disheartened over not getting close to their intended goal of registered voters. Fear is such an overpowering emotion, and Sov-Com practiced whatever tactics they deemed necessary to instill it.

One evening when Joseph was depressed, he called Sarah to tell her about the abundant amounts of sacrifice and loss that summer. "You would not believe what we are dealing with every day," Joseph told her. "There have been homes burned to the ground and bombed. They even bombed and burned churches that offered us support. There have been shootings, riots, and murders of innocent people. I, along with many civil rights fighters and others who stood with us, have been beaten with billy clubs and fists."

"Oh my God, Joseph! Are you OK? I think you should come home," Sarah said. "I am so worried about you. Your mother will not be happy."

"I'm OK, but I can't leave now. We're not done. The national media has finally showed up to capture all this violence. We are thrilled. It's what we needed."

After they talked a while longer, Joseph told Sarah good-bye and that he loved her. Back to work it was. Sarah worried immensely about him, but she was proud.

21

The Boys of Summer

Yes—the national media had finally pointed their lens in the right direction. The magnifying glass on the rabid racism in the Deep South had been switched on, and it was powerful. The rest of the country was now seeing the immeasurable violence that went on. But why this sudden interest?

It all began one day that summer when Joseph and three of his fellow volunteers were out working the civil rights trail in Mississippi. The four boys had become more than just coworkers on the road; they were buddies. Joseph had mostly worked in the areas of northern and central Mississippi, but he often had the privilege of volunteering with Michael and two other fellows who had become close and dear friends of his: Andrew and James. This was not the same James who was a role model to Joseph, but true to the name, this James was not only a friend; he, too, was someone Joseph admired.

Joseph had grown to have immense respect for all three of these guys. The uncertainty that Joseph had once felt for Michael had long dissipated. These men had shown dignity, kindness, and respect to every human being they met. They would do something as simple as hold the door open for someone, all the while fighting for their rights. They wanted the best for everyone regardless of color, money, religious background, or origin. They were handcrafted by God from the finest of moral fibers.

They also knew how to have fun. When the four guys got together, they had the best of times. One night, they were in a hotel room relaxing with a few beers after a hard day. They had not known each other for very long, but they felt they could be fully themselves, with no fear of judgment or persecution. It was as if they had bonded almost instantaneously. The jokes and intimate stories rolled magically with them together in that room. It was similar to the magic that unfolds when you mix these four ingredients: grits, water, butter, and salt. Every time they were mixed together, it was perfection in a bowl.

There were several nights when they might have rejoiced in their camaraderie a little too hard, resulting in having a bit too much to drink. However, when this happened, it was always surrounded by their laughter and the happiness of just being together. The only thing that exuded from their bodies was pure love for one another—and sometimes tears and, on rare occasions, maybe a bit of vomit. They were not just coworkers by any means. They were more like best friends and family, the sort that's carried with you for the rest of your life.

They had traveled all over small-town Mississippi on their campaign trail, but they often gathered in Meridian to orchestrate new target locations or to devise fresh strategies. This Saturday evening was different, because this time, they were not just planning; they were also going to Longdale, Mississippi, the following day to investigate a church that had burned to the ground in someone's fit of rage and hatred. This church had been set on fire, and its congregation had been beaten in the name of the Lord by none other than the Klan. This was all in full compliance with Sov-Com, which also was run by the hypocrisy of people who claimed to be Christian. There were no rules, and hatred was the fuel that fed the flames.

This was a welcoming church that had graciously agreed to stand up in revolt against the injustice. They were standing for the children. This church was to host one of the freedom schools that would teach the innocent children who would otherwise not receive a proper education. It was an act of love, but Sov-Com and the Klan had different plans, which included using God to fuel their own repugnant and detestable desires.

Joseph was headed down to Meridian to help with the planning of the next day's trip and to see his buddies. He was really looking forward to seeing them again, even though the reason for his visit was less than a time to rejoice. When Joseph arrived that evening, his buddies greeted him. They took a moment to briefly discuss what the next day's plan would be.

Then Michael said, "Let's set aside the atrocities we will face tomorrow and celebrate life, each other, and our friendship. We don't get much time together, so let's enjoy it."

They all agreed, and from that moment on, it was pure happiness. The laughter that they shared that night was transforming. They laughed and talked into the wee hours of the morning. It would have gone till daylight, but Joseph found a responsible bone deep down.

"We have a big day ahead of us investigating the church fire and consoling those that we can," he said. "We'd better head to bed. It's going to be a long day."

That morning, they were ready to head out to Longdale, although they were exhausted and a little hungover. It was nothing they couldn't overcome with a hearty breakfast, coffee, and some glasses of water. Not for Joseph, though. He had had a little *too* much fun the night before and could not get out of bed.

"Guys, I'm so sorry. I feel absolutely horrible. I'm afraid I would only hold you back if I went. I'm going to get some rest and help out later today when y'all return."

Joseph was able to pull himself out of bed just long enough to wave them good-bye as they drove off in their station wagon, blue as a robin's egg.

Right before they left, Michael said something to Joseph and a few other CORE workers. "If we are not back by four o'clock, start searching for us."

When the wagon pulled out of the drive, it was back to bed for Joseph. He was feeling quite ill.

Joseph napped most of the day. He woke up for lunch and then went right back to bed. Like countless people in his state, Joseph lay there promising himself he would never drink again. Certainly it would be a promise not kept.

As the day lingered on, he started to feel a bit better. By midafternoon, he knew his buddies would be back soon, and they would have more work to do. He pulled himself out of bed and hit the shower, which was like a rejuvenation portal. He felt like a new man, ready to face the day . . . well, face the evening, that is.

He scrounged around the kitchen for something to eat and found enough food to have a good meal prepared for everyone when they arrived back in Meridian. Joseph knew how to cook quite well, but only when he wanted to. He decided tonight was a good night since he had been too sick to help out that morning. He wanted to make up for it, even though no one was angry that he had not been able to make the trip. It would be fuel for them to playfully pick on him once they got back. Joseph knew that he wouldn't be living this one down anytime soon.

Joseph wanted to have the meal ready by the time they walked in the door, but he knew he was almost out of time. It was almost four. The minutes ticked by, and soon the spaghetti was ready, but there was no sign of the guys. More time passed, and the food was now getting cold. Joseph decided to go ahead and eat, telling himself that sometimes these things happen, but he was starting to feel panicked.

"They might have gotten caught up consoling the church members," Joseph told himself, along with a plethora of other scenarios.

Joseph, along with the other volunteers, had become restless. They moved into action mode. They had already called all the places they knew to call and had searched the bumpy route the boys usually took to go to and from Longdale. They had also called the police, but that was rarely any help. Most of the police were in Sov-Com's pocket.

The evening crept into the wee hours of the morning, and Joseph was beyond stressed. He and the others could not sit still. They were pacing back and forth, feeling helpless. No one was sure of what other action to take. All their outlets had been exhausted. At this point, they feared the worst, but no one could have imagined what the worst really was.

Joseph called Sarah to let her know he was staying there in Meridian till his friends returned. She was thankful he was safe and let him know he could stay as long as it took. Two full days passed without a word. Of course, there were many rumors floating around—one being they had been arrested—but nothing substantial. None of the rumors held anything positive.

Those who were not pacing the room sat around in a semicircle on the chairs and the couch. Every ring of the phone shot fear and anticipation through their bodies and through Joseph's heart. Then came the call that rang out so loudly in the room chock-full of sweaty anxiety. Alex, a volunteer, answered the phone. By the end of the call, everyone in the room could tell that something horrendous had happened by how Alex was holding the phone, dangling by the cord in his hand. Once again, the evil beast of hate that lurked within the South had raised its ugly head to show its true malice.

Joseph finally spoke up, his voice shaking as if it knew that this was about to open the floodgates of tears and emotional agony. "What is it?"

Alex's voice was full of shock and disbelief. "They're dead. They are all dead."

Joseph slid off the couch like all the muscles in his body had dissipated and there was nothing left to hold him up. He went to his knees with his head in his hands. The screams came as rivers poured down his face. "Why? Why? Why? Why, God? Why?"

His body was trembling; he could not catch his breath. Sally, one of the other volunteers, came over to rub his back to calm him down. Everyone was in shock, but no one had been as close to the three young men as Joseph. He could not catch his breath no matter how hard he tried. He was hyperventilating.

"Breathe, Joseph, breathe. Someone get me a cold rag. Calm down, Joseph. You have to breathe," Sally said.

None of this was helping. He had just lost his three best friends, and he could not pull out of this. All that was flowing through his head was that he would never see them again and that it should have been him, too. "Why not me?" he screamed in anger. "I should have been there with them!" This was all he could utter once he caught a bit of breath.

Joseph left the next day to travel back to Lee to be near his family. As soon as he got back home and walked in the door, his mama and Sarah immediately grabbed him as tightly as possible and just cried. He tried to stay strong, but once their loving embrace melted into his body, the tears began to roll. Sarah silently cried and held him tight, and his mama could just say one thing.

"Thank God, thank God, thank God; I have my baby. Thank you, Jesus, for my baby."

Claudia's whole body shook as she held him, praising Jesus in selfish but honest relief. Jeremiah and William stood back, trying to hold in their raging emotions. They both stood separately with a hand covering their faces. You could tell they were crying by the strong sniffling coming from the corners of the room. Finally, one at a time, they broke and walked to the huddle. Jeremiah and William embraced them, holding the huddle strong and placing a protective barrier of love around them with Joseph in the center. They all held each other and cried tears of pain and tears of joy. The pain was very real, but it was an honest joy, too. They felt pain for the horrific acts that had taken the lives of three amazing people, but they also were so thankful it had not been Joseph; it had not been their boy. His mama would always get on to him if he drank too much with his friends, but in this moment, she could not be more thankful that he had done so.

The FBI was the call on the other end of the line that day, and throughout the next couple of months, all the details of what had happened came out one by one all over the national news. Michael, Andrew, and James had all been murdered on their way back to Meridian. The Klan and local police had hatched a demented plan to "take care" of them. The church burning had originally been set to kill Michael, but to their surprise, he was not at the church. So what was the next best thing to do? The local police arrested the three boys as suspects in the fire that the police themselves had set. After a night spent in jail, the three boys had been released. They must have felt relief while walking back to their car, deluded into thinking that they had evaded what could have been a horrific situation, as if it wasn't horrible enough.

The reports on the national news said that when they reached their car, all they'd wanted to do was get back to Meridian as fast as possible after that frightening experience. They then decided to take the highway instead of the bumpy back road they always took. This was why there had been no trace of them when the volunteer search parties went out looking—not to mention that they had also, at one point, been sitting in jail.

The search parties had searched the boys' usual path to and from Longdale, but this time, the route they had taken was far from the usual. The local sheriff said that they had been speeding, but who knew if that were true? If it was, they'd had a damn good reason to be speeding away from that horrible situation, but the plan was already hatched, so whether or not they were speeding, there was no intention of letting those boys out alive. All that was known from the news was that the three had been shot by a gutless mob that included police working alongside the Klan. Their lifeless bodies had been loaded into their blue station wagon and driven to a dam, where they were carelessly buried and disgracefully left to rot. Their car had then been driven off and set ablaze in an attempt to burn away all evidence of this reprehensible act, disgusting to all humanity.

What had happened that night was unfathomable to so many sitting around their TV sets and watching it all unfold. Later, the numerous men responsible for the three deaths were given brief sentences, if not acquitted altogether. Many were sent to live out their pathetic lives free from penance for these acts. The highest penalty given was a mere ten years in prison for one of the most methodical criminal murders of all time, but as the judge presiding put it: "They killed one nigger, one Jew, and a white man—I gave them all what I thought they deserved."

How could this have happened? The horrific incident became known in the media as Mississippi Burning. That was what it felt like while watching it unfold. Mississippi was burning itself to the ground in front of the nation, one racist and hate-filled act at a time.

It took months for Joseph to get back to a certain normal, but he would never be the same. These were not deaths that could be prepared for like with a terminally ill person. His heart and brain were in shock. Joseph believed that this—losing them unexpectedly—was the worst way to lose someone. How they'd died was terrifying. He could never forget or fully let go of what had happened, but eventually, life started to shine with a semblance of normalcy. The summer was over, and he was back in school with classes, studying, and being taunted.

22

Love Wins

It was December 1967, and Joseph was finishing up his undergrad. He was planning on attending law school to achieve his goal of becoming a civil rights lawyer. He really loved the law. It gave him the means to use his mind as a weapon against the kind of horrific and unjust acts he had witnessed over the years. His family and Sarah were all immensely proud of him. His mama exuded pride when speaking to others about her boy. "My boy, the lawyer," she would always say, even though he was not yet in law school. No mind the particulars; she was one proud hen with her chest puffed out.

Another thing: when he met Sarah, Joseph had known without a shadow of a doubt that she was the one. She was his partner for navigating through life. He knew their souls could not flourish without one another. One day, Joseph sat his mama down to reveal his plan to her. He needed her approval.

"Mama, I have something to tell you, and I want your blessing. I plan to ask Sarah to marry me once I graduate."

"That's so exciting."

"But I don't think I can wait."

His mama had the biggest smile on her face.

"I'm so happy for you, Joseph. Of course you have my blessing. I can't wait for me some grandbabies."

Joseph knew his mama had just jumped a bit too far ahead of herself, but he was thrilled they had her blessing. Joseph was now ready for his big move.

Yes, Joseph knew exactly what he wanted, but attaining it would be a little trickier than one might think. It was not a simple proposal followed by planning the wedding at your local church and walking down the aisle eager to marry your love and best friend. No, it was not that simple at all.

One night in late May of 1966, Joseph drove Sarah out to the very field where they had met years earlier. He told Sarah every step of the way where they were and what was going on so she could "see" what he was seeing.

"We are passing the little yellow house with the tick hound in front that you always hear howling," Joseph described like a tour guide. "We are now passing the church you told me you went to that one Sunday after you moved here."

It continued like this for the whole ride—except he kept one little detail to himself. Sarah was confused as to what his intentions might be. Soon, they pulled up alongside the barbed-wire fence and climbed through. Joseph ducked her head under to ensure she would not be cut. The smells and feel of the ground were all so familiar to her. Joseph had sandwiches and a water canister filled with sweet red wine. It was the very same water canister he had been carrying the night they met. Joseph had saved it as a reminder of what true kindness and love felt like.

Once they were standing in the place where they had once lain hand in hand as two lost and scared kids, Joseph dropped onto one knee and began to flood Sarah's heart with his soul. "We once lay here in this spot hand in hand, praying for the night to never end. That night, for the first time, I no longer felt alone. My soul had found its partner, its mate. I was taught what true love and kindness were by you. I brought this canister as a symbol of that, filled with the blood of our love. We barely knew one another, but our souls were instantly bound together, falling into place seamlessly like they knew where they were always meant to be.

"Even though we separated and I found myself lost again, I finally found my way back to you. This is where I belong, hand in hand with you forever. You have been my rock, my best friend, and my teacher through so much, and I would like to spend a lifetime repaying you. Will you spend a lifetime allowing me to do such? Will you marry me? "

With tears welled up in her eyes, Sarah said, "Yes. Yes. Of course."

They both kissed with tears of joy falling down their fresh young cheeks. That night, they again lay there hand in hand under the twinkling stars, sharing their wine and bliss. Joseph described the beauty of the night's sky to Sarah, star by star. They gently drifted off to sleep, comforted by each other, as this was the first night the universe had pulled them together; two people, gentle souls, who were misunderstood, lost in life, the cycle of abuse, and the pursuit of happiness.

The next morning, they jumped up to drive back home and tell everyone their amazing news. As they drove back, it dawned on them: Whom could they tell besides those very few closest to them? This was a time to share and shout their love from the rooftops, but they could not. They had to think about who would really be happy for them and who would push "God's" unwilling judgments on them. Joseph felt a cloud of sadness descend on him as he remembered his three best friends, who would have been elated with their news. They would have thrown him the best of parties and not missed the wedding for anything.

A foolish interpretation of the Bible had been forced into the laws there in the South, and it dictated people's beliefs. Because of this, Joseph and Sarah did not know whom they would invite to the wedding. Who should they invite, who would judge them, who would take the news well, who would take the news poorly, who would lash out at them, who would alienate them, and who would throw their misconceived version of the Bible—along with their condemnation to burn in hell eternally—in Joseph's and Sarah's faces? These were not the thoughts that should run through a couple's minds when they think of sharing their news of being engaged, but it was a reality for them. This was the society they lived in, and that would not change overnight.

Joseph and Sarah opted for a very quaint wedding in California, far outside the South. They had no option. They would have much rather wed in the place where they fell in love, but ignorance did not allow it. They could be fined or imprisoned if someone learned of their relationship.

Their wedding was a commitment ceremony in which they committed themselves to one another for a lifetime. It was beautiful. Sarah was stunning in a white sundress, and Joseph was in his best blue suit, looking dapper. The trees embraced them on a patch of emerald grass near the foothills of a mountain. There were Easter lilies all around and one in Sarah's hair. The smell was intoxicating. In attendance were Joseph's mama, William, an aunt of Sarah's, and two of her cousins. They had asked Jeremiah to officiate their ceremony, not wanting a stranger to perform an act they held sacred. It didn't matter that Jeremiah was not a preacher. It did not affect the legality of their wedding; it would have been null and void in Mississippi anyway.

They struggled greatly with the fact that their marriage was not legal. A few days before their ceremony, Joseph and Sarah talked about how hurt they were by this.

"I know our love is no different than others," Joseph said in a huff.

Sarah grabbed Joseph's hand.

"I know. It hurts me, too," she said. "Why can't people just see the love we share without throwing their flawed judgments at us?"

Those who were not clouded saw the deep love and beauty between Joseph and Sarah. It was magnetic and contagious and could definitely be felt the day of their ceremony. It was truly a special day— one filled with joy.

Three years later, they were able to legally wed thanks to the federal government, which again lent a helpful hand dealing justice, so infrequently seen in the South. The law prohibiting their love had been struck down two years before, in June 1967, but most churches and men of the cloth refused to perform ceremonies of those who were "living in sin." Joseph and Sarah were able to rejoice in the fact that they were finally legally partners for life, but they rejoiced quietly. The hatred that surrounded their marriage was still pungent and lingered for years to come. Would the malicious judgment ever end? Consequently, they felt shame and feared holding hands in public or publicly celebrating their love in any capacity. Joseph would shy away from Sarah's touch. He feared the backlash, not the intimacy. He hated the looks, words, and judgments that came along with a simple pat of the back. Would this evasion of affection eventually damage their relationship? Time would tell. They were being punished by an entire society for loving one another, but ironically, one another's love was what helped them through it all.

23

Spreading Viruses

After a long and bitter battle, Joseph conquered his dream by graduating from law school at the top of his class in the spring of 1971. He was finally a lawyer, and a very bright one at that. As he thought back on the hell he had endured to get to this place in his life, he was reminded of the Bible verses that speak of walking through the valley of the shadow of death. Joseph had spent many of his days literally being shadowed by death, and he could not believe he had finally made it out alive, defeating the obstacles and overcoming the challenges in his way. The dream that had pushed him to reach out and touch the stars had become a reality, and he was finally there, dancing on the moon.

This was short-lived. Despite all his accomplishments and feelings of being on top of the world, beginning his career in this predominantly white field made him feel like a frightened little boy again. Even though he was not proud of how small the number of African-American lawyers in the South was, he was proud to belong to this group. Joseph was proud to be a part of changing the course of history, altering society, and leading the way for others to do the same, but this journey was also frightening and, at times, lonely. Joseph did not have the luxury of peers who were going through similar experiences and who could relate to his successes, hardships, and failures, helping to validate his feelings while he navigated through them. No, Joseph was a lone black wolf, and many people did not take kindly to this proud, successful black man being in "their" town.

Joseph and Sarah had married, but Joseph had not stopped fighting for equality. He had told Sarah before their wedding that he was there with her for better or worse but that his worse might be more prevalent than that of others. He would wage bitter battles within the civil rights fight that would grow rampant over the years. Sarah had no desire for Joseph to stop this honorable work toward equality, but she did worry. She had seen firsthand the sickness that could thrive within the South. She had seen firsthand close friends murdered in the name of Jesus, of all things.

Joseph's days in court consisted of wins and losses, ups and downs. These were not simple cases of fender benders and public drunkenness. These were the victories and failures of human rights and much-needed societal changes. This affected his mood and positive outlook, but he had no intention of slowing down or stopping. Passion was what drove him. He remembered how irrelevant he'd felt and the misery that had been pressed upon him when he was forced into the role of a little slave boy for the Kingsleys and the senator. He did not want a single other person to feel that same repression ever again, so he worked diligently on his cases.

One of his clients was an African-American gentleman who wanted nothing more than to teach, but he was being shut out of every school to which he applied. Joseph was fighting for this man's right to be employed at the school of his choice. Joseph could see himself in this man, and he was empathetic. That made it difficult to separate himself from his work.

Most days, Joseph would be at the office late into the evening. Sarah missed having Joseph around, and it took a toll on their relationship. She would often lie in bed wondering if he was going to come home or if something horrible had happened to him. Unfortunately, she could not go to the local police if something were to happen. Racism was strong and prevalent. It was almost impossible to know who to trust in Mississippi law enforcement and the local government. Sarah was very much scared, alone, and isolated. Joseph and Sarah shared the same feelings of fear and isolation.

Every night Joseph came home late from work, he quietly eased into their bedroom and dressed for bed. He came home very late most evenings due to his commute to Memphis. He'd hired on with a civil rights firm there, and it was a great opportunity, so he made the hour-and-twenty-minute trek twice a day. Sarah was usually asleep by the time Joseph got back home, but it was a light, restless sleep. One night when Joseph came home, Sarah was not in bed. She was sitting on the edge of the couch waiting for him with her legs trembling, biting her nails. Joseph was well aware of her nervousness about his coming home late, but on this particular crisp winter night in late February, something was undoubtedly different.

Once Joseph made it inside the front door, he instantly saw it in Sarah's face. Her eyes were filled with tears. Joseph was usually very much in touch with people's emotions, especially Sarah's. Not tonight. He could not tell if Sarah's tears were from joy or despair. Joseph always liked to know what was going on, and he welcomed the feeling of being in control of a situation. The fact that he could not read Sarah threw him into a panicked state.

"What is it, Sarah? What's wrong?"

Sarah began to cry uncontrollably. When Sarah tried to speak, all that came out was indistinguishable mumbling. Joseph's face dropped and his forehead wrinkled as he intently tried to comprehend the gibberish coming from Sarah's mouth.

"What's going on, Sarah? You are scaring me. What, baby; what is it? Please tell me. Who died? I can handle it. Please just slow down and talk to me. Are you OK?"

Sarah continued to utter incoherently. Tears of fear, sadness, and concern began to form in Joseph's eyes. He was helpless, feeling the brunt of all that this moment entailed as he continued pleading for answers.

"Calm down, baby, calm down," he said to Sarah. "Please tell me—what is it?"

"It's happening."

Over the past week, Sarah had been feeling ill, so Joseph had urged her to go see a doctor the night before. Normally, Sarah did not run off to the doctor every time there was a scratch in her throat, but there was a nasty virus going around town. She also felt something strange was going on with her body. No matter what it was, Sarah wanted to catch it in the beginning stages before she became too ill. So Sarah had taken herself to the doctor's office earlier that morning to pick up some antibiotics, and she was met with some very rousing and unexpected news.

Joseph soon realized Sarah's tears were a mixture of pure joy, love, relief, and gratefulness. The phrase "It's happening" echoed in Joseph's head. He knew exactly what those sweet, sweet words meant. He was relieved to finally know why Sarah was crying and not making a lick of sense, and he was overjoyed. Joseph pulled Sarah into his warm, loving arms and squeezed her as tight as he could. Well, as tight as he could without snapping something or injuring the little miracle growing inside of her. They both sat on the couch in their living room and held each other while they shed tears of humble joy.

For the past two years, Joseph and Sarah had been diligently trying with all their young bodies had to offer to create a baby. They had begun to believe it was hopeless. They had feared they would never have the joy of bringing a beautiful child of their own into this world.

They had almost given up, so they decided to take a hiatus from all the pressure for Sarah to become pregnant they had placed upon themselves. The mixture of this pressure and the pressures from Joseph's work had taken a toll on both of them, so they had placed their shared dream of having a baby on the backburner, until that day at the doctor's when she learned that the stomach bug called pregnancy had bitten her.

24

Wisteria Is in the Air

The months passed, and another well-known Mississippi summer began creeping in. You could feel the sun caressing your skin while a gentle sheet of moisture delicately layered itself on top, securing your youthful appearance. The smells of sweet honeysuckle and wisteria twirled through the air. With the wonderfully fragrant lavender flowers it boasted once a year, wisteria had always been one of Sarah's favorites, but this time the sweet, potent smell was proving to be too much for her weak, pregnant stomach to bear. Whenever she caught a whiff of it, she could feel vomit rising, tickling the back of her throat. This was quite an unfortunate predicament because wisteria grew wild in the South and was abundant. Lucky for her, the fragrant flowers only lasted a few weeks, but these few weeks were the most miserable she could remember.

Sarah was having a difficult and uncomfortable pregnancy, to say the least. She'd always heard women speak of the gift of pregnancy and how much they loved the artful sensation of being pregnant. She was not experiencing this assumed fable of pleasure. She was downright miserable. Sarah already felt like she was lugging watermelons around on her ankles, and she was only a few months into this self-proclaimed personal hell. She was swollen all over and not looking forward to this hot summer. On top of the discomfort of housing a human being in her body, she was packing up boxes in the sticky heat. Spring didn't hang around long in Mississippi. The Mississippi weather liked to jump straight to the point when it got to be around summertime, and that point was sweat-lathering heat.

Joseph had had great success in his first two years out of law school while working with the Memphis firm. He'd been so successful that Sarah and Joseph had decided he should venture out and open his own firm. The daily travel back and forth to Memphis had become too rigorous, especially now that Sarah was pregnant with their first child. Joseph wanted to be close to home at all times in case Sarah needed him. Opening his own business had become a possibility because of the good wages Joseph brought home, and he had been vigilant with their money. He loved to save.

They'd purchased a little office building there in Lee, and they were boxing up his stuff for the move. Sarah thought it would be a good idea to move some things from their house to make his new office a little more homey because he would be spending a good deal of time there. Sarah enjoyed this type of activity because she liked decorating and being creative. Most of all, she enjoyed making Joseph's space a happy place for him to be.

Against Joseph's wishes, Sarah insisted on helping him pack. As much as he enjoyed having control in situations, when it came to Sarah, Joseph was definitely the passenger. He liked nothing more than for her to be happy. Sarah had informed Joseph that helping him pack was better than lying around dreaming of the day this baby could make its way out of her. They both dreamed of the day when she would give birth, but she fantasized about it a little beyond what Joseph did.

Unfortunately for Sarah and her already miserable experience, their baby became a demanding little thing as it grew inside her. She was only allowed to sleep and lie in a certain way that Its Highness approved. If she went against the baby's wishes, it would kick her and scrape its sharp little heel against the inner lining of her uterus until she complied. It felt as if the baby's heels were made of jagged arrow-head shards. She was sure it had to be doing some sort of damage, as it felt as though the baby's heel were ripping straight through her. So yes, Sarah liked to keep herself distracted to help the time pass. She was determined to help pack up the old office no matter what Joseph insisted.

Joseph and Sarah worked throughout the summer, and the new office started to come together nicely. Business was slow, however. Joseph used to have steady work when he was with the Memphis firm, but he was sure not overflowing with clients now that he was branched out on his own. He knew he had to build his name and reputation while pushing against the racism of the area, although he'd assumed business would be a little more abundant. He was not terribly far from Memphis, where the clientele flowed generously, but in this small town, he was having no such luck.

Potential clients stumbled into his office from time to time in search of counsel. Oftentimes, these people had looked in the telephone directory to find themselves a lawyer. They had seen Joseph's name and given him a call to set up a consultation. He didn't "sound black" to them, so they felt there was no cause for hesitation. All too often, however, that optimism turned to astonishment and disgust once they stepped into his office and saw that he was black.

It was uncommon to walk into a small-town Mississippi law office and find the person in charge to be a black man, and many—too many—liked it this way. Some of them were no-holds-barred racists who flew their racism flags high and proud, while some of them had racism quietly trickling through their veins. Silent racists were becoming more common. Because they didn't yell racial slurs or strike physical violence at people of a different race, they did not consider themselves racist. They refused to look within and see the darkness lurking. The quiet way they would pull their bodies back from being near to or touching a person who was black was telling, as were the unconscious looks of condemnation and repugnance as they passed nonwhite people in the street.

This form of racism was all so discreet, comparatively, yet its trumpet of disdain blared. This was the new, more hushed racism at work. Outspoken racism was falling out of fashion, but racism itself was alive and well, breeding in the quiet corners of small social gatherings. It would be passed on from parent to child, friend to friend, and even church to congregation. It just found a new way to manifest itself. A black man in charge made those people downright uncomfortable.

This made it extremely difficult for Joseph to be successful with his own business. Some of those people who stumbled upon Joseph's law office turned and left in silence. Others stayed and took the initial meeting—at no charge—but then left and never returned or called. Some grumbled to themselves as they abruptly left; others made cruel and hateful comments before storming out, slamming the door behind them. They all went home to pass along gossip of the Negro lawyer in town, almost ensuring Joseph's fate of a failing business.

Joseph quickly learned that it was harsh being in business for himself in this small southern town. He had managed to pick up a handful of clients, all of whom were African Americans. Many times, he took cases out of the goodness of his heart, knowing that the person had a true need but didn't have a method of payment. He quickly found out, however, that his generosity and good intentions weren't paying the bills for his own family.

Joseph aspired to find a way to make money to support his family and help out those that needed it the most. Some days, he just wished someone would come to salvage him and his drowning young business. At times like that, Joseph would look up from his desk at the picture frame hanging in the office. It bore an inspirational quote carefully positioned over a cotton blossom his mama had painted for him on a piece of old wood found in a cotton field behind their home.

Be your own hero.
Berta King
1868–1953

Reading Berta's words would change everything for Joseph in such moments of despair and self-pity. He had told his mama of Berta, and this one phrase from her had gotten him through so much in his life. It had kept him strong when the fiercest of men would have crumbled. This helped remind him to live for each day he was given and to remember that no matter how hard things got, God would give him a path to be his own hero. He reminded himself to stay positive for his wife, himself, and their unborn child. Things were difficult now, but they had to trust that a better path would unfold before them, because soon their lives would again change as they embarked on a whole new chapter.

Anyone who has had children knows how the birth of a baby changes the entirety of one's world. Those who don't have children might not understand to the same magnitude as those who do, but everyone can imagine. This marvelous baby was about to come into their lives, and this new adventure would be for better or for worse. A little bit of both can creep in as you guide and teach your child and as your child in turn teaches you things about yourself and the world around you that you'd never considered. The future of this tiny embryo was now in Joseph and Sarah's hands, and they felt its magnitude.

25

The Beginning of
a New Era

The summer of '73 had finally passed. Sarah felt like she had barely made it out alive due to her constant swelling and discomfort, enhanced by the sweltering heat. Autumn had been much more merciful, but she was ready to put the burden of her pregnancy behind her. Her body felt like it was going to burst.

Joseph had come to the realization that the need for him to be there for his wife and child might be behind his shortage of clientele. Joseph's business still had not really picked up much, but now, that was not Joseph and Sarah's main concern. Sarah's screaming and screeching were deafening to those within earshot and were distracting them from all other thoughts.

Sarah was in labor, and the pain had her screaming louder than was thought humanly possible. Her pregnancy had been difficult on her, and by the sound of it, apparently her labor was going to be no different. Joseph and Sarah had just whipped into the hospital driveway directly under the big red emergency sign. Joseph ran around the side of the car, jerked open Sarah's door, and supported her arm as they both tugged to pry her pregnant body out of the car. She felt like a stubborn cow being pulled from a livestock trailer: large, awkward, and difficult. Joseph helped walk her into the hospital as fast as she could go. He was overly eager and nervous, tugging at Sarah's arm, but she could not move fast.

"Joseph, this isn't a race. Slow down," Sarah spouted in a tone that made it clear she was irritated with the entire world.

As soon as they walked through the emergency room doors, Joseph started shouting for help and a wheelchair. Their interracial marriage screamed louder than they did. Their cries for help were ignored, but the stares were conspicuous. Being an interracial couple was still taboo, but so was being black. Finally, a sweet young nurse came to help after several other nurses had snubbed them—and not a minute too soon. The normally polite and tranquil Sarah was going to get irate with the whole situation if one more contraction wrapped its clutch of sheer torture around her. She was going to snap like a dry, fragile twig in its day of reckoning.

In a voice that sung out sweet tenderness, the little nurse said, "Ma'am, let's get you in to see a doctor. It seems as if you are goin' to have you a baby today."

Normally, Joseph would have been quick to act defensively and be protective of his relationship and wife. He had almost been conditioned to do so, but he could feel the tenderness and kindheartedness exuding from this nurse, Alice. Alice escorted them into a curtained area, while Sarah periodically screamed from her new set of wheels, a wheelchair.

Alice calmly told them, "The doctor will be in shortly."

As Joseph waited, the intensity of pain and the nerves became more pronounced. Every time Sarah felt a contraction, she squeezed Joseph's hand tightly and dug her nails into his tender flesh. He swore one time—or maybe a few times—that he could feel bones crack and blood drip down, and he was not quiet about it at all. His whining was getting on Sarah's last struggling nerve. Joseph had been through a lot in his life and had always been a strong character, but in this delivery room, he was being a big baby.

The doctor came in just in time, it seemed. Alice was by his side to assist with the birth of Joseph and Sarah's baby. After a whole lot of pushing and screaming on both parts, this little miracle finally made its appearance. Joseph was a proud papa, overwhelmed with emotions of joy.

"Is it a boy? Is it a girl? Is it OK? All ten fingers and toes?" he asked.

The doctor passed the baby over to Joseph.

"Congratulations, sir; it's a boy."

It was a beautiful baby boy, and he was perfect. There was something very special about this one. The doctor and Alice even stopped to admire him as if there were something drawing them in. He had such a strong presence, and everyone in the delivery room was drawn to him like a light. The doctor had birthed many babies, but this one was different. Joseph and Sarah both cradled him together like the precious gift that he was, and again they cried as they had done the day they found out Sarah was pregnant. They boasted huge smiles as tears ran into their mouths. Alice cried along with them. Even the doctor had tears in his eyes. No one was sure why this birth was so special or touching, but it was. Everyone could feel it, even the doctor, who, like so many, still shamefully carried the belief that it was wrong to marry someone of a different race.

Joseph and Sarah needed a name for their baby boy. They'd thought of many, but none seemed to fit his strong character. Joseph had felt like God had spoken to him many times in his life, but in this moment, he had never been more positive that God was speaking directly to him. Just as God had whispered the name "Joseph" directly into his mother's ear, he was now whispering into Joseph's: "Isaiah." It was as clear to him as if someone had put a hand on his shoulder and spoken softly to him. Then Joseph remembered a dream he had experienced several times over the years.

"Sarah, we have to name him Isaiah," Joseph said. "This baby boy of ours will bring wisdom and knowledge to people."

"How do you know this?" she asked.

Joseph smiled with confidence.

"Because this is what I was told. I have had this dream time and again. He needs to have a strong name."

Sarah was a little taken aback, but she knew Joseph was a dreamer. Too many times, his dreams and intuitions had proved to be truths, so she obliged. She, too, felt that there was something truly special about this baby, other than just being their child.

When Joseph had these types of dreams, his subconscious always filled in the blanks for him. He assumed his son's cause would be to help in the battle for civil rights and humanity that Joseph had known and struggled profoundly with. Sometimes we fill in our children's blanks with our wishes, but these are *their* blanks to fill. Joseph never thought for a second that a new generation would have a whole new civil rights battle on their hands.

Isaiah had a "typical" childhood. He had two parents who adored him and provided for his every need. He had a wonderful grandmother, Mama Dove, who indulged his every want, and an Uncle William who took every chance he could to play with little Isaiah.

Isaiah never got to meet Jeremiah. Jeremiah had passed away ten months before Isaiah was born. He was an elderly man with a lot of health complications. He held on as long as he could. The last years of his life were the happiest, though, because he got to spend them on his terms with the ones he loved. He spent those years not just enjoying his family but also indulging their every desire. He did for them whatever they asked. Everyone was devastated when he passed, but they knew he was ready to go. They did not want him to suffer any longer.

In the last few years of his life, Jeremiah had found himself enthralled with gift giving. Gift giving had been tricky while living on the plantation; there was no money, and the senator didn't allow it. Jeremiah had now been able to give to his heart's content. He was always giving William, Joseph, Sarah, and Claudia little gifts that were so special and individualized to each person. He paid attention to what each one of them wanted and needed, and then he would surprise them at the most unexpected times. He loved the look of happiness these gifts brought. Sometimes he felt a bit selfish because he believed that it might bring him more happiness to give than for them to receive. But no matter—he loved it all the same.

Once Jeremiah passed, they all believed he had entrusted to them one last special, unique gift. It was a month after his death that Sarah miraculously became pregnant; she and Joseph had been trying without success for two years. All four believed Jeremiah had gone to heaven and sent down little Isaiah as one last gift of his love.

Joseph and Sarah wanted the best for their little gift. That's why, when Isaiah was just twenty-two months old, his parents decided to sell Joseph's business and move to Jackson, Mississippi, where Joseph could better financially support his family. They sold their house in Lee and bought a little house in Lakeview, right outside Jackson.

There, he was offered a position in a nonprofit law firm, Southern Rights Law. The firm provided legal assistance to those who needed it most while struggling against injustices brought upon them by being denied human rights. It was a newly formed nonprofit, rapidly growing, and it needed to bring on talented lawyers to keep up with the demand. They fought against major white supremacist groups, for exploited workers, and for those who were treated maliciously or unequally. This was exactly what Joseph had gone to law school for. He was now able to help those in need and provide for his family. It was a win-win.

When Joseph, Sarah, and Isaiah moved, it was not much of an adjustment for Isaiah; he was too young at the time to notice they had moved halfway across the state. Before they moved, Sarah and Joseph explained to Isaiah that he was going to have a new room and a new house. They thought he understood. They always spoke to him as though he were a little adult, saying things in a manner a toddler would understand but without all the baby talk. If someone used baby talk with him, he would glare at the speaker with an indignant look, as if to say, "How dare you talk to me like I am stupid." His parents always found this look endearing and funny while he was young, but that would change when he turned that look on them as a teenager. For now, he was a very bright young toddler, and a cute one, at that.

Isaiah always knew what he wanted, and he was allowed to express his opinions and will. Well, to a point. His safety and well-being were top priority. All in all, he was a well-adjusted little fellow. His parents were doing a fantastic job raising him despite the hell and turmoil in which they both had been raised. They would often say, "What would my parents do?"—then they would do the complete opposite. Joseph did not include his mama, Claudia, in this "how not to" guide on parenting. She had never been granted the opportunity to raise her boy. Sarah and Joseph wanted the best for Isaiah, and that included his mental well-being.

Sarah and Joseph's mutual decision to break the cycle and raise Isaiah completely different than how they had been raised took great insight, bravery, and courage. Many parents continue the cycle of abuse, or whatever dysfunctional cycle it might be. These can be very difficult to break, but Sarah and Joseph chose to ditch the dysfunction and chaos in order to better the world for themselves and little Isaiah. He was a happy, well-adjusted, intelligent little guy with a world of opportunities in front of him.

26

The Dilemma

Joseph was enjoying his new job at Southern Rights Law. He loved helping others while providing for his family. However, there were new aspects to this job that Joseph was not prepared for or comfortable with. One morning, a new client came into the firm, and it made Joseph anxious. This client had Joseph questioning his devotion to God. He knew this client deserved and needed help, but he wondered if helping this client would keep him aligned with God and the church teachings he had received. Joseph was not prepared for this at all.

Here's the story. This charming and well-spoken young man, Robbie, had a gut-wrenching case involving his rights as a human being. One day, Robbie was walking back from a convenience store, where he had picked up some eggs, flour, sugar, and peaches for his grandmother. She was going to make him some good ole peach cobbler. On the way home, he made the nearly fatal mistake of "looking" gay to some passersby. These were three guys in their midtwenties driving around in an old pickup truck that sputtered and spat smoke. Two of the young men were perched in the bed of the truck with their mullets swaying in the wind while the third drove along, spitting black tar out his driver's side window. It's a wonder the two in back didn't have tobacco spit in their long locks. A rebel flag plastered on the back window of the truck accentuated their prideful ignorance. It was an omen and a banner of the hatred and violence sure to come. Robbie was noticeably shaking while he unveiled his horror.

"They pulled alongside of me and started to scream out, 'Hey faggot, you're not welcome in these parts. Take ya sissy ass back where you came from.'

"I quickly dropped my head down, looking only at the ground. I continued to walk faster and faster. The truck sped up beside me. I knew that these three were up to no good. I feared for my life as I threw down the groceries and began to run. The truck again sped up and cut me off. The two boys in the back jumped out of the pickup, grabbing me and flinging me into the back of the truck. My head slammed hard against the back window, where the flag was.

"The next thing I remember is being pinned against a barn wall. I can still smell the scents of hay, blood, urine, and sweat. Everything was a haze. I heard one of the boys scream to the other, 'Hey, Billy, get me my nigger beater out of the truck.' My mind was screaming, but I had no strength to fight. I lost consciousness again. I faded in and out of consciousness as they took turns brutally beating me within an inch of my life."

"Did they leave you alone then?"

Robbie looked physically ill, and a pale, grayish color took over his face.

"No, they began raping me with the short, thick wooden bat they got from the truck. I screamed and pleaded in agony, but they wouldn't stop. I kept screaming for help, but no one heard my cries."

Robbie's unconscious body was left there in that barn covered in blood, semen, spit, and tears to be found by the owner of the barn a day later. God was the only thing that kept him alive that day.

What happened to Robbie was a horrific story of hatred and brutality in the worst of ways, yet no one heard of it on the local news. Zero arrests were made for this barbaric cruelty. It was shoved into that closet and sealed up airtight until months later, when Robbie was finally able to walk again—directly into Southern Rights Law, looking for justice.

The word "gay" was something Joseph had seldom heard, especially on TV, back in 1976. He wouldn't begin hearing this word on TV till many years later. This was not something publicized, especially in the South. When the news finally did begin to cover these grossly disregarded people, it was only in connection with AIDS. Most of this news emerged from San Francisco, but not there in Mississippi. You wouldn't hear the word "gay" on the local news for decades to come.

Gay people of the South were tightly concreted in their closets. If you asked around, most people would say they'd never known or even met a gay person, because the people who were gay never announced that fact. This was to avoid the inevitable discrimination and hatred. Everyone knew someone gay without knowing that the person was gay. It was exceedingly hush-hush. However, around these parts, you would never verbalize the word "gay" to be able to conduct that poll. It was a never-ask-and-never-tell policy.

Joseph, like many heterosexual people, was not aware of the struggles and persecution that LGBT (Lesbian, Gay, Bisexual, and Transgender) people faced. Mum was the word in order to avoid religious and social persecution and possible death, like what Robbie had experienced when viciously attacked.

Being gay was so repressed in the South that many people denied that part of themselves so intensely it would morph into pure hatred for gay human beings and themselves alike. What a horrendous feeling, to hate yourself so intensely that you would take on the position of brutality toward those made from the same cloth. You would not know if you met someone who was gay around those parts because the consequences of speaking the truth about oneself could be deadly or could at least mean being shunned from the community like an ulcer-ridden leper.

Joseph had been taught that being gay was a sin, and he did not want to budge on his beliefs. However, he believed this man's mistreatment was inhuman. It reminded him of how people he'd known growing up had been victimized and how he himself had been mistreated. He saw a similarity in the way this young man was targeted and regarded like the filth of the earth. Joseph remembered those feelings well, and for a brief time, he related to this man on a richly personal level. This threw a hinge in his belief system and marked the beginnings of an internal battle exploring what was right and what was wrong.

Robbie's case never made it to court. The doctors and nurses who treated Robbie refused to speak out, and the case withered to a he-said, they-said death. The police and the district attorney never wanted to pursue this case, so there was no chance of a win. Robbie was forced to retreat home, where he had to try and heal himself physically and mentally without a lick of justice being served. The only thing that helped Robbie through was the thought that, one day, those three in the truck would be judged and punished by God.

Joseph and everyone involved were happy to drop the case. Joseph would be able to stop pondering the rules of morality and the rights and wrongs of what he had always been taught in church. He was not hesitant to go about his merry way without solving his moral dilemma. Who likes discomfort, even if it helps you grow as an enlightened being? Robbie never did get that peach cobbler. His grandmother died shortly after his attack. Her heart was not strong enough to suffer through her grandbaby being brutalized. Thankfully for everyone else, they could breathe a sigh of relief over being able to rid themselves of the discomfort of dealing with their own inner demons.

27

How the Birds and Bees Flutter

I saiah was growing up so fast. Everyone who met him adored him, and he ate up all the attention he was given. He was such a little ham, smiling and batting his beautiful hazel eyes, which were enhanced by his bronze skin and light brown hair, streaks of gold dancing among his curls. People would often stop to comment on how beautiful he was. "He is gorgeous. What a beautiful little boy." These were the welcome phrases that were most often heard.

When Isaiah started preschool at the local church, Pine Creek, his teachers adored him. Most people were immediately drawn right to him. There was the occasional misguided person who had an issue because he was mixed, but his being so young and his striking attractiveness seemed to outweigh that fact, or so it seemed.

Preschool was a breeze for Isaiah. He was intelligent, and his teacher allowed him to do about whatever he desired. She thought he was too cute to tell no, and he knew how to play this to his advantage. He was working the system and working it well. If he didn't want to participate in an activity that the other kids were being forced to participate in, his teacher would scoop him up and keep him right by her side where he wanted to be, lathering in that attention.

Isaiah enjoyed preschool, but first grade was another story. There were all these new rules and regulations, and he had to be there practically all day. This really cut into his time of doing what he wanted to do, which was play outside. He was not pleased about being treated like just another kid. The horror.

This transition to all-day schooling was particularly difficult for him. At home, he was so well behaved, but he was an independent little fellow. Joseph and Sarah encouraged that independence. They relished the fact that he had his own ideas and little personality. However, these traits did not fare so well in the first grade. His independent side didn't appreciate being told by practical strangers what to do. He had also become a tad spoiled from his preschool experience. All the "awwws" and doting were fading away, and he didn't embrace where this was headed.

This was a new experience for the irritated Isaiah. He was very respectful, but he had been a willful child since before birth. He had impeccable manners and was very polite to everyone around him, but in his mind, someone's character must prove to be deserving of his trust and utmost respect. Respect has many elements of trust, and courtesy was just common decency.

Isaiah always said "Thank you" and "You're welcome." When he was a bit older, he always was polite in other ways, such as holding the door open for someone or waving if they stopped to let him cross the road. Respect, though, was something he gave to someone he looked up to and admired, as he did his parents. It was something to be earned. Because Isaiah had not known his new teachers well enough to develop admiration and respect for them, he had obedience issues. His independent spirit and strong character would be a great asset when he became an adult, but they were making his first grade experience a trying one.

Because of Isaiah's strong character, even stubbornness, he found himself in trouble from time to time for talking without raising his hand or for his lack of obedience. When he got in trouble with his first grade teacher, little Isaiah would be forced to hold buckets in each hand while standing on books in place of recess. No sun or play for Isaiah. Instead, he was busy performing a strange form of corporal punishment. The tingling and burning in his little arms did not teach him the intended lesson, which was obedience. The only thing Isaiah took away from it was that some people were cruel and untrustworthy. Isaiah still did not understand why he'd received such a punishment, but that did not make those buckets any less tangible. His parents would not have been pleased about this form of punishment, to say the least, but only if he had told them. He'd been afraid to leak a word since he had found himself in trouble at school.

As Isaiah progressed through first grade, other kids began to bully and ridicule him, mocking him for having a white mom and a black dad. All kids are picked on from time to time, but Isaiah was singled out and targeted daily for being different. This significantly added to his dislike of school. He was made to feel dissimilar; there were no other visibly mixed-race children in his school. There were not many other races at all in many schools in the South. The children's taunts began to make him feel like he was a sore thumb sticking out there, the gray sheep in the middle of two herds: a black herd and a white one. Isaiah's self-esteem was taking a hit. The kids in preschool had never seemed to notice the difference. They all just saw each other as little human beings, as it should be. It was a beautiful occurrence that carried so much peace among them, but the teachings of parents and society, whether intentional or unintentional, indoctrinated kids into noticing the differences and holding them in scorn.

"Mommy, that little boy is my friend."

"Which one, son, that little black boy over there?"

Something as simple as a parent uttering that seemingly innocent phrase raises awareness of differences and separation, which children otherwise don't notice.

Isaiah had difficulty fitting in with any group. He was not readily accepted, and he was confused as to which group he should choose: the white kids or the black kids. It was apparent to him that this was a decision that he was forced to make, as evidenced from the segregation in the classroom. It was perplexing, to say the least. He had grown up in a home filled with love, and it had been two races colliding that had created that beautiful devotion. Isaiah felt like he was being compelled to pick between his momma and his dad. This was not a decision he could make and a dilemma he should not have had to struggle with at all. The only dilemma Isaiah should have been facing was to find which kid or kids he best got along with. It should not be a racial issue, but it was, and that was how things were constructed to be. It was no matter that the schools were no longer segregated; society had done a terrific job securing this segregation.

Joseph never really had any trouble with this distressing issue growing up because he was dark skinned. Isaiah was not dark skinned, which ironically made things more difficult for him in school when he was younger. However, as Isaiah got older, it became easier for him to make friends—maybe because Isaiah's charm won them over; or maybe because he learned that life was full of difficult, nonsensical decisions; or maybe because the kids acclimated to him over time; or maybe because society was evolving a bit. No matter the reason, Isaiah and his parents were thankful.

Second grade was a bit smoother for Isaiah. He had learned how he was expected to act in school, even though he was still not a fan of attending. Around third grade, he started to get into the groove of this whole school thing. It also didn't hurt that his teacher was very nice to him. Isaiah was shown respect and kindness and was not forced to perform strange forms of punishment. Isaiah was quite drawn to that teacher. He wanted to impress him, so he started performing exceptionally in class. Before, his grades had been mediocre because he felt there was no one to impress or please, but he really wanted to make his new teacher proud. His parents had great hopes that this marked a new beginning for his school performance.

The very first day of third grade was when Mr. Turner came marching in, and Isaiah's whole attitude changed. Mr. Turner sure caught Isaiah's attention as he walked in the door, smiling. At times, Isaiah would stare at Mr. Turner, and he wanted nothing more than to please and impress him. Isaiah's new goal was a shocking one. He aspired to gain Mr. Turner's respect, and in return, he now sought more positive attention from his new teacher than the other kids received. Isaiah once again desired to be treated specially. This might be the definition of teacher's pet, but don't tell Isaiah that. He would never want to be called that or have anyone insinuate that he would ever do such a thing.

At this ripe age of eight, children do not analyze their every action, which must be liberating. There is no thought process to ask the question, "Why did I just do that?" Beyond the basics, Isaiah—or any third grader—couldn't even begin to gauge why his teacher might be so special to him. If you'd asked Isaiah why he liked Mr. Turner so much, his answer would have been along the lines of, "Because he is nice to me." Third graders don't have the depth of thought to venture beyond these very simple answers. Things are still black and white, and ironically, that made things much easier in this situation. Even though Isaiah was aware he was staring at his teacher, doing it did not make much sense to him. Nor did he give it a second thought. Isaiah was a normal child with a fascination for another person. There was nothing for him to ponder.

Parents of young children often make comments referring to their child's fascination with another person: "Aw, he must be flirting with you" or "She can't quit staring at him; she must think he is cute." This is as typical as the day is long. Isaiah was no different in finding Mr. Turner attractive. He was unaware that his church or society would view his attraction as anything but an innocent act and also unaware of the struggles he would have to face in his future trying to make sense of the madness of being rejected by his church and society. At this time in his life, Isaiah still innocently believed that his feelings and thoughts about Mr. Turner would be considered as adorable as two babies kissing or as natural as the birds and the bees. Fortunately for Isaiah's sake, no one ever noticed his innocent fascination with Mr. Turner; therefore, he was not met with the kind of ignorance and hate his father had experienced growing up. How could children instinctively have it so right and society have it so dangerously wrong?

28

Alarming Accusations

Isaiah eventually became very active in church through his frequent attendance. His parents had begun taking him often. They started attending a local church, Pine Creek, where Isaiah had attended pre-school. What better place to call their church "home" than where Isaiah had received his grand dose of doting. Joseph and Sarah wanted their little boy to fit in and be happy.

Joseph, meanwhile, was becoming a very successful lawyer. He won most of his cases, he was becoming well known in the community, and he was making decent money. His success seemed to tone down his "differences" to people in the community and the church. People began to see success and money instead of black and white. Joseph was now seen as successful in the community. Because of this, he was starting to be seen as a person instead of a black person.

As the family's apparent acceptance in the community grew, so did their attendance at church. They were going like clockwork: Sunday morning, Sunday evening, and Wednesday evening. Sarah even started to teach Sunday school to the four-year-olds. They really started to feel like they had a church "family." It took some years for Joseph and Sarah to establish themselves and defeat the ignorance, but it seemed to all be coming together quite nicely.

Not everyone was settling in nicely, though. Just as Joseph and Sarah finally started to settle in, Isaiah was beginning to feel unsettled in his surroundings and within himself. He was starting to develop this itching sense that he might be different from most of the others who surrounded him, and the anxiety was causing a rash. It was a difference that was not visible to the naked eye, unlike his mixed race, which so flamboyantly stood out. It was a difference that he could hide deep within himself. It was a burden he could attempt to conceal. Joseph had not been able to mask his societally appointed burden, but Isaiah could hide behind a suffocating veil. Was this an advantage or a curse?

Isaiah had begun to notice his increasing interest in certain other male peers or young adults he found himself drawn to, as with Mr. Turner. It was not a sexually motivated lust; he just found himself wanting to be around them and impress them. He would see someone whom he thought was "cool," and he then would challenge himself with the task of becoming his friend. The question that was always in his mind was, "Am I good enough?" Trying to make friends became like a game where the prize was feeling validated as a person. He assumed this was how all children made friends. Wasn't it?

Unfortunately, while Isaiah was at a crucial point in molding his sense of self, Pine Creek had already done a fine job of teaching Isaiah to hate himself and deny himself the right to be who he was created to be. Isaiah remembered all the Sundays and Wednesdays at church, where the messages had made him feel berated to the point that he began hating himself. Isaiah started to believe that something as simple as his finding his teacher attractive or being drawn to others like himself was among the worst things a human being could experience. These messages told him he should feel no better than murderers and pedophiles. He profoundly feared that his innocent actions would send him directly to the fiery gates of the inferno, with Satan himself there to welcome him with blazing streamers and all the hell and damnation imaginable. The message of damnation for gay people that Isaiah had heard had made him assume that Satan himself must be gay as well.

Isaiah often wished he had a friend or someone he could talk to about all the feelings and thoughts he was having, but the church had taught him that something was terribly wrong with him. He was afraid to tell anyone what he was thinking and feeling. The questions he would ask someone, if he could, were, "Isn't this who God made me to be? If the messages I have heard at church about God not making mistakes are true, then how can my church be telling me that something really bad is wrong with me? Am I not God's creation?" Isaiah was even afraid to talk to his parents or grandmother about this because he wouldn't be able to take it if they turned him away and stopped loving him.

By treating Isaiah the way it did, was the church not condemning God himself and his love for diversity, as had been the case with Joseph in the past? Isaiah wondered if his grandmother had felt the way he did when she was denied her freedom and treated less than human, or if his father had felt this way when he was turned away from churches and told, "Niggers are not welcome here."

As was common in the South, Isaiah swiftly learned to suppress his feelings, to hate who he was, and to deny parts of himself that he wanted to never be exposed. Isaiah started to hold anger and hate within himself, which was poisoning him slowly every day. It was a part of himself that he wanted to reach in and rip out through his chest like a lamb in slaughter, but he could not. It was part of him.

Isaiah had not made any friends at the church since he graduated from kindergarten, but he had made some new friends in his neighborhood. A new family had moved in next door to the Doves just about the time Isaiah was starting the second grade. They had three sons, one of whom, Jonathan, was Isaiah's age and, just like Isaiah, loved to play outdoors and explore. Isaiah spent most of his time with Jonathan and Jonathan's brothers, Justin and Josh. Isaiah loved to have playmates. Playing alone got tiresome even though he was an expert at it. Josh was younger, so most of the time, it was just three of them: Isaiah, Jonathan, and Justin. They would spend days out in the woods near their houses building forts and climbing trees—stuff like that. They would bike ride, roller skate, and even play a mean game of street hockey, stopping from time to time to let cars go by: "Game off. Game on." They had the best of times together. These were some of the best years of Isaiah's young life. He loved all the action and activity.

Over the last two and a half years, the boys had spent every day together. They often ate dinner together, and most days during the summer, they had lunch together. Jonathan spent many nights at Isaiah's house and vice versa. The families even vacationed together on occasions.

By now, it was 1984, and these years of friendship bliss had passed by quickly. Isaiah was already in the spring semester of the fourth grade, and Sarah and Joseph could not believe their eyes at how big their baby had gotten.

One dreary afternoon, abruptly out of the deep blue like a ship being slammed by waves, Isaiah's world of contentment was rocked. It all began while Isaiah, Jonathan, and Justin were watching television when a rainstorm had driven them inside, making them miss their next great outdoor adventure. Isaiah was as happy as could be right there among friends who had become like brothers to him.

Just when he felt all was right with the world, Jonathan turned to him and said, "Isaiah, you are soooo gay. You are such a faggot. I caught you staring at that guy on TV. You couldn't take your eyes off him. I saw you."

Isaiah was mortified and defensive.

"No, I wasn't. Shut up. I am not a faggot!"

Jonathan and Justin both chimed in with their taunting voices like a choir.

"You're a faggot. You're a faggot. Isaiah's a faggot."

Isaiah turned a revealing, crimson shade of red as he screamed, "No, I'm not! Shut up! Just shut up!"

He felt tears forming in his hazel eyes, and he knew he must get home before he unveiled how much this name-calling had wounded him. He knew that if they found out how much it bothered him, then that would confirm their taunts, and the ridicule would become that much harsher. He ran home as fast as he could, but it all felt like a blur, with a stream of humiliation trailing behind him. He went straight to his room in a safe nook of the house and curled up on his bed, where he cried his ten-year-old self to sleep.

The next day, Isaiah was still upset, but he wondered if he had indeed been staring at the guy on TV without realizing it. Maybe Jonathan had picked up on something without even knowing he was right. This experience stayed with Isaiah for years. It never became clear to him what had been different about how he'd watched TV that day, but it changed everything.

Unfortunately, this was not an isolated occurrence. The name-calling became a ritual. They would often say they caught Isaiah staring at a guy, which was always followed by calling him a faggot. Isaiah never noticed whether he was doing so. The taunts seemingly came out of nowhere. They stayed right there, haunting Isaiah and attacking when he least expected it. This made certain that Isaiah no longer allowed himself to relax, just be a kid, and be himself. He found it strange and tremendously humiliating that they would constantly berate him with these awful names. Being called gay was among the worst of offenses, one said to carry an eternal sentence. However, Isaiah was incredibly forgiving. He always tried to brush it off. He didn't want to lose his only friends even if he did have to take some abuse every now and then.

Isaiah now often cried himself to sleep as part of a demoralizing routine. He was not just hurt; he also was confused and feared for his eternal life and his family. What would the church say if they caught wind of what he was being accused of? Would it be the death penalty? Isaiah had hard questions for God.

"God, why would they say these horrible things to me? Why do they hate me all of a sudden? I thought they were my brothers. Am I going to hell?"

Isaiah would obsess over these unforgiving thoughts, which circled in his head like hungry vultures while he lay in his red racecar bed, soaked with his own tears of self-betrayal. It made no sense to him. He often questioned, "How am I different from them?"

Jonathan and Justin would now mock Isaiah every chance they got.

"I caught you staring at that guy's package, sicko."

Sometimes they would purely make up a scenario. They would claim that Isaiah was staring at someone even when they knew he wasn't, just to see Isaiah panic and squirm. They knew it horrified him.

"You must love that guy, because you can't quit staring at him."

When accused, Isaiah never remembered committing these offenses—or maybe he just didn't realize. Maybe it was because he had parts of himself buried so deep within him, and those parts of who he was were screaming to get out. This suffocation brought misery, hatred, and anger. Was his subconscious betraying him?

Isaiah felt deeply ashamed. He felt less of a human being than others. He was an outcast in society and within himself, and he now felt like an outcast to his own little siblinghood, which he cherished so profoundly. He had considered the three of them a pack with a strong, unbreakable bond. Suddenly, the pack was turning on him and would tear him apart piece by piece because they'd sniffed out his "weakness." He found himself marked with a scarlet *F*.

Isaiah had quickly relearned to play alone. The ridicule had become so harsh he was no longer welcome in the pack. Nor did he want to expose himself to that abuse any longer. It was tremendously hurtful. One day, Isaiah returned from school and went to ask his momma something that had not been asked for a while.

"Momma, can I go out and play?"

She was happy he was finally going out again. For the past month, Isaiah had refused to leave his room after school, and he'd refused to talk about why.

"Of course you can, sweetie."

When Isaiah was granted her blessing, he swiftly headed to the woods across from his house. It was there that he met his queer-bashing fate. As he was playing alone in those woods that had once held the good memories of friendship and acceptance, he found himself surrounded by his formerly sibling-like friends and their two buddies. Just as Isaiah had predicted, here came the slurs of ignorant, offensive hatred spewing from their uncomprehending mouths. They were just bully kids and did not understand the gravity of what they spewed, but the words were sharp like spears nonetheless. The attacks escalated. Maybe they felt the need to show off in front of their friends. They surrounded Isaiah as they chanted, "Faggot, faggot, faggot, faggot." The chanting sounded like a dark ritual that had commenced against Isaiah's will. Jonathan began the ritual persecution by shoving Isaiah so hard that his neck snapped back as he stumbled backward. An exposed root caught his heel, and he tumbled to the ground. Jonathan really lashed out. Maybe he had something to prove because his name had been associated with Isaiah's. Jonathan wanted nothing more than to prove that he was not a faggot too. Isaiah saw the anger and fear in Jonathan's eyes as Isaiah shuffled backward with his hands dug in the tough, cold earth.

"Get up, you sissy. You're not a man. You are just a little faggot. Get up, I said!"

Isaiah just lay there, his heart aching too severely to fight back. He was silent as the torment persisted.

"Fine, you little fag. Just lie there." Jonathan lashed out again. "That's all you want to do with another guy anyway. You're sick. Come on, let's go, guys. If we stay here any longer, we might get AIDS."

Isaiah could have fought back, but he still felt love for Jonathan and his brother. Isaiah could never attack someone with whom he had once so closely bonded. Instead, he just lay there, surrounded by the dirt and leaves that had once held his childhood joys, while he watched them walk away. He felt a true sense of betrayal—not just from Jonathan but also from himself. Isaiah felt like he himself was to blame for the attacks and the loss of his only friends. The self-betrayal that Isaiah was haunted by was a hard pill to ingest. He was hurt and in shock. The push that Jonathan delivered had been a hard hit, but the hit that was more difficult to endure was that Jonathan was the one and only friend Isaiah had ever known. Betrayal from the inside out never felt so real.

Later that evening, while Isaiah was eating dinner with Sarah, he looked at his momma with confusion festering.

"What is it, son?" Sarah asked.

Isaiah gulped with fear. He sure didn't want to ask in front of his dad, but luckily for him, Joseph was still at work that evening.

"Momma, what's AIDS?"

"Where did you hear that, Isaiah?"

"The neighbors said I had it. Am I OK, Momma? Am I sick? Am I going to die?"

Sarah's heart was shattering inside her chest at the thought of her baby being bullied by the boys who had once been his only friends. She wanted to run next door and grab them by their shirts and scream in their faces for hurting her little baby, but she knew that was not an option. Fighting the tears, she answered:

"No, baby, you don't have AIDS. Those boys were just being mean. If they are mean to you again, come get your dad or me. Some people are just bullies because they are jealous or not happy with themselves. You are perfect just as you are, Isaiah, and don't let those boys bother you or get you down."

Isaiah slept that night with a bit of relief, but he still knew something was going on inside of him. But what?

This weighed heavily on Isaiah for a long time. He did not understand why they'd turned on him and called him such names. Such understanding would only come many years later. For now, as a ten-year-old, he only blamed himself.

29

The Refusal

Isaiah had learned a life of solitude. He was quite good at playing alone, but nowadays, he also had a lot of other distractions to keep him busy: church and school. This did not mean that Isaiah did not long for a friend, but it was not panning out for him at Pine Creek. He was beginning to despise attending Pine Creek. He was cast as "different," and he knew this by the way he was shunned by the other kids. This was also how he learned to view himself, and he began to feel comfortable this way. The truth was that he *was* different. Although parts of him wanted to fit in desperately, a little voice deep within told him he did not want to be just like some of them. He had witnessed the way they treated people, and he saw through the façade.

Isaiah was raised in this Southern Baptist church, where he was continuously made to feel like an outcast. His peers and others at the church sensed he was a little "funny." They shut the door of reception in Isaiah's face as the whites-only churches had literally done to Joseph. There was no "Love thy neighbor as thyself" going on. It was "Love thy neighbor *if* thy neighbor is just like you."

Joseph and Sarah had taken Isaiah to church since he was very young because they had wanted the church's teachings incorporated into his daily life. They believed the morals and guidance the church could offer was a great motivator and unparalleled to other forms of teachings. Although Pine Creek offered some valuable teachings to Isaiah, it seemed to bring more harm than good. Joseph and Sarah did not know about this, or they would surely have given him leniency on his mandatory attendance. They would not have wanted him to experience the self-degradation that was part of his life at Pine Creek.

The level of Isaiah's self-hate was unimaginable. Not only did he loathe himself, his peers at Pine Creek sniffed out that Isaiah was not a cookie-cutter mold of them. It became a destructive and uncaring environment for him. Isaiah's experience was the polar opposite of what was preached at Pine Creek. Every Sunday, love and acceptance were shouted from that pulpit, and every Sunday, Isaiah felt like he was in a ring of bulls snorting and scuffing their hooves to get a piece of him. Thankfully, he had hidden his scarlet *F*.

Isaiah constantly received this masked form of treatment, which he encountered from the very people who preached acceptance and held hands while singing of Jesus's unconditional love. They would preach, "The gays are going straight to hell! They are an abomination and are not welcome here in this Christ-like church home of ours." They preached that while singing, "Jesus loves me, this I know, for the Bible tells me so; let his little child come in." The bull's horns had Isaiah torn inside and confused. The messages of disdain screamed much louder than those of love.

Isaiah had learned to lend himself the same message of masked hatred that he was sponging up three times a week. However, through the three-times-a-week teachings, he had unmasked his self-hatred and had become his own worst bully and abuser.

"You're not good enough. You're ugly. No one likes you, and why should they? You're going to hell because you're a horrible person who doesn't deserve love. No wonder no one wants to be your friend. You're disgusting. You don't deserve to live."

This sweet-faced boy berated himself with these little mantras on a regular basis. Isaiah became increasingly unhappy and began to religiously fight his parents about attending that church. The three of them engaged in the same argument every Wednesday and Sunday.

"I don't want to go to that stupid church," Isaiah would say. "Just because y'all like to go doesn't mean I have to. I don't have anyone to talk to there."

"Isaiah, you're going to church," his parents would counter. "Have you tried making friends with the other kids? Just talk to them. You will see how easy it is to make friends."

"Just because y'all made friends doesn't mean I will. We are different. Those kids hate me, and I don't want to go. I don't need them."

This blatant refusal was wearing thin for Joseph and Sarah, but the truth of it was that Isaiah was never able to make friends his age or feel accepted—not to mention that the church's boastful claims of love were filling Isaiah with anger and teaching him to hate.

Isaiah's one friend at Pine Creek was Mrs. Betty, a lady who had befriended Isaiah years earlier when he first started attending the church. She was a slightly older lady with moon-colored skin and hair as black as night. She had it colored, of course.

Mrs. Betty was a bit on the fluffy side. This might have been because of her ability to whip up the most incredible fried chicken you would ever set your taste buds on. She would batter up some of her chicken for many of the church events as well as for Isaiah whenever he liked. Boy, Isaiah loved that chicken, and he didn't mind that Mrs. Betty was a bit pudgy. This made her hugs all the more marvelous.

Mrs. Betty had a younger daughter and son-in law who also attended Pine Creek. They were a newlywed young couple twenty years of age. They would always speak to Isaiah and gave him the most honest smiles when they saw him.

"Hey, Isaiah. You're looking sharp as usual," one member of the young couple would say. "You're welcome to come sit with us during the sermon."

Isaiah felt so loved and special when they talked to him. They were truly a kind couple. Mrs. Betty always spoke lovingly of her daughter and son-in-law. All three were such giving souls. They consistently gave to other members of the congregation and charities. You name it, they did it, all without the desire for recognition or praise. Most of their generosity was never known to others. Boast-free donations and generosity—what a concept.

Over the years, Isaiah became very close to them. Isaiah loved being around Mrs. Betty. He was always relieved when Sunday school was over and he could go into the "big church" to sit with her. She loved his company as he did hers. They formed such a close bond that Mrs. Betty was invited over to the Doves' house on many occasions, and she cherished every moment. She had even become Isaiah's new sitter when Sarah and Joseph needed a night alone, much to Isaiah and Mrs. Betty's delight. Her daughter and son-in-law were the only family Mrs. Betty had left, but she was praying daily for a grandbaby to love and dote on. Mrs. Betty and her family were the reason why Isaiah continued to try and appreciate the church.

Mrs. Betty would always tell him, "Isaiah, you have to give these good people a chance. Maybe you could go to them and reach out your hand in friendship. This church has always been good to my family and me. I have no doubt they would be here for my daughter, son-in-law, and me in a time of need, and I feel the same about you. They would be there for you, too, Isaiah, even though you might not believe it. People show their true colors in a time of need. You will see one day."

Because of Mrs. Betty's praise of Pine Creek and the friends she had there, Isaiah was resilient and had not given up on the promises of the church—the promises of family, unconditional love, and acceptance. But Isaiah was a very shy fellow, and it took a lot to put himself out there for fear of rejection. That was all he received at Pine Creek these days, other than from Mrs. Betty, her daughter, and her son-in-law. Nonetheless, he made himself vulnerable to the lion's den and marched into that church, destined to make a friend.

On one particular Sunday, Isaiah entered Sunday school wearing his pants of valor and intent on having a conversation with just one other kid. He would turn this den of lions into kittens. As he entered the room, Isaiah slowly walked over and sat down ever so meekly at a round little table filled with other children. With his head tucked down and puppylike eyes peering up at the kids around him, he was showing submission and the desire to be part of the group. He so badly wanted to fit in and be included. He was too nervous to even speak, but he pushed words out of his mouth into the air for all to hear. It came out in a small, meek voice that headlined fright and timidity.

"Is it OK if I sit with y'all?"

The others at the table quickly looked at Isaiah with obvious disgust. Just as quickly, they turned back around. It was if he had never spoken. All his effort had been in vain. There was definitely no magic going on with the conversion of the feline species. No, it was a cold place. Isaiah bowed his head in disgrace and scampered to sit in his unwarmed chair at his lonely table in the back corner of the room. It was a dark corner. Even though Isaiah sat there every week, they hadn't once turned on the back corner light. He sat every week in shunned shame and dark solitude, praying for acceptance.

Despite all this, Isaiah was persistent. He tried time and again, and every week, he was shot down. This went on for years. Every time was like whispering into his ear, "You're not good enough; you're not like us." Sometimes he would cry, but never in front of others. Isaiah quickly learned to hide all his vulnerability. Come to think of it, Pine Creek had taught him to hide a lot.

One Wednesday evening, Isaiah went to his momma for her counsel.

"Momma, why don't the other kids like me?

"I don't know, Isaiah. I wish I did. You're a cool and funny guy and a good person. You're a good friend to have."

He thought to himself, *I am a good friend. I'm loyal, honest, fun, and I don't smell funny.* Maybe the others smelled the sin on him. Whatever the reasoning, children and adults alike shunned him. The adults would saunter right past him with their conceit leading, ignoring the fact that no one in Sunday school would even communicate with him and that he sat alone. Isaiah was no longer that irresistibly adorable little toddler.

It was a warm Easter Sunday in 1989. Years had passed, and Isaiah was still in steady attendance at Pine Creek, his friendship with Mrs. Betty strong as ever. Isaiah was sitting in church decked out in his shined shoes and Easter best, patiently waiting for Mrs. Betty's arrival, when she suddenly came running in. She had her oversized white hat covered in flowers and lace flopping in her hurried breeze while she carefully held on to it with one hand throughout her sprint down the aisle. She was almost out of breath by the time she reached the pew where Isaiah was seated.

"Isaiah, guess what? I'm gonna have myself a grandbaby!"

Isaiah's eyes lit up with excitement.

"Are you gonna help me babysit my grandbaby when it arrives?"

Isaiah was as thrilled as if it was his own flesh and blood.

"Of course I will!"

They both sat there dreaming and planning of the baby's arrival until the sermon began, and even then, they could barely keep still and quiet. After that day, the months seemed to fly by. Right after Christmastime was the baby's due date.

The much-anticipated due date had finally arrived. Joseph and Sarah were going to take Isaiah up to the hospital when they got word the baby was on its way. Now they had to wait for word of the birth. Time ticked by so slowly as Isaiah continually glanced at the clock.

He was convinced the minute hand must be broken. An hour passed, then two hours, and before they knew it, the clock struck 8:00 p.m. Moments later, the phone finally rang. Isaiah knew this had to be the call, the moment of truth. Time to go see this baby. He ran into the kitchen, screaming, "Is it time? Is it time?"

Nothing in the world could have toned down his excitement, or so he thought. His momma hung up the phone. As she turned toward him, Isaiah saw the look on her face. It was not a look of joy.

"What's the matter, Momma?"

Isaiah soon wished he had never asked that question. The answer he received was nothing short of devastating.

"Jenn lost the baby during birth. I'm so sorry, Isaiah."

She leaned in to hug Isaiah, and Isaiah pushed her away and ran off to his room in tears.

During this desperate time of need, Pine Creek and its congregation showed their true colors, as Mrs. Betty had predicted. Mrs. Betty's words echoed in Isaiah's head as he watched the truth unfold. The prophesized support and unconditional love were nowhere to be found. There were no calls of outpouring comfort and love as preached every Sunday. Isaiah believed that Mrs. Betty might have been the one to feel the full brunt of this heartbreak, because she'd truly felt the church was her extended family. Instead, besides Isaiah and his parents, Mrs. Betty was left all alone. Luckily, Jenn and her husband had not made Pine Creek their main support system, so the church's lack of support and empathy didn't hit them as hard.

Mrs. Betty could not swallow the thought of this being the truth. Through some tough convincing, she got Jenn and Jenn's husband to accompany her to Pine Creek the following Sunday. As they entered, silence overtook the pews, and heads turned away to shun the newly mourning family. Isaiah knew the feeling well, but he could not stand to watch the people he cared for so dearly go through the same.

It was on this Sunday a few months after Isaiah's fifteenth birthday that he refused to ever return to Pine Creek. Pine Creek had boasted false claims of family to the congregation every Sunday, and Isaiah was thankful that at least he knew what genuine family was about and what it truly felt like: love, acceptance, and kindness. This had been last straw in a sea of many.

Like Isaiah, Mrs. Betty never returned to Pine Creek. Neither did her daughter and son-in-law. Isaiah and Mrs. Betty slowly drifted apart due to their loss of Sundays together, but he would never forget her. Isaiah would always treasure the relationship they'd had and how she was the one who made him feel welcome. Without her, Isaiah's Pine Creek days would have been unbearable. She was an angel who truly walked in the footsteps of what Jesus preached.

30

Fágard's Revenge

Isaiah was now attending the only high school around, Lakeview High. Isaiah was excited to be starting at a new school. Here, he was able to seek out others who were also "different" and who did not fit the bill of the mainstream crowd.

Since this was such a small town, all the Pine Creek kids also attended Lakeview, as did some others who had not attended Pine Creek. This was a delightful treat for Isaiah; he was just sick and tired of being shunned. He was weary of the empty promises of acceptance and the repetitive rejection. When Isaiah and the kids he had known for years from Pine Creek passed each other in the hallways, they would avoid all eye contact with each other.

Despite Isaiah's profound distrust and lack of respect, deep down, he still wished one of them—just one—would befriend him. It was strange that Isaiah still felt like he needed their approval and acceptance, as if he had been trained and brainwashed to do so. It's like the old saying: "You always want what you can't have."

Isaiah had been wrong to think this school would offer him a level playing field. He was attempting to form his own little set of friends while developing a sense of who he was, but that was proving to be difficult.

Isaiah's neighborhood reputation was beginning to leak over to the high school, slowly polluting his pool of potential friends. Even the few friends he had made were slowly turning on him. They had been poisoned by society screeching in their ear that gay was equal to revulsion, and Isaiah agreed. He was revolted by the names he was called, and he was revolted by what he felt within. The bullying was cranking up again. Isaiah found himself pushed and shoved into lockers on a daily basis while being called a faggot. It almost became a numb word to him because he had heard it oh so often. The colorful and "clever" phrase "You're so gay" became something like his theme song.

Isaiah was growing weary of the daily abuse, and his parents could tell that something had shifted within him. He was no longer the fun-loving, charming, talkative little boy they had always known. Instead, he was quiet, withdrawn, and cold. His parents begged him to share, but he refused. Many of the teachers would turn the other cheek when they heard Isaiah being taunted, abused, and called names. One teacher in particular should have been suffering from whiplash by now. As she so eloquently put it, "It's not my place. Kids will be kids." This kind of ignorant view was what got Isaiah into this situation, in which others could bully him without repercussions. No one deserves to be bullied, taunted, and mistreated. No one deserves a free ride to harm another human being, verbally, physically, or otherwise. Apparently this teacher, Ms. Fágard, had views on morality that varied a bit from those of people who understand what morals are.

Ms. Fágard was a bitter lady who had never fulfilled her youthful dream of being one of the popular kids. She was a high school teacher, and that is exactly where she belonged: high school. This fatuous lady spent her days flinging herself shamelessly at the popular boys in her classroom and having her hair and nails done by the popular girls. It was like she was in her very own salon of free child labor, Narcissistic Nails.

This was what her days consisted of. Teaching? Wait, she was supposed to teach? There was no telling this to Ms. Fágard. To this day, Isaiah was not sure she knew how to teach. Her immature behavior suggested a lack of substantive intelligence. Ms. Fágard had dull, straw-like brown hair that straggled down her back and around her neck, constantly clinching itself to her cheeks, plastered there by a thick, shiny, goo-like substance rumored to be makeup.

Ms. Fágard seemed to loathe Isaiah for reasons unknown. She often sat and watched other kids pick on him, seemingly gaining pleasure from the taunts, laughing as the fifteen-year-old was ridiculed and bullied. Isaiah reasoned that she must have been bullied herself once upon a time, and maybe she was still in exile and mocked as a young adult. Isaiah wondered if the revenge for her bullying and lack of love was to allow him to be subjected to the same. Or maybe he threatened her because he would not follow her blindly. No matter the reason, she despised him. She enjoyed nothing more than watching him squirm and suffer.

The daily dose of abuse Isaiah received was intensifying and becoming unbearable. He dreaded the time between classes, when he had to walk the singing halls of torment that echoed: "Fag, queer, faggot, sissy, fairy, fudge packer, twinkie." He found himself rushing through the halls in a mad dash to arrive at his next class. Although the darts of malice were still carefully slipped past the teachers, they were dulled during these times. For most, class was the lull time between socializing; for Isaiah, it was a little piece of sanity—except for Ms. Fágard's class.

One Wednesday afternoon, Isaiah found himself noncompliant with his normal turn-the-other-cheek self. Exhausted from all the inner and outer torment, he was butting heads with his breaking point.

All he wanted was some silence. The bell rang, and Isaiah knew what this meant: yet another perp-like walk through a volatile prison. He never knew when or from where the strikes would come. He felt like he had to constantly walk on eggshells to conceal himself while making his transit, but the eggs shattered against the floor anyway. This time, the dreaded walk to the even more dreaded class had Isaiah annoyed. Each step, he tiptoed harder and harder until he was stomping down the hall. The slurs just bounced off him. He was livid with his life. When he arrived at the door of Ms. Fágard's classroom, Isaiah went in huffing and slammed down his backpack. One boy immediately took notice, and he threw his jousts across the room.

"Oh, look at the little sissy boy trying to act tough. Do you think you're a big man now, huh?"

Isaiah suddenly felt a wet sting to the side of his cheek. Spitball. He wiped his hand across his face, smearing the vile spit from the rolled-up paper that had been expelled from this boy's mouth. The classroom was filled with giggling. Isaiah turned viciously red and melted into his seat.

"What, you ain't got nothin' to say? You came storming in here like you owned something. What's wrong, you faggot? Are you scared?"

Isaiah felt the sensation of warm anger consume his entire being.

He was flushed with pure adrenaline as he screamed, "Shut up, and leave me alone!"

This was out of character since he always tried to stay invisible to avoid bullying, but he had been pushed too far this day. His anger felt so real. The rest of the class, however, erupted into a roaring laughter of mockery at his devastation. Isaiah was mortified and wished that he could kill himself at that very moment. Maybe his blood splattered all over their faces would surely shut them up. They would feel regret then.

As soon as Isaiah shouted, Ms. Fágard sprang from her salon chair and marched over to Isaiah, grabbing his arm and digging her witch-like, freshly painted nails into his tender flesh. The classroom laughter continued as she dragged him out, slamming the door behind her and nearly catching his fingertips as he held on to the doorframe, hoping to save himself from what was to come. He felt like he was on the front lawn of the courthouse being demonized by all the townspeople before his hanging. As he looked up to Ms. Fágard with wounded and confused eyes, she sharply responded to his gaze of despair with the words that carried the tune of his anthem:

"Come on, you little fag. You're going to the office."

Isaiah had never been so humiliated. He was horrified and scared and had not been in trouble at school since the first grade. As he lay in bed that evening, he noticed the marks of red from Ms. Fágard's fresh coat of paint still prominent on his arm. They were there as fresh as the wounds of this day, which would stay fresh with him. Isaiah never quite recovered from this sheer ridicule. It changed a part of who he was becoming.

31

Black, Shiny Salvation

This first year of high school was a tough one for Isaiah. Fortunately, he did have one friend sticking by his side through all the mockery and persecution. Isaiah had met him in an unexpected way. One morning, he was in the middle of his daily bashing in the hallway at Lakeview when this boy walked up and demanded the heathens stop torturing Isaiah. Isaiah was in shock at how this boy, a stranger, was willing to put himself in harm's way to rescue him. Of course, the boy was quickly met with a ferocious shove, which flung his petite body backward into the metal lockers, making a chilling crunching sound. Oddly, the boy seemed unfazed by this brutality. He looked up at Isaiah with piercing blue eyes highlighted by pale skin and hair as dark as midnight. His smile revealed his pearly whites as well as his pride in what he had just done. Isaiah's heart pumped with glee that someone cared. Austin was Isaiah's hero.

Austin and Isaiah quickly became dear friends. They were much alike in many ways, and they had a great time together. Joseph and Sarah called the boys two peas in a pod. Austin's family was always very busy, so he started to ride the bus home with Isaiah after school. This allowed them to spend every weekday afternoon together. They shared their deepest darkest secrets with one another. Well, almost all of them.

Austin, too, was a castaway forced on the outside of the ring with Isaiah. He was not welcomed into the "cool" circle. The bully stick prodded Austin like it did Isaiah, deeply bruising him with each jab in the halls. The students called him similar names as they did Isaiah, but they were not as harsh with Austin. Austin's dad was a very prominent fixture in the community, so the harassment was dialed back a notch. The teachers and parents were quick to discipline those who intimidated Austin. No one wanted to be on the ugly side of Austin's father, the mayor. This gave Austin the upper hand when being ridiculed around teachers, unlike poor Isaiah, whose taunting never seemed to ease up.

These two comrades were not just bonded by their likenesses in interests; they strived to shield each other from the hateful slurs in the hallways. It was their own personal battle zone out there at Lakeview High. They endeavored to shield each other from the bullets with their mutual admiration and love.

Austin became increasingly protective over Isaiah, making it his mission to protect Isaiah from as much harm as he could. He would rush to alert teachers when Isaiah was pinned in the hall by a harassing group of tyrants, and he would run to the principal if his first method failed. These alleys of attempted protection were not working to Austin's approval, so Austin tried to take his mission to the next level—the mayor.

One afternoon, Isaiah rode home with Austin after school for a change because neither of Isaiah's parents would be home till later that evening. Austin's mom had agreed to pick up both of them. It had been a grueling day of bullying at school. Austin decided this was a perfect time to take his concerns to the top, especially since his father was actually coming home for once. The mayor was always working, and if he came home at all, it was late in the evening after Austin was asleep.

When Austin's father, Mayor Higginbotham, got home that evening, Austin went directly into his office to expose the horrible things that Isaiah was encountering at school. He just knew in his heart that telling his father would change it all. Isaiah was against leaking a word to the mayor because he did not want the spotlight of attention on him. Austin assured Isaiah that this would show the people at school, including the bullies, who they were messing with. Isaiah was still not sold on the idea, but Austin was adamant that this would change everything for them, for the better.

Isaiah stayed safely tucked in Austin's room while Austin marched down the stairs to his father's office. Austin laid it all out there for his father. He wanted him to view all the evidence of the horror unfolding at Lakeview High. Austin told his father of the physical abuse and the name-calling that had been occurring directly in front of the teachers and the entire class. Austin focused on telling his dad about what had transpired in Ms. Fágard's classroom of vengefulness. Mayor Higginbotham tilted his head slightly to the side and furrowed his brow. He stood there in a quiet contemplation.

"Dad, did you hear me?"

Austin could tell that his father was dissatisfied. The mayor's protruding, furrowed brows carried a thickness that ensured the conveyance of his disappointment, but Austin was confused as to his reference of irritation. "Dad, did you hear me?" Mayor Higginbotham grunted to clear his throat. It was a low grunt that could easily be misconstrued as a growl.

"Son, you need to quit hanging out with that boy. I have told you time and again that he is a little light in his loafers, and nobody wants to be associated with that. I don't know how he got over here in the first place. He is not allowed here ever again. Do you hear me? I don't want him to rub off on you from your hanging around him. He is a bad influence, and I don't need you shaming this family by his association. You know I am running for reelection, and being associated with that fruit could ruin my chances. I feel ill even thinking about it. We will no longer discuss this. Go to your room."

This was not the first time Austin had heard this or a similar speech from his father, yet each time he heard it, it still brought much anguish and an aching sadness upon him. These piercing words were coming directly from the man who should be his number-one protector—a man so many respected but Austin barely knew.

"But, Dad."

Mayor Higginbotham's head snapped up with a look of dismay that his orders had not been followed.

"Go, Austin! Now!"

Austin walked sullenly to his room to cry, but he sucked it back in before reaching those bedroom doors. He didn't want Isaiah to see his tears. Austin was extremely thankful that only his mother knew with whom he rode home every day so he would not be kept from his true ally and best friend. That would be a little secret he kept to himself.

Austin's father was never supportive of him and was always too unavailable to be a dad. He was so busy waving for the cameras and pretending to be a great family man that he forgot to actually be one. This had weighed heavily on Austin for years, although he still had hope. It had left a true lack of self-worth burrowing deep within Austin's soul. Longing for love and yet feeling undeserving of love created a destructive tornado that was tearing Austin apart at his core. This allowed the torment at school to affect Austin on a more profound level, even though his torture was not as intense as Isaiah's. Austin, like many, never felt a deep urge to protect himself because, deep down, he did not believe that he deserved protection. He'd never felt he deserved much of anything, including a friend, until he met Isaiah. That was why Austin felt such a strong pull to protect Isaiah. Isaiah made him feel accepted and worthy. Was Austin solely protecting Isaiah out of selflessness, or was he also protecting little parts of himself he saw in Isaiah?

As Austin walked toward his room, he felt a liberating and fearful anger encroach on his body. He felt the sudden urge to vindicate not only Isaiah but himself as well. His father was never there for him, but Isaiah was. How could he have been so cowardly as to let that man degrade the only lifeline that Austin felt he had? These thoughts ran through Austin's head as he whirled his body around and headed right back into his father's office. He felt this burning within him screeching to be released like a teakettle with flames scorching beneath. When Austin entered the office, his father snapped with a growling tone.

"What do you want?"

Austin immediately felt like a scared little boy all over again, but his bravery helped to hold his spine stiff.

At the same time this was going on, Isaiah, bored but curious, had lifted himself from the comfort of the beanbag chair and crept down the stairs so he could listen in on what was going on. When Isaiah reached the bottom step, he could hear Austin and his father in the middle of a heated argument.

"But, Dad, he is my only friend," Austin pointedly said to his father. "He is my best friend. He is not like that. He is just misunderstood. He can't change who I am just by my being around him.

"That's not how it works, and that sounds so stupid. If I were gay, would you not love me anymore?"

Mayor Higginbotham scowled and released an earth-trembling grunt.

"Don't you joke about those things, Austin. Don't you dare shame this family with that disgustingness. I feel ill even thinking about it. We will no longer discuss this. Go to your room and never speak of this sickness again."

There was a long pause, and Austin was frozen until his father's abruptness shook him.

"Did you not hear me, son? Go to your room now!"

Austin took a deep breath, almost like he was meditating, and when he released it, he expelled all the demons holding him captive.

"Dad, I am gay."

As his father's blood boiled, Austin began to cry with fear and a great, freeing release. With his crimson-red face, Mayor Higginbotham began to shake. His eyes bulged and his mouth frothed.

"Get out of my house! Get your things, and get out of this house!" the mayor yelled. "I want you gone for good by the morning. This sickness will never be welcomed here.

"You are no longer my son. You are dead to me. Dead to me! Do you hear me? *Dead!*"

As soon as Isaiah heard all this, he quickly turned to run back up the stairs before he could be caught. His mind was racing too fast for him to process this information. His immediate thoughts were of sorrow for Austin and disbelief that Austin's father would speak to him with such hatred. Then Isaiah's mind took a twisted journey. He questioned where Austin would live. Isaiah believed that his parents, Joseph and Sarah, would surely take him in, but he began to consider that, if that happened, then the kids at school would take that as an admission that Isaiah was in fact gay. The ridicule would be over the top and beyond unbearable. Isaiah had convinced himself that he could not bear anymore ridicule, so Austin living with his family was not an option.

By the time Isaiah reached Austin's room, his feelings had gone from sympathy to fear, and his fear quickly turned to anger as his only shield of defense. *I'm not gay, and I won't have this fag living with me and ruining my reputation any more.* This all transpired so quickly that by the time Austin reached the top of the stairs, covered in tears and heartbreak, Isaiah was not in a state to offer comfort. Isaiah had become the opposite of what Austin needed at the moment. Austin reached toward Isaiah for a hug, searching for human connection. He was searching for a reason to live, but Isaiah shoved Austin's arms back down by his side. He looked at Austin with cold, fearful eyes and said, "Don't you ever touch me, and don't ever speak to me again, faggot."

Isaiah stormed out, leaving devastation in his dust as he walked out their front door toward home.

When Isaiah arrived at school the next morning, there was somberness in the air. This was no normal day. No one taunted him on the way to class. He arrived at his first class and sat down at his desk just as the bell rang. He looked to his left and noticed Austin was not there. Isaiah wondered where he might be. The guilt had already begun to set in with Isaiah, and Austin had a big apology coming his way. Just as Isaiah started to unpack his backpack, the intercom rang out like a shot in his heart.

"I don't know if everyone has heard the tragic news this morning, but we would like to take this time to have a moment of silence for Austin Higginbotham."

It turned out that after Isaiah had stormed out, Austin had not been able to handle the loss of his family and his best friend. Austin had always strived for his father's attention and to make him proud. All he'd wanted was his father's love and acceptance. Instead, this time, all he got was his father's words echoing in his head: "This sickness will never be welcomed here. You are no longer my son. You are dead to me."

A few minutes later, Austin had reached into his father's night table drawer to find his black, shiny salvation from this cruel life. He was in too much pain in that moment to see the future or another avenue to survival. He'd just played over and over in his head the words he was berated with every day at school, his father's words, and his own. "Faggot. Fag. No one will ever love you. You're not good enough, your sickness is not welcome. You are dead to me. I want you gone for good by the morning." All the words of degradation and hatred felt like a bullet going through him. His body trembled as he released all his sadness and watched it puddle on the carpeted floor beneath him. He could not stop the plaguing words that his brain kept circulating like a tape on repeat. Austin just wanted it all to stop. It was incessant and deafening. He just wanted peace and quiet, so he put a bullet in his brain to silence his demons once and for all. Austin obliged his father's wishes and ensured that his father would never find him in their house again. He left them at 9:15 p.m., never to return.

Isaiah left school early that day. He was overwhelmed by emotions of guilt, grief, and shame. Isaiah cried out quietly, "What have I done? What have I done?" What had he done? He had let his fear of being his true self shove a friend away during a crucial time of need. Isaiah felt like he had single-handedly killed his best friend, his protector, his pea. Isaiah was now living in an empty pod. If they had both just been allowed to be themselves without an entire society shaming them, this would have never happened. This weighed heavily on Isaiah daily. He could not shake it no matter what he tried. He was lonely, and he felt it was no one's fault but his own. He knew something must change, but what?

32

The Daunting Realization

That summer, Isaiah felt isolated like never before. He spent every day locked in his room, surrounded by his own desperation. On top of that, he had developed a bad temper toward his parents. He yelled and argued with them about almost everything. His anger at himself had also worsened. Holding one's true self captive as a prisoner in one's own body tends to make one depressed, angry, desperate, and suicidal. He was rotting from the inside out.

This was how Isaiah was dealing with the murky devastation of losing his best friend. He was lashing out at his parents more than a normal teen, and he was breaking things throughout their home. No matter how many holes the walls were graced with, he could not crush the pain within. Joseph and Sarah feared it would escalate out of control. Everyone was plagued with a feeling of shattering helplessness, and what can you do to fix helplessness?

Joseph and Sarah were having a difficult time fumbling through how to approach and deal with Isaiah. He refused to talk to them. He would not open up about what was going on at school or the inner turmoil he was battling. Joseph and Sarah experimented with different parenting strategies. How do you parent a child who shuts down and refuses to be parented?

Joseph had adopted the more authoritarian style of parenting. He was abrupt with his words, and he expected Isaiah to follow rules without offering explanation. It was Major Joseph reporting for duty. This militant style of parenting was not working in the least, however. This did nothing more than anger Isaiah and shut him down even more. Sarah, on the other hand, had adopted a more authoritative style. She would sit down with Isaiah and question him on what was making him act out with such anger.

Neither approach was working very well, although Isaiah was somewhat more responsive to his mother. There was a sliver of opportunity there. He did not wall her off as he did his father. All Joseph saw was a cold anger in Isaiah's eyes when he approached him with such force. Sarah, though, was able to peek in and see her baby's hurt and desperation. No matter their techniques, they were both devastated to not understand what was going on with their boy, and they were distressed that he would not allow them to help.

Isaiah spent most of the summer at his house alone. Both Joseph and Sarah worked, and Isaiah, being fifteen, was well equipped to care for himself during the day. When summer was ending and it was time to go back to school, Isaiah had no desire to return to Lakeview High without his only friend, someone whose death he felt responsible for. Joseph and Sarah both assumed Isaiah's reluctance toward going back to school was that it was too strong a reminder of Austin. This was true in part, but there was a hall full of reasons why Isaiah wanted no part in this school.

One evening in early August, two days before school would start, Sarah, Joseph, and Isaiah were having one of their now-infamous fights. Isaiah came walking into the kitchen with what felt like the world weighing on his shoulders. Joseph was sitting at the kitchen table talking with Sarah as she cooked dinner. Isaiah walked into that kitchen ready to make a stand and make his point of not returning to school crystal clear, but somewhere along the way, that point got jumbled, like his emotions and thoughts.

"I am not going back to that stupid school, and you can't make me!"

"Isaiah, why is school so stupid?" Sarah questioned. "You need an education so you can get a good job when you grow up."

"Fine. You and Dad can homeschool me."

"Isaiah, we both work. We can't homeschool you."

"Y'all don't understand."

"No, we don't, because you won't tell us what is going on. Why don't you tell us what's going on, and maybe we can help find a solution."

"Y'all would never understand, and you can't fix it. You can't fix me."

"What do you mean we can't fix you, Isaiah?"

"You can't fix me. No one can."

"Son, I don't understand. Explain it to me. I want to understand."

"Don't worry about it, Momma. Just forget it."

"You don't need fixing, Isaiah. You are perfect as you are."

"You would hate me if you knew."

"We could never hate you. Isn't that right, Joseph?"

As the back and forth occurred between Isaiah and Sarah, Joseph had been getting increasingly aggravated. Joseph had quit listening a while back because he had had enough of what he referred to as nonsense. Joseph pushed his chair back from the table, taking his stand.

"Isn't that right, Joseph?"

"Isn't what right? I think that's enough of this nonsense. Isaiah, you respect your mother, and you're going to school. That's the end of it."

207

"Fine! See, I told you y'all would never understand. I hate you. I hate both of you!"

Isaiah immediately fled to his room, and he refused to come back out till the morning.

That night, Isaiah cried and cried. He cried himself sick and then cried himself to sleep. His body and mind were exhausted.

Waking up the next morning was a relief until the daunting realization of it all came rushing back to him, slamming him like a brick to the skull. His whole world was once again jarred into dysfunction. Isaiah wished he had never woken up. All he felt inside was devastation and desperation as he walked to the empty kitchen for his breakfast. His mother had left him a plate of steak and eggs in the microwave. She never liked to leave her baby hungry before she went to work at the bank.

Isaiah took his plate back to his room to eat in solitude. As he cut through his steak, blood oozed out, seeping off the plate and onto the floor. Overwhelmed, Isaiah's feelings suddenly came crashing down on him. He threw his plate, sending it flying across the room and crashing into the wall as the food exploded all over. The mess smeared all over the walls and floor was just a symbol of how he felt inside, and he could not handle seeing the realization of it all. In this moment of desperation, Isaiah firmly grabbed the handle of the steak knife with both of his shaky, unsure hands and slowly brought it toward his stomach.

He was having a battle within himself. Part of him wanted to push the knife in and end his life, and the other part wanted to push the knife away. The more Isaiah felt the force of hopelessness in him, the closer the knife got to his bare stomach, but then it seemed he felt another force pushing the knife away. However, Isaiah's sense of hopelessness was a powerful, relentless energy. The cold, sharp tip of the knife made contact with his delicate skin, tearing through the tender layer of meat. Isaiah looked down and saw his own blood on the knife mixing with that of the uneaten steak.

He threw down the knife and collapsed onto the floor with his face hugging the cold ground as he screamed, "Why, God? Why? Why am I like this? I have tried to change, and I can't. I just can't. Why did you make me like this? I hate myself, and you hate me, too. You hate me, don't you? Why would you make me like this? I can't change, and I don't want to go to hell. I'm a good person. I am, but I can't get this out of me.

"Please help me. Please, God, please. Please just help me save myself. I just want to be normal. I want to have a normal life. I don't want it. Take it from me, please, God. Just take it from me. I don't want these feelings. I don't want this to be me. Please, just help me. Please. I will do anything. Just take it away."

As Isaiah lay there terrified and pleading for his salvation, a calm suddenly came over him. It was an unexplained peace that swept over his body, and for once, he felt OK. He felt like he had as a very young boy, before he had been taught to hate himself. Some of the demons within him had been released to fly far away, but the demons were not from Isaiah being gay. The demons were Isaiah trying to battle against God's creation. He was battling against the person God had made him to be.

For the first time in years, he felt like everything was going to be all right. God did answer him; it was just not the answer Isaiah had expected. For the first time in his life, he heard God, not the hateful screeches of Pine Creek claiming to be God's voice. Instead of hearing the lies that said God hated him and that he was going to burn in hell, Isaiah heard his creator tell him that he was loved and perfectly made. That day, Isaiah picked up his Bible voluntarily for the first time ever. It was not the church forcing him to see through its eyes; he was able to begin seeing through his own.

He opened the Bible like he had never seen this book before. A mystery was laid in front of him. As he began to thumb through it, he landed on one specific scripture that rang out to him: "Blessed are you when others revile you and persecute you and utter all kinds of evil against you falsely on my account." That could have not resonated louder to Isaiah in that moment, and he did suddenly feel blessed—blessed to be alive.

33

Late Awakening Is Not Too Late for Everyone

After that day of self-destruction and slight personal resurrection, Isaiah was learning to accept and love himself. He felt a bit more at ease within, but the road was still a long and bumpy one. You can't completely accept overnight what you have spent a lifetime being taught to hate, but Isaiah was finally on the right track. He was forging along on his destined path.

The thoughts of "what could have been" were frightening. If Isaiah had not been pushed away from the church at the expense of his friend, Mrs. Betty, he might never have had the strength to see through their lies and reveal the truth to himself. He might never have been able to hear God's voice telling him that he was loved and created perfectly. If he had not been pushed away, his eyes might still have been sealed shut, and he would be lying on his bedroom floor, left drowning in his own blood of self-disdain for Sarah and Joseph to find. They would never have known the truth of what haunted Isaiah. They would only have known that they had lost their little boy, the love of their lives.

Gratefully for everyone involved, Sarah and Joseph were not left with having lost their child, the biggest tragedy a parent can face. Instead, the opposite was blossoming. Isaiah's relationship with his parents was improving slowly. Joseph could not have been more ecstatic to see the smile that occasionally revealed itself on their little boy's face, and Sarah felt euphoric hearing the happiness creep back into his voice. Neither Sarah nor Joseph knew what had transpired or the root cause of Isaiah's misery. Isaiah still was too frightened to talk to them, but Joseph and Sarah were just happy to see that Isaiah was improving daily.

With each day of Isaiah's swelling self-acceptance, his relationship with God was strengthened. It was the polar opposite of what the church had always dictated. They always claimed gayness was a disease and a demon from Satan that would tear him away from the Lord. Ironically, when Isaiah started to accept whom God had made him to be, the demons began to flee him. The only demons he'd ever had were those from the devastating words and actions of Pine Creek and society that had lurked within him, turning Isaiah against himself and those like him. Those haunting demons were not spoken of, even as they destroyed one innocent life at a time. They were invisible except to their host, who could not silence them.

One demon Isaiah was particularly concerned about was not an internal one but a goop-lathered witch scraping her freshly painted nails on the chalkboard of Isaiah's core—Ms. Fágard. Since he was now in the eighth grade, Isaiah would no longer be tormented in her classroom, but he held concerns for the next poor sap she dug her child-labored nails into.

Isaiah spent weeks trying to avoid seeing Ms. Fágard or walking past her classroom. He knew that one day walking past the room that haunted him so would be inevitable, but he avoided it at all costs for as long as he could. He still would wake up covered in his own sweat and haunted by nightmares of the public humiliation and abuse he'd received. Each time he relived these nightmares, he awoke from his body jolting itself forward, and he would be left dripping and breathless. He was always immediately relieved to remember that he was no longer in her dreaded class of harassment and discrimination, nor should he be forced to enter there ever again.

Isaiah's nightmares were happening so often that Sarah was in the habit of waking up in the middle of the night to comfort her baby. She would rub his face and head while singing him a song in her calming and gentle voice till he realized it was just a dream and could relax back into a peaceful slumber. Isaiah never once felt too old for this euphoric tranquility given to him from his momma's comfort. He was transcended into a place where only lullabies could exist.

Isaiah's nightmares were the only way his mind knew how to release the trauma that he'd once experienced daily. His body wanted to expel all the damage and emotions he had been forced to hold inside. Each day of school brought Isaiah to a new level of comfort. Not only was he no longer forced to attend the hyena's den (otherwise known as Ms. Fágard's class); the torment in the hallway had severely lessened. The prejudicial slurs slung at him and his daily slams into the lockers had diminished. He was beginning to feel that it all might be a thing of the past.

One seemingly normal school day, Isaiah moseyed into his new class like he had done many mornings before. He set his backpack down before sitting at his desk, which so eagerly called his name. He didn't like to stand too long once he'd entered the classroom, as Isaiah was not a fan of drawing attention to himself. He safely slid into his desk and was ready to learn whatever was being served as the lesson of the day.

Just as Isaiah was getting settled in, an overwhelming urge struck. Isaiah had forgotten to head to the restroom before class. Just as this revelation rung, so did the bell. *I'm stuck,* he thought. The only way he could relieve himself now was by raising his hand and therefore attracting the attention of the entire class. He told himself in a scolding tone that he was just going to have to hold it until this class was over.

Mrs. Palmer began the daily lesson, and Isaiah could not hear a word she was saying. He normally liked to listen intently, as he loved to soak in knowledge, but not today. All Isaiah could hear was his bladder screaming at him, warning him that, without an immediate trip to the bathroom, he was going to be soaked in something else. Isaiah was dreadfully thinking he would need to raise his hand. *Everyone's going to turn and look.* His thoughts were panicked. *All eyes will be on me. If I can hold it just this once, I will never force myself to hold it again. Come on, you can do this.* Isaiah was bargaining with his bladder, but nothing was working. He knew he must buck up and raise his hand or else. Isaiah raised his hand meekly in the hope that he might not be seen but also with the knowledge that if he was not seen, there would be an urgent situation at hand. Isaiah's raised hand caught the eye of Mrs. Palmer.

"Yes, Mr. Dove, how may I help you?"

Isaiah meekly asked, "May I please go to the restroom?"

What came next was a shock that Isaiah was not prepared for.

"Yes, Mr. Dove, you may, but I need you to drop this packet by room 605 while you're up. Could you do that for me?"

All Isaiah could hear was 605; everything else went silent. He was met with sudden panic.

Isaiah knew that room number too well: it was the room that still haunted him. He knew a good verbal bashing was in his immediate future. He had been sent on a death mission right into the den of Ms. Fágard, and Mrs. Palmer had no clue what she had just done. He must buckle up for the ride and face his fears. With all that anxiety racing through Isaiah's head, he had forgotten to respond to Mrs. Palmer's question, and the entire class was now staring.

"Mr. Dove, is that too big of a request for you?"

Isaiah shook his head as he raised himself from his desk and walked over to the packet extended in Mrs. Palmer's hand. He reached out for it with a shaky hand and turned to leave the classroom on his dreaded mission.

Isaiah walked slowly down the hall, fearing that moment of impact when he would face his biggest bully head-on. The walk down to 605 seemed endless, yet at the same time, it seemed to occur at the speed of light. How this happens is a mystery, but it seems to happen to everyone at one time or another.

Isaiah stopped before entering the room to conjure up a plan to slip in and out without incident. Isaiah took a deep breath in an attempt to inhale all the courage around as he turned the corner into this beauty shop of horrors. To Isaiah's surprise, Ms. Fágard was not there. Her classroom was sporting a brand-new teacher, and this teacher was standing up and doing the unthinkable: teaching. This classroom had not seen actual teaching in years. Isaiah felt neither sadness nor disappointment when he learned of Ms. Fágard's absence, and it was a bittersweet moment when he learned the facts behind the demise of Ms. Fágard's career.

After Isaiah learned of Ms. Fágard's fate, he was able to let go of just a bit more of the anger and fear that had resided within him. It had been exhausting mucking through all that pain and fear. When depression rushes in, it often brings its friends. When one is depressed, it seems everything becomes a personal tragedy. This often happened with Isaiah. With that sting of pain Isaiah felt while reminiscing on Ms. Fágard's cruel treatment, Austin often leaped into Isaiah's thoughts. He wondered if Austin's father had ever become aware of what had transpired. Did the mayor take this tragedy as a time to awaken? Isaiah might never know, but he sure prayed that something positive would come out of his best friend's tragic death.

Isaiah would have been delighted to know that Austin's words had finally cracked their way into his father's heart, splitting it open to allow his emotions to leak out. Mayor Higginbotham was devastated after he found his son lying on the floor. Austin was lying there lifeless next to the bed where his father and mother had conceived him with great love in their hearts and great plans for his life. That was all a distant memory now, and the mayor's regrets haunted his soul. Somehow, he had allowed his plans for his son to overshadow the love that he'd concealed. He had planned Austin's entire life, never once considering what Austin wanted or who Austin truly was. That did not fit into the mayor's plans.

Being gay was not what the mayor had envisioned for his son, but what he hadn't realized was that his son had been the same person all along. There had been no demonic transformation. The mayor just hadn't wanted to open his eyes to see that the person who was standing before him saying, "I am gay," was the same little baby he had held in his hands minutes after his birth, whispering promises of giving Austin the best life a father could. He had whispered promises of unconditional love, but when it truly counted, he had yanked that love out from under his child's feet and persecuted him.

Through this tragedy, the mayor had realized his grave errors. The bottomless pain and regret wreaked havoc on his heart, soul, and mind. Austin's mother was filing for divorce, and the mayor saw his shambled life. He knew it was no one's fault but his own. It was a travesty that his own son had had to take his life in order to deliver a jolt of awakening to his father. Now, the mayor wanted nothing more than to live out his son's dying wishes, which were to protect Isaiah from further harm.

Mayor Higginbotham's new mission took him straight to Lakeview, where he demanded a school meeting with all the board and faculty members present. This meeting resulted in the firing of Ms. Fágard—and a good riddance it was. The other faculty members were reprimanded and began to take appropriate actions when they were informed of or witnessed bullying. The mayor even took his new mission a step further. He created an antibullying campaign in his son's honor, and he championed a new law to protect those who fell victim to the same torment his very own son had experienced: Austin's Law. Yes, his actions to save Austin—and possibly his marriage—were too little, too late, but the mayor realized he could use his position to help be a solution for other children facing the same torture. His awakening might have been too late to save his son, but not too late to save others.

Isaiah could not have been happier to know that his best friend could finally look down and see that his father truly did love him. This helped Isaiah realize that if Mayor Higginbotham could make a positive difference out of something so horrific, why couldn't he do the same? Isaiah started to feel a strong pull to help others who were in the same predicament he had lived for the past few years. He especially wanted to help all the Austins in the world. This became his dream and his destiny. Through this, Isaiah began to slowly forgive himself and heal from what he believed he had done.

Isaiah believed he had murdered his best friend with actions deeply rooted in fear, and he was finally beginning to release himself from the prison of guilt. Isaiah realized he could try and create a wave of change, one tortured child at a time. He wanted to take a similar path to the one his father had taken to help those whom society bore against. Isaiah would have his chance, but for now, he had to finish high school in one piece.

34

Society Told Me So

Austin's death really shook the school. It affected a lot of students. Many had never dealt with death, especially suicide. Isaiah felt the shift more than anyone. It seemed as if most of his fellow students had softened toward him. There were still a few assholes, but Isaiah was in a better state mentally to handle this kind of ridicule since he no longer assisted their bullying by attacking himself. He tried to let those muffled voices buried deep within him shine through. These were the voices that had once told him he was a good person. These voices from long ago were like strangers to him, an ancient myth, but they glimmered inside, just waiting to be polished so they could shine. Isaiah had to reacquaint himself with that self-esteem and self-love, and he was now working toward it instead of combating it.

That newfound confidence in Isaiah shined through, and shiny things tend to attract people. Isaiah had begun to make a few friends—and one girlfriend. Yes, Isaiah had a girlfriend. Isaiah was like so many who face the daunting task of "coming out." He found it easier to break down the barrier walls in his mind and in society by doing it a small step at a time. In itself, the act of coming out was an overwhelming barrier. There should have been no such process, but that was not how society had set up this little gem. The simple task of being himself had been turned into an anxiety-ridden announcement that was forced upon him. This announcement would bring instant relief, but it could also bring a lifetime of prejudice and bigotry.

For Isaiah, coming out was a necessary evil and inexplicably difficult. He feared ridicule, hatred, beatings, abuse, and even death. He did not want to be cast out of the societal boat. One thing he feared worse than death or being cast out was that he would face rejection and hatred from his very own flesh and blood. Those people who were always rumored to love him no matter what and always have his back could turn on him in an instant with their pitchforks sharpened and torches blazing.

Because of all this, Isaiah felt this whole coming-out deal was easier done in tiny increments. Maybe if it were done this way, no one would notice. It was a marathon of social and self-acceptance that might not ever be over, but for Isaiah, coming out of the starting gate with rainbow flags flying was too much for him to handle. A step at a time was his path to finally being himself.

All of this social pressure was why Isaiah had found himself a pretty girlfriend. He knew this was the only thing that was socially acceptable because society had told him so. Thankfully for Isaiah, finding a girlfriend so that he could appear "normal" was not all that difficult, even with the rumors that had been so buoyant. Let's not forget how strikingly beautiful Isaiah had been as a boy, and he was becoming blindingly handsome as he blossomed into a young man. This made the task of finding a girlfriend pretty easy.

Isaiah and his girlfriend, Rebecca, had become very close. He felt strangely comfortable with her, and ironically, he felt more like himself around her. There was no pressure from her to be anything he was not, and Isaiah had even admitted to himself and to her that he was bisexual. After being shackled in the closet of shame for so long, admitting to himself or anyone else that he was gay was too difficult, but being bisexual didn't seem as bad. He still naively envisioned that he could marry a woman, have children, and live a normal life. This was a much easier pill to swallow. Also, being bisexual meant he would never need to tell his parents. He had heard so many fallaciously explain how being gay was "just a phase." He greatly wished that, yes, maybe this was just a phase, but he was wrong. Isaiah would slowly learn that what was inherently in him could not be, as they put it, just a phase.

The first person Isaiah told of his newfound fractional freedom was Rebecca, and she was very sweet about it. She had heard the rumors, but they were just that, rumors. She was shocked, but not in a judgmental way. She could even be described as happy about this revelation. She found it cool that she had a new best friend to talk with about the boys in school, and she swore to never tell a soul of the secret that Isaiah had entrusted her with.

Rebecca didn't have many other friends, so having a friend in Isaiah meant the world. Like Isaiah, Rebecca had many self-esteem issues. She felt like she was not pretty enough for a boyfriend. She felt fat, and she believed she didn't deserve the same things as the cool girls in school did. Rebecca actually was a beautiful person. She just couldn't see it.

Isaiah sat her down one day and told her how he saw her.

"You're so beautiful and such a great person," he said to her.

"No, I'm not."

"How can you not see it? Don't tell yourself that. You're amazing; you let me be myself without being mean to me. You are a good person. You should feel proud that you are not just pretty on the outside; you are on the inside, too. That's where it really counts."

"Thanks, Isaiah," Rebecca said. "That means a lot. You're not too bad yourself."

Isaiah always made Rebecca feel beautiful. He helped mold her self-esteem into something that she deserved, and she did the same for him. Isaiah had never been able to mentally or verbally express his attraction for the cute guys in school. Rebecca gave this gift of personal freedom to him. It was liberating to finally allow himself to feel this without the shame and internal threats of hell that had so eloquently been taught to him. Rebecca, too, had never had a friend that she could be around and feel so comfortable with. This was a perfect friendship fit. They lifted each other up.

One evening, Isaiah and Rebecca went to the movies. It had been a good night filled with laughs. As the credits began to roll, Isaiah hesitantly leaned in toward Rebecca, perspiring as he repeated to himself, *Just do it already.* Rebecca realized she was about to get her first kiss; they both were. Their nerves were flying when their virgin lips touched, and one could see their lack of experience. It was a truly awkward moment for them both. They had zero intimacy with one another. It definitely was not a night to remember.

The first handholding experience and the first kiss can be the most uncomfortably awkward thing one experiences as a young person, but after that evening, Isaiah and Rebecca realized they had the perfect setup. They could kiss and talk about boys at the same time. There was no pressure of sex and no pressure to be a perfect kisser. They could practice kissing all they wanted free from all that romantic and sexual pressure. It was a nonthreatening way for both of them to learn about relationships.

Their relationship did not last. They dated for almost two full years, but as they grew up, they quickly learned that romantic relationships entailed more than just hanging out with a buddy. Both of them were becoming more mature and needed something more. Their relationship had served its purpose, and they both were in search of a relationship with more depth than just friendship. Nature was calling out to both of them.

Isaiah's endearment and affirmations gave Rebecca the personal strength to know she deserved more. He had helped bolster her self-esteem, and she could not have been more grateful. Rebecca had given Isaiah freedom to grow in his evolution of personal acceptance. Even though their dating relationship ended, they remained great friends and held such gratitude for one another. There was never a blowup of emotions or a tear-filled breakup. As a couple, they couldn't have that kind of passion because Isaiah could not form that kind of bond with a girl no matter how hard he tried. Over the last years of high school, Isaiah had several girlfriends, and he became good friends with all of them, but there was no further connection. Isaiah never experienced true love or heartbreak while in high school, but that would all change for him one day.

35

Walk Back Into the Light

Isaiah's last few years of high school went relatively smoothly in comparison to what had come before. A few of the self-proclaimed cool guys in school still taunted him, shoving him around while calling him a faggot, but something powerful happened when he began to accept himself. This self-acceptance helped shield him a bit from the ridicule. By no means did the beginnings of self-acceptance make the bullying free of pain or trauma, but it was a bit better without his inner bully joining in on the fun. However, Isaiah was a very tender soul, just like his parents, and there were still many days when he went home and crawled his almost manly teenage body into bed and cried. No matter how old or large he was, the hateful slurs broke his gentle heart. He stored all his torment as ammunition to become a strong, successful man and help those who were bullied, mocked, victimized, and denied the equality that they so rightfully deserved.

Graduation day finally presented itself in all its glory. Isaiah had been working for twelve long years toward this goal, and he could not believe it had finally arrived. In his mouth, he had the taste of sweet freedom from the institution that had left him with such a blemished palate. His parents were there cheering him on as he walked with a huge sense of pride and a smile to secure that diploma in his eager hand. His smile covered his face and soul. He still hated being in front of a crowd, but he knew that this was the dash for home plate. He was done with the anxiety-inducing harassment of high school once and for all. There had been many times Isaiah, Joseph, and Sarah thought he might not make it to the end, but there they all were, crowning Isaiah with his victory.

As their little boy walked across that stage looking like a grown man, Joseph and Sarah could not help but feel boastful. Sarah began to cry tears of joy and relief while Joseph secretly wiped away the mist forming in the corners of his eyes. Just as Isaiah reached out his hand for the diploma that signified the end to his high school desolation and a new beginning to his life, Isaiah heard one last cry of hateful discrimination.

"Faggot!"

His heart sank as his glowing crown fell to the ground, shattering his bliss. Three of Isaiah's long-time and relentless bullies had not so cleverly faked a cough, muffling the word "faggot." The vile slur was meant to be heard by just a few, but it rang out loudly in that auditorium like a menaced bell tower. Isaiah heard gasps from around the room, accompanied by childish chuckles that sent a dagger straight into his tender soul. In that moment, he wanted nothing more than to disappear. He achingly envisioned melting into the floor where he could no longer be seen.

These three boys' foul ignorance had just stolen one of the scarce minutes of joy Isaiah could remember ever experiencing at this school. They had smeared their ignorance all over his diploma, and that horrid memory was now ingrained into its fibers. He could never look at his diploma with a prideful gaze. All he saw was humiliation and scorn staring back at him, mocking his efforts to be like them—to be "normal."

Joseph and Sarah's joy was also stolen in this moment of selfish ignorance. Joseph wanted to go down and beat all those boys for the cruelty they had shown his son, but his restraint was sound. Sarah was livid, and the call of ignorance echoed in that auditorium as it did in her ears, puncturing her eardrum as it pounded at her breaking heart. Joseph and Sarah were finally able to get a small glance into the reason Isaiah had always loathed attending that school so vigorously.

While looking around the auditorium before the ceremony started, Isaiah had had a brief moment of melancholy for this chapter's close. That momentary sadness was quickly dissipated with the eruption of hate he knew all too well. With that kind of send-off, Isaiah was reminded he would not miss a thing. All that was left in him for this fleeting school experience was relief to leave his twelve-year sentence behind him like dust in the wind.

Even though Isaiah had graduated, the stinging lingered long after. He had experienced too many tribulations growing up for them to just be wiped away. Sometimes he thought that maybe things could have been different if he'd felt open to communicating with his parents. He knew that they, too, had dealt with unspeakable hardships and heartaches. *Surely they would have understood and supported me. They may have even offered me helpful advice, but I guess I'll never know.* Isaiah kept his anguish to himself as a little keepsake of sorrow. He was ashamed of the names he was called, and he believed it would be a burden on his family.

No matter how well Isaiah believed he concealed his aching, his parents felt his agony to the marrow of their bones. Any good parent will hurt when their child hurts. Joseph and Sarah did just that: they hurt, but they allowed this hurt to corrupt them. In the past few years, this hurt had found a way to morph itself into a struggle to stay connected. They quickly forgot their battles to marry and the passionate emotions of love that they once felt so strongly.

Isaiah felt this disconnect in his support system, and he was drenched in silent anguish. He could see the wedge that had been driven between his parents, and he wanted nothing more than to remove that mass. He could not help but feel that the wedge was his doing, something constructed of his own trials and tribulations. It was not. It had been crafted by his parents' own defense systems, set in place to defend them in times of crisis. What Isaiah did know was that he wanted his guiding forces to reunite into that one strong orb of love that had helped him survive through so much even when they weren't aware of the gravity of their impact.

Due to their different pasts, Joseph and Sarah had different ways to deal with stressful situations. Sarah found Joseph to be very hostile, while Joseph found Sarah to be distant. Through all Joseph's abuse growing up, he had learned to react in anger, which had protected his tender heart but made him seem hostile. Due to the constant need to flee from the screams of terror Sarah had heard from her bedroom window growing up, she had the power to disconnect. This made her seem distant.

This was how they both survived, but no one had told them that they no longer needed to use their old ways of coping to survive. They were not able to see that the ways of protecting themselves they had learned as children were the very things that were keeping them from being able to lean on each other for support.

Joseph and Sarah's marriage had reached the point where they were losing the light at the end of the tunnel. They hoped that now they could rebuild and repair the profound relationship they once shared. It would take time, but they would put forth a valiant effort to save what was worth a lifetime of sincere partnership and love. This chapter in their lives was closed, and all three hoped to grow and heal from what had been endured. It was time to walk back into the light.

36

Different but Equal

During Joseph and Sarah's walk back into the light, they were learning to trust again and growing as individuals to produce a stronger bond as one. They were not just learning about themselves but also learning more sweet tidbits and pieces about their amazing son. They learned of Isaiah's plan to help those who had been targeted by society as somehow less than human. They both radiated so much pride for him, and they couldn't help but feel a bit of pride for themselves. He was, in fact, the child they'd raised with moral fibers made of gold. Sarah said he sounded just like his dad. However, they did not know the truth behind those Isaiah wanted to help—those that were like him. All they knew was he wanted to help those who were striving for human rights, which should be all that mattered. If they knew the truth, would it alter their pride?

Joseph and Isaiah were both seeking to change the injustices of the world, each in their own way. They both felt strongly about the pursuit of civil rights. They believed everyone should have basic human rights and be treated with basic human decency. Isn't that what we all are: Human beings navigating through this life together in the boat of humanity? Isaiah had the gift to see further than his father did. Joseph focused on an issue that was literally black and white—a search for equality. That was Joseph's purpose and his mission. Isaiah had a similar mission, but his civil rights issue colored outside the lines that had been drawn before him. He wanted to strive for the equality of race, but there was also a new mission at hand. This mission had the same purpose—for all humans to have equality and be treated with kindness—but Isaiah's mission was more difficult to navigate. It was not black and white. It encompassed a gray area tremendously complicated to explain.

There was no denying the fact that Joseph and Joseph's mama were black. They had been born so. There was no coming out as black, and there was no hiding it; they just were. Which, for Joseph and his mama, could have been a gift or a curse. Maybe it was a bit of both. If Joseph could have hidden who he was, this could have saved him a lifetime of hurt and abuse—or would it have?

For Isaiah, there was no hiding that he was mixed race, but he did try to hide that he was gay. The abuse and hurt he suffered for being gay was minimal compared to what many like him had experienced. Maybe the hardest part was that he could not share his struggles and the prejudices against him with anyone. His loved ones and friends had not rallied around him. He didn't have a church to back him in supportive love followed by a hymn of "We Are One." Other than his short-lived friendship with Austin Higginbotham, Isaiah had not experienced any of the support Joseph had had from those who shared in his fellow kinship. Unlike Joseph, who had his family to turn to, Isaiah feared that the discrimination against him for being gay could mean that at least part of his family would join in the hatred and discrimination against him. Would they quit talking to him? Would they shut him out? Would they deny him love and acceptance? Would he be alone to fight this horrible disease of prejudice? Would his family and friends think being gay was his choice?

Isaiah wondered if it were true that God hated him for being gay. If that were true, did God hate Joseph for being black? What about other people who were different? Isaiah wondered about the struggles other people faced to be treated equally. He saw that these two civil rights struggles held differences, but they had one large thing in common—the fight to be treated equal.

Isaiah remembered hearing the stories about the journeys of his grandmother and father to get to the place they were now in their lives. Isaiah hoped and prayed that maybe this was just a part of his journey and that God did have a purpose for his life, just as there had been a purpose for his father's life. He just wished he had someone to talk to about it.

37

Full Circle

With all this desire and drive under Isaiah's belt, he was off to college to become a newly birthed man. He could barely wait. He felt a fresh start to life and a fresh journey were just what the doctor ordered. Likewise, Joseph and Sarah had begun getting counseling to help them along on their path. Their psychologist had told them that this fresh start could be healthy for Isaiah and his self-esteem. The doctor had literally ordered it.

Isaiah could almost smell the sweetness of the fresh air at a new school, one where no one knew his name or his reputation. He would be free to roam the campus without the daily dose of being kicked, hit, or slammed into a locker while being called a faggot. The fear and the lacerations on his soul would still linger for some time, but Isaiah was learning that he finally might be free to spread his wings and discover himself; free to let his beautiful qualities shine without the tarnish that haunted him from Lakeview; finally free from the binding shackles of the religious and social persecutions he had faced. Isaiah also realized that he was free to choose what college he wished to attend. While all the other freedoms felt invigorating, this one was confusing. With so many choices, which one should he choose?

Joseph and Sarah were thankful to be one step closer to having the house to themselves, yet they felt a deep sadness. It felt almost like a loss that was to be mourned. In fact, it was a loss—the loss of their little boy. He was no longer a baby or a boy. Isaiah was reaching out into the world to become a man, and that was just what he resembled. It was a bittersweet time for Joseph and Sarah's emotions. Their heartstrings were being pulled in two opposite directions like a mean game of tug-of-war. They would miss their little boy, but they were proud of his tenacity and the man he was becoming.

Joseph and Sarah greatly wished for Isaiah to attend Old Dixie. No matter how horrible Ole Dixie had been for Joseph, that was still his alma mater, and he had pride in what had been achieved there. He held high expectations of the progress that had been made at the university. They would never have wanted to send their son into that den of hell if they did not believe things had undergone some change. Joseph wanted Isaiah to follow his legacy so badly that he was on the border of being a bit pushy on the subject. He knew that would repel Isaiah like water from oil, so he controlled his urges to push.

Isaiah was never one to have his path dictated for him. He was strong in pursuing his own journey without the interruption and intrusion of others' dictations, even if those dictations came from his parents. Isaiah always wanted to make his parents proud, but he would do that through the triumphs and successes of his own journey and path, not one forced upon him.

Isaiah loved and greatly respected both of his parents. Many children in such circumstances tend to follow in their parents' footsteps. Sometimes this is forced, and sometimes it is a personal choice made out of similar interests, paths, and admiration. Isaiah had made the decision, his own decision, to strive to become a lawyer as his father had. Joseph and Sarah had never felt it was appropriate or correct to force their child into a path that was not organically his, and they were right in believing so.

Isaiah considered attending Ole Dixie. Joseph had left a strong legacy there, and Isaiah was proud of that and of him. However, Isaiah was not looking to be in the same grueling and horribly racial situation. Even though there had been some progress at the university and in society, Isaiah was still not sold on the idea; he had already done his schooling hardships. No, Isaiah was looking for another school in Mississippi with a law program, and he found one: The College of Mississippi. It was close to home, so he could easily be with family for get-togethers and yet still experience that coveted freedom to be on his own and discover himself.

Joseph and Sarah told Isaiah how excited they were when he revealed his choice of school. It was not their first pick, obviously, but the more they thought about the logistics, the more they appreciated that they might like this choice even better.

"It's way closer to home, which means your dad and I can see you more," Sarah said.

Joseph was especially excited because he periodically went to The College of Mississippi as a guest speaker in the law department.

"When I come to campus, I can take you to dinner or lunch, and we can spend some quality time together," Joseph told Isaiah.

Sarah and Joseph both loved the campus. It was safe, and they thought it beautiful with its abundance of flourishing oak trees and rosebushes. Yes, this seemed like it could be the perfect fit for all involved, but things aren't always what they seem.

Isaiah's acceptance to The College of Mississippi (CM) came quickly. It was official; he was a college student, and he couldn't have been more excited. Sarah and Joseph's hearts were filled with pride as well, Joseph's especially. He knew what he had been through with his struggles to enroll in college, and he could not be more ecstatic that his son could simply send off an application and be accepted to attend like all the other students, as it should be.

The purpose of Joseph's noble struggles all felt very real to him in that moment when he saw the freedom he had fought so hard for paying off in an enormous way with his son. Joseph was given the gift of seeing the outcome of his struggles come full circle. Over the years, he had become numbed by his work; this reignited that passion that he'd once held so strongly. He felt in this moment that all the persecution and abuse he had suffered was well worth it for his baby boy to not have to experience that prejudice that would deny him an education. What Joseph didn't know was that a different set of prejudices threatened to do just that—to take away Isaiah's ability to attend college.

Packing up Isaiah's belongings for him was a time of joy and tears. Sarah cried a bit on and off, and Isaiah was filled with a boyish excitement. Sarah was helping Isaiah put some of his things into boxes as she grilled him on how to stay safe. It was like a demands list of what to do and not to do.

Don't ride with anyone if they have been drinking.

Don't get into cars with strangers.

Don't do drugs. Stay away from that crowd.

Don't get so caught up in your freedom that you quit goin' to your classes.

Call us every day, and we expect to see you every Sunday.

Isaiah looked exhausted and a bit irritated.

He huffed, "OK, Mom, OK. Gah, calm down. I will be fine."

Sarah nodded and said, "I know, Isaiah, but I am still your momma. Your dad and I will always worry about you no matter how old you get."

Isaiah nodded and smiled through the irritation; deep down, he knew it felt good to be so loved. He knew his momma was just worried about him, but that did not change the fact that he was a full-on teenager. He could not yet fully appreciate things like the love of amazing parents, which not everyone gets to experience. At Isaiah's age, it was hard to see outside of his little world so that he could truly appreciate what he had, but he was working on it.

In one day, Joseph, Sarah, and Isaiah had packed up all of Isaiah's things, and now all there was to do was wait on the big college move-in day. Joseph and Sarah sat back and stared at the packed boxes as if they were a mirage. The fact that eighteen years had passed by in the blink of an eye felt so surreal. There was nothing that could have prepared them for how the years swept by them so quickly. It was unfathomable to them that they had a grown boy going off to college in only a week. This was nothing that could be immediately absorbed. This would take them some time.

38

Prince Charming

Move-in day at The College of Mississippi came quickly. Before Isaiah knew it, he was helping his dad lug a bookcase up the stairs of Rattledge Hall with his momma in the background sounding like an instructional video on how to navigate a stairwell while hoisting furniture: "Pivot." Isaiah could not have been more ecstatic about moving into his new dorm. It was where he hoped to forge lasting memories and friendships. That was what he had always heard about college—that it was a place to build memories and friendships that would withstand the test of time.

As soon as Joseph and Sarah had Isaiah all moved in, Isaiah, like a typical teenager, was ready for them to leave. He wanted to explore his new campus and his new independence. It was a tearful good-bye. Well, at least on one end. Sarah was crying in a manner suggesting she had just moved her son across the world instead of just across town. Isaiah was a bit embarrassed.

"Mom, I am only thirty minutes away. I will see you Sunday," Isaiah said.

Sarah replied in typical mom form: "I know, Isaiah, but my little boy is moving out and becoming a man. It seems like just yesterday your dad and I welcomed your naked little bottom into this world."

"Mom! Shhh, that's embarrassing."

Joseph couldn't help but giggle as he watched this exchange between his beautiful wife and son. Sarah grabbed Isaiah tightly and kissed his cheek. Joseph pulled Isaiah into him and kissed his head as they all said their good-byes. As soon as they were gone, Isaiah quickly turned to head out into the wild world of the college campus.

Isaiah strutted off with a bit of confidence in his gait. He felt like a grown man now, out in the big world on his own. He was off to discover himself. Isaiah had embarked on the journey of self-revelation that we all have once we go out into the world unsupervised for the first time. He was no longer being told when to do things and how to act. He was now dependent on his own self-governing to live and be a moral human being. For some, this is fear-evoking, but for Isaiah, it placed a fresh breath of liberation under wings that had long awaited their moment to fly. Isaiah had always desperately strived for independence because he had always been forced to suppress and suffocate parts of whom he truly was. Since it wasn't safe for that part of himself to be free, he constantly strived for freedom in other areas of his life. When you lack control in one area, you overcompensate in another. Isaiah just wanted personal freedom and liberation from the shackles that had been placed upon him from being born into a society that made him feel different. That was a personal prayer that could not be fulfilled at this time, so the freedom that college could offer would have to do for now.

Isaiah set off to trot around and discover his new world like a spunky young colt, but first, he had a stop to make. He walked straight over to Bishop Hall, conveniently located right next to his dorms. Isaiah was practically skipping and whistling on his way over. He would have been engaging in both if he didn't feel that would be just too embarrassing, but the smile that was radiating from him could not have been hidden.

Bishop Hall was a women's dormitory, the new home to his closest friend, Rebecca from Lakeview High. She had just moved in hours earlier. When their eyes made contact, you would have thought they had been torn from one another for years. There's something about seeing someone you know in a new place that puts a whole new spin of excitement on it. It was no matter they had seen each other just days before; they ran toward each other, screamed with enthusiasm, and hugged. After their grand reunion, the two walked all over campus, excitement propelling their every step. They walked and walked while taking it all in. This was their new life, college life, and they loved it so far.

Isaiah and Rebecca walked around until the sun was setting. That was when their stomachs not so discreetly reminded them that they were now in charge of feeding themselves. No one was going to call them anymore when dinner was ready, so they decided to wander over to the cafeteria for some supper. They had loved gossiping about all the cute people they had seen on campus that day, and just as they were walking up the steps to get some grub, they spotted the cutest guy they had seen all day—possibly ever. Rebecca and Isaiah were both consumed with giddy outbursts of giggles.

"Isaiah, he is so cute. Go talk to him."

Isaiah playfully shoved Rebecca and, in a giggling tone, said, "No, you go talk to him."

This playful banter went back and forth until it caught the attention of "him." This guy that had Isaiah and Rebecca so animated looked up and smiled at the two people playing around like a couple of teenagers, which they so conveniently were. They both melted when they saw his rich chocolate eyes. They had never seen eyes so dark and mysterious. He was even more beautiful than they had expected. His head was buried in a book when they first walked up, so all they originally saw was portions of his face and hair as black as a Mississippi night waving effortlessly in the warm, humid breeze. When he looked up, Rebecca and Isaiah both felt uncontrollable smiles capture their faces. There was no hiding their reaction, which led to their faces taking on the color of a crimson sea. This striking fellow's smile had captured both of their hearts, and that did nothing to stop their playful bickering.

"Rebecca, go talk to him. He is smiling at you."

"No, Isaiah, you go talk to him. He is smiling at you."

This went on, back and forth, all the way up the stairs into the cafeteria, where the conversion shifted.

"You should have gone to talk to him, Rebecca."

"No, you should have gone, Isaiah."

Eventually something captured both their attention that managed to unsnag the record, thankfully for everyone within earshot. Isaiah and Rebecca's Prince Charming drifted out of their forefront . . . for now.

Classes had begun, and it was down to the nitty-gritty—down to business. Well, mostly down to business. Rebecca and Isaiah had several classes together, and this was not the best venue for their education. Sitting next to each other in a classroom made paying attention a tad difficult. Like schoolchildren, they giggled at the smallest things. Just a few months prior, they had been just that: schoolchildren. Now they were college kids whose behavior was expected to magically transform overnight. As we all know, however, that just does not happen. Maturity takes a while to, well, mature. These two were proof of that as they giggled their way into being thrown out of class. The disappointment and embarrassment they felt was short-lived. They didn't like algebra anyway. They quickly learned that no one would find out about this and that they were free to roam the campus and explore a bit more.

The two spent the entire afternoon talking while they roamed their new lair. They talked about anything and everything. One would have thought they would run out of things to talk about, but they never did.

"Did you hear that Mike didn't get into State?"

"Rebecca, you're kidding."

"Nope. My mom is friends with his mom, and she told her last night."

Isaiah was turned around backward, strutting along while they gossiped about the latest news in their little worlds. Isaiah was too involved in what Rebecca was saying to concern himself with turning around to see what was or was not behind him. Rebecca suddenly called out to Isaiah:

"Watch out!"

Just as Isaiah was about to turn around to see what Rebecca was warning of, he collided with something that jarred his whole body. The impact was enough for Isaiah to bite his tongue. The jarring stunned him, and he quickly turned. He wondered why Rebecca's face had transformed into this dumb, blank expression. It was a mixture of giddiness and googly eyes. Isaiah quickly turned around, and what he saw was like a mirage of his boyhood fantasies. It was the dark-haired, handsome Prince Charming from the other day. Prince Charming flipped his charcoal locks out of his face and looked up at his offenders.

"Good to see you two again," he said with a smile.

Isaiah could not formulate words properly, but Rebecca pulled herself together and managed to speak.

"Hi, there. Sorry we ran into you."

Isaiah realized he should chime in at some point since he was, in fact, the one who had almost thrown this guy to the ground.

Isaiah nervously uttered, "I am so sorry. I was turned around and didn't see you coming. Let me get your book for you."

The guy smiled.

"No—if I had not had my head buried in a book, then I would have seen you coming."

Isaiah had a huge smile on his face.

"I am Isaiah, and this is Rebecca."

Rebecca giggled to herself and smiled as she was introduced. Prince Charming reached out his silky, golden hand.

"I am Kamil."

The three quickly became friends. They hung out every chance they got. Kamil fit in perfectly with these two. Isaiah and Rebecca were quite surprised that Kamil did not have other friends. He was sweet, funny, trustworthy, intelligent, and fun to be around. Not to mention that he was beautiful. They could not believe he did not have other friends there or that a girlfriend had not scooped him up.

It turned out Kamil was not from around there. He had gotten a full scholarship to attend school at The College of Mississippi; because of this, he had come a long way from home. Most of his family and friends were all back in California. This was only the second time he had been to Mississippi. The first time had been when he visited the campus the previous spring.

Kamil loved the new smells he'd been met with that spring. Nothing could beat the smell of freshly growing honeysuckle, but it was August now. Kamil was not adjusting to the humidity and heat as easily as he was to all the beautiful countryside he saw, and he was finding out that a lot of people did not as quickly adjust to him. Most looked at him strangely in the beginning since he did not look like most others in the area, but he found that many warmed up quickly to show him that southern hospitality he had heard so much about. Isaiah and Rebecca never needed a warm-up period. Those two started out warm. They couldn't fathom why anyone would not just fall in love with this amazing person they had befriended.

Over time, Isaiah learned that Kamil was missing his family and that he was a bit homesick.

"It's so beautiful here, and even though you guys have been so great toward me, I miss home. I miss my family."

Even though Isaiah and Rebecca welcomed Kamil with open arms, Isaiah wanted to do more to make this California native feel at home.

"Why don't I show you around this weekend, and you can come home with me for Sunday lunch if you want," Isaiah said.

He decided to take Kamil under his wing and show him the ropes of the area. The two started to spend most of their free time together. Isaiah even began bringing Kamil home every Sunday for lunch with the family. Kamil really appreciated this since he missed the connection with his family back home. It was nice to experience that feeling, even if it was through someone else's family.

Kamil was a big hit with the family. Joseph, Sarah, Mama Dove, and William all loved him. They began inviting Kamil to everything they did as a family. He was quickly accepted, and he fit right in.

Kamil had the pleasure of meeting William and Mama Dove. The old gang was back together. Some years earlier, William and Mama Dove had moved down to the Jackson area to be closer to their family. They spent every holiday together before the move. After the move, they had Sunday lunch together every week after church. Everyone was so thankful to have their extended family in the same town again. Family was so important to all of them, but family was not the only important thing.

Back when Mama Dove and William moved down to the Jackson area, Mama Dove had insisted they find a new church they all could attend. They tried out many different churches until they all had found a church they enjoyed. It was a task to please everyone, but they made it work. Sarah and Joseph's main rule was that Pine Creek was off the table. The whole gang went out to find a new church to attend, and that they did. The whole family attended the new church, including William's wife and daughter.

Yes, William had married just three years after Sarah and Joseph had been able to legally wed. His wife was Ruth, a beautiful and in-

telligent woman. Her mocha skin exuded confidence, and her glasses radiated the intelligence that lingered behind her maple eyes. Her
large curls were just long enough to tickle her shoulders, and one was
left to imagine whether that was the reason behind why she smiled
so much. She had a very caring smile, but that didn't mean she was a
pushover. She was not.

Ruth was a wonderful aunt to Isaiah. She was always loving and
full of good advice, but she'd also been quick to correct him if he was
out of line when he was younger.

"We don't talk like that."

"Where are your manners?"

When Isaiah was around his Aunt Ruth, he knew he'd better follow the letter of the law, or else. Her gaze of disappointment would
break his heart. Isaiah, at times, found himself nervous to go to
Aunt Ruth with news of his wrongdoing. No one likes to be glared
upon with scolding eyes, but all she did was done with love. Ruth
was stern when she needed to be, but she was loving and a delight
to be around.

On top of being an excellent aunt, Ruth was also a great mother
to her and William's daughter, Kayla. William and Ruth had had difficulty conceiving a baby, just as Joseph and Sarah had. Kayla was their
little surprise, born a full fifteen years after Isaiah. They believed that
this kind of gift could never come too late.

Kayla was not only her parents' best gift but also Isaiah's pride and
joy. She was Isaiah's one and only cousin, and he was delighted in her
addition to the family. Isaiah seemed to have such a paternal instinct
about him. He was so gentle and caring with his little cousin. He just
loved to babysit. Isaiah took every chance he could to be a big part
in Kayla's life, and as Kayla grew, she looked up to Isaiah with such
admiration. Isaiah felt Kayla was more a little sister than a cousin, and
he would do anything for her, which included setting foot in places
he'd sworn never to again.

Sometimes in life, we make bold statements and promises to ourselves that we can't quite keep. It's the curse of the "never." Once the words "I will never . . ." leave your lips, you can almost assure yourself that you will end up doing what you said you would *never* do. It's a little joke that the universe must enjoy playing. Well, Isaiah had never quite learned his lesson, and he'd sworn he would never again set foot inside Pine Creek. What would you know—Isaiah had to suck it up and do what he'd sworn he would never do again.

Yes, Isaiah would do anything for his little cousin Kayla. This included taking her to Sunday school at Pine Creek. Kayla had a very different experience at school and at that church from what Isaiah had endured. Isaiah was not one to tarnish someone's positive experiences based on his own vastly negative ones, so he kept to himself what he had lived. He allowed Kayla to enjoy her own unique experiences. Kayla was quite popular, and most of her close school friends attended Pine Creek. Because of this, Kayla had begged to attend Pine Creek instead of the church that the rest of the family attended. William and Ruth did not put up much resistance; there were way worse things their child could want than simply going to church with her friends. They agreed to give Kayla her wish if she could find a ride to and from church every Sunday. Kayla was a smart girl. She knew just who to ask: Isaiah. Isaiah felt plagued by this request, but with a little pouty begging from Kayla, his resistance melted away.

Isaiah began to take Kayla to Sunday school every week. He would drive around or sit in the parking lot, patiently waiting on her till it was over. This was dreadfully boring, but he had learned how to pass the time by listening to music and studying. Every once in a while, Isaiah lucked out, and one of Kayla's friend's parents offered to give Kayla a ride home. However, this did not happen as much as Isaiah had hoped. Isaiah had another boredom-beating trick up his sleeve, though. He had somehow convinced Kamil to run this errand with him almost every Sunday. This also gave the two a lot of spare time to talk and really get to know one another. Their bond quickly strengthened through all this quality time together, and they found themselves secretly enjoying this Sunday-school purgatory. That is, until the day it turned into a little slice of hell.

39

Murderers, Pedophiles, and Gays: Oh My

One Sunday just like every other, Isaiah and Kamil drove Kayla to Sunday school at Pine Creek, and Isaiah parked the car in the very back of the parking lot close to a heavily wooded section. Many Mississippi towns have these little wooded areas. It's your own little slice of heavenly nature plopped in the middle of everything. Isaiah loved these undisturbed animal and nature sanctuaries, but although that was a bonus, that was not why he parked his car close to it. He did this to ensure that he did not take up parking for those wishing to attend service or Sunday school. He was a thoughtful guy who always tried to think of others. It was a very rare event for the parking lot to ever get full enough to come close to the wooded section where they nestled every Sunday morning.

This was where Isaiah and Kamil patiently waited it out like they had become accustomed. This day in particular, they were in high spirits. Both had just done well on exams the week before, and they were enjoying this beautiful, sunny day free from studying for once. They were listening to their new favorite song on the radio, "I Will Always Love You," and enjoying each other's company when they heard an unwelcome and startling rap on the driver's side window of the car. They both jumped a bit. They had been wrapped tightly in the joy of their own world, and they had not seen the dark shadow of a man approaching the vehicle. Isaiah's head whipped around so fast that he could have caused injury to himself. He looked up at the ominous character towering over him, and he recognized him immediately. It was none other than Christopher Henryson, the pastor of Pine Creek.

Pastor Henryson's mother, Mrs. Henryson, was a gossipy ole gal who had spent many a day sipping tea with none other than Mrs. Kingsley. She had been there as a compliant accessory during the abusive slap to Joseph's face that had jarred his life into a new direction. Yes, she had been there facilely agreeing with Mrs. Kingsley's rant on the weary troubles of finding good help. This was the foul residue Mrs. Henryson had left behind to remember her by. That, and the fact that she had two children: Christopher and Jean. She tactlessly raised these two children with the same ignorant pride and bigotry that she had exhibited that day.

In the South, you come to learn that it is a small world—a small world indeed. You will find someone who knows your momma, daddy, grandparents, cousins, aunts, or uncles most everywhere you go, especially at church. No matter what Southern Baptist church you choose to enter, there will be direct threads attaching someone there to someone you know. That's just how it is in the South. Usually, it's not a hard connection to make; you might just be talking about someone at the church on one of the other three corners of the block.

The churches down south are not few and far between. Not by a long shot. One of the very first questions you might receive from a complete stranger is, "What church do you attend?" This is the local gauge to discover what mutual acquaintances you might have. It's also a litmus test to find out if you are a heathen or not in the eyes of the Southern Baptists. So it was not a far stretch around here to believe that Pastor Henryson would be a part of one of Isaiah's defining life moments just as his mother, Mrs. Henryson, had been a part in the life of Isaiah's father.

The day when this ominous figure towered over the boys in the car would be a changing day, a truly upsetting day, a day that exposed to Isaiah just how far prejudice and malice could spread their foul wings. When Isaiah saw who stood at his window, he quickly rolled it down. He was expecting to be questioned along the lines of why they were just sitting in the parking lot and not coming into church. Isaiah was preparing his excuse of why the two were not attending, but a beckoning into church was not what they received.

"Yes, sir?" Isaiah muttered with a questioning tone.

"Could you follow me and bring your little friend with you?"

Isaiah quickly realized this was more of a demand than a request.

"I need to speak with you inside," the pastor said, with disdain glossing over his eyes.

Isaiah and Kamil looked at each other with confusion and apprehension. They shrugged and slightly nodded in hesitant conformity to comply with Pastor Henryson's demands.

The two boys walked quietly behind the pastor in nervous contemplation of what could possibly be unfolding. They were led into a room that Isaiah had never seen before, even though he had spent more than a decade attending that church three times a week. Isaiah nervously wondered what this room could be, what it was used for, and why he had never known about it. It must have been the pastor's secret lair. As soon as Isaiah and Kamil walked into the room, they sensed this was an unforgiving and threatening situation. Isaiah thought to himself that surely his instincts were wrong. He was, in fact, in a church, but he could not deny the feeling that they had walked into a sinister room.

Isaiah and Kamil were "asked" to sit down. Again, being "asked" to sit was more of a demand than a polite question of will. There were five others sitting around in their chairs of arrogance. They looked eager and aroused for what was about to happen. Isaiah and Kamil's chairs were positioned facing the others. It was set up in a courtroom fashion, but this was a courtroom where they had no defense and had committed no crime. The others sat high on their judge's panel, looking down at the two on trial, but in their eyes glared the word "guilty" before the trial had even begun. Isaiah realized that this was no trial; this was an execution.

The panel seemed haughty, and their pack was one of prideful ignorance. It was obvious that their pride leader was Pastor Henryson, who could do no wrong in their eyes. He had waited till he had his victims helpless, isolated, and surrounded before his attack. He was too spineless to face these boys alone. Who would fill him with this illusion of grandeur if not his flock?

The pastor's hair was the color of a lion's mane, and his canine teeth seemed to be accentuated as fangs for shredding Isaiah apart. Isaiah felt like an injured gazelle, surrounded, but these creatures that surrounded him were not noble like lions; they were cowardly.

The pastor whipped his mane around, focusing his predator-like eyes on Isaiah. "Isaiah, I brought you two here today because we have taken notice of you and your little friend here sittin' in the parking lot every Sunday. We know what you two are up to, and we feel that what you boys are doin' is disgusting and somethin' that needs to be addressed. We have discussed it in detail, and we have decided to confront you about it."

Isaiah barely had time to question what this man was speaking of before the pastor's terrorizing rant continued.

"It is a sin that will be punished for eternity in the fiery gates of hell. Do you understand that? You will spend your eternity with the agony and stench of your flesh meltin' off your bones."

The others in this flock all nodded and murmured, "Amen," blindly and vacantly following. Isaiah was confused as to what this sin might be, but he had more than a sneaking suspicion what the "good" pastor might be referring to. However, how this pastor had made the giant leap from two friends hanging out while performing the good deed of taking Isaiah's cousin to church to the two fornicating in the car was beyond any reasoning. The good pastor didn't seem to mind taking the plunge.

One can only assume that the pastor had heard the puerile gossip of the reputation bestowed upon Isaiah as a child. The truth didn't matter. Pastor Henryson had already made up his mind, and there was no changing what he believed. He had already turned the innocent into what he so recklessly believed to be evil, and he was on the attack with his smite.

"Sir, I don't have a clue what you are talking about," Isaiah huffed in an irritated tone.

He was sick and tired of being accused of something he had not done. He was also growing increasingly weary of the fact that, if he or others wanted to fully be themselves, this was surely not something that should carry an accusatory tone or persecution. That was exactly what had led to the death of Austin. Isaiah felt strongly that he and countless others should not have to live in fear. Sadly, no matter how irritated Isaiah may have sounded, it was fear that was driving his anger. Anger had become his defense.

The pastor whipped his eyes down at Isaiah, judgment bolting from them like daggers. "Tell the truth, son. Isn't it true that you are gay? Tell us here now. Isn't it true that you are livin' in sin? Isn't it true that you have allowed yourself to be an abomination to this world, a sickness that is corruptin' us, and a disgrace to God's name? Tell us. We are all sittin' here to hear you say it."

The panel of five looked eager. This would be splendid gossip to spread to all their friends and acquaintances throughout the church and community.

Isaiah paused as fear continued to consume him. He felt attacked, persecuted, and condemned for their sick entertainment. This forced the transformation of his fear into fury. Isaiah believed that he could not escape this persecution, no matter if the accusations were the truth or lies. These beasts were out for blood, and they would get their taste, no matter the cost—even if at the expense of traumatizing two boys. This was an attack that could change Isaiah's entire life path and even shove him toward suicide, but blood and a good show was what they so desired.

After his talks with God, Isaiah knew there was no longer a reason to hide. God had given Isaiah this gift to allow himself to be who he was created to be. This would be no easy feat, treading against society and what he had been taught, but he knew in that moment more than ever that there was nothing wrong with him. He was tired of being looked upon as if he were less than a human being and treated as if he were the filth underneath their nails.

Isaiah's face became flushed, and he felt a warmth come over his body. Everything in the room became a blurry sea of red. Isaiah's rage and anger overtook him. *They want a victim to attack, so why not give it to them on my own terms. I will no longer be ashamed and hide,* Isaiah thought. He took a deep breath before blurting out what he had trapped in for almost two decades.

"Yes, I am. I am gay," Isaiah said with great pride in his voice—but this pride was being chased vigorously by fear.

The fear quickly consumed the pride. The fear won. How could it not? With anxiety all over his face, Isaiah turned to look at Kamil. He did not want to lose yet another friend. Isaiah had lost friends in the past simply for being accused of being gay. This time, he did not deny the accusations. He stood strong in who God had made him to be, yet it was God's self-proclaimed people who were attacking him so viciously. They had helped mold society to treat Isaiah as a leper and a demon. Love thy neighbor was out the window. It was all hammers and nails on deck.

Pastor Henryson smirked for just a moment when Isaiah stood firm in who he was. This smirk was patronizing, and it also seemed to be filled with eagerness for the punishment the pastor believed he now had the right to inflict on Isaiah.

He reeled in his demeaning sneer as he began to preach. "Son, you know that this is a repulsive and sickenin' sin. The only things that compare to the sin of being gay are the sins of murderers and pedophiles. You are as sick and filthy as they are, and you will burn with them in hell if you don't repent. You need to get on your knees and beg for forgiveness. I don't know how you're even allowed to take a child to Sunday school or have them in your care. This is unsafe. Children should never be exposed to these types of perversions."

Isaiah was speechless and horrified to his core. The sweet release he'd felt when he finally stood strong in the person he was born to be was quickly overshadowed by this hatred and darkness being forced on him. He felt betrayed by the church in which he had grown up. Isaiah should have not been surprised, but he was at the level of betrayal and hurt. Isaiah felt like there was a ton of bricks on his chest, forcing it to cave in and crush his heart. He couldn't breathe, and he started to panic. He knew he had to get out of there quickly.

Pastor Henryson continued preaching. Whose words he was preaching was unknown, but they sure were not the words of Jesus. The others sat in their semicircle on their high horses reveling in every moment, and their eyes were filled with awe as their great leader assailed two innocent boys who had not provoked any of it.

"Isaiah, I have known you for a while, and I only tell you this because I care what happens to you, just like I care what happens to my sister. She claims to be gay, and I hope she is saved one day. I don't want her to have to burn in hell with all the other wicked of the world. I've had to banish her from my life until she repents, just as with you. The acts you are committin' are disgusting, and you both are revoltin' to me. I wish there were a way to burn your flesh and release your demons from your body. I wish all the gays in the world would repent so they could be cleansed from their evil. I then could have a sister again, but just like you, she refuses to repent for this wickedness. Isaiah, you and your perverse little friend are no longer welcome to set foot on the grounds of this church ever again. Do you hear me, boys? You are never welcome back here! I will pray for your souls, and I will pray that you are rid of this immoral disease. Until then, we cannot risk havin' you here, infectin' us with your filth."

Kamil was in shock of all that was unfolding. He could not believe that he'd just watched someone who claimed to be a man of God attack and spew such hatred toward someone so innocent. He was confused at how the phrases "I care what happens to you" and "We cannot risk having you here, infecting us with your filth" could even be in the same speech, not to mention everything else the pastor had said that directly contradicted what Jesus taught.

Everything Kamil had heard growing up about God was the complete opposite of what he had just witnessed. He had been taught that God was to be the only one to judge his flock, but he'd just watched the "good" pastor play the role of judge, jury, prosecution, and executioner. Isaiah had no chance when he walked into that den of smite. Kamil knew that God created everyone in his image; wouldn't that include his gay children? Even though Jesus was friends with outcasts, Kamil was witnessing them being cast out. Kamil wanted to know where the church's claim of open doors and "everyone is welcome" went. He wondered if these were just lies and manipulation used to appear holy. It all seemed like bigotry to him. Kamil had always been taught that you could not judge a book by its cover, and he was realizing that this didn't just apply to people.

During the pastor's continual preaching of damnation, the sensation of Isaiah's chest caving in was intensifying. His body was shaking, and everything was going dark. He suddenly jumped up and bolted out of the room. His escape seemed like a blur. When he reached the parking lot, he lost all traces of composure. Isaiah had no idea what happened in that room after he left. He just knew he had to get out immediately. He could not hold in the pain any longer, and he felt like he was going to pass out. Once he reached the parking lot, he could barely breathe as he began crying.

Kamil walked out of the room right behind Isaiah, turning to give them all a look of disgust as he left. Once outside, Kamil's shock continued to set in, but when he saw Isaiah, he quickly shook free from it. He knew Isaiah needed him and that he must stay strong. Kamil walked over to Isaiah and placed his hand on Isaiah's back, gently rubbing it.

"Why am I being treated like this? I am just a human being like them," Isaiah said, sobbing.

"I don't understand why this happened. Why were these people so hateful to me, and why did they attack me when I had done nothing wrong? Why would anyone believe that I am a horrible, filthy person? I know I'm a good person with a good heart. I know that God loves me like I am."

Isaiah's heart was destroyed, and he seemed to have forgotten how to breathe. He began hyperventilating through his tears, and his heart felt physically heavy in his chest. Isaiah felt as if he could feel his heart ripping.

Kamil offered encouragement. "It's going to be OK. Calm down and breathe. You're OK, Isaiah. Don't listen to that idiot. He has no idea what he is talking about. He is misguided and lost in his ignorance. I am here for you, and I want you to know that being gay is not a sin. God, or whatever you choose to call him, would not create us this way if it were wrong. It is not wrong. Love is love. There is nothing wrong with love. Love is the purpose of life, and love is what is right in this world. The ignorance and hatred that you just experienced is what is wrong with the world. That's what people are killed over and how wars are created."

Isaiah looked up at Kamil though the haze of his tears. All that Kamil had just said escaped Isaiah except for that one word: "us."

Kamil had just said "us"—as in "we." Isaiah's mind raced. *He said "us,"* Isaiah thought.

Isaiah forgot for a moment what he was upset about as he stared at Kamil, who was staring back at Isaiah with his gentle and consoling eyes. Without someone who supported him, Isaiah could have easily turned to suicide after this bashing. Isaiah saw that Kamil exhibited the compassion and love that Jesus preached of. Kamil had not run or shied away.

The thought seeped into Isaiah's head that, because of how he'd turned on Austin when they were kids, he did not deserve this. That had been a time when Austin desperately needed someone, as Isaiah did in this moment. These thoughts were too much for Isaiah to process, and he began to shed more tears of shame for what he had done. Isaiah's head was bowed in disgrace when Kamil took his hand and lifted Isaiah's chin.

"Isaiah, none of this is your fault. You have to let go."

Isaiah took a deep breath. When he exhaled, it was like his shoulders melted off his neck. He was finally able to catch his breath. He looked up at Kamil with eyes that were defeated, bloodshot, and teary. He stared directly into Kamil's eyes, which were filled with such gentleness and compassion. Kamil reached out with his other hand and gently touched Isaiah's face with such tenderness. He leaned in slowly toward Isaiah. There was a hesitation filled with fear, but that was overcome as their lips met. It was a warm kiss filled with love.

All Isaiah's fears and shame melted away. He knew in that moment that this love had been made by God. There was no other explanation for this feeling of pure bliss. Isaiah felt warmth tingling throughout his entire body, and just like that, in a church parking lot, Isaiah was reminded what true love really felt like. It did not come from the pastor or his band of thieves but from the beautiful brown boy who'd graced his life just a few months earlier. Isaiah's Prince Charming was there to help rescue him from the prison he had been trapped in his entire life.

41

Equality and Justice for All

Isaiah and Kamil's relationship took a devastating hit immediately after that beautiful moment they shared in the parking lot of Pine Creek. How could it not? Isaiah was still terrified of who he was. He had some serious adjustments to make before he could allow himself to be happy. Before that day in the church, Isaiah had not yet fully admitted who he was to himself, much less to others. How much more horrid would his church and schooling experience have been if he had?

As Isaiah grew older, he would hear stories of kids like him being bullied far worse than he was, not just by other children but also by the children's parents, the faculty, and the administration—all because these kids were brave enough to reveal who they were. The level of hatred and alienation these kids experienced was astounding. He wanted to step outside the fear so he could help those kids and himself.

Even though Isaiah had blurted aloud that he was indeed gay while surrounded by the attack pack, he was still deep in that closet, suffocating and scared. That self-hatred lingered because of the lies he had incessantly been fed since he was a young boy. He was learning to stand up for himself and to stop listening to or believing in the lies. It took bravery to turn off all the noise that constantly flooded in.

One of the more difficult lessons for Isaiah was grasping that being taught things throughout his life did not make those things right. Some people are never forced to question these lessons, but when everything you have been taught goes against who you are as a person—like it did for Isaiah—a light starts to flicker. The truth is all you seek. There was no guide on this journey besides what Isaiah felt to be right inside him and from God. That made for one bumpy ride, and Kamil became a casualty as part of this ride. Kamil did not quite know what he had signed up for, but he was there for Isaiah when Isaiah was ready to reach out his hand.

Years before, Isaiah had taken the terrifying step of revealing to Rebecca and himself that he was bisexual, but that was not the whole truth. That was only half correct. He had not yet fully been able to let go of this imprisoned part of himself that was ripping and clawing to be free. Revealing that he was bisexual was the stepping-stone that Isaiah needed to climb that mountain to freedom. Claiming he was bisexual was his crutch, but no matter how hard Isaiah tried to believe it, he could not be something he was not. Isaiah was not bisexual.

The word "gay" was and is so taboo and thought of in such a horrid way by so many. Isaiah had just found out it was a terrifying thing to directly say, "I am gay." He had learned that, in some countries, he could be imprisoned or executed for simply being who he was born as. He was lucky enough to not live that horror-inducing fate, but he still had numerous dreadful obstacles to overcome. He would live his entire life outside the "normal" box that society had prescribed for everyone at birth, meaning he could live his entire life facing inequality, rejection, prejudice, hatred, and fear of being attacked. His mind was flooded with thoughts of fear.

What if my parents reject me? What if my family rejects me? What if my friends reject me? What if me holding hands with Kamil grosses them out? What if they say that revealing who I am is inappropriate and I should keep it to myself? What if someone asks why I am not married? Will they lash out at me if they learn the truth? What if Kamil is the one I want to marry? That's not possible, so what do we do? What if a group of people on the street notices I am gay and attacks me? What if they beat me to death? What if some guys come to service the air conditioning and notice I am gay? If I'm alone, will they rape me to show me what a faggot I am or attempt to rape the gay out of me?

These are just some of the fears Isaiah faced, but living in the prison walls that had been built within him was worse torture. He was always lonely. The torture would never cease until he was freed. He wanted to love himself and be allowed to live his life as the person he had been created to be, free from fear and hatred, but with society chastising him so severely, that was not possible. This was why he found the "bisexual" stepping-stone so imperative for his process. He was too afraid to deal with all the layers upon layers of fears and challenges at one time. Not everyone who is gay takes the same path, but this was Isaiah's.

Just like there are taboos around the word "gay," there are also taboos around "bisexual," but Isaiah believed that, by claiming he was bisexual, he still had a chance at a "normal" life with a wife and kids. He felt that he could repress who he was and live a lie. He did not take into account the toll this would have on his body and soul.

Isaiah's attempts at what he and society viewed as normal were failing, but there was nothing normal about how he had been living. What was normal about suppressing and suffocating the person God made him to be? What was normal about screaming out to

God in frustration why he won't take it away? What was normal about praying for death and hating every fiber of his being? However, Isaiah was learning that living a completely "normal" life when LGBT would not happen until society evolved. He realized that we are all human beings made from the same cloth, and we all desire love, friendship, and compassion.

People, by design, want to share closeness with others, have families, and share their lives. This innate drive does not stop just because one is born gay, but society tries to put a halt on Mother Nature by shaming, judging, casting prejudice, practicing intolerance, showing hatred, disowning children or family members, and victimizing human beings through vicious verbal, emotional, and physical attacks. No matter the victimization, someone who is LGBT—someone like Isaiah—cannot change who he or she was born and meant to be. Mother Nature and God's designs cannot be controlled by what religion or society has deemed as right. Equality and justice for all—so many would like to see that very bold statement hold some truth, and Isaiah so desperately wished to one day live it.

42

The Power of Denial

Until that moment at Pine Creek, Isaiah had not fully admitted to himself—much less others—that he was, in fact, gay. Pride was something he would need to strive for, but he was one step closer to loving himself for who he was. That was a brilliant feeling, even if it was just for a second, to finally let go and be himself. He had begun the road to healing, but it would be a treacherous, lifelong road. However, Isaiah was taking small steps in the right direction.

Right after Kamil had kissed Isaiah, Isaiah was immediately filled with an explosion in his heart. In that moment, he felt like all the pieces in his life and inside him finally fit, and he felt like he was finally, sincerely himself. The feelings that flowed through him were overwhelmingly wonderful, but a whisper of fear and shame flooded in swiftly until it was screaming, *You will burn in hell!* Isaiah panicked and shoved Kamil away. Kamil was confused and hurt.

"Isaiah, what's wrong? Why did you shove me? I know you felt what I just felt. I have never felt this way before. I thought you felt the same way. Don't you?"

Isaiah had shut down, becoming distant and silent.

"Isaiah, talk to me, please. Why won't you talk to me?"

Kamil felt this overwhelming sense of grief and heartbreak come over him, and he began to cry. He was not only hurt but also felt rejected and confused.

"Why don't you see what we have? Answer me."

Isaiah finally opened his mouth to speak, but it sounded like an animatronic version of him. He sounded dead and detached inside.

"I don't know what you are talking about, Kamil. It was a mistake, and I don't know why you are crying. Stop crying. You look foolish."

Kamil felt like a dagger had just gone through his heart. He could not understand why Isaiah would say such hurtful things when he knew they both felt the love and power of what had just happened between them.

Kamil tried to look unaffected, but he could not hold in the tears streaming from his crying heart. Sunday school was beginning to let out, and when Kamil saw Kayla walking toward the car, he quickly wiped away his tears.

Kayla could tell something strange had happened, but she did not ask any questions as they drove her home. She sensed an awkward silence, so she, as children like to do, filled that silence with childish jabber. Isaiah was acting strange and closed off; Kamil was quiet and somber. The ride to drop Kayla off seemed like an eternity. All Kamil wanted to do was talk out their issue, and all Isaiah wanted to do was escape these petrifying feelings he had within.

These feelings Isaiah had could have been the beginnings of inner peace and true love, but they were mixed with shame and self-loathing. They were battling within him like a civil war. One wanted freedom, and the other wanted him to be enslaved to the corrupt laws and false declarations of the church and society. Isaiah knew what he was feeling was sincere, but these feelings did not fit into his plan of marrying a woman and living a "normal" life. How do you avoid what you don't want to acknowledge? You shut down emotionally, and you play a fierce game of denial with yourself.

After finally dropping Kayla off, the silence between Isaiah and Kamil was broken. Kamil spoke up in an unstable voice.

"Why won't you speak to me or look at me, Isaiah? Did I do something wrong? I thought that was something we both wanted. It felt right, and it felt amazing. You can't deny that."

Isaiah refused to look at Kamil as he spoke, and his response was stone cold.

"Kamil, I don't want to talk about it. This is stupid. It was nothing. Just drop it. I don't think I can be around you for a while. I need a break from you."

Kamil was devastated.

"What have they done to you, Isaiah? Why can't you just accept yourself and realize that this is how you were made? You were born this way, and there is absolutely nothing wrong with you. You are not living in sin, you are not dirty, and you are not a monster. You are a beautiful person inside and out. You need to start recognizing that."

Isaiah's eyes began to swell with tears as he desperately tried to hold them back. "Kamil, I just can't live like this. This was not my plan. This is not who I want to be."

Just as they arrived back at campus, Kamil grabbed Isaiah's face, forcing him to look into his tear-covered eyes.

"But Isaiah, this is who you are, and you are amazing."

Isaiah pushed Kamil's hands away from his face, and he ran as fast as he could, but he would soon learn that running away from Kamil would not fix his problem. The problem was not Kamil; it was within himself.

Isaiah tried to avoid Kamil at all costs, but he was drawn to him, and the more he stayed away, the more he hurt. He kept thinking about the kiss and about Kamil's hands touching his face. He was torn inside, and he wore that pain on his face like a battle wound. They both struggled in the losing battle of trying to hide their pain. Rebecca knew something must have happened, and she was on a mission to find out what.

One day while Rebecca and Isaiah were at lunch, Rebecca started asking questions.

"Why are you avoiding Kamil?" she asked.

Isaiah immediately tensed up. It was no matter that Isaiah had talked with Rebecca about boys for years; his shame had him beaten into submission. Isaiah felt he could never breathe a word to Rebecca about what had unfolded in the Pine Creek parking lot. Talking about it and acting on it were two different worlds. Rebecca was a very obstinate gal, and she pestered Isaiah until he finally gave in.

"Fine, Rebecca. I will tell you, but not here. I will tell you when there isn't anybody else around."

Rebecca was proud of her perseverance, and she was so eager to find out what had happened. She finished her meal as quickly as possible, shoveling in every bite, then very impatiently watched Isaiah take his time, chewing every piece till it nearly dissolved in his mouth. As soon as Isaiah put the last bite in his mouth, Rebecca jumped up.

"OK, let's go outside," she said.

Isaiah looked at Rebecca with an irritated glare, but his face quickly shifted. It filled with anxiety.

The two walked outside and into a cotton field across from the school. Isaiah wanted to get far away from the possible lurking ears that he, in a paranoid fashion, thought might linger. Isaiah kept walking deeper and deeper into that field until Rebecca grabbed his arm to stop him.

"OK, Isaiah, no one else is around. What is it already?"

Isaiah's nerves were showing, and he was pale. He took a couple of deep breaths, like he might be in the beginnings of hyperventilation.

"I . . . I . . . I . . ." Isaiah stuttered.

"Isaiah, spit it out already."

Isaiah took another deep breath. "I . . . I kissed Kamil."

"You what?" Rebecca shrieked in an excited tone. "Oh my God, Isaiah, that is so exciting. Tell me all about it. Where were you? How was it? Was he a good kisser? I bet he's a good kisser. He looks like he would be."

Isaiah looked stunned and confused.

"Rebecca, you're not shocked or disgusted?"

Rebecca furrowed her brow.

"Shocked? Why would I be shocked? I have known for years that you liked guys. I assumed one day you would have your first love. I am so excited for you, but not shocked. And why would anyone be disgusted? That's just stupid. Now tell me all about it. I want to know all the juicy details."

Isaiah could not help but begin to cry. His head had been overwhelmed by the negativity and prejudices he had always heard his entire life. They had drowned out the part in him that knew this was not just OK but normal. It was an absolute shock for Isaiah when he heard Rebecca talk to him like he was just a normal guy experiencing a normal first kiss with someone he liked and cared for. As they stood there among those cotton blossoms in full bloom, it was the most moving and beautiful occurrence he had ever experienced. Isaiah had built up all this tension and fear, anticipating people's reactions and what they would say, and then he was met with Rebecca's ability to see through all the prejudices and hatred to notice that it was just love. Her best friend in love was all she saw, and this made her heart smile.

Rebecca realized that Isaiah's fear and shame were keeping him from the man he loved. She could not believe his ignorance in this moment, and Rebecca quickly began to scold Isaiah for ignoring Kamil for the past two weeks.

"Isaiah, you go talk to him now! You don't want to lose him. He is awesome, and he is amazing for you. You two are so cute together. I see how close you have gotten. I can see it in both your eyes that you love each other. Don't be stupid, and go talk to him now. You shouldn't care what other people think."

Isaiah knew this would be easier said than done. Isaiah stood quietly in contemplation of all that Rebecca had just left him to absorb. He was scared, but he knew Rebecca was right. He didn't want to lose the best thing that had ever happened to him.

Isaiah went to Kamil's dorm room right after Rebecca scolded him into seeing his ignorance. That was the first step in Isaiah's healing. He started to recognize the madness in hating himself and denying who he was. Kamil accepted Isaiah's apology that day, and they were both elated to have one another back in each other's lives.

Even though Kamil was Prince Charming, their reunion was no instantaneous happily ever after. There would be many peaks and ruts over the next couple of years. The two took it slow in the beginning because Isaiah still had too much fear to totally let go. It was questionable whether he would ever completely let go of what was so deeply embedded in him, but he was sure trying now. There were several times when Isaiah's wall began to crumble a bit more. He began to be his complete self around Kamil, and his love for Kamil shined when this happened. These were the times when things took the next step in their relationship.

It was a natural progression, but with each step forward, Isaiah had overwhelming panic that regressed them several steps backward. Isaiah would push Kamil away by shutting him out and breaking up with him. In these times, Isaiah reverted to the scared little boy in denial. He ran from himself and administered a hefty dose of self-hatred. Through this, Isaiah ended up pushing Kamil away in a brutal way. He would lash out, trying to get Kamil to run far from him. If Kamil were out of the picture, Isaiah believed he would no longer have to deal with these feelings he had in himself.

Thankfully, Kamil could see through Isaiah's actions. He knew Isaiah was fighting a war within himself and that it had nothing to do with him. This helped Kamil stay strong and stick with Isaiah during these times, no matter how hard Isaiah pushed him away. Isaiah's fighting against himself and living in denial eventually subsided, but not before it almost broke them both. The power of denial can be an astounding thing.

Isaiah had a lot of demons to conquer, and after battling through many of the demons, Isaiah and Kamil found themselves more in love than ever. It took several years to reach this point, but they did it. They persevered. Even though they were in a great love story, they saved this love and affection for when they were out of the eyes of others. Still, they feared what something as innocent as holding hands in public might mean for them. The possibilities were bleak, and they would very soon get a taste of how bleak they could actually be.

43

A Table for One

Isaiah and Kamil had been enjoying the college life together, and they enjoyed being in love. To be in love felt incredible, and Isaiah was finally allowing himself to feel it deep within his soul. It was a healing feeling he had once thought he would never experience. Even though there were few opportunities for them to fully express their affection for one another, it was still immensely sweet when they could.

As Isaiah and Kamil's relationship blossomed, hiding it became more and more of a burden. They longed to just hold hands or even hug one another. It was so intense sometimes that it hurt. Their feelings of love drifted into sadness from the realization that they could never show affection like a "normal" couple because they feared being attacked by those with deeply embedded and maybe even unrecognized prejudices.

At times, they would turn on each other because they did not know where to place these feelings of injustice, which felt like a burden that no one should have to bear. Isaiah and Kamil believed that no one should have to calculate what distance from your loved one is considered safe in order to protect yourself from outside attacks. They knew that love was the only thing that could fight these vicious assaults, but ironically, it was their love that was hated and being forbidden.

When you're in love, you want to hold that person's hand. You want to gently touch that person's arm or face. You want to kiss them when you feel that sudden eruption of emotion that reminds you what an amazing person you are with. You want to simply hold hands and be able to say, "I love you," without fear of backlash.

Like Joseph and Sarah had once had to do, Isaiah and Kamil had to distance themselves from each other, even emotionally. What choice did they have? If Isaiah and Kamil did not distance themselves, it could let those feelings of love and admiration erupt while in public. It sounds ridiculous that they even needed to think this way, but it was for fear of the very real and daunting ramifications they knew all too well occurred daily in the world around them.

Isaiah and Kamil did a good job of keeping their relationship a secret. No one else knew except for Rebecca. They were both so thankful that they had such a great friend in her. While they were both extremely grateful, Isaiah might have been a bit more so, because Kamil was not as trapped in the closet as Isaiah was.

Years before moving to Mississippi, Kamil had revealed to his parents and a few of his closest friends back home that he was gay. He had already dredged through the muck and painful agony of coming out, and through this, he had found a few other people he could share his experience with. He had a small network of friends he was able to talk to, and this helped him navigate through his coming-out process. He was also able to hear their coming-out experiences and know that he was not as alone as he felt on the inside.

If Kamil had not come out, he would have not survived, for he was drowning. He was to the point of contemplating suicide. Even though Kamil's parents had not been immediately supportive, through coming out, he finally felt a sense of wholeness and freedom. Because of this, Kamil was much better adjusted than Isaiah. However, this did not mean Kamil did not still have difficulties.

When Kamil moved to Mississippi, he found it unfathomably difficult to put the shackles back on after he had just freed himself from them as far as society would allow. However, Isaiah was not ready for the parade just yet. On top of Kamil's sensitivity for Isaiah's feelings, there were times Kamil feared letting himself shine. There were situations where he felt that his life could be threatened if he revealed the truth. He had also heard a rumor that being himself—a human being who happened to be gay—was illegal at their college. Kamil took this rumor with a grain of salt, because how could this ludicrous and prejudiced rule even be possible? But he did keep this piece of knowledge in the back of his head, just in case.

Pushing oneself backward was a painful process. Once a proud person, Kamil started to again find himself filled with that fear of being himself that he had felt as a child. Just a few years before, he had learned to not care as much what people thought of him. This was what had finally allowed him to begin to be happy with how he had been created. Now, with each whisper that told him to conceal himself, he was taken right back to that dark place where he felt shame for who he was. He began to believe that he needed to suppress himself and that he should yield to other fallacies. This was agonizing for Kamil. This agony and suppression was something he believed he could not talk to Isaiah about because, quite honestly, he didn't completely understand it himself and did not have the vocabulary to vocalize his distress.

Kamil didn't understand that all these whispers were making him slowly start to fear being himself again. He did know something felt off and very wrong inside him, and he wanted to be free once again. He had tasted it before, and he knew that he and Isaiah both deserved to love freely. Kamil and Isaiah spent years and years of their lives hearing the same song and dance of oppression, and they were damn tired of the two-step. It always seemed to be two steps backward when all they wanted to do was dance to the finish line, where they would be treated like equal human beings.

Kamil and Isaiah were both on this rollercoaster to personal freedom, but for now, they needed to hide their love. Besides, Isaiah was not ready for his family to know, so that played into his hiding. It was painful to see everyone else allowed to love freely while their love was forced into this coffin where it was sentenced to die.

They could not brag to people about how wonderful the other was. Isaiah could not boast to his family that he had met someone amazing whom he wanted to spend the rest of his life with. When Isaiah was asked if he was dating anyone, he would have to tell them no. This led to numerous family members, church members, and others trying to set Isaiah up on dates. "Oh, I have someone perfect for you," they would say. It was irritating to Isaiah, and he loathed that he could not express that he was in an amazing relationship. He wished he could just scream it at the top of his lungs, but he was instead forced to whisper lies that made his heart ache.

It was also upsetting to Kamil because he was proud to have Isaiah as his boyfriend. Kamil hurt when he was denied a part in Isaiah's life. He was tired of Isaiah being auctioned off by anyone who thought he was lonely and needed to be set up with a granddaughter, daughter, or niece. Kamil and Isaiah both wished that they could just say, "No, we are in love."

They felt like they were eternally single to the entire world. Even if they had been together for twenty years, they would still be checking the single box at the doctor's office. Some days, Isaiah felt like he was going to live his entire life asking for a table for one, because that was how he was seen in the eyes of society. It was painfully hard on them both. Kamil and Isaiah tried to push all that to the backs of their minds. For now, they just suppressed themselves and the fervent force of their love to the best of their ability.

44

Southern Fried

Isaiah and Kamil were enamored with thoughts of the next time they could hold each other. It was a hard feeling to shake, but there were times that something drifted in and managed to grab their attention away just for a moment. One fall day in the early afternoon around lunchtime, when their stomachs were howling, that was just what happened: Isaiah and Kamil's attention was grabbed tightly.

About a year or so after Kamil and Isaiah moved into their dorms at The College of Mississippi, they began meeting up with each other on campus after their eleven o'clock classes. This one time, they were both walking from opposite directions, and just at the moment they laid eyes on each other, it happened. Why it had never happened before was something that they would be confused about for years. Just as their noses were at the peak location, they both caught a whiff of something so fantastic that they could not shake it. An overwhelming desire to seek out this salivation-inducing smell dug its nails in and would not let go. Thankfully, neither of them had a class next, so Isaiah and Kamil wandered around the outskirts of campus sniffing out this heavenly smell like a pair of bloodhounds. They continued to sniff it out until they stumbled upon the source.

It was a quaint little home-cookin' restaurant within a short walking distance of their respective dorms' front doors. This walk was made even quicker when they found a shortcut through the cotton field across from campus. The decadent smells led them right to the entrance of this little treasure. The fried chicken, fried okra, fried catfish, and homemade biscuits and gravy could be smelled for miles when the wind caught them just right, and the food was incredible. It had kept customers coming in again and again since they first opened their doors twenty-five years earlier. It was called Southern Fried.

Kamil's first experience eating there was more fun for Isaiah because Kamil was not used to all the southern cookin'. Isaiah reveled in watching how Kamil's eyes lit up with every extravagant bite he took. Kamil, in turn, was amazed at how someone could take such simple ingredients and make something that spectacular. Flour, oil, and spices equaled a little slice of heaven. Kamil was hooked. This became a regular spot for them to dine at least once a week. They tried to keep it at less than two times a week, but it was a battle with their cravings to do so.

This became their spot to dine and study, and after a while, everyone knew them when they walked in the door. One of the waitresses took a particular liking to them. She was a sweet lady in her early thirties with curly, dirty-blonde hair always in a ponytail. Beatrice had a sweet face, but she looked like she had lived a rough life. Her face was worn, and her eyes looked tired. She always referred to Isaiah and Kamil as the "doctor-types." Every time they walked in the door, she would holler out, "Well, there's our doctors." They were not really sure why she referred to them this way—maybe it was because they were always studying—but they knew they could be called worse. They just hoped that they wouldn't be called to service if someone started choking.

A few years had passed since Isaiah and Kamil, now college seniors, had found their little treasure. They had even introduced Rebecca to it. She went with them on occasion, but she was not as taken with it as the two of them were. Isaiah had introduced his family to Southern Fried when they came into town to visit. The people that worked there seem quite pleased with the business that Isaiah brought them. He was becoming their best advertising tool.

One day, Isaiah and Kamil were headed over to Southern Fried after a brutal round of exams. Nowadays, they just referred to it as "our spot" since they had been going there at least once a week for about three years now. Isaiah and Kamil were in the middle of the spring semester in their fourth year of college, and their taste buds had not changed one bit since the day they stumbled upon this little gem. They also loved the routine of going to their local diner to eat and study. However, there came a day it was far from routine.

Isaiah and Kamil walked into their spot on a seemingly typical Wednesday. Everything was normal except that they were free from books and stressed faces because their midterm exams were over. As they entered, they were greeted with the routine, "Well, there's our doctors coming in for lunch." They smiled and had their typical chit-chat as the waitress walked them to their favorite booth. As they sat down, they noticed an unfamiliar face staring at them. After a few minutes, Isaiah looked at Kamil with concern.

"Have you noticed that guy over there staring at us?" Isaiah said. "He has been staring since we came in."

Kamil nodded and said, "I know; he is creeping me out. I don't get a good vibe from that guy at all."

Isaiah and Kamil did not hang around long after lunch as they normally did. They were trying to leave as inconspicuously as possible in hopes this creep would not notice. They were both a bit freaked out, but as they were walking out, the waitress called out to them.

"You guys aren't staying for a while today?"

"No, not today," Isaiah replied while looking out of the corner of his eye at this strange guy who just kept glaring at them.

"See y'all next time, boys!" the waitress shouted, waving to them from across the restaurant.

"So much for not being noticed," Isaiah whispered.

Since attention had already been drawn to them, they were not as cautious while flinging open the door, which was adorned with bells. They quickly realized that there was no quiet escape from this place. As they began to briskly walk away from the restaurant, they could hear the bells singing them adieu, a ringing reminder that they were still too close for comfort.

Once back on campus, Isaiah and Kamil spoke about how odd it was that the guy would not quit staring at them with an unsettling glare.

"Have we ever met him before?" Isaiah questioned.

"It seems like we made him angry for some reason," Kamil said.

They were positive that they had never seen that creep. This confusion and unease stayed with them for a bit, but they soon forgot about it and moved on with their day as normal.

Since Isaiah and Kamil had not been allowed to fully enjoy their Wednesday's meal, they decided to make this week a two-day attendance. They would go back to Southern Fried for lunch that Friday. By lunchtime Friday, they were both salivating. Eating there never got old for them.

As they walked in, they were both instantly reminded of their last unpleasant experience. This influenced them to both do a quick scan of the place to ensure the coast was clear.

Shortly after they got settled in, the man with the unsettling aura showed up again. They both noticed him the second he came sauntering in with his arrogant gait. Isaiah and Kamil made eye gestures at one another, and Isaiah let out a frazzled sigh. Like last time, this man began to give them a sinister glare, which darted from young brown eyes surrounded by skin that had been weathered by life. The red flames growing from his scalp at times overshadowed his weathered skin. It was as if he had a tracker embedded in his lifeless eyes to locate exactly where they were in the restaurant, because he scowled at them the second he walked in without the need to search around. Isaiah and Kamil had no clue why this guy was targeting them, nor did he have any logical reason to.

Whenever they now went to Southern Fried, the creepy guy was there, staring at them. They could not understand where this guy came from and why he would not go crawl back into his dark hole. They began to feel intensely uncomfortable and unsafe, but their food cravings continued to drive them there. They did not want to allow this man to control them and stop them from continuing a ritual they had practiced for years. Their persistence and resistance was valiant or stupid. Maybe it was a bit of both.

After a few weeks, the bullying began to escalate. This foul fellow began to mumble prejudicial slurs at Isaiah and Kamil as they walked by him. Every time he came in, he seemed to perfectly position himself between them and the door.

One afternoon, as this man mumbled his cowardly slurs, he inched his foot out from beneath the table just as Isaiah and Kamil were walking past to leave. Isaiah always looked up and away when walking past their terrorist, and because of this, he did not see the attack that was creeping up from below. Isaiah tripped on the carefully placed foot, and he almost fell. Kamil caught him just in time before he was laid out for all to see. Isaiah's face and neck rushed with colors of crimson from the embarrassment and anger. This insolent fellow sat back in his chair with a smirk on his face for what he had accomplished.

Isaiah and Kamil's favorite waitress, Beatrice, caught a glimpse of what had just unfolded. She called the boys over and asked them what in the world was going on. They filled her in about the last few weeks' occurrences. Beatrice looked appalled at what she had just heard. She could not believe that had been happening to her little doctors right under her nose.

Beatrice marched over to that fellow's table.

"Billy, you need to leave right now. Our customers will not be treated like that."

Isaiah and Kamil instantly felt a sense of relief. They were impressed with Beatrice's bravery, and they continued to thank her over and over. She just smiled with a bit of pride for the good deed she had done seeping through. Isaiah and Kamil felt special that she would stand up for them.

Even though Isaiah was thankful for Beatrice's actions, Kamil felt especially appreciative because of how his first encounter with Beatrice had gone years earlier. The first time Isaiah and Kamil had walked into Southern Fried, Beatrice had kept Kamil at arm's length. In Mississippi, the racial diversity was slim, and Beatrice was a small-town girl with a limited view of the world. Kamil was neither black nor white, so she saw him only as "different." Her world had just been expanded, and she needed a moment to take it all in to realize that different did not equate to bad.

In the beginning, there were no affectionate greetings of "sugar," "darlin," or "sweetheart" for Kamil, as she had expressed with Isaiah. After being around Kamil a few times, Beatrice allowed herself to let go of her prejudices. She began to see Kamil in the same way she saw Isaiah—just another "darlin'" customer. Her intention had never been to be hateful; she was just ignorant. When she saw the hurt in Kamil's eyes brought on by her attitude toward him, Beatrice didn't like the way it made her feel, so she changed.

Beatrice had come a long way from that original encounter, and Kamil was thankful. Even though Isaiah and Kamil were forever grateful to Beatrice, those thoughts began to fade as they were overtaken by curiosity. Isaiah and Kamil wanted to know who this guy was. They decided to ask Beatrice since she had addressed him by his name, Billy, when scolding him out of the restaurant. When they asked her who he was and whether she knew him, Beatrice dropped her head with shame and nodded with embarrassment in her eyes as she said, "Yes, I know ole Billy Conner. He and his mama live down the way from me. We grew up together. I am sorry he acted that way toward you boys. He has always been a cruel boy. He once killed the neighbor's cat just out of spite for her tellin' his mama that he was smokin.'"

Beatrice lifted her head and smiled as she assured Isaiah and Kamil of their safety.

"You boys don't have to worry about him no more. We ain't lettin' him in if he is gonna act like that to our little doctors," she said.

Isaiah and Kamil were thankful to know that they would be safe in Southern Fried, but what would happen when they left? They waited till that Billy Conner fellow had plenty of time to get a safe distance away before they headed back to campus. They waved bye to Beatrice as the bells tolled once again, signaling their exit. As soon as they were out the door, Isaiah turned to Kamil and began to vent his frustration at what had just happened.

"That was scary. What an asshole. I can't believe he tried to trip me," Isaiah said.

Kamil shook his head in disbelief.

"I know. Thank God you're OK. You were almost laid out on the floor."

Isaiah took a moment from his anger and smiled at Kamil.

"I would have been if it weren't for you catching me."

Kamil smiled back with a loving grin. Even though they were angry, they briefly got caught up in their love, but that moment faded as their venting continued.

Isaiah and Kamil were almost back to campus. They turned to cross through the cotton field, the shortcut that led them to safety, but as they made the turn, they both got an eerie feeling that was almost overwhelming. They looked at one another with questioning and uneasy eyes. All they wanted to do at this point was get back to their dorms.

They picked up the pace to make it through the cotton as quickly as possible. They were as jumpy as one would be after watching a horror flick. They were both speed walking to the best of their ability, and their pace was gradually increasing. Just before breaking into a run, Isaiah suddenly hit the ground. His body slid, and there was no time to stop his face from planting into the dusty soil. His mouth was filled with dirt, and his eyes were filled with fear. They heard a grunting voice coming from within the crops.

"Got ya that time, you fuckin' mongrel. You and your little sand nigger here are goin' to pay for gettin' me kicked out of *my* restaurant."

Isaiah was still on the ground as he looked up at Kamil. Both of them had stark fear bleeding from their eyes as Billy continued his tirade.

"There's only a few things I hate in this world. One's a nigger, one's a sand nigger, and the other is a fuckin' faggot. You little queers seem to have all three now, don'tcha? You can't hide that queer, just like you can't hide that dirty skin."

It was hard to believe these were the only things that Billy hated, and if you were to bet that he hated others, too, you would hit the jackpot. However, this seemed to fit his criteria for now.

Billy's rage seemed to be intensifying as his rant continued.

"You think you can get away with what y'all did. Naw. You nigger faggots gotta pay."

Billy Conner pulled his foot up as high as he could. He positioned it perfectly to come down right on Isaiah's head, stomping his skull till it crushed. Before stomping down on his victim, he stopped and gave a vile grin to Kamil with his unkempt teeth glimmering in the sun. Kamil noticed how unsteady Billy must be with one foot high in the air, and without a second thought, Kamil took what was their only shot at escaping their ill fate. Kamil raised his arms, and in a catapult motion, he shoved Billy as hard as he could. Billy went flying backward into the cotton plants.

"Come on, Isaiah! Get up! Get up!"

Isaiah scrambled to his feet in sheer panic. He was slinging dirt everywhere as he dug his nails and feet into the earth, trying to get up. The two boys ran as fast as their bodies would carry them. The cotton kept snagging their clothes as they ran. They jerked free each time, leaving rips and snags in their shirts. Nothing was going to slow them down in their mad dash to get away from what could have turned into a deadly situation. Billy got up from the shove that had left him on his back and in shock. He had not been prepared for them to fight back. He wiped the dirt from his face as his screams echoed through the field.

"Y'all fuckin' faggots! We'll be seein' each other real soon!"

Isaiah and Kamil made it back safely onto campus in a sprint that seemed like a marathon. They were so relieved to be back. Once they made it onto the campus grounds, they were able to slow to a walk. They got quite a few stares for bolting out of a cotton field with tattered and dirty attire, but they didn't care. They were safe. They followed the sidewalk around, which offered the security of a well-beaten path. It led them right to the front of their dorms.

They were both terrified and shaken as they sat down on a brick wall just outside Isaiah's building, where they could finally have a moment to catch their breath. As they sat there with their clothes dirty and torn, they both took a deep sigh of relief. Isaiah began to tear up.

In a panting, shaking voice, Isaiah said, "Kamil, we could have just been beaten or killed. I'm so scared. What if he comes to find us? What if he knows where our rooms are?"

Kamil looked at Isaiah, and in a supportive and soft but out-of-breath voice, he said, "We will be OK. Nothing is going to happen to us."

Kamil's eyes began to well with tears as he saw the pain and terror in Isaiah. As Kamil consoled Isaiah, he reached out his hand and placed it on Isaiah's. In Isaiah's panicked state, he was not worried about others and their judgments. There is nothing like a life-threatening event to jerk you right into the moment. Isaiah began to hold Kamil's hand in return as he reached out with his other hand and placed it on top of Kamil's.

"Kamil, thank you so much for saving me. If it was not for you being so brave, who knows what would have happened?"

Kamil interrupted Isaiah and looked at him with such compassion. "Isaiah, it's OK. You don't have to worry now. It's over."

In this moment, Isaiah was finally not concerned what others thought. He was solely focused on what had just happened, and he was thankful they were OK. He was thankful that he had this wonderful person in his life who had saved him in more ways than one. Isaiah had never been more in the moment or more in love than he was right that minute. As they sat there holding hands, consoling one another, there was an abrupt clearing of the throat encroaching behind them. This was not a normal grunt, like when a person has allergies. This was deliberate, so as to grab someone's attention. Kamil and Isaiah felt their hearts drop into their stomachs as they slowly turned around to reveal their fate. It was going to be an unexpected one.

45

Unexpected Fate

Isaiah and Kamil sat on that brick wall outside Isaiah's dorm still tantalized with terror. They were rattled from their possible near-death experience in that field. When they heard that abrupt throat clearing intruding on their safety corridor, it startled them to their core. All they had set out to do that day was relax and enjoy the day. For once, they did not have to overwhelm themselves by cramming for yet another exam. Isaiah and Kamil had both been so busy with school. There seemed to not be a second of the day left to relax. There had been many tears of joy, frustration, and disappointment. With the study loads that both of these guys took on, it was a wonder they had made it this far without breaking.

Isaiah and Kamil both had managed to keep impeccable GPAs. They were very intelligent and excelled at everything they did. Well, almost everything. Math was not Isaiah's strong suit, but he excelled in everything else. He was still searching for something that Kamil did not do perfectly, but he had yet to find it. Without the good graces of math on his side, it was thankful that Isaiah was striving to become a lawyer like his father instead of a mathematician. The only X that needed to be found in law was a valid point to argue and win. This was one X that Kamil noticed Isaiah had no problem finding.

All Isaiah and Kamil seemed to be able to talk about these days was finals and how close they were to graduating. They both wanted to feel like they could just breathe for a moment. They had suffocated themselves in books and studying for years. Both of them were on the path to graduate with honors, and they were so proud of one another.

At the start of this day, they had set out to have a day of much-needed relaxation, but it turned into something far different. When Isaiah and Kamil heard a low, buffalo-like, rumbling grunt invading on them, the panic was starting all over. Isaiah and Kamil looked at each other with horror. Their eyes questioned, *Could it be? Did he find us?*

Both took deep breaths as they slowly turned. They just knew in their gut that it was Billy Conner coming back to finish what he had started. However, when they turned around, it was not at all what they expected to see. It was none other than Dean Morgan, the dean of The College of Mississippi. It was a shock to see the dean standing there with his puffed-out belly and silver hair glistening in the sun. Isaiah and Kamil's immediate reaction was relief, but then the paranoia set in. Why would the dean be there grunting at their backs like a bull? When they looked up at him, his bushy brow was furrowed, and he looked less than pleased.

In a very abrupt, grumbling voice, Dean Morgan said, "Boys, we need to talk—now! Follow me."

Kamil wondered if the dean had heard what had happened to them and was there as their protector. Was the displeased look because of his deep disapproval for the foul treatment of two of his honor students? Isaiah and Kamil would learn very soon that playing the role of their protector was not Dean Morgan's forte.

Isaiah had a sneaking suspicion the dean was not there because of Billy Conner's attack. Just as they began their long walk behind the dean to his office, Isaiah suddenly remembered he had been holding hands with Kamil right there in public for all to see. Isaiah was ravished with fear. He had a lot of experience in this department, the Department of Discrimination.

As Isaiah and Kamil scuffled behind Dean Morgan, Isaiah turned to Kamil and began to whisper. His whispers screamed out with his fears.

"Kamil, he saw us holding hands. He knows. He knows."

Kamil looked at Isaiah with confidence as he assured: "There is nothing to worry about. Even if he did see us holding hands, A: he will understand that we just went through a traumatic experience and were consoling one another, and B: it's not illegal to hold hands. There is nothing he can do to us. Don't worry. Everything is going to be fine."

This did settle Isaiah's fears a bit, but they were still in there, stirring around and making him uneasy.

They finally arrived at the dean's office after what seemed to be the great migration across the Serengeti. The dean sat them down in a huffy manner. The buffalo was back; the boys were just praying he was not going to gore them. Isaiah was nudging Kamil in hopes that, after seeing the glares from the dean, he would begin to rethink his rationale on what this little chat might be about. Kamil stayed strong in his beliefs. At least, that was what his exterior led Isaiah to believe. He wanted to appear strong so Isaiah would not panic. On the inside, Kamil's shell was beginning to crack and let his apprehension seep in.

The dean walked over to his desk and sat down, leaning back in his chair. He scowled at the two boys as he began to shake his head ever so slightly back and forth, expressing his grave disappointment.

"Boys, I don't even know what to say. How could you bring this into my school? I just . . . I am just speechless."

Even though he claimed to be speechless, it seemed like he had a hell of a lot to say. "Disappointment is not even adequate enough to describe how I feel toward you two right now. You had such promise and bright futures, even despite Kamil being Muslim. Why would you throw all that away? You know this here is a Christian college, and we play by God's rules. We don't allow ourselves to fall into the pit of Satan. I was already takin' a big chance on you, Kamil, with your alternative beliefs, but this is far worse than I anticipated."

Isaiah and Kamil were beyond confused and infuriated. Kamil finally spoke up in an agitated manner. He could not handle this mental torture. "Sir, what exactly are you referring to?"

The dean looked shocked this question could even be asked. "Son, I am referrin' to the sexual improprieties that you two engaged in on *my* campus."

Isaiah and Kamil both knew what "impropriety" meant, but they could not fathom an act that they might have committed that was improper or that could ruin their futures. Surely holding hands would not be exacerbated to this extreme. Even Isaiah thought this was outrageous, and he had witnessed some pretty ridiculous stuff. Isaiah and Kamil both became very defensive, which only angered the dean.

"What do you mean by sexual improprieties?" Isaiah questioned.

Kamil backed up Isaiah by saying, "We have done nothing wrong."

The dean stood up out of his cushy chair and hollered. "That's enough! You need to respect who you are talkin' to. I will not tolerate this tyranny in my school, and I will not tolerate your horrid behavior. I don't know what Allah, or whoever, teaches, but this is against God. It is unnatural for two men to hold hands, and I will not allow it. Homosexuality is specifically listed in your handbook as sexual impropriety and as an expellable offense. That is exactly what you two are. You are both expelled and banished from this college."

Kamil's face turned red, and he began to shake as he became even further enraged, while Isaiah began to cry helplessly with desperate tears. After four years of intense work and determination, just weeks from graduating, they were now being told that they wouldn't graduate or obtain those degrees so vigorously fought for. All because they had been seen holding hands. There were couples on campus who spent their time between classes in steamy make-out sessions on display for all to see, but Isaiah and Kamil's hand holding was considered offensive and indecent, an impropriety. Isaiah and Kamil were two of the brightest students at that college, but it was all lost for nothing more than loving one another and consoling each other in the immediate aftermath of a near life-threatening tragedy.

The dean was standing with a puffed-out chest to show his dominance over these two students he had just victimized as he raised his finger, pointing forcefully.

"You have one day to have your things out of here."

Isaiah and Kamil turned to leave the dean's office, and both of them were devastated. They could not fathom what had just occurred. Discrimination had never rung so loud for either one of them, and Isaiah felt like he was going to snap.

On the walk back to their dorms, Kamil was irate, and Isaiah just cried. Isaiah knew he had to think fast, because they only had one day before they had to be out. He thought of many scenarios in which this could all play out. One of those was the frightening thought that if he was expelled, his parents would find out why. Isaiah was not ready for that; his parents just couldn't know. He began to shake with rage; then he turned around and began to run. Kamil whipped his head toward Isaiah and yelled out.

"Isaiah, where are you going?"

"This is something I have to do!" Isaiah yelled back.

Kamil nodded, but he was in a state of confusion as to what had just happened. He wondered if Isaiah had just snapped, but he let Isaiah go. He watched Isaiah run off and wondered if he had just made a grave mistake not stopping him.

Isaiah ran as fast as he could back to the dean's office with dried tears adorning his face. He ran up the staircase and into the office, slamming the door behind him, rattling the windowpanes and the walls, which were adorned with deer heads. The dean's look screamed shock and a bit of fear. He was speechless at first. The dean could see Isaiah looked devastated, and he had a slightly absent look in his eyes. Isaiah felt broken and lost. The dean began to speak in a degrading manner toward Isaiah.

"Why are you here? You shouldn't be here. I already told you to leave. Get out of my office."

In that moment, Isaiah did what he believed he had to do. He felt there was no other way.

Kamil, meanwhile, had found Rebecca so he could fill her in on what had just happened to them. It had been one insane day. First there was the nearly tragic attack from Billy Conner, and now they were both expelled just weeks before graduation. Rebecca was appalled and in shock. After venting to Rebecca, Kamil began to worry about Isaiah.

"Where did he go? What is he doing? Do you think he is OK?" Kamil said.

Rebecca shrugged her shoulders. Kamil and Rebecca got up to begin walking in the direction that Isaiah had dashed off toward. Rebecca suddenly screamed.

"There he is, over there!"

Isaiah was running back in their direction. The closer he got, the more they realized something looked off. Something was not right.

"Kamil, is he covered in blood?"

They both began to run toward Isaiah, but it felt like their legs would not move fast enough. When they got close enough, they noticed he was not only covered in blood but also appeared drained and breathless. Kamil's heart stopped.

"Isaiah, what did you do?"

Isaiah was desperately trying to speak through his panting.

"I fixed it."

Isaiah slowed down and took a deep breath.

"I fixed it for you, Kamil. It's going to be OK."

Kamil began to cry.

"What's going to be OK, Isaiah? What? What did you do? Are you OK?"

Kamil grabbed Isaiah's face.

"Talk to me, Isaiah! Talk to me! What happened? What did you do?"

Isaiah looked up at Kamil and smiled.

"I fixed it. You don't have to leave the school. It's all going to be all right."

Isaiah did not want to tell Kamil how he'd fixed it. He did not want Kamil to carry that.

Isaiah had gone into the dean's office, and when the dean began to degrade him, Isaiah snapped. He broke down and began to uncontrollably weep. All the degradation that he had received throughout his entire life had been held in him, and it all came rushing out in that moment. However, Isaiah knew what he must do. He had to suck it all back in and play this wicked game. Isaiah stood strong and took all the shaming and degradation that the dean dished out. He had figured out what the dean wanted. If Isaiah was going to get what he came for, then he had to play into the dean's narcissism and grandiose view of himself. The dean wanted someone to acknowledge his "superiority" and praise him for it. The dean wanted someone to fall at his feet to beg and plead, and Isaiah gave him just want he wanted.

"You are sick, and you need God in your life. What you two boys are displaying is disgusting."

Isaiah took a deep breath.

"You know what, sir, you are right. I need to seek help. Thank you for showing that to me. Please forgive Kamil, though. It was me who lured Kamil in. He doesn't deserve to be punished for my sickness; I do. Without me around, he can find a nice girl and become a successful young man. Maybe he can even find Christ. If he leaves this Baptist college, his chances are limited without your wise guidance. He will just go home to a Muslim household where he won't get a chance to know Jesus's love."

This all appealed to the dean. Isaiah had played to the dean's pathetic desires so that he could secure what was most important to him. Isaiah pulled the dean's strings like a marionette. The dean thought he was in control, but he was sadly mistaken.

Isaiah wanted nothing more than to finally save Kamil, as Kamil had done for him many times. There were times that Kamil had saved Isaiah just by being there, and he didn't even know it. Isaiah was willing to do what he had to so that he could help his true love. After the dean got what he desired, Isaiah was able to negotiate with him that he would leave the campus without a fuss and never return if Kamil could just graduate. After the dean's ego had been stroked, he agreed to Isaiah's terms. No matter all that had happened, in this moment, Isaiah felt victorious.

After Isaiah negotiated the biggest deal of his life, he had been so elated to tell Kamil the news that he'd run all the way down the stairs back out of the building that housed the dean's office. Upon exiting the building, Isaiah had tripped and fallen down the three concrete stairs that led to the sidewalk. He had scraped himself up and sustained a gushing bloody nose, but he jumped up and continued to run. His news was far more important to him than a little blood. This all played into his dramatic entrance upon his arrival back to Kamil and Rebecca.

Kamil and Rebecca's thoughts had ventured to a very dark place when they saw Isaiah covered in blood, but Isaiah immediately relieved them of their darkest fears. Who could blame them for those thoughts creeping in? However, deep down, they knew Isaiah was too strong to falter to that kind of evil. Isaiah told them all about his nasty spill outside the building. However, he would never tell them what he had done for Kamil to be able to stay and graduate. Although Isaiah tried to keep it a secret, Kamil had a sneaking suspicion of Isaiah's sacrifice, and he was so grateful. Kamil looked at Isaiah with appreciation and affection in his eyes.

"I love you so much, Isaiah."

Isaiah's face was overtaken by an undeniable smile that exuded love.

Before this day, Kamil had believed that he could never love anyone more than he already did. He was proven wrong. Their entire day had been one unexpected occurrence after another. This day, Isaiah and Kamil's fate had shifted, and it, too, was unexpected.

46

This Child of Mine

The horrible day that left Isaiah and Kamil attacked and expelled seemed to never end, although, thanks to Isaiah's tenacity, Kamil would be allowed to stay at The College of Mississippi to graduate. It was still one hurdle after the next. They were both exhausted and longed for the second their heads could hit the pillow and it would all be over. The true dream was for those pillows to be touching the same bed, letting them lie next to one another and feel comfort and love throughout the night. However, for today, both of these dreams were not a reality.

Isaiah still had a daunting task ahead of him, a task he had been dreading most of his life: talking to his parents and revealing the truth of it all. He must reveal his expulsion from school, which would be terrifying on its own, but with this reveal would come the questions as to why he was expelled. These pending questions felt like a ton weighing on Isaiah's chest and mind, and they were just piled on top of the day he had already endured.

Isaiah was proud of his grand performance in the dean's office. He had held strong when all he wanted to do was break down and lash out at the horrid injustice. Isaiah was proud he held this kind of strength and selflessness to help the one he loved. His parents had raised him well. However, the victory that had left him feeling empowered quickly began to fade as the nasty reality set in.

Isaiah's mind began to spin at the hideous truth. He was being forced to leave college in a bout of pure, raging prejudice. The path and future Isaiah had envisioned for himself was being shredded, and so was his tender heart. He was being forced to lose four years of hard work, sweat, and tears—and for what?

Other students could walk around flaunting their love, taking for granted every step of the way that they could hold hands without the lynch mob chasing behind them. People expressing their love did not upset Isaiah and Kamil; they just wanted the same right. It was unfathomable how someone could lash out in such a discriminatory and hateful manner toward love while claiming to bathe in the love of Christ. The irony seemed to not be comprehended by those lashing out.

The rules dictated to Isaiah and Kamil were that they could turn to one another in tragedy, but at a "safe" distance, so that others would not be affected and disturbed. They learned that a top rule was, no matter what tragedies they were facing, they dared not touch, because it made others uncomfortable. This sounded as insane as making a rule that everyone must stop eating ketchup because you don't like it and it grosses you out. This was the type of ignorance and prejudice that Isaiah and Kamil had to fight against in order to simply live their lives in peace and happiness.

This was a razor blade of a pill to swallow for Isaiah, slashing him all the way down. Isaiah just could not fathom the fact that he was being forcibly expelled from college. Isaiah and Kamil's love was banished and lynched in the eyes of society, sentenced to dangle there and struggle until the execution was carried out. There was no cheering section rooting for Isaiah and Kamil's love to succeed.

This discrimination and hatred were all becoming very apparent to Isaiah, and he no longer felt victorious. He just couldn't help but think: Where was someone to fight for him and all those like him who were being degraded, discriminated against, and prohibited from living happily ever after?

It was hard for Isaiah to move past these feelings of rage until his terror set in. It came to him like a freight train plowing through his chest: he would now need to call his parents and tell them that he had been kicked out of school, and they would want to know why. Billy Conner suddenly felt like a walk in the park on a nice spring day, watching butterflies flutter by. Isaiah was terrified of what his parents might say, but he knew what he must do.

Isaiah picked up the phone to dial, his hands shaking. He wanted to just hang up the phone, pack his things, and run away. As Isaiah pressed the last number, he raised the phone to his ear, hoping to hear the normally numbing sounds of repetitive beeping. The busy signal, usually annoying, would have been welcome. However, after only a few short rings, someone answered the phone. It was a familiar voice, but not either of his parents. Mama Dove had answered the phone, and it was a pleasant surprise. Isaiah felt some of his fear melt away at the sound of Mama Dove's voice. He was not sure why he felt relief, but deep down, it might have been because he thought Mama Dove would be more understanding and supportive since she always had been.

When Mama Dove answered the phone, her gentle tone sang to Isaiah's ears. "Isaiah, is that you?"

Isaiah tried to squeeze out a response, but it was hard to get it past the lump in his throat.

"Yes, ma'am, it's me," he said meekly.

"Well, isn't this a nice surprise. When is my favorite grandson goin' to come see me? I miss you. Are you coming this Sunday to dinner?"

297

Mama Dove always called Isaiah her favorite grandson, which was true, but he was also her only grandson. She loved that joke, but Isaiah could not laugh today or answer her questions. He only had one thing on his mind.

"Mama Dove, I need to talk to you, and I need you to not tell anyone, not even my parents."

"Well, what is it, son? You can talk to Mama Dove."

Isaiah hesitated and stuttered a bit.

"I need you to promise me you won't tell a soul."

"All right, Isaiah, I promise, but you have to promise me that you will tell them if it is somethin' they need to know."

Isaiah hesitantly agreed and took a large gulp, trying to add some type of moisture to his throat. After his failed attempt, Isaiah just blurted out his small confession. The larger and more frightening confession still needed a bit of prepping time for Isaiah to not pass out.

"I was expelled from school today."

"Why, what happened?"

He could hear in her voice that she believed her grandson surely could not have deserved this type of punishment. He was, in fact, her favorite. Isaiah began to try and ensure his safety before continuing with his terrifying confession.

"You can't get mad, OK?"

"Isaiah, I can't promise to not be disappointed, but I will love you no matter what. You're my only grandson, and I can't trade ya in now, can I?"

"No, ma'am."

Isaiah mentally chanted a prayer that she meant what she had just professed, and he took a deep breath.

"Mama Dove, I was expelled for . . . well, they said it was because . . .You remember Kamil, right?"

"Yes, Isaiah, I do remember him well. He seems like a real sweet boy. He didn't do anything to hurt you or get you in trouble, did he?"

Isaiah appreciated all his grandmother's supportive words, but he just wanted to get this beast out of its prison. For far too long, it had been tearing at him to be free. He was ready to release it.

"No, ma'am, he didn't do anything. He and I . . . I feel like I . . . He is my . . . I got expelled for holding his hand."

After Isaiah had finally barely squeaked the words out of his throat, the pause on the other end of the line felt like an eternity. Isaiah began to panic.

"Mama Dove, are you there? Did you hear me?"

Mama Dove said in a very calm tone, "Isaiah, this is somethin' you need to tell your momma and daddy. You come on home now, and we can talk about this some more. I love you now, ya hear?"

Isaiah felt relief for having told his grandmother. He felt on top of the world until he realized he now had to go home and face the daunting music of his reality.

Isaiah walked to his car, got in, and headed to his house. The drive was all a blur due to his intense anxiety. He was imagining all the possible outcomes. He was remembering the stories his parents had always told him about their excitement and happiness when he was born and how they'd praised his arrival. Would that excitement still exist?

He drove around for a while, prolonging the inevitable as much as he could stand. He knew what awaited him, and he was scared to death. This would forever change his relationship with his parents, for better or for worse. If all his dreams came true, and they accepted him for who he was, then their relationship would blossom. They could have a chance to get to know all of his beauty, not this closed-off son he had been forced to project. Isaiah felt fear to his core that he would be disowned by his parents like others he had heard about. All he wanted was his parents' love and approval. The thought of disappointing them was almost too much to bear. It was time to let the curtain of shame drop to reveal himself. What a terrifying and liberating experience this would be.

The drive to his house was agonizing. By the time Isaiah decided to quit driving around and pull into the driveway, he was almost relieved to be there just so he could get it over with. He was ready to know the outcome instead of this constant broken record that kept replaying the worse possible scenarios over and over.

Isaiah stepped very slowly and carefully out of his car. He shut his car door with caution to ensure the noise did not alert the world that he was there. He felt like he was outside of his body, floating while watching himself tremble with sheer angst. The feelings that precede coming out are not for the faint of heart. Thankfully, Isaiah was a strapping young fellow whose heart was in fine shape besides being broken by all the unjust treatment.

Isaiah stopped shortly before walking in the front door. He held his breath, said a little prayer, then began to feel dizzy, like he might pass out. He leaned forward, grabbing the doorframe for support. Just as he leaned into the doorframe, bracing his shaky body, Sarah opened the door.

"Isaiah, is that you?"

Isaiah remained very still and quiet for just a moment longer. He was allowing his mother time to cherish the last few moments before he shattered everything they'd believed about him his entire life and the life they had pictured that he would lead. Isaiah took a deep breath, preparing himself for what was to come.

"Yes, ma'am, it is."

Sarah responded with a smile:

"I thought that smelled like you. You always smell so good. Your dad just ran out to the store, and you just missed your grandmother. She was in a hurry to get to her Wednesday night church group, but she said she will see you Sunday. Your dad will be excited to see you when he gets back."

Sarah continued to chat as she and Isaiah walked toward the living room. As Sarah was talking, she began to notice that something was off balance. She could sense something was very wrong with her baby.

"Isaiah, why are you being so quiet and breathing so heavily? Is something the matter? You know you can always talk to me. I am here for you no matter what. Sit down, baby. Let's talk."

Isaiah sat down on the couch across from his mother. All he could think was that he desperately wanted to believe his mother's words of support, but in this case, he held immense fear that she would not stick by him after finding out his dark secret. Twenty-two years was a hell of a long time to hold a secret that had chewed at his insides, attempting escape.

"Momma, I have some really bad news. I don't know if you will still love me after I tell you. It is really, really bad."

Sarah's face showed a look of fear and concern. She wanted to know what had happened to her little boy. Sarah tried to reassure Isaiah of her unconditional love.

"Isaiah, nothing you could do would ever make me stop loving you. Please just tell me. You are worrying me."

Sarah was unable to see that Isaiah was pale and had the look of someone about ready to vomit. Either that, or pass out. Even though she could not see it, she could feel her baby's angst.

Isaiah took a long and deep breath, although that did little to slow down his heart rate. He knew it could possibly be the last breath that he would take while having a relationship with his momma. Isaiah's eyes filled with tears when he began to speak his truth.

"Momma, I was expelled from school."

Sarah gave a relieved sigh.

"Well, Isaiah, that is not that horrible. Relax, son. We can figure this out."

Isaiah shook his head.

"Momma, that's not all. I was expelled for touching Kamil's hand."

Sarah's face expressed a deep level of confusion at what Isaiah was trying to say. The fact that he'd touched someone's hand and been expelled made no sense

"Isaiah, what are you trying to say?"

Isaiah sat with his head buried in his hands, wallowing in dread and disgrace as he uttered, "I am . . . I am with Kamil. I . . . I . . . I am . . . I am gay."

Sarah took a deep breath, trying to fathom what her son had just revealed to her. Her mind raced with many different questions. *Has he always been like this? Why has he not told me before? What will his father say? How will people treat him? Will people treat him differently? Will they be mean to him? How can I protect him from this? Will he go to hell? He is an amazing person. Surely he would not go to hell. Was he born this way? If so, why would God make him this way just to send him to hell? Nothing makes sense. What do I say to him? Is he OK? Will he be happy?*

Sarah was not sure what words should come out of her mouth. There was no training course for this, so she just spoke from her heart. It was the best she could do to break this silence that was killing her boy.

"OK . . . OK . . . OK . . ."

Sarah just kept repeating herself as she took some deep breaths. Each time she repeated the word "OK," it was in a different tone, as if her mind was trying to work through it all in one-word segments. Sarah took another deep breath and placed her hands over her face with her middle fingers buried in the corners where her nose and eyes met. Isaiah looked up at her and saw the sheer stress on her face. She was at a loss for words, but then she began to find them. She found them for her son, whom she did not want to suffer anymore.

"OK. This is OK. You're OK. We're OK."

Sarah took another moment to process, and Isaiah sat there, petrified. Sarah suddenly looked like she'd come to an agreement with the battling voices in her head.

"You know what? All that matters is that you're alive and well and that you are happy. I love you, son, and I want you to be happy. I am scared for you, because I don't want anyone to ever treat you differently or be ugly to you, but I believe you are the same son I gave birth to and raised. I am proud of you for who you are, and I will work through the rest."

Sarah had a lot to work through. She, too, had always been taught in church and by society that being gay was a sin and wrong, but this was her son. This was now personal. It wasn't about some kid she saw on TV or read about in the newspaper. This was her son, whom she loved unconditionally. She knew her son was an amazing person, and she believed that this was not anything novel just because he'd revealed a secret to her. This was a secret he had been holding his entire life, which meant he had been the same person his entire life, the same person who stood before her now. She began to see this, and through that revelation, she began to see that maybe, just maybe, all that she had been fed and taught was misinformation and lies. She knew the one thing that rang out to her from all of her teachings in church was that love and kindness were number one. Sarah believed this to her core, and she sat back with a bit of peaceful silence coming over her. She knew she still had immense amounts to work through, but she thought to herself, *All I know is, I will always love this child of mine.*

Isaiah was moved and elated by his mother's words of love and support. He began to cry tears of relief and joy. He was relieved to finally have this colossal secret out to his mother. He was one giant step closer to freedom. Isaiah was so incredibly thankful for how his mother had reacted. So many parents react with such hatred toward their children . . . *their own children.* They scream at them, call them hateful names, shame them, and shun them from their own home and from receiving that motherly and fatherly love ever again. What a horrific travesty it must be for those who are shunned and have hatred spewed by their own parents, the people who are supposed to love them unconditionally in a world full of conditions.

Through this experience, Isaiah realized that he wanted nothing more than to go help those who needed someone to tell them they were normal, important, and cherished, no matter what had been falsely and cruelly conveyed to them. Just as Isaiah was reveling in his thankfulness and sheer happiness, it dawned on him that he still must tell his father. This put that lump right back in his throat and knots back in his stomach. Now he must sit and wait for his father's return. He sat quietly in purgatory, awaiting his sentence. Would it be heaven, as it was with his mother, or hell?

47

His Silence Speaks Volumes

As Isaiah sat there quietly on the couch, contemplating his fate, he could not help but fear what his father's reaction might be. He could welcome Isaiah with open arms, or he could shun him, leaving Isaiah profoundly damaged. This type of damage is not gentle and short-lived like skinning your knee. It stings and lingers long after the initial strike. There is no bandage that will patch up this wound.

Isaiah knew that, when reacting to this type of news, there was little to no middle ground. In most circumstances, one is either for their child and their child's deserved happiness or against. It's that simple. If there is a "neutral" response, choosing to not comment one way or the other, that means the silence is left for interpretation, and the child hears, "I do not accept you or wish for your happiness in life. You have disappointed me so drastically that I cannot speak." This was one scenario among many that Isaiah had considered.

No matter Joseph's response, if there were no acceptance and love, then Isaiah would be left aching with an unimaginable pain only a parent's rejection could bring. This pain strips the feelings of love, acceptance, security, self-worth, and self-esteem right from the heart. Though this pain may never be spoken of or shown to the outside world, it is in there, casting darkness while rendering the victim helpless to the constant questions berating their existence. *Am I good enough? Do I deserve love?*

Over the years, Joseph had become sterner and less understanding. He was slowly becoming, as many say, "set in his ways." Isaiah had noticed that it had become a fallacy that was just accepted as a fact that behavior could not be helped or changed. The only time this belief might hold some relevance is if dementia is involved, but most of the time when this excuse is used, there is no dementia involved— only denial. Joseph was on this path of becoming a set-in-his-ways person, but he had a strong soldier to battle against. Isaiah would not just roll over and take his father's hostile transformation.

Isaiah often wondered how his father had become this way. When Isaiah was a boy, Joseph had been a lively and softhearted fellow always up for learning and experiencing the world. Isaiah wondered whether maybe Joseph's hardening and the isolation of his emotions and mind were the result of all the heartache he had suffered and whether, because of these experiences, he had shut himself off from outside influences. Maybe Joseph held trepidation of letting it all in for fear of being hurt, or maybe he arrogantly believed that, since he had lived so much of life, no one else could add anything to his knowledge or views.

Isaiah knew his father's actions were a choice, and he was determined to connect with his father once again. Maybe sharing this deep secret with Joseph would reconnect them to the place they once had been when Isaiah was just a boy. He missed that relationship with his dad desperately. They had both been closed off to one another for quite some time. Reconnecting was a dream that his fingertips were desperately reaching out for.

Isaiah was, in fact, being banished from college for being none other than himself. He was reminded of the stories his father once told him of Ole Dixie, and Isaiah could not help but think of how uncannily similar these two acts of discrimination and prejudice were. They were two humans both rammed by prejudice and ostracized for being born into those lives and bodies. When Isaiah realized the similarity of this mutual experience, it led him to a sense of comfort. His father surely would see this parallel they shared. If his father could not see these similarities, then he truly had shut himself off from the world and reality.

Isaiah felt grand hopes and provoking fears as he continued to wait in limbo. His mother could hear him constantly rustling around in a nervous manner. She was painfully learning that she could not protect her son from everything. He was an adult now, and she could not protect him from things as well as she could when he was just a boy.

Isaiah suddenly felt his angst pushing up and projecting itself out of his body through his mouth. He ran to the bathroom as quickly as possible, barely making it to the toilet in time. He threw his head down, spewing his angst all over the toilet bowl. He hoped this would relieve some of the tension in his body, but all it did was add burning flames that were now scorching his esophagus. Isaiah stood to wash his hands and splashed some cold water on his pallid gray face. He stared at himself in the mirror, questioning whether he had the bravery to go through with this or whether he should just run.

Just as Isaiah was drying his hands and contemplating his actions, he heard the front door open. Joseph was home.

"I'm back. Is Isaiah here? I saw his car in the drive."

Joseph walked into the kitchen, where Sarah was preparing dinner. He handed Sarah a bag.

"Here are the rolls you needed for dinner."

Sarah turned to Joseph to thank him, and Joseph saw in her eyes that something had happened.

"What is it, Sarah? What happened?"

Sarah turned her head toward Joseph, swallowed hard, and said, "Isaiah needs to speak with you, honey. Just remember, he is our son, whom we have raised and love unconditionally."

Joseph shook his head rapidly back and forth in confusion. He turned and began to call for Isaiah.

"Isaiah, I heard you need to speak with me?"

Isaiah began to cry there in the bathroom mirror, but he knew he must pull himself together. It was showtime. For better or worse, he would be free of this secret that had plagued him for decades. He would have a little sweet taste of freedom, but he hoped he would not be served with the death of his and his father's relationship as a side dish. He didn't think he could handle losing that love. Isaiah took the towel and wiped the tears from his eyes, but he could not wipe away the pallid look of fear. He said a little prayer before heading out of the bathroom to meet his fate.

As Isaiah exited the bathroom and turned the corner into the living room, he saw his father there, sitting in the chair that was permanently claimed as his. Joseph looked up at Isaiah, confused, but he did not want to let that show. He quickly gathered himself and, in a stern voice, asked Isaiah to sit down. He couldn't let the confusion linger and risk the chance of looking what he considered weak. Isaiah's knees were shaking and threatening to collapse as he went to sit down.

Joseph looked at Isaiah and said, "I hear from your mother that we have something to talk about."

"Yes, sir," Isaiah squeaked.

"Why don't you start talking, son?" Joseph questioned in a more demanding tone.

Isaiah nodded his head, but he seemed to forget to stop. His head was faintly bobbing, and his hand found its way to his chest. He could feel his heart pounding through his chest. As Isaiah sat there holding his heart in his chest and nodding his head, he focused his eyes on his father's shoes and began to unveil his truth.

"Something happened at school, and I don't think you are going to be happy, but please promise me that you won't hate me."

"Isaiah, what is it?"

Isaiah knew it was now or never. At this point, he just wanted it to be over as he began saying the most terrifying sentences of his life.

"I've been asked to leave college."

Joseph shook his head in aggravation at what he believed to surely be the mistreatment of his son by CM.

"Why on earth were you asked to leave college? Do I need to go down there? I can draw up a letter with intent of our actions for your mistreatment if they do not reverse their decision. What was their reasoning?"

Isaiah knew the time had come. He grabbed both knees and tensely strummed his fingers on one knee. He looked like he was trying to hold himself up from tumbling forward off the couch headfirst. Isaiah took a deep breath and began to spill it all.

"Dad, I am going to tell you, but you are going to be disappointed."

Joseph nodded, awaiting Isaiah's response.

Isaiah nervously uttered, "I was expelled for . . . well, the dean saw me touching Kamil's hand, and that's why I was expelled."

Joseph's confusion and his fear could not be hidden now. "In what way were you touching his hand, Isaiah?"

Isaiah briefly shut his eyes and then slowly opened them, directing them back down toward the ground. He could not dare look his father in the eyes. He was too ashamed as he revealed his truth. ·

"I was holding it. I was holding Kamil's hand. He is my . . . my boyfriend. It is not Kamil's fault. I have always felt this way my entire life."

Joseph was in shock.

"Isaiah, this better be a joke. Is this a little phase you are going through?"

Isaiah shook his head and, in a glimmer of pride, looked his father in the eye.

"No, Dad, this is me. This is part of me, part of who I am, and it always has been."

Joseph could not handle what he was being told. It ruined the life he had planned for his son. He never once took into concern that the life he had planned for Isaiah was not the life Isaiah had been born to lead, but that was no matter to Joseph. He couldn't see past his own desires, insecurities, and delusions. Joseph, like a sullen child, immediately turned to stone. He refused to speak to Isaiah any further and left Isaiah hurting. Joseph had cast Isaiah out into the wintery weather projecting from his heart and actions. Isaiah attempted to speak to him, but Joseph was cold and shut off.

"Dad, Dad, please talk to me."

His dad was gone, and Isaiah was left with this frigid figure staring through him with his cold, dark eyes. The conversation was over. The relationship was over. Joseph was shut down. Isaiah tried to talk to him and reason, but Joseph reached for the TV remote and drowned Isaiah out.

After Joseph's actions, Isaiah felt like his life vest had just been ripped off of him, leaving him treading water in an unfamiliar sea. Where would he go? What would he do? He could not flee and escape to college; nor could he stay there with this empty shell of a father. Isaiah did know one thing for sure. He needed to get out of that house.

Isaiah jumped up to escape. He went to hug his mother, holding in the flood of tears that were slowly cracking that levee. He told her that he had to get out of there, and she knew what must have happened. It was what she'd feared in her heart for her son. Isaiah fled the house, running out to his car.

Once he was safely in his car, he just drove. Isaiah drove till he found an empty park close by, and he parked his car. Isaiah needed to get it all out. He needed to just scream and cry with no one around. He was devastated, and he felt like he would never recover from this pain.

After sitting in the park for about an hour, Isaiah decided it was time to pull himself together and figure out where he would go. He pulled out of the park and continued to drive for a while longer, this time in a daze of disbelief, until he found himself at his grandmother's. She'd had a feeling he would be coming, so she had skipped church to cook him his favorite meal, chicken 'n' dumplings. When he was upset as a child, she had always made it for him. As he sat at her kitchen table with his eyes blurred from all the tears, he ate his food, and it comforted his soul. It tasted like love. It was the best meal he had ever had.

Isaiah continued to stay with Mama Dove while he sorted things out. He felt welcome there, a far cry from what he felt when he was near his father. Isaiah took this time at his grandmother's to think about his future. He knew he had to figure out his next step. What would he do now? He was lost for a path and direction, but Mama Dove kept assuring him that one would present itself if he allowed it. He just needed to be patient and live for each day. That was a difficult concept for Isaiah right now since his life had been on this sure-paved path, and now everything was disorganized beyond recognition.

To Isaiah, the continued silence of his father sounded like pure chaos. How can you dust off and move forward with the screaming of your parent's disappointment and disdain echoing in your head repeatedly on a bullhorn? Even though Joseph refused to speak, his silence spoke volumes.

48

Clearing the Brush

Isaiah was dealing with the devastation of his father's silence every day, but he knew he had to pick up the pieces of his life and move forward. He needed to sniff out his path again to feel sane, but it would be tremendously difficult starting from scratch even when he once felt he knew exactly where he was headed. That is a fallacy that we all succumb to: believing that we know exactly what our path and future holds. Isaiah often went to his mother, Mama Dove, and Kamil for counsel. They were supportive, but they, too, could not offer him much direction. They could, however, offer him support and love when he most needed it.

Isaiah still held a great passion for law, and he had such a drive to pursue that field. He wanted to help battle the injustices in the world like Joseph had. Becoming a lawyer had once been a smooth and direct path, but now it was all jumbled and full of obstacles. Isaiah was pulling himself together one day at a time. He was gaining strength to fight, and through this strength, he decided that these obstacles were not going to hold him back any longer. He would conquer the discrimination chasing after him, trying to tear him down. With this newfound confidence under Isaiah's belt, all he needed was a lead in the right direction—just a hint that could get him on his way.

One Friday afternoon, Sarah was struck with an idea that she believed could help her son find his track. She wanted desperately to do more, but he was an adult now. Sarah picked up the phone to call Isaiah with her thoughts on a possible solution to his dilemma of stagnancy. His momma had the great idea of Isaiah searching for a job at a law firm and then reenlisting in college—but at a new college, not one with hate and discrimination tainting the veins of the laws and people that ran it.

Although Isaiah thought the job was a great idea, he was not sold on attending a new college just yet. He was still very bitter from the hatred and discrimination he had been shown, but he was excited to have a slight push in a direction that brought promise and hope to his dreams. When Sarah suggested pursuing a job at a law firm to Isaiah, he had a light that flickered inside of him. He knew exactly where he was going to go, even if it meant facing some demons of his past.

Mayor Higginbotham, Austin's dad, had stepped down from his duties as mayor. He felt he could no longer ignore what was left of his family. He needed to be more present, especially while he and his wife grieved. His wife saw this and wanted the one person there for her who could understand what she was going through, so she did not divorce him. Their son's death was a true tragedy, but through that came growth and the chance to change himself and help change the community and possibly the country. Mayor Higginbotham embraced that opportunity for growth and change. He embraced not feeling sorry for himself and not letting his son's death be in vain.

Mayor Higginbotham had opened his own law firm, and he was still actively pushing hard to have Austin's Law adopted to protect all those being bullied and wading through the dark muck of hatred. In the process of advocating for Austin's Law, the former mayor took on pro bono cases here and there to help fight for those who were bullied and treated unequally. He took on those cases along with taking for-pay clientele. He needed these clients to keep his doors open so he could continue to fight the good fight, which, for him, was Austin's Law.

When Mayor Higginbotham began advocating Austin's Law, it was a great shock and surprise to him that he quickly found himself battling the people he had shared a church with for years, including one certain pastor: Pastor Henryson. The pastor was, of course, the opposition's mouthpiece against Austin's Law becoming an actual law. The former mayor could not believe that these former friends were now his biggest foes. They turned their backs on him, his wife, and his son's memory.

The former mayor was confused and deeply saddened at how someone would fight against Austin's Law, all because they did not want children to feel that it was OK to be themselves—or, as opponents put it, heathens, sinners, and gays. Mayor Higginbotham tried time and again to show them that this proposed law would protect all children from hatred and bullying, but they simply could not see past their own agenda, ignorance, and insecurities. This helped the former mayor see just what his son had battled against, and it made his heart break. It also made him realize that his work was far greater than he had ever imagined, and he quickly learned he would need help.

It was not as easy as one would think to acquire help for this kind of battle. This was still small-town Mississippi. The church ran most of these types of towns' every breath, and seeing as the church was his biggest opponent, he was having trouble finding the help he so desperately needed. Mayor Higginbotham was a Christian man himself, but he found himself having to relearn what it meant to be Christian. He learned that what mattered above all was love and treating all humans equally, with dignity and respect. He wanted to bring this to the world, but first he found himself praying for God to send him some much-deserved and needed help for his plight to protect innocent children and show them that they did matter—a small gesture that his own son had been denied.

Isaiah had caught wind of the former mayor's new law firm, and he thought this would be the perfect place to get experience working in the legal field, if the former mayor permitted him. Isaiah's original plan had been to work with his father over the summer after his graduation and before he began law school. That was no longer a possibility, especially since there would be no graduation and his father wouldn't even look at him, but Isaiah was excited and nervous about this new possibility.

The former mayor and Isaiah had not seen each other since Austin's horrid death. Isaiah feared that Mayor Higginbotham might hold him in part responsible—he still felt guilty and as if Austin's suicide had been in part his fault. At times, he believed that if he had not been so homophobic toward himself, he could have reached out to help Austin, and Austin would still be alive. Since Isaiah was now dancing with the thought of walking into the former mayor's office, this guilt all weighed on Isaiah much more heavily than it had in years. He had to prepare himself to walk into that office and brave whatever might come his way. Luckily, he had a few days to prepare himself. It was going to be one tough weekend.

Monday came all too quick for Isaiah's liking. He was standing in his room, adjusting his tie in the mirror, wondering what he was going to say to the former mayor and how Mr. Higginbotham was going to respond. He wished Kamil could be there with him to talk him through it, but Kamil was taking his finals and preparing to graduate. Isaiah was so proud of him, but that did not change the fact that he wished he were there.

As Isaiah was preparing to leave, Mama Dove had some inspirational words for him.

"You go out there and get what's yours, ya hear?"

Isaiah knew exactly what she meant. He knew she did not mean to literally go take what was his but rather to stand strong and forge the life that he desired, earn the respect that he deserved, and find his pride and dignity once again. It was time for him to reclaim them. He headed out the door, turned, and smiled at Mama Dove. He was so very thankful to have her love and support pushing him to succeed, like a warm wind at his back.

Isaiah's drive to the law office had been a tense one. He was now sitting in front of the law offices of Joe Higginbotham. Isaiah had not realized how difficult this was going to be until he pulled up. He was not just facing the father of his best friend whom he had not saved but also facing his old demons, which had made him hate himself and shun a friend in desperate need. He sat there in his car, fighting back the tears, while he gave himself a pep talk.

Isaiah knew the former mayor as a man who had, much like his own father, shunned his child in his greatest time of vulnerability. Isaiah feared that the former mayor would now turn and do the same to him, but he knew that he must try. Even though it might not seem like what Isaiah wanted, God knew what was best and gave him nudges toward his purpose. This was what his parents and Mama Dove had always taught him: that you must trust your instinct and that little voice inside, because those instincts were one of God's many tools used to guide us.

As he was walking up to the door, Isaiah treaded lightly on the gravel so as not to disturb what could be a sleeping giant inside that building. When he reached the door, he was not sure if he should knock or just turn the knob and walk in. If this were a normal office building, he knew the policy would be to just walk in to find a receptionist, but this was no normal center-block building. It was a cute and quaint older house that had been repurposed into an office. He loved the feel it gave, but it made him hesitant to just open the door. He would never just walk up to someone's home and walk in.

He stood there at the door with his hand on the doorknob, pushing for some courage. He had begun to use this slight dilemma as a procrastination tactic to prolong his encounter, but his pause was cut short when the knob began to turn. Isaiah quickly looked down at the knob and then up at the door. What he saw startled him. There in the door's window stood Mayor Higginbotham with all his stature. Isaiah swallowed hard as the door swung open, but as it did, he felt the energy shift drastically. Mayor Higginbotham looked at Isaiah with tears in his eyes. In a bout of nerves, Isaiah just blurted out:

"I came about a job, if you can help me."

The former mayor did not speak, but he reached out, grabbed Isaiah, and pulled him close in a deep embrace. In the warmth of this embrace, Isaiah began to tear up. He could feel the sorrow, guilt, and pain flowing between their two bodies and souls. Neither had been able to forgive himself, and being brought back together was allowing their bodies to release a bit of that guilt and sadness for the loss of the one they'd loved. This embrace brought healing through one another. Isaiah could feel that, in this moment, they both let go of some of that blame they had held within themselves for all those years. The former mayor grabbed Isaiah by his shoulders, and pushed him back lightly, just to where he could see Isaiah's face.

With tears in his eyes, the former mayor said, "You are what I have been praying for. Thank you. Thank you."

That day was the beginning of the former mayor and Isaiah's new relationship. Mayor Higginbotham and Isaiah quickly forged a close relationship working alongside each other day in and out. He even asked Isaiah to simply refer to him as "Joe." Isaiah had trouble with this because he was, in fact, southern. Those rules and teachings of respect don't fly out the window that fast, so it was "Mr. Joe" for Isaiah.

Mr. Joe became Isaiah's mentor, and it was immensely helpful having him there in his own father's absence. By no means would Mr. Joe ever compare to having Isaiah's own father there for him, but it did help having that one extra person in his corner to guide him. Mr. Joe had made a great new impression on Isaiah, and he had even brought Kamil on to work that summer. They needed the extra help. Kamil was able to get that experience under his belt before law school, and he was able to be near Isaiah while he did so. This scored a whole lot of points for Mr. Joe in Isaiah's book. He loved being able to be by Kamil's side every day, working toward something they were all so passionate about. Isaiah's life was back on track, and he was headed down the road, clearing brush out of his way.

49

All the Children of the World

That summer working with Mr. Joe and Kamil at the law firm was amazing for Isaiah. They were able to help so many, and this made them all so proud. Due to the extremely high level of discrimination and the society's refusal to talk about such subject matter or utter the word "gay," most times, they had to find their victories in other places. One of those victories was the simple fact that some of their clients felt good just having someone there for them and someone to listen. Feeling like you have no one in your corner can be a very dark and scary place that leaves you feeling like you're the only one who cares about you, and if no one else cares about you, then why should you? These are very dangerous thoughts; they can lead to exactly what was being fought against: Austin's fate. You begin to feel the deep ache of unimportance, like you don't matter. This was where Mr. Joe, Isaiah, and Kamil found most of their victories, letting these individuals know they did matter and that they were not alone in struggling with the archaic fallacies that said they were devious, sick, and evil.

All three of these men brought a different level of experience and different qualities to the law office. Each of them had walked his own path, which had led them here and given them all different areas of expertise and skill sets to help guide those who needed direction or a friend. All three loved to feel like they were helping a community in which this kind of help was unheard of and frowned upon. They were doing what many called "the devil's work," but ironically, it was God who was leading them.

Even with all the setbacks and futile resistance from the community, Austin's Law made some strides that summer. It now had three hands on deck, but it was not making strides in the originally intended way. The original purpose of Austin's Law had been to have it passed so that all kids would be protected from bullying, no matter their circumstances, but it was shifting. That original plan of it becoming an actual law was making no advances, so it evolved, like all things are designed to do. Survival of the fittest was in play, and Mr. Joe knew it must evolve or let Austin's legacy die out.

Austin's Law, like the law office, was becoming more of a foundation and a safe harbor. The possibility of it becoming an actual law anytime soon was miniscule, so Mr. Joe shifted his focus. Even if the law were passed, these teens and kids still needed someone to confide in and to assure them of their worth. Mr. Joe realized that if he paddled with the current that God was providing him, he could strive for a larger venue and much larger audience. He would not be localized to just the one town as he was when trying to pass a local law. He now was beginning to realize that he could possibly reach further if he started a nonprofit that reached out to these struggling people.

Some days at the firm were excruciatingly tough that summer. Some of their clients came in with stories beyond heart wrenching; actually, most of them did. The stories ranged from parents disowning their children to extreme levels of abuse, thoughts of suicide, and prayers for death. Before that summer, the law office had been just that—a law office—but somewhere along the way, it had morphed into more.

It was becoming an unofficial teen-counseling center and a strong advocate for LGBT rights in the least likely place you would dream of finding one, the heart of small-town Mississippi. But this was exactly what this town needed. Whether they were LGBT or not, all these bullied and abused teens needed a voice. They needed to feel like they mattered to someone. They needed to know that they were not alone in this daunting and confusing time. They needed to hear and feel that they were normal.

No one can define what it is to be a normal human being. It changes by culture, community, and region. It even changes throughout social groups, but there is a need for so many to feel "normal." Could normal be just a feeling? Isaiah believed that what may be defined as normal was the feeling within that you fit in somewhere and that you had people around you who lifted you up and made you feel like you mattered. He felt there was no set, prescribed guidelines. Normal was to want to be accepted and loved no matter what society or social group you found yourself in. Wasn't that just being human? That was how Isaiah, Kamil, and Mr. Joe wanted to make people feel: like they were not alone—like they were normal.

Isaiah's silence and refusal to speak about being gay was still very piercing; mum was the word. He felt like a muzzled dog, spitting and spewing to have the freedom to simply speak his truth. This religion-based community was a hard nut to crack, and Isaiah still had the stinging memories of how it had felt growing up all alone in this community that sprayed bigotries at people like him daily.

The bigotry was not intentional acts for everyone, but it was deeply ingrained in the societal fabric. Most were not aware of their prejudices or the acts of discrimination that they oozed. Then there were people, like Pastor Henryson, who were very aware and intentional in all their hateful actions. All Isaiah, Kamil, and Mr. Joe wanted to do was crack that hard, exterior nutshell and let some light shine in. All the three could do was keep pushing and striving. They just wanted to come together as a community, hold hands, and sing "Jesus Loves the Little Children" in this boat of humanity to help those struggling with life. Remember, it does say, "All the children of the world."

While growing up, Isaiah had seen many people singing this song every Sunday and then teaching it to their children, but he saw that these were empty praises. These people were just going through the motions. They were not living by the words they preached or sang. That song held no validity for their actions. The song that many people who Isaiah, Kamil, and Mr. Joe encountered should actually have been singing was what their conscious or unconscious actions were singing already:

> Jesus loves the little children
> All the children of the world (mostly the United States)
> Only if we decree that they are worthy
> Jesus loves the little children of the world.

> Jesus loves the little children
> All the children of the world
> Red and yellow, black and white
> White sounds good, but the others, we'll smite
> Jesus loves all the little children of the world.

> Jesus loves his little children
> All the children of the world
> If you're gay, you may not stay in church with us today
> Jesus loves all the little children of the world.

This song was the real song that Joseph and Isaiah, along with too many others to ever count, had both lived. Most others who heard the song's real words still would not speak the truth because they were filled with fear. Consequences could be boundless.

It was hard pursuing this line of work in a small town. Isaiah, Kamil, and Mr. Joe began receiving death threats and extremely hateful letters and calls. Some of the letters and calls they received seemed to have words that had been made up by their authors solely because they had run out of harsh and hate-filled terms to use. It could also be a strong lack of education on some of their parts. Sadly, these threats escalated as their success and the word of their mission spread. It was terrifying, especially the first few times, but after the first month, the threats seemed to all run together like a soup of hate brewing in the corner.

The threats were not Isaiah, Kamil, and Mr. Joe's only hurdle. On occasion, the three would be offered some help to counsel the people in need. These offers of "help," if that's what you wanted to call it, were no help at all, offered by people trying to push their own anti-gay agenda. They wanted to witness to the people who were struggling and force them to change their filthy gay ways. Some would hand out a colorful pamphlet covered with people burning to death in flames with the words "hell" and "gay" in bold lettering. Were the childlike drawings and coloring supposed to make this "revelation" any easier for someone struggling with that very lie? Was it meant to brainwash the children early on into believing that gays were evil and that if they were gay, then this was their fate—burning in crayon? Their offer was not meant to help people love and accept themselves, which is what was truly needed. The world and this community needed more love, less hatred and division.

Isaiah, Kamil, and Mr. Joe were not looking for the kind of help that entrenched more darkness into its victims; they had all seen firsthand what that could do to a person. They would rather let those in crises see the shining light and set them free of the prison they were shackled in. The type of "help" that was being offered was the same type of "help" that Pastor Henryson had offered Isaiah, and it was the same type of "help" that had led to Austin taking his life. This was not help at all; it was destruction of the soul.

A lot of changes happened in their lives that summer that helped Isaiah blossom. His entire life, he had felt like he was dissimilar and an outcast. He'd felt as if he were the only person out there in the world like him. He felt he was the only one struggling with this "sickness," as Pastor Henryson had so eloquently put it. This summer, though, was when Isaiah discovered that he was not alone and was indeed very natural. He found that he did have a place in this world.

Throughout the summer, Isaiah was exposed to many teens and even some adults who were struggling. As word spread, they began coming from all over the South. They were struggling with the same teachings of the church and society that Isaiah had been swindled into believing—that he was "less than." As thrilled as he was to finally realize he was not alone, he was even more ecstatic to let these people know that they were not. He tried to convey to each one of them that God had created them and that he had created them all in his image. Isaiah didn't want them to have to isolate themselves because they believed they were going to hell. He wanted to help them crawl out of the flames.

Isaiah treasured the times when he was able to help build the foundation of self-love within these kids and adults. He wanted to help give them the tools to stop looking at themselves with loathing in their eyes. Isaiah loved that he could reach out his hand and let them know that they were not sick and were not going to burn in the fury of hell. They were slowly learning that and that they had many people there to reach out to when they needed support. This would be a very long road to undo a lifetime of lies, but Isaiah was finally telling them the truth—a truth that he was still learning. For many, it was the first time they had ever heard the truth their entire lives. They were finally hearing that they mattered and were loved just as God had made them.

Isaiah was discovering himself, and he was discovering that he loved himself. That was a powerful feeling. He finally felt whole. Through helping to counsel and lend a supportive hand to all these people, he was learning more about himself than he'd ever known, and he was learning his true path. He decided that he did want to go back to college. He'd known that he wanted to get a degree to fight for those who needed help, but what he learned was that he wanted to fight for them in a different way. He wanted to help them learn that they could be advocates and fight for themselves. He wanted to become a counselor.

When the summer came to an end, Kamil headed off to law school, and Isaiah applied to finish his last semester of undergrad. Mr. Joe had managed to negotiate with The College of Mississippi to release Isaiah's transcripts and allow all his previous semesters and grades to stay intact. This left Isaiah repeating only his final semester instead of a full four years. Dean Morgan was reluctant, but Mr. Joe could be very persuasive—not to mention that he had been a very prominent mayor not too long ago.

On top of this success, the law firm was continuing to morph along with the purpose of Austin's legacy. Mr. Joe had learned he wanted Kamil and Isaiah to finish their education while continuing to help him along the way, if they would be willing. The three made a great team, and they were building a foundation of love right there in their community to counter the hate. They all had a feeling that this could be something great.

50

Silenced

That summer, Isaiah, Kamil, and Mr. Joe were able to help shift people's lives and possibly save a few. It was life changing for all involved, especially Isaiah. They all had doors opened for them that summer. Some of the doors that were opened were in their hearts and minds, while some were for opportunities out in the world.

Several doors had opened for Isaiah. One was the opportunity to finish college. Isaiah didn't want to go too far to attend college because he wanted to stay close to Kamil and be close enough to still help out at the law firm on the weekends. They say distance makes the heart grow fonder, but it can hurt, too. Taking this information into account, Mr. Joe knew the perfect place for Isaiah to attend. It was, in fact, where Mr. Joe had obtained his undergraduate degree. It kept Isaiah close by, as he wished, and as a bonus, they offered degrees in the field of psychology. Isaiah did his research and agreed that this was the answer to his riddle and the best place to continue his education.

Isaiah applied and was accepted to the University of Southern Mississippi (USM). He was beginning his final semester of undergrad in the spring, and then he was planning on applying to USM to continue his education and become a counselor. However, he still had a full semester to wait until he could go back to school because the fall semester had already begun, but he had plenty to keep him busy until then. He was going to pack more experience under his belt while continuing to work with Mr. Joe. Once again, Isaiah saw light on the horizon, and he was excited for what the future held.

That summer brought many life changes, one of them the continued blossoming of Isaiah and Kamil's love. You could see the depth of love they held for each other in their eyes when they looked at one another or spoke of one another. It twinkled brilliantly. Before this summer, even though Isaiah loved Kamil and deeply cared for him, it had been hard to let those emotions blossom because he'd still held fear of what others thought and what his family would think.

By summer's end, a lot had shifted. Isaiah was out to his parents, and through counseling of others, he was recovering parts of his shattered self, piece by piece. He had been intact at birth, but throughout his life, he had been forced to snuff out pieces of himself along the way to where he was barely recognizable to his true self. Through the consoling that he would lend to those who came in broken, he could see himself in all of them, and it helped him to shake free of the shackles that had been placed on him.

Through this newfound piece of freedom, Isaiah was allowed to love with his full heart, and it felt incredible. He'd never believed he would find this kind of love; he'd never believed it could be this powerful; and he'd never believed he deserved someone as amazing as Kamil. When he was young, he had imagined the person he was supposed to be with, and he'd never imagined them to be this incredible. God had way more in store than his mind could have fathomed. Isaiah and Kamil were soul mates, and they knew it from deep inside. Isaiah had learned that this was a strong force field created by God from which he could not pull away no matter how hard he tried.

Isaiah was finally at ease with his and Kamil's relationship taking the natural progression it was designed to take. Before, he had been too afraid, and every time Kamil took one step forward, Isaiah had jumped ten steps back, shunning that part of himself as he had when they kissed for the first time. That was over now, and Kamil was extremely thankful. It had been unimaginably difficult for Kamil, but he did not hold a grudge. He understood because he, too, had had that fear instilled in him by society.

Isaiah and Kamil were both happier than ever, and their love radiated a beautiful prism of light. Kamil had been waiting for years for Isaiah to begin learning to love himself. He could see the momentous shift in Isaiah unfolding right before his eyes, and it made him weep. He finally knew it was time. He was ready, and he prayed that Isaiah was, too. Kamil knew it was meant to be. He could feel it in the depths of his soul.

One perfectly beautiful, warm, starry night in the early fall, Kamil took Isaiah to a stream out in the country he knew Isaiah adored going. It was a place where Isaiah could go and meditate to feel as one with nature. It brought him great peace and silence during those times in his life he most needed it. Isaiah had always said that this place was one of the few places in the world where he felt complete tranquility. He was always able to just sit and be while out among the universe, where he could sense the oneness amongst it all.

This stream was also where Isaiah had taken Kamil on their very first date several years before. In the past, Isaiah had revealed his true self to Kamil in spurts of bravery, such as asking him out on a first date. Kamil knew this place had such significance for them both, and it brought such stillness to the chaos. He wanted the serenity of nature to help bring more meaning to that night that extended beyond the realm of this world. Kamil knew that out there in Mother Nature was where Isaiah felt a deep peace. Mother Nature welcomed and embraced their love with serenity and acceptance, and Kamil wanted their love to be a part of that reception. Their pure love didn't receive this type of warm embrace in most places, and Kamil wanted this night to be solely about love. He did not want anyone's hate projected onto it.

Kamil had planned this evening for months. He was just waiting on the perfect night, when the stars and moon were hanging just right in the night's sky. Isaiah did not question why they had gone out to the stream to have dinner. They often went there for silence and clarity or just to get away from it all. Isaiah did, however, wonder why Kamil was taking them to a different bank along the stream and why he was acting so strange.

Kamil was jumpy and uneasy. Isaiah asked several times if everything was all right, and the responses he received left him with further confusion. Kamil was so nervous, he answered Isaiah in a blunt fashion with one-word responses. Kamil was usually a pretty laid-back fellow, but not this evening.

The drive was never-ending in Kamil's book, but for Isaiah, it was just the same ole same ole. That is, until they arrived at the stream. Kamil's normal relaxed fashion was in the wind. He was fumbling his words and everything he touched. Isaiah stared at him with confusion.

"What's with you tonight?" Isaiah asked. "You are acting so strange. Are you OK? You don't want to break up, do you?"

Kamil knew it was now or never. Isaiah was beginning to become too inquisitive and a bit insecure. He did not want that for Isaiah, so in the warm, tender breeze under the bright moonlight, Kamil went down on one knee.

"Isaiah, from the moment we met, I knew you were the one. You help me want to be a better person. I am my best self around you, and I never want to quit trying to strive for better. You help me do that. You encourage me to want to better the world. Every day, I am honored to be in your presence. This life is a constantly flowing journey, just like this stream, and I want to take that journey with you by my side.

"Since we met, we have traveled that stream together, reaching new banks and fresh waters. We are on a new bank now, and I want to begin a new journey with you. You are the love of my life, and I want our journey side by side to be never ending. Isaiah, will you marry me?"

Isaiah could barely hold back his tears of sheer joy. He wanted nothing more than to marry Kamil and spend the rest of his life with him, surrounded by that love they shared. In that perfect moment out there, surrounded by everything God had created, Isaiah's fear was silenced, the hatred toward their love was silenced, and the gross injustices and inequality that they had faced and would face were silenced. It was just two human beings embracing what life is truly about—sincere and pure love.

51

This is Tom, Nancy's Friend

The moment of Isaiah and Kamil's engagement was one of the happiest times of their lives. They were thriving in their love and their intent to spend their lives together. They had never been happier and more in love. They were making strides toward becoming a true family. They seamlessly floated in the love they shared for each other, relishing in each moment. It was like walking on a cloud filled with joy. They were living this high to its fullest, as they should have.

They rode that high for a while, but with every good high, one must come down. In their case, they were knocked down. After an engagement, you should float on that joy and happiness through your wedding day and honeymoon at the least. The whole experience of an engagement and the day you marry the love of your life should be enchanting and exciting. However, unlike other engagements, Isaiah and Kamil's had an ugly side that would soon bare its nasty teeth, ripping into their happiness.

Isaiah and Kamil began to realize that an actual marriage between them might never happen. They also realized that sharing their joy with others was not as simple as the experiences they had witnessed others share. It was beyond painful when Isaiah and Kamil once again remembered the reality they lived in. Their union might never be complete, and they might never be able to openly share that love with family and friends. That reality was soul crushing. They tried to stay hopeful as best as they could, but at times, it was hard with what seemed to be the entire world fighting against them. At times, they believed their optimism might just be ignorance, but that did not deter them from loving one another. No, Isaiah and Kamil were both willing to fight and strive for their love and equality.

They quickly began to realize that there were many layers to this onion, and all of them brought tears. Isaiah and Kamil had mostly kept their relationship to themselves, so their reality got a jolt when they began trying to spread the joy of their engagement. They were met with more prejudice than they had ever expected. They had both experienced many prejudices in their lives. They were both gay, Kamil was Arabic, and Isaiah was of mixed descent, which included African American. Discrimination was their middle name, but this love they shared brought prejudices that were a shock to both of them. It was unexpected and definitely unwanted.

One expression of these many prejudices was all the whispers that told them to not be "so gay" when around each other. They were told to not be themselves because it "affected" others. It would ignite the negative reactions or opinions of people. As absurd as it seemed, they were expected to change who they were to make others more comfortable. Isaiah and Kamil were told to keep their love and happiness to themselves because it was no one's business. It would be like someone saying to a newly engaged woman, "Katie, now don't you mention to anyone about you and Derek getting engaged. It's just nobody's business. They don't need to know about your personal life. You keep that to yourself." That sounds ridiculous. Isaiah knew that no one would ever say that to a straight couple.

There were many times when people's actions were contradictory to their words. Their words would say, "I am OK with you being gay," but their actions screamed quite the opposite. "This is Kamil, Isaiah's friend," they would say. This was how Isaiah and Kamil's relationship was disrespected and belittled time and again. If they only had a penny for every time they heard this, they would never have to work again. No one in their right minds would say, "This is Tom, Nancy's friend," when Tom was in fact her fiancé or husband. It would be seen as weird and incredibly disrespectful to Tom and Nancy's commitment to one another.

Isaiah and Kamil did notice that there were times when a person's omission of the fact that they were a couple or gay had come from a place of protection and fear. These people feared that Isaiah and Kamil would be attacked if others knew the truth, just as Isaiah and Kamil themselves feared the cruel actions of others—but staying in that closet was helping no one. The whispers were silencing their bravery. Whether the whispers were out of someone's ill intent or the goodness of someone's heart, it was hindering Isaiah and Kamil. It was pushing them slowly back in the closet and intensifying their fear of being themselves.

An engagement is a happy time in everyone's lives, right? In addition to spreading the happy news of an engagement to family, friends, even to bank tellers and cashiers in convenience stores by flashing your ring or a smile that cannot be dimmed, most people in this culture have the luxury of experiencing an engagement as a celebration among family and friends. Everyone pulls together to show love and share in your happiness. Your closest friends throw engagement parties, bachelor parties, and bachelorette parties, and you are adorned with lavish gifts of love. Then it is all topped with an extravagant ceremony, followed by an additional party and then the honeymoon vacation of your dreams. This was what Isaiah and Kamil had seen other people experience, but they were not afforded these luxuries.

Their love was labeled as "less than" and not "real," so they did not get the same experience others were fortunate enough to have. There was no running out with sheer excitement to call and tell everyone in their families. There was no spreading the good news to all of their friends. Instead, there was a strange emptiness where happiness should have been inserted. It was a longing to experience what they had seen everyone in their lives experience since they were born. It was part of their culture, but their culture did not want them. People did not accept their love with open arms. It was the same love, but for some reason, it was treated like treason.

Not only did Isaiah and Kamil not get to experience these things, they also feared simply telling people of their happiness because of the very real consequences that they would suffer. They would have backlash and hatred spewed with piercing tongues in the face of their love instead of being adorned with gifts and celebrations.

Isaiah and Kamil began to notice that many believed their love and their relationship were not valid—that their relationship was not a real relationship. Many viewed Isaiah and Kamil's love as a phase, a sickness, a mental illness, the devil's work, a sin, an abomination, or just not as important and sacred as love between two people of the opposite sex. Because of these unenlightened beliefs, people were led to believe that Isaiah and Kamil's love did not deserve any respect, and subsequently, they as human beings deserved no respect. People spat on their love with intense spite. What an arrogantly ignorant view to believe that one can know and define another's love.

This was the struggle that Isaiah and Kamil encountered. They had to hide a lot about their relationship, but their love was not the only thing they had to hide. They also had to hide their symbols of commitment to one another. They had matching gold rings that symbolized their profound love. Kamil had bought two rings, one for each of them. The rings were identical because he felt that this badge of commitment should also symbolize their unity. He gave one to Isaiah when he proposed and slipped the other on his own finger. This was their way to signify their lifelong commitment, and this might be the only way they could ever display it. They knew marriage might never happen, so matching rings were all they had.

They were beautiful rings that symbolized such a level of love and commitment. They also held Isaiah and Kamil's struggles and angst. The rings were engraved with a beautiful inscription of *Always and* إلى الأبد, which meant "forever" in Arabic. Always and forever was the commitment that they wholeheartedly professed to one another. Kamil wanted the engraving in two languages to honor both of their heritages in some small way. As beautiful as the rings were, unfortunately, Isaiah was ridden with gut-churning anxiety over wearing his. The rings were something that signified their eternal love, but they both feared the hatred that they could bring.

The anxiety Isaiah felt from the ring was because of the questions he knew would be asked. The questions themselves, however, were not the real problem. It was the frightening responses his answers would bring if the questions were answered honestly. Oftentimes, when Isaiah wore his ring, he would be bombarded by the questions he knew he must answer—but would he be true to himself? "Oh, are you married? What's your wife's name? Maybe I know her. Is she here? Did you two young lovebirds just marry? What church were you and your wife married in?" Someone just married or engaged might be delighted in answering these questions, but this kind of rhetoric was what Isaiah and Kamil feared. Kamil was always hesitant, but he usually didn't lie. Isaiah felt his soul crushing when he uttered, "Her name is Kathy," but he was too afraid.

Isaiah and Kamil were trying to tear down the barricades holding them in the closet, but the barricades never stopped piling on. They were constantly trying to claw their way out, but it was never-ending. Each and every time Isaiah or Kamil met someone new, they were burdened with the agonizing act of coming out again. The simple act of meeting new people could bring such anxiety. *What is this person going to think? Are they going to be OK or lash out at me? Am I going to be safe?* These were the thoughts that ran through their heads.

Neither Isaiah nor Kamil wanted the fear of a verbal attack that came with honesty, but lying was almost intolerable. It was like lying to themselves and about who they were. Lying felt like they were ashamed to be who they were born to be, that they were spitting in God's face. Lying shoved them back into that closet to suffocate, but telling the truth brought a whole other set of gut-wrenching consequences. Even when someone did not say a word when they heard the truth, the shock and horror on their faces was enough to scar one's soul.

Crude stares and verbal attacks were not all that Isaiah and Kamil feared when it came to sharing their exciting news. Physical abuse and death were very tangible consequences for expressing love and joy. They had read and heard stories of attacks on people who were gay or thought to be gay. Some of these brutal attacks had even been carried out by police officers. This was something they would never understand: how such hatred, to the point of murder, could come from someone being themselves and expressing love, the complete opposite of hatred. Loving without fear—what a powerful feeling that must be. Isaiah and Kamil hoped to feel that one day before their lives were done.

Some people mocked Isaiah and Kamil's engagement. Neither Isaiah nor Kamil found this to be anything that should be taken lightly, but to some, their engagement was nothing more than a joke, something to poke fun at and ridicule. Many ridiculed them, but what was surprising was when a person they knew to be gay ridiculed them for their decision. This ridicule was almost the hardest to stomach for Isaiah and Kamil.

One day shortly after their engagement, Isaiah sat down with a guy he had been helping teach to love himself. This guy, Jeremy, was also struggling with being gay. On this day, Isaiah sat down with him not for a counseling session but to tell Jeremy of his fantastic news. Isaiah was so pumped to have someone he could freely share his news with. That didn't happen often, so this was going to be a real treat.

"Jeremy, I have some great news to tell you. Kamil and I are engaged!" Jeremy's face did not reveal the excitement Isaiah was expecting, which confused Isaiah.

"Jeremy, what's wrong? Why do you look like that?" Isaiah said.

Jeremy furrowed his brows and shrugged his shoulders.

"I guess I just don't get it," Jeremy said. "What's the point if you can't get married? It's not a real engagement anyway. It's a waste of time."

Isaiah was crushed hearing these words from someone he'd entrusted his good news to. He had to quickly leave the room in order to hide his tears of betrayal. Jeremy was a person with whom Isaiah had spoken in detail about accepting oneself. Isaiah and Kamil had both shared so many personal stories with him while striving to make his life more peaceful. Jeremy should have been one of the people standing in solidarity with them, but he was turning his back, casting a dark shadow on them. This has happened throughout history and in everyone's lives at some point. Jeremy had taken a different stance than Isaiah and Kamil would have ever imagined, a stance that hurt them personally. Any such ignorance is also detrimental to society. It gives those who are against human equality more fuel for their scorching fire.

Jeremy's criticism of Isaiah and Kamil's engagement was not just shocking but also extremely hurtful. Isaiah knew many people expressed their mockery through ignorance and a lack of understanding, but Jeremy had experienced daily the lack of respect and equality they were all shown. He should have been the last person to mock the love for which they had fought so hard. Isaiah and Kamil could not wrap their heads around it. Jeremy's ignorance spoke with a thick accent, and it was difficult to understand. Unlike verbal accents, this one held no beauty.

Even though getting engaged was, to some, a pointless gesture because Isaiah and Kamil could not legally marry—and to others a capital offense worthy of death by flames—Isaiah and Kamil found it to be more of a spiritual gesture. They did not need others to define their relationship and solidify their love. They knew the intense feelings they shared for one another were not something to take lightly. They were not something from this earth. No matter the setbacks and resistance, Isaiah and Kamil still shared in the great hope that, one day soon, they would be able to legally marry one another and legally solidify that commitment. It felt criminal that they were not allowed that right.

Even though they could spiritually marry without the law on their side, Kamil and Isaiah found themselves oddly traditional in some ways in the sense of societal customs on marriage. They wanted the legal binding of marriage to solidify them and protect them in times of need. If Isaiah fell ill, Kamil wanted to be able to hold Isaiah's hand in the hospital. If Kamil died of old age, Isaiah wanted to be able to inherit their home together without the fear of it being taken away. If Isaiah were in a horrible accident, Kamil wanted to be able to be by his side and make the decisions he knew Isaiah would want because Isaiah had always told him what he wanted. They would grow to know each other more than they knew anyone else in the world. They would share a loving life together, but if one of them fell deathly ill or died, the other would be no more than just a friend in the eyes of the law and society. They would have no rights. All rights had been stripped away because they were nothing more than just a couple of fags. Isaiah and Kamil did not want to face this fate. They wanted the privileges that came with legal marriage. It was their civil right as human beings.

The sobering fact that Isaiah and Kamil had to accept was that they could not marry because, for reasons beyond comprehension, their love brought so much hatred and fear into other people's minds. They had often thought about and talked about the things that could happen to them. They knew that some people would lash out with ignorance, demonstrated by hurtful and hateful words. They had heard the horrible curses thrown at others as well as themselves. "You fags are goin' to hell. It's gonna be hot where you're goin'. Homosexuals need to repent for their sin, or you're goin' straight to hell. If you don't believe you're goin' to hell, that doesn't make them flames any cooler. I'll pray for your soul. It's Adam and Eve, not Adam and Steve, fag. I will pray for you and your salvation from Satan."

There was not true concern in any of these statements. Isaiah and Kamil surely would not be welcomed into the churches of the people who spewed this hatred. If these people truly believed in Jesus and understood what Jesus stood for, they would not attack Isaiah and Kamil; they would welcome them with open arms. Love and acceptance—wasn't that what Jesus taught? There were innumerable times throughout Isaiah's and Kamil's lives that they were told all of these reprehensible things for nothing more than falling in love with their soul mate or being the person God made them to be. Ironically, the only things from which Isaiah and Kamil needed salvation were the persecution, discrimination, and hatred slung at them by "God's people." Many argued that it was Adam and Eve only, because God did not make mistakes. To that, Isaiah and Kamil questioned why others were fighting against their love and against them, because God had created them as they were.

52

The Great Doctor

The "jagged little pill" continued to rip at Isaiah and Kamil's insides. All the thoughts of not being able to share the joy of their engagement flooded through their heads, almost drowning every sprig of happiness. Isaiah craved the ability to tell his family about his great news, but he was scared. *Would they think it was great news? What would they say? Would they accept it?* Isaiah knew his father, Joseph, would not take kindly to the news. Joseph had still not spoken to Isaiah since Isaiah had been brave enough to reveal his truth.

Kamil was also nervous to tell his parents about his engagement, but he did not hold as much fear as Isaiah did. His parents had known about his being gay for a while and were a bit more comfortable with the truth. Kamil, however, could not tell his extended family. At his parents' request, they still did not know he was gay. His parents did not want them to know for the "shame" it would bring upon the family. It felt like a dagger to the heart when Kamil's parents told him that he would bring shame to the family. What a harsh thing to hear from the people who are supposed to love you unconditionally. Kamil learned that day that his family's love did indeed have conditions, and one of those conditions was that he had to be the person *they* wanted him to.

Isaiah wrestled with the decision of whether to tell his family, but for now, he decided to hold off until he was brave enough to do so. Isaiah decided for now to cling to the optimism or delusion that soon, very soon, his engagement would be normal. He planned to focus on the positive with Kamil. They were going to start planning a wedding in the hope that, one day soon, they could fulfill that dream. Isaiah and Kamil had succeeded in the area that so many strive for. They had found love in a world that could be scary. They had found someone to navigate life with when life could be hard and unforgiving. They had found someone to lean on in all the tough times and someone to laugh with in all the good. All they wanted to do was marry that someone they'd been lucky enough to find. This was the dream, the dream they did not want to see snuffed out. It was a simple dream. They weren't asking for much.

One of the most exciting things about getting married, for many, is planning the wedding. Isaiah was really getting into the planning. He was channeling all his anxious energy about someday having to tell his family into planning a wedding that might never happen. Kamil watched as Isaiah began to live more and more in denial about their situation. He had seen other people do this same thing when they were feeling helpless about something important in their lives. He realized that Isaiah was beginning to live in a fantasy world and ignore the truth around them. That was how Isaiah handled everything. He was too nervous to tell his family of his life-changing news, along with being devastated that he and Kamil could not marry, so he internalized his feelings and immersed himself in another world.

Kamil was so worried about the day Isaiah's fantasy world of having a "normal" engagement and wedding would crash around him, leaving him in the rubble. Then he would be left with the same problem and a sense of devastation. Kamil also knew that now was not the time to confront Isaiah about his fantasy. He was not ready to face the truth of their situation.

One sunny morning in late September, Isaiah sat on his bed in Mama Dove's house, flipping through a wedding magazine he had scored at the Jitney Jungle, a super market in town where they often shopped. Isaiah's eyes gleamed with excitement as he flipped through the pages. While looking through the magazine that hosted his dreams, Isaiah decided to watch some TV as he fantasized of the perfect wedding to Kamil. Isaiah got up and walked over to the television and flipped it on. The national news station was blasting. Just as the TV flipped on, he heard something that crushed all his hopes and dreams. His desire to have a normal wedding was collapsing around him while the screaming sounds from the television deafened his hopes. It all began to crumble into rubble. On September 21, 1996, a federal law was passed that defined marriage as between a man and a woman, effectively banning Isaiah and Kamil from ever having a marriage in the eyes of their home, their country.

Isaiah's faint hope of living the life that so many others had the privilege to live was gone in an instant. He stormed over to the magazine in a fit of rage, shredded it, and threw the pieces across the room, just as the news had done to his heart. Isaiah fell onto his bed and began to cry. It was just one more act showing him that he was not worthy of being a human being. He was not good enough to have equality and marry the person he loved. That was what the nation had just told him; he was not a person of worth, and he was devastated by it. Can you imagine being engaged to your soul mate and planning a wedding that will not happen? Isaiah tearfully grabbed the phone to call Kamil.

Kamil had not been in denial of the reality like Isaiah, but he was still devastated by the news. He'd known that they would not be able to marry soon, but he had not been prepared for a national law against their love. It was a punch in the gut and spit in the face. They couldn't comprehend what was so scary about their love that a national law needed to be in place to prevent them from being equal. Shouldn't love be what defines marriage? Isaiah and Kamil could no longer pursue a more binding relationship when previously they had had hopes that society was evolving. They had reached the ceiling and were trapped by ignorance and fear. Isaiah and Kamil would not lie down, though. They would keep pounding with fists in the air till they shattered those barriers. They would march, they would protest, they would fight until they got the same rights as every other human being in this country. They would fight for equality, but for now, Isaiah was devastated and needed someone to hug him and tell him it was all going to be all right.

Isaiah went into the living room in search of Mama Dove. He called out to her in a shaky, unstable voice. She did not answer, but as he looked up with tear-filled eyes, there she stood with her arms open. She knew exactly what he needed. Isaiah cried into Mama Dove's arms as she comforted his soul. He tried to hold it in, but as soon as her arms wrapped around him, he crumbled.

"It's OK, baby. Mama Dove's here."

She held him for a few minutes until he pulled away and wiped the tears from his face. Mama Dove sat him down to talk. She wanted to know what was wrong. She was worried about him. He was nervous to tell her about his and Kamil's engagement, but he wanted her to know. He couldn't hold it in any longer. He needed to tell someone because he needed someone to talk to. He wanted the whole world to know, but that was not possible.

Isaiah fumbled for his words as he attempted to tell his grandmother something that should have just leaped out of his mouth with pride, but for Isaiah, it was fear that was holding his tongue hostage. Isaiah was met with hesitation before he began, but then he found his words.

"Mama Dove, something has happened, and I don't want you to be disappointed. OK?"

Mama Dove furrowed her brow in confusion and concern.

"Well, what is it, Isaiah? Tell Mama Dove."

Isaiah took a breath before he quickly spat out his words.

"Please don't be mad, but Kamil and I are engaged."

Isaiah felt as if there was a long pause, but in reality, there was not much of a pause at all. Mama Dove took a minute to comprehend what Isaiah had said because he'd spat it out so quickly. Mama Dove's face, which had been consumed by concern, turned into happiness. She responded in the perfect way to ease Isaiah's concern.

"Isaiah, that is great news. I am glad you found you somebody. He seems like such a sweet boy. Does he treat you good? He don't want Mama Dove to whoop him, does he?"

"No, ma'am, he doesn't," Isaiah responded with a giggle. "He is a real good boy, and he treats me well."

Isaiah was so relieved and thankful for his grandmother's reaction. He'd received the reaction that he had seen others receive throughout his life. That was how the news of a loving engagement should be taken. Isaiah had a smile that lit up the room. It was radiating what his heart felt. Mama Dove was excited for Isaiah, but she wondered why he was so upset.

"What was all the cryin' for, then, if all you had for me was good news? I hope all that hoopla wasn't for that."

Isaiah nodded his head back and forth as his excitement was once again countered by the thought of the devastating news.

"Well, Kamil and I just found out that it's illegal for us to get married."

Mama Dove looked confused.

"Isaiah, didn't you know that already?"

Isaiah somberly nodded his head.

"Yes, ma'am, but this morning, they passed a law that defined marriage as between only a man and a woman. We can never be legally married in the eyes of our country. This took away all our hope of ever sharing that bond that others get to experience. We thought the world was changing and finally seeing that we are just people like them."

Mama Dove sat back as she told Isaiah a story—one that he needed to hear. "Well, son, let me tell you about a couple I knew not that long ago that couldn't get married. The law told them it was illegal. People told them it was wrong, it was an abomination, and it was sick. They told that couple that God was against it. They told that couple that they could go to jail for such awfulness. That couple loved each other dearly and could not stand to be away from each other. They didn't understand why people couldn't just see their love when they looked at them. They couldn't hold hands or touch while out amongst others. When they got engaged, it was one of the happiest days and the saddest days for them, because they realized again in that lovin' moment that they were not equal. People hated their love, and they could not understand why. It broke their hearts, but they did not give up."

Isaiah look shocked. It all sounded so familiar. He was going through the exact same thing now. "Mama Dove, I didn't know you knew a gay couple."

Mama Dove smiled as she said, "I didn't."

Isaiah look puzzled. "Well, then, who are you talking about?"

Mama Dove began to nod and grin as she revealed the truth to Isaiah. "I'm speakin' of your momma and daddy, son."

Isaiah was shocked. He had never heard this story. It made him want to run over and talk with them and share in their struggles. He was almost excited for what he heard. Not because he wanted his parents to have hurt, but because he had someone who understood what he was going through. He wondered why Mama Dove had never told him before.

"Why tell me now, Mama Dove?"

"Isaiah, what I'm tellin' you is that it's not hopeless. Keep fightin' for your equality. You see your momma and daddy livin' happily ever after, don't you? They didn't give up on their love just because of the ignorance and fear of those around them. Don't let this loss defeat you.

"You have always been a strong and determined boy like your father. Your equality may be buried a bit, but it's possible. That's one thing I have learned from watching your father. He never gave up. He kept pushin' forward. He was inspirational. He gave me hope when I had accepted what I thought was my fate. I had given up on that plantation, and he gave me courage to fight. Your father marched with Dr. King and stood strong against all the hatred thrown his way. Without people like Dr. King, your father, and others who demanded equality, there would be no platform to speak on. Their courage in fightin' for equality is why you now have a platform to stand on. They have led the way for people like you and people who are not treated equal. March forward with your head high, son, and don't give up."

Isaiah felt so inspired by his grandmother's words. She was right. Then he paused and thought for a minute. "But Mama Dove, my father doesn't love me. He would not stand for this."

Hearing Isaiah say this, Mama Dove's eyes welled with tears. She wanted to make her sweet grandson feel better with her words. "Oh, Isaiah, your daddy does love you so much. He is just lost in his denial and ignorance. He has forgotten his way. He's forgotten who he is and where he came from. He's forgotten what he stands for. He's forgotten what the man that he admired so much, Dr. King, taught him: 'Injustice anywhere is a threat to justice everywhere.' He will come around, Isaiah; he will come around. I will talk to him for you, if you would like. Your father just needs to understand that you are his son. The same son Sarah gave birth to. He needs to understand that what he fought for all those years and what you are fightin' for are not two separate causes. They are the same cause, a human cause that's goal is for people to be treated with dignity and respect—to be treated equal. He is bein' silent and not standin' by you, which is not right. The great

Dr. King said, 'There comes a time that silence is betrayal,' and maybe your father needs to be reminded of that. He needs to stand with you in this battle.

"Now, wipe your tears, and don't give up on marryin' that boy. Don't give up on your love because of others' hate."

Isaiah knew what he must do. He could not live in denial anymore, but he could change the reality. He might not defy the barbaric laws of a university or stand on a podium to give the world hope, but he was finding his own way to help change the world. For now, though, he must start with changing his life. He needed to tell the rest of his family of his good news, and he needed to have a long overdue conversation with his father.

53

You Never Forget the Way Someone Made You Feel

Isaiah was prepared to do what he knew he had to, and that was to tell his family of his and Kamil's engagement. Even though he knew what he must do, it didn't make it any easier. Pulling himself off Mama Dove's couch, which offered so much comfort, was difficult. He knew he must tell the rest of his family and confront his father. That's one hell of a day.

Isaiah wanted to call his cousin, Kayla before heading to his parents' house. He wanted to share with her this part of himself. She was one of the most important people to him. Knowing who he fully was as a person was the only way she could truly be part of his life. Isaiah was not as concerned with telling his aunt and uncle. He wanted them to know, but Kayla and his parents were his first priority.

Isaiah nervously picked up the phone. His fingers hesitated and trembled as he dialed. His stomach had found a new home in his throat, and he was finding it difficult to swallow. The phone began to ring. One ring, two rings, three rings. With each ring, his anxiety grew, and his bravery was faltering. Just as Isaiah was reaching for the hook to hang up the phone, there was an answer. It was a great relief to hear Kayla's voice at the other end of the line. As nervous as he was, he hadn't wanted to have to ask for her if she had not picked up. That would have added another layer of anticipation.

"Hey, Kayla. I have something important I need to tell you, but I'm nervous." Without hesitation, he just began to tell her his truth.

"Kamil and I are together as a couple, and we just got engaged."

As Isaiah told Kayla about being gay and his engagement to Kamil, Kayla responded without hesitation.

"That's so exciting! I'm OK with you and Kamil being together. I'm excited that now I will have two uncles."

She was very supportive and open. Her response was perfect. Her response mirrored what everyone's response should be: happiness for the one you love.

Isaiah could have not been happier. It was such a huge relief to him, and he felt so much closer to her now. He'd hated lying to her for all those years. It should not be anything to lie about, but society had morphed it into the unmentionable. To work up the courage to tell her took a lot out of Isaiah. He was relieved and so thankful that she'd responded the way she did because he couldn't dream of disappointing her. They had always been so close, and he'd always held a special place for her in his heart.

After Isaiah got off the phone with Kayla, he let out a huge sigh of relief. He felt like the weight of the world had been lifted off his shoulders. He needed a minute to recoup before heading to his parents' house, and it was lunchtime. Isaiah grabbed himself a sandwich and walked to sit down at the kitchen table. Just as Isaiah began to relax from all the anxiety and sit down with his lunch, the phone rang. He called out to Mama Dove.

"I'll get it."

Isaiah got up and walked over to the phone.

"Hello?"

"Isaiah?" said a disgruntled voice.

It was Isaiah's Uncle William, and he sounded furious. Isaiah couldn't fathom what might have happened for him to be angry, but he was worried.

"Uncle William, is everything OK?"

With a fierce grumble, he responded, "No, everything is not OK. How dare you tell a child about that kind of stuff. She is just a child. She is too young to hear about those kinds of things. I can't believe you would do that to this family."

Isaiah hung up the phone. He was stunned, and his heart felt like it was smashed to pieces. He knew what his uncle was referring to, but it made no sense. There was no reason his uncle should be so angry. He could not understand anything besides the immense pain he was feeling. This hurt beyond words. He turned around, and once again, there was Mama Dove with arms wide open. Isaiah was hurt, but then the anger took over as he ranted:

"How dare he say that to me. He said a child shouldn't know of these things. These things like me? He is saying that who I am as a person should be shielded from people and children. That would be like someone telling us to not tell their child that we are black because they aren't ready to deal with it yet.

"There is nothing scandalous or horrible about me. There is no reason to shield anyone from me or who I am. It hurts so bad. Why? Why does it hurt so bad? I was there for his daughter when he was not. I taught her so much, and I have protected her from so much. Now he wants to sit all high and mighty and act like he needs to protect her from me.

"No, fuck that and fuck him! He made me feel like I am a criminal. He made me feel like what the preacher said I was, and I am not that. I will not be made to feel that way."

Isaiah's anger deteriorated, and again he was left with agonizing tears of palpable pain. That was all that his anger was. It was just pain.

Mama Dove grabbed Isaiah's face and said, "He was wrong, Isaiah, and you pick up that phone and tell him that. Tell him how you feel. There can't be change without a conversation." This was the opposite of what Isaiah would ever do, but with Mama Dove's encouragement and all that had already happened that day, Isaiah picked up that phone.

It took some time for Isaiah and his Uncle William to get back their relationship. Isaiah's hurt did not just dissipate, and his uncle never understood. Their conversation that day was the last one they had on that subject. They were never going to see eye to eye. Uncle William could not let down his defenses to see, and Isaiah gave up trying to show him. After that day, everyone pretended that nothing had ever happened, but Isaiah's heart still knew what had happened. Isaiah forgave his Uncle William in his heart, and he eventually forgot the words he'd said, but he never forgot the way he'd made him feel.

54

Unsullied Son

Isaiah had had a rough day, but it was not over. His heart was bruised, and his body was tired. Trauma to your heart and life can take a whole lot out of you. Isaiah was feeling the effects for sure, but he was still anxiously waiting till his father got off work to go speak with his parents. He was restless and just wished five o'clock would come on. When your anxiety has encouraged your avoidance of a situation and you finally get the courage to go through with what you have been avoiding, you just want to get it over with. That was how Isaiah was feeling. He wanted to get it over with, no matter the outcome.

As Isaiah sat there on the couch, staring blankly at the TV, the clock ticked slowly until five finally arrived. Isaiah jumped up and told his grandmother he was off. Mama Dove gave him a big hug. She whispered in his ear, "No matter what happens, know that I love you, and I am always here for you." She kissed his cheek and sent him on his way. When Isaiah pulled up in the driveway, he noticed his father's car was missing. He had not made it home yet. *No matter,* he thought. This would just give him time to tell his momma separately. This made him a lot less nervous, for sure. Isaiah went in, sat his momma down, and he unveiled his news to her.

"Momma, Kamil and I are engaged. We want to spend our lives together."

When he told her, she paused and then began to cry. Her crying was not because he was engaged. She was crying because she did not want him to live a harder life than he already had. She was still coming to terms with the understanding that this was not a choice, but that did not change the fact that she still didn't want him to get hurt. Isaiah looked hurt and puzzled. He knew she had previously told him she loved him unconditionally and would accept him, so he could not gauge where her tears were coming from. She quickly wiped them away and decided to tell Isaiah that she was crying because she was so happy for him.

Sometimes, it's OK for a momma to tell a little white lie to protect her children from unnecessary pain, but Isaiah knew she wasn't being honest in what she had just said to him. He loved her for trying to protect him, though. She was scared for him but happy in knowing that he was in love with someone who loved him so dearly. She was ecstatic her baby was happy. She expressed to Isaiah her happiness about Kamil joining the family, and this made Isaiah's heart smile. He felt like he was on cloud nine with the love and support he had received from his momma, Mama Dove, and Kayla. He almost felt whole again.

All Isaiah had to do now was confront his father, and for that, he was terrified. The wall that Joseph had put up seemed impenetrable. His father was a tough crowd nowadays, but Joseph's shield had recently been pierced. What Isaiah didn't know before heading over there that evening was that his father had had a horrible experience a month earlier. Joseph had been coming home every night overwhelmed and traumatized from work. In the beginning of August, he had been asked to help weigh in on a case with the district attorney.

Joseph had not known before he signed on to help what the case was about, but when he found out, he felt sick. The first time that Joseph read the files on this case and saw the pictures, he had to run and throw up. His body could not handle the vile evil that came from this case he was now a part of.

The victim was a three-year-old boy named Zachary, a typical three-year-old. He liked playing with dolls and trucks, enjoyed going outdoors, and he loved to color and play games. That is, until Zachary made the deadly mistake of "acting gay." What exactly is "acting gay" for a three-year-old? You would have to ask his mother, Jessica, because she said that her three-year-old "acted and walked gay." So she labeled him as such.

Jessica had an ignorant and ludicrous stereotype in her head of what "acting" and "walking gay" was. That was the worst thing you could be in her illiterate book—gay. These were messages that she had received from the society that she lived in. These messages, mixed with sheer ignorance, fear, hatred, and pure evil, were what led to this little boy's fate. What did being marked with a scarlet *F* mean for that little boy? He had to die. He had to die a slow and painful death that he couldn't understand. He couldn't understand what he did wrong as his mother watched while her boyfriend, Brian, kicked him to death. As this happened, Zachary, with his soft skin and dark, pleading eyes, stared up at his mother for help, and he received no mercy. She jumped in on the festivities of beating her child to death. He was a faggot in his mother's eyes, and faggots didn't deserve to live, so he was beaten to death the day before his fourth birthday.

Joseph had not been filled with this kind of stomach-churning anger and utter disgust in a very long time. He didn't know how to tolerate it. This time, it was the child's own mother. No matter how angry he was at Isaiah, he could never, ever do this to him or any other person. There was no fathoming what had happened to this innocent little boy. Being in the presence of that kind of sheer hatred day in and day out was exhausting, but he couldn't get the images out of his head at night to sleep.

While this was going on, Joseph withdrew from Sarah because he couldn't talk. They only thing that ran through his mind was that little boy, and he didn't want Sarah to have to bear that kind of horror. Thankfully for Joseph, they didn't need his help on the case for long. He couldn't handle much more, having seen the ignorance and corruption in that mother and her boyfriend's way of thinking. He'd seen the evil and hatred that they displayed in a sickening way. For Joseph, the seed had been planted in his head—the seed that would help him see the light.

When Isaiah went over that day, he did not know that his father's wall had a brick that had been cracked, but he did know that he was filled with fear with Joseph about to come home. When Joseph's car pulled up, Isaiah's heart jumped, thumping his throat. He felt a bit sick, but he knew he must be brave. He wanted a relationship with his father. He wanted his dad back.

Joseph was shocked to see Isaiah's car there. He was not sure if something had happened, but he was not in the mood for light pleasantries. He still could not look his son in the eye and speak to him, but his hand was about to be forced by a very strong young man who took after his father.

Isaiah sat anxiously on the couch till Joseph entered the house. He was facing the door when Joseph entered. Isaiah's leg was shaking uncontrollably, and his hands were sweaty.

Isaiah looked up at Joseph and, in a meek tone, said, "Hey, Dad. We need to talk."

Joseph was not having it, and he rudely grumbled something as he walked past.

Isaiah then stood up, and in a firm voice, he said, "I said, we need to talk. *Now.*"

Joseph was taken aback by his son's firmness, but so was Isaiah. Joseph turned around in an irritated manner.

"OK, what is it, Isaiah?"

Isaiah took a deep breath and began to let out what he had been wanting to say to his dad for months.

"We need to talk about me. We need to talk about us. I need my dad back. I don't need whatever you have been for the past few months. I need you to listen to me and understand me. Kamil and I are engaged now, and I want your blessings and support. I need that."

Joseph's jaw clenched at the thought of Isaiah's engagement. He couldn't understand it, so he feared it. His fear had morphed into anger at the one he loved the most.

Joseph turned away and refused to look at Isaiah as he vehemently stated, "I can't support this. It's against God. It's just not normal. It's just not, Isaiah. The Bible says it's a sin."

Isaiah began to cry. He knew it was not a sin. He could feel it. He knew it as a truth, but he didn't know what to say. He didn't have the words to respond to his father in this moment. Isaiah stopped, and he closed his eyes so tight that all the tears fell down his face. He began to pray and asked God to help him find the words to say to his father.

In that moment, Isaiah felt a change. There was calmness, a passion, and a bravery that had not previously been there. Isaiah opened his eyes, and now he had words in his mouth, given to him by something other than himself. His sentences were coherent, and he could speak the truth to his father, so that maybe, just maybe, Joseph would understand, and he could have his dad back.

"Dad, you can't pick and choose which rules of the Bible to follow. Religious society has chosen which rules fit their lifestyle. You can't do that and use it to exclude entire genera of people.

"Times have changed, and religious society needs to evolve with it. Just because you were taught things growing up does not mean they are right or moral. If you followed what you were taught growing up, then black people would be subhuman. They would not deserve the same things that white people deserve, but you saw the truth and fought for it.

"You saw through the lies about yourself like I have about myself. The murder of your wife is a punishable offense now, but the Old Testament says to murder your wife by stoning. The Bible was written in the climate of that time period. Minus Jesus's words, it was filled with a bunch of laws made up by man. Not by God or Jesus. If the Bible had been written here one hundred years ago, it would say, 'A man shall not lie with a Negro.' That is just ignorant now, isn't it, Dad?

"I know that you believe that's not right or moral. Now you can see what I live every day. People choose to hear and see what they want to. They use whatever verse supports their cause. Forget the part that says, 'Above all, love.' That doesn't prove anyone's political or personal point. People claim Jesus or Christianity like it's a competitive sports team. Christianity is supposed to be about loving everyone equally and not throwing on your armor of judgment and defense. That is what Jesus did. He loved everyone. It's time we start doing the same. Don't you think, Dad?"

Joseph was looking frustrated. He began to shake his head. He started sputtering, "I can't. I can't. Why can't you be normal? It's just embarrassing. You are shameful and an embarrassment."

Joseph's words fueled Isaiah, and Isaiah began to nod his head:

"That's what the mother who raised you used to say to you, isn't it? Mrs. Kingsley used to tell you that you were an embarrassment and that you were shameful. You brought shame to their family. That's what she would tell you, isn't it? She would tell you that you were dirty. You knew you weren't, just as I am not. I am not dirty. You knew what she said was a lie. You knew that God smiled down on you. How did you know that? Because you could feel his smile. You could feel his blessing, just as I can. I can feel it, too. You were such a brave man who fought for equality.

"What happened to you? When did you put up this wall and lose your passion? You tell me I am wrong. How can you sit here and be such a hypocrite? You fought for the same damn thing! Equality is all I want. You always said: 'How can all these people be so hateful toward others who were also made by God?' I ask you the same damn question, Dad! How can *you* be so hateful to me for being born how God made me?"

Joseph was turning red. It was as if his heart was fighting with the things his brain had always been taught. He was not ready to submit. He was not ready to admit that he had been so wrong all this time. As he turned red, he began to shake a bit, and his eyes were showing all the white.

He looked scared as he screamed, "It's not the same, Isaiah!"

Isaiah, too, was yelling as his passion flared. "It is the same! The exact fucking same! Why won't you love me?"

Isaiah broke down in tears that streamed down his soft cheeks. Isaiah was no longer yelling. He now sound defeated as he pleaded. "Why won't you love me? If you don't love me, who else in this world will? I am your only son. If I don't deserve your love, then whose do I deserve?"

Isaiah could not stand any longer. He dropped down onto the floor. He felt like that scared little boy on his bedroom floor all over again as he pleaded. "Why, God? Why did you make me this way, where even my own father hates who I am?"

For the next few minutes, the only sound was of Isaiah crying. Every now and then, you could catch a faint sniffle from Joseph. After a few minutes, Isaiah picked himself up off the floor, and he left. He had said all that was in him, and he was done.

After Isaiah left, Joseph sat down and cried for the first time in a long time. He couldn't help but think that he did not like what he saw in himself, but he couldn't admit it. Something in him reminded him of what that "mother" of that little boy, Zachary, must have been thinking. She, too, didn't want her son to be gay. Joseph began to think, *If I can understand her way of thinking, then maybe I am the one in the wrong. Maybe it is me that needs some soul searching. I'm the one with the same thoughts as that beast.* Joseph could not believe what he had just realized, and he was sickened. He was not ready to let go, though. His fear was holding on and could not let his vulnerability come out, so he just shut down once again. His fear and ignorance lived to fight another day, but they were weakened.

55

Love Is the Light

A year passed, and Isaiah and Joseph still had not spoken. Even when they were at the same table on Sundays, there was tension between them. It was a little sadness, a little anger, and a little resentment. Joseph resented Isaiah for making him feel the way he did. However, it was no one's fault but his own, and on some level, he knew that. He knew that his stubborn ignorance was making him miserable, and he resented himself. Joseph's stubborn ignorance was not making just him miserable; it also affected all those around him. Sarah, in particular, was tired of it. They all were, including Joseph. Sarah wanted the man she'd once known before. Joseph had imprisoned himself in misery, and he was not sure how to turn the key to freedom. Joseph, too, was in a closet, but he was in one of his own making. Family get-togethers had become quite awkward. No matter how awkward they got, though, they were still family, and there was still love present.

Throughout Isaiah's life, he had struggled a lot with accepting and loving himself. He was now finally in a good place. Perhaps he would never be free of all fear, but he was close. A little fear would probably always linger, because the truth was that most of the world would not accept him. Some people were accepting; those he cherished. Some were only tolerant because they felt they had to be. Others wished him dead. Not knowing the wishes of each individual by simply seeing their faces or trusting their words would always leave Isaiah with some fear of being 100 percent his own person in public. That was a very devastating reality, but that was exactly what it was—reality.

No matter how far things had progressed from when Joseph was a boy and since Isaiah was a boy, there still was so much work to be done. Joseph and Isaiah had experienced racism and prejudice almost every day of their lives. Isaiah had even experienced it from his own family—his own father. The realities of society were difficult to see for some, but Isaiah noticed them. Isaiah saw that some just chose to live in the dark because it was easier. However, that did not change the truth that hatred, racism, and prejudices still linger in the shadows of our societies.

Some linger by whispering "fag" and "nigger" in the privacy of their home or once they have had one too many to drink. Some walk with their chest puffed out on the street, waving a flag and screaming "faggot," "nigger," and "sand nigger." There are many more names that can be used, but all these words have two things in common: ignorance and hate. Some of these prejudices are shown through words and others are shown through actions. It can be a significant action, such as joining the Ku Klux Klan, or a small action, such as giving someone a disgusted look for holding their loved one's hand. They all still hurt the same. Hate is hate. Inequality is inequality, and it all hurts. Our hearts are all made from the same flesh. Society needs love. Human beings need love. Isaiah had realized this, and he wanted to share that love with the world.

Isaiah had grown so much since meeting Kamil. He had really blossomed into the man God created him to be. He was going to school in order to help as many people as he could to not struggle as he had. Isaiah always knew he wanted to change how society thought.

One day, Isaiah was talking to Kamil when he realized something very profound. He was complaining about society and how unfair it all was. Then he stopped himself and said, "We keep blaming society, but society is you and me. *We* are society." With that, his problem suddenly seemed much smaller. He finally saw how he could begin to change the world. He just needed to show those around him love and stand up for what was right. There was the light he had been searching for. Now he just needed to help others see it, too.

56

The Cotton Blossom

Over the past year, Isaiah had been attending USM, and he was excel-ling at everything. He knew psychology was the right field for him. He knew this was how he was supposed to help people, and it felt great.

Kamil was enjoying law school, and he already had a job lined up with Mr. Joe for after he graduated. Actually, they both did. Mr. Joe was working on the law firm becoming a nonprofit law, counseling, and help center for bullied youth. Mr. Joe, Kamil, and Isaiah were all found-ers of this project. They prayed that they would have the ability to help many people. It was all coming together, and they couldn't be prouder. This was what they all had strived for: to help.

Kamil and Isaiah became great activists for human equality: LGBT rights, racial issues, and prejudices. You name it and they wanted to help. Isaiah never wanted a single person to feel what he had felt grow-ing up, so he dedicated his life to helping in any way he could. That boy was a good one for sure. One of the causes they fought so hard for was the right to marry. Isaiah and Kamil did not know when they were ever going to be able to legally marry one another, but they did move in together. They were more in love than ever before. Isaiah was doing well, and he was trying to enjoy life, but he missed his dad.

One late Saturday afternoon that summer, after working all day at the law office, Isaiah and Kamil drove over to Mama Dove's because, earlier that morning, she had promised him and Kamil a good home-cooked meal. Isaiah loved it when Mama Dove cooked. As he left the office, his mouth began to water, and his heart began to swell. Mama Dove had always been there for him. She'd never once turned her back on him when he needed her, and she always seemed to know what was best. Kamil couldn't help but feel a tad jealous that he didn't have a grandmother like that, but as Mama Dove said, "Kamil, you do now." That was her heart: loving and accepting. It made Isaiah so proud to call her his.

When they pulled up, Isaiah leaped from the car like an excited kid on Christmas. He had not seen Mama Dove in a few weeks, and he missed her and her cookin'.

Isaiah flung the door open and shouted out, "Mama Dove, we are here!"

As Isaiah entered the house, he smelled something burning. He knew Mama Dove never burnt her cookin'.

"Mama Dove?"

This time, there was no excitement in his voice, only panic. Isaiah ran into the kitchen and found Mama Dove lying on the floor unconscious. He fell to the ground and began shaking her.

"Mama Dove, Mama Dove, wake up, wake up! Call 911!"

She was not waking up, and Isaiah was hysterical. Isaiah did not know if Mama Dove was dead or alive. He couldn't feel a pulse, but his hands were too shaky. Kamil called 911, then stayed right by Isaiah's side.

Mama Dove was rushed to the hospital, where she died the next morning. She had suffered a stroke that Saturday. She was only sixty-eight years old, but she had lived a hard life. Yet it had been a full life as well. She had had enough stories to fill three lifetimes and had gained enough wisdom to fill them, too. Her last years with her family had been the best she could ever remember, and they were all devastated to lose her. She had been their rock.

Mama Dove was beautiful, intelligent, loving, and accepting. Despite all the pain and hardships she had been through in her life, she still had never lost sight of what was important: acceptance and love. She'd also fostered forgiveness. She did not forgive Senator Westridge or Mr. Kingsley in order to give them a pass for what they had done. No; she forgave them to free herself and her body of that ugliness. This was something Joseph and Isaiah were still learning. Mama Dove had taught them so much. She had been the true description of what an amazing human being is and what one encompasses. Isaiah and Joseph knew this. Her entire family, blood and adopted, knew this. They all were enamored by everything she had accomplished and all the love she had shared.

Joseph took the death of Mama Dove particularly hard. She had been taken from him when he was a baby, and now she had been taken from him too early as an adult. He couldn't understand why she was gone, and it hurt. Besides the struggle of loss, Mama Dove's death hit Joseph particularly hard for other reasons. He had been sheltering himself from reality and pain for so long that when she died, everything was shattered for him. He couldn't eat or sleep. When he did eat, he could barely keep food down. Sarah was worried about him, but she wondered if this was the awakening he needed. Sometimes it takes tragedy to awaken a person. All Joseph saw was despair. He was gasping for air and reaching out for a hand to help him. Someone did see him reach, and a hand was there to help him.

The day of Mama Dove's funeral was a hard day for them all. There was a strong energy surrounding them as they laid her to rest. As they stood around her coffin with tears in their eyes, they could feel her. Not only could they feel her, but in death she also gave them a final gift—the gift of love and acceptance, one last time.

Through Mama Dove's death, Joseph was awakened. It was her hand that reached out to his when he was desperate. He finally saw his son whom he loved so dearly standing there in front of him. He saw that Isaiah had never changed but was still the same little boy Joseph had held in his arms and rocked almost every night. Joseph saw that Isaiah was the same little boy he would play catch with in the backyard and the same little boy he would risk his life for. There stood his little boy. He realized that his little boy had never been lost; he was the one who had lost his way.

There in that cemetery, he looked at his beautiful son, and he wept. Joseph walked around the casket, which was covered in flowers and surrounded by emerald-green grass, and he grabbed his son tightly and cried.

He softly whispered in Isaiah's ear, "I love you, son. Please forgive me. I've been lost, but I am here now."

Isaiah, with tears in his eyes, said, "Welcome back. I've been waiting on you."

They both turned with tears in their eyes and smiles on their faces because they knew Mama Dove had done that. She had brought them back together, and in that very moment, Isaiah could feel her hug him tight that one last time. Joseph and Isaiah had one final gift to give Mama Dove. They walked together to lay one last flower on her casket before her spirit left. There, on top of all the other flowers, they laid a beautiful yellow cotton blossom in full bloom.

Cotton blossoms had been Mama Dove's favorite flower since she was a girl. When she'd worked in that field like an animal, she would, for a while, lose her will to live; then she would look up at the beauty and the life that the flower held in its soft petals. She admired the flower and respected its strength. It symbolized everything she was as a person. She could look past the negative and see the beauty in everything.

All of their lives were represented in that flower. The flower carried the sins of racism and the prejudices of the ancestors in its veins, but it still projected the beauty and love that life had to offer.

Joseph and Isaiah carried the journey of that blossom within them as Mama Dove had. To them, Mama Dove was the beauty and the love that helped hold them all together. She was their cotton blossom.

Matthew 5:11 "Blessed are you when others revile you and persecute you and utter all kinds of evil against you falsely on my account."

About the Author

J. C. Villegas was born and raised in the South, spending most of her days in Mississippi. Since childhood, she has been a strong advocate, seeking justice and the humane treatment of animals and people. Throughout her lifetime, she has seen and experienced a great deal of prejudice, more often administered in minute ways as opposed to the grand gestures of hatred we hear about almost daily in the news. No matter the size of the gesture, she has seen how prejudice affects people on a personal and family level, as well as how it affects our society. Although she has been described as a natural storyteller, J. C. Villegas had not planned on writing a book. But, as strange as it may seem, this story came to her in a dream. She did not act on the dream immediately. In fact, it took almost nine months of continually having this persisting and strengthening dream before she took action. With this action, *Journey of a Cotton Blossom* was born through her.